*   *   *

"THE PRESIDENT HAS AIDS"

*   *   *

"THE PRESIDENT HAS AIDS"

Enemy plot, accident, drug abuse, or sex: how did the
Commander-in-Chief acquire this HIV infection?

LESLIE C. NORINS, M.D., PH.D.

ISBN: 0692758003
ISBN-13: 9780692758007
Library of Congress Control Number: 2016912058
Medvostat LLC, Naples, FL

Medvostat LLC
4301 Gulfshore Blvd. N., Suite 1404
Naples, Florida 34103
USA

* * *

PREFACE

When I revealed this book's title to my literary friends, they opined that it was daring and would draw a lot of attention. But a couple of cautious ones asked, "Are you sure you want to go with that title? Even such a plot? You could get criticized."

"Criticized for what?" I asked.

"Well, it could sound like you're trying to stigmatize AIDS patients. And maybe you're also trying to smear the reputation of _____ (insert name of any current or former presidential candidate or White House inhabitant)."

My short answer to any such accusations: Totally wrong. Read the book and see why.

Here's the full story. It all began in 1966, when I was appointed as director of the Venereal Disease Research Laboratory at the federal Centers for Disease Control and Prevention, in Atlanta (known widely as CDC). It was one of the government's oldest public health laboratories, and it was the nation's reference lab for studying and testing patient samples for syphilis and gonorrhea, which were at the time the two major sexually transmitted diseases.

Herpes and chlamydia would come into the spotlight next.

The outbreak of AIDS was twenty years in the future.

The top brass knew I wasn't a world expert on venereal diseases. But because I had studied immunology with Nobel Laureate Sir Macfarlane Burnet, in Melbourne, Australia, they hoped that I could help integrate newer immunological findings with existing methods for diagnosing these two classic infections.

Raised in a middle-class family, and having been somewhat sheltered, I had only medical books and clinical sessions to learn about "VD." In fact, it took my father (born in 1895, and a veteran of the First World War) several years to be able to tell his friends what, exactly, I worked on. Based on his own upbringing, at first he could not say aloud the term "VD," or the "S" and "G" words. He would tell his friends, in a soft voice, that his son the doctor was researching "social diseases," the semi-polite term current in his own youth.

I'm sure he wondered why his sacrifices for my medical schooling had taken this strange turn.

As far as understanding what could and did clinically go on in the arena of sexually transmitted diseases, I had to substitute "book learning" for field observations. Certainly personal experience was a non-starter.

The top VD officials in higher-level positions had risen through the ranks in earlier decades. They had "shoe leather" experience in such things as checking bordellos to control venereal infections and discreet, personal tracing of syphilis contacts in urban areas so that penicillin could be administered to the afflicted.

Fortunately for me, the findings they made were recorded in reports and file notes. Names of patients were omitted, but I could see diagrams of diverse epidemics. Sometimes there were chains of fifty or more individuals whose contacts with each other, and with strangers, were traced out and displayed in neat charts.

My initial reaction was, "Wow, there's a lot of sex going on," especially when compared to my rather Spartan life at the time. But on closer inspection I could also see that in the "real world" captured in these documents there were relationships far beyond the "usual" one-to-one, male with female. Every variety of partnership was represented, and sometimes the same individual had several types ongoing at once.

Thus, I do consider myself fully informed about most permutations of sexual contact extant. But I do not claim personal life experience with them. I have been happily married, monogamously, for over twenty years. If you deem this a shortcoming to write about AIDS in high places, so be it.

As for my bosses' attitudes toward sexually transmitted diseases, as physicians, they felt their job was to control infections, the most serious at the time being syphilis. (Gonorrhea cases were more numerous, but that disease was considered less dangerous.) They strongly imbued us with the concept that the "germs" were the enemy, not the patients who carried the microbes or transmitted them.

Thus, nobody in my professional environment considered that speaking or writing about the realities of syphilis in the life of citizens was in some roundabout way denigrating those who carried or transmitted the microbe. In the same spirit, I reject any suggestion that this book's title and contents somehow denigrate those with HIV or AIDS.

Yet, only a naïve person would deny that, even in today's more accepting environment, the presence of certain diseases can sometimes trigger public opprobrium. Here's the explanation. Because certain microbes are spread largely by sexual contact, their appearance in a person can serve as a surrogate indicator that the individual in question had sexual relations with somebody who was infected.

But the crucial point is that the mere identification of the germ is not, in and of itself, the cause or inciter of disapproval. The adverse publicity comes from the fact that the sexual behavior thus revealed is incongruous with the public image the infected person has claimed as his or her own.

Let us compare two hypothetical men: (a) Wild rock musician on tour, entertaining numerous groupies, and (b) apparently staid, upright public official, supposedly happily married and monogamous. Suddenly, each is found to have AIDS, and must begin anti-retroviral therapy. Then this information somehow becomes public.

It's likely the musician's infection would cause hardly a ripple. Maybe some comments like, "Bad luck." In contrast, the public official's medical development could be a front-page scandalous item in newspapers, or at least in tabloids. Voter disapproval could skyrocket, and he might even be pressured to resign.

Would it be valid for the public official to claim his critics were "stigmatizing AIDS?" Certainly not. They were criticizing the official's obvious hypocrisy. The microbe was merely the indicator that brought his extramarital sex to light.

While this account of AIDS in high places is fictional, I hope I have been true to the scientific and medical aspects of the disease as currently understood. This story is not meant to cast aspersions on anyone or any group. Still, over the decades, enough unusual things have happened at the White House, or in connection with it, that I believe this tale will provoke interest and spur healthy conversation about the risks of this pernicious disease.

Leslie C. Norins, MD, PhD

Chapter 1

*   *   *

As he perused the breakfast menu at the Charter Yacht and Sailing Club, Dr. Martin Riker sensed that someone had approached his table and was standing quite near. Rather than looking up and making contact with his visitor, Riker deliberately kept his eyes fixed on the food and beverage choices neatly printed in gold letters.

It wasn't that Riker was by nature antisocial; to the contrary, he enjoyed the company of his fellow citizens, including the club members, who, while mostly being ten or twenty years his senior, were a companionable bunch. A few of them were even pretty good sailors, although owning a boat and having experience on the water was not a prerequisite for acceptance. Unlike more than a few of his fellow members, Riker had joined the Charter Club not because he wanted or needed social status. He owned a sailboat—a twenty-foot vintage pocket cruiser—and was a skilled helmsman. He viewed his club affiliation as a practical means to an end as well as a convenient place to take his meals when he wasn't in the mood to cook at home. Since his wife Rebecca had passed away, cooking at home often aroused bittersweet memories of delicious dinners that they had made together.

The club gave him a mooring for his boat, a place to eat, and agreeable companionship, for which he paid ten thousand dollars a year in dues. Since the weather on the Gulf Coast of Florida was suitable for sailing year 'round, Riker considered it to be a pretty good deal.

On this particular morning, Riker was eager to set sail, and he wasn't in the mood for chitchat.

"Hello, young fella! Mind if I join you?"

Riker glanced over the top of his breakfast menu. Standing next to his table was Howard Fodson, a retired insurance executive from Louisville, Kentucky, who had moved to Naples over a decade ago with his wife Irene. Howard was eighty years old, which is why he addressed the fifty-eight-year-old Riker as "young fella."

Mrs. Fodson was not in attendance. She often did not leave the house until her tennis lesson at eleven in the morning.

"Flying solo this morning, Howard?" said Riker with a friendly forced smile.

"Yep," replied Fodson as he pulled out a chair. Riker watched in dismay as Fodson planted his bulky frame and scooted forward so that his belly pressed against the edge of the table. It was early December, and Fodson was wearing a Hawaiian print shirt under a blue blazer and white slacks, which Riker thought was pushing the limits of seasonally appropriate attire. While Riker had lived in sunny Naples for three years, he was a Yankee by birth, and the local habit of wearing white slacks and colorful shirts after Labor Day was something that he had never gotten used to.

Fodson slapped the morning newspaper on the table. Then he looked slyly at Riker. "Think it's safe to read? Should I wear a surgical mask?"

Riker eyed the folded copy of the *Naples Daily News*. He sighed. Howard Fodson wasn't the first of Riker's friends to make this joke since he had smashed a deadly terrorist plot to contaminate newspapers with smallpox virus.

"Yes, Howard, it's perfectly safe," replied Riker.

"Okay—but only because you say so!" Fodson smiled at the success of his joke.

Mercifully, Robin, one of the regular morning servers, appeared at the table. Riker ordered two eggs over easy, whole wheat toast, a banana, and a large orange juice.

"And for you, Mr. Fodson?" she asked.

"I'll have the eggs Benedict with extra hollandaise sauce, a side order of bacon, a cinnamon doughnut, and coffee with cream."

Riker glanced at his breakfast companion. He could only imagine the condition of Fodson's arteries. The man was lucky he didn't have diabetes. But if anyone asked Fodson about his diet, Riker knew exactly how he would respond: "I've lived my four score years, and I'm going to eat whatever I damn well please!"

Fodson picked up his newspaper. Riker was happy, since the paper provided an effective diversion from human interaction.

But not for long.

"Have you seen this?" said Fodson.

"Have I seen what?" replied Riker.

"President Ralston. He's got the flu or something."

"So what?"

Fodson jabbed at the paper with his finger. "It says here that yesterday he cancelled his appearance at the Northeast Trade Association luncheon. He was admitted to Walter Reed Medical Center for tests. Press secretary Julie Bishop said that the president came back to the White House late last night. He's expected to resume his normal schedule, including meeting with the ambassador from Ireland at two o'clock today."

"The flu is going around," said Riker. "We're in the peak season, between December and February."

"Are you telling me that the president of the United States didn't get vaccinated?"

Riker shrugged. "I assume that he did, but the shots aren't one hundred percent accurate. There are countless strains of the flu virus. The people who formulate the vaccine each year try to anticipate which one will be the most prevalent. If they're right, great. If they guess wrong, a flu shot would provide very little protection."

"Hmmph," said Fodson. He leaned forward. "Say, do you think the Chinese are trying to poison him?"

"What?" replied Riker with a trace of annoyance.

"I'm telling you, Martin, you can't trust those bastards. They beat us at every game we play. Manipulate their currency. Take our jobs. Dump their products on our shores at below cost. They'll do anything to screw us."

"But Howard, I thought you told me last week that President Ralston was a weak appeaser of the Chinese, and that he had signed terrible trade deals that sold us out to them."

"True!" said Fodson as he slapped the paper on the table.

"Then if he's in their pocket, why on earth would the Chinese want to get rid of him?"

Fodson rubbed his chin. "Maybe it's the Russians. They know how to do this clandestine stuff. I read all the time about how people who oppose the Kremlin wind up dead from mysterious illnesses, like that guy who was poisoned with radioactive material."

"Alexander Litvinenko," said Riker.

"Right!" said Fodson.

"Listen, Howard, the Russians did not poison the president. He got the *flu*. The president has a very robust and secure security system that keeps him quite safe."

"Keeps him *safe*?" exclaimed Fodson. "Are you kidding?"

Riker saw a few other diners at other tables glance over before returning to their meals, no doubt thinking, *Oh, it's just old Fodson getting excited again. Well, Riker can handle him.*

"How about when he nearly got killed in that auto accident in Kenya?" continued Fodson. "And when he goes jogging around Washington? And last year he had some sort of secret operation—"

"If *you* know about the operation, then it wasn't so secret," interrupted Riker. "Howard, listen to me. While it's true that Paul Ralston is the president of the United States and lives in a security bubble, he's still a mortal human being who, every once in a while, gets out of it. Sometimes things happen that can't be helped. Remember when President George W. Bush was giving a press conference in Baghdad and a guy threw his shoes at him? Luckily the president ducked. And how about when President

Obama was playing basketball and cut his lip, and the doctor had to give him twelve stitches?"

"Oh, yeah, I remember hearing about that," said Fodson. "And didn't Bush Senior toss his cookies into the lap of the Japanese prime minister?"

"Yes," said Riker. "He did, at a state dinner in Japan, before passing out cold. Later, Bush's doctors said he had the flu. So you see? Despite the security cocoon, presidents still live in the real world."

To Riker's immense relief, Robin arrived with their food. After dumping the extra hollandaise sauce on his eggs Benedict, Fodson took up his fork and began to eat, noisily chewing and slurping. Aside from that, the table was silent.

Riker finished his breakfast before Fodson, who had ordered a second doughnut. "You should try one sometime," he had told Riker. "They make 'em right here at the club. Fresh every morning. Cinnamon, chocolate, buttercrunch, raspberry—really terrific!"

Riker promised Fodson that he would try a homemade doughnut the next time he came for breakfast. Then he made a show of looking at his phone. "Howard—please excuse me," he said as he stood up. "I'm late for an appointment. I'll see you around, okay?"

"See you," replied Fodson as he dabbed the cinnamon from his chin.

Riker walked out of the sunny Bayside Room, as it was called in contrast to the more formal Main Dining Room, and strolled past the placid swimming pool, beside which a lone woman sunned herself. On the long hook-shaped dock he walked past the moored boats of the other members—rows of sleek white motor yachts, each forty or fifty feet long, with their tall deep-sea fishing rods pinned against the brilliant blue sky. They looked like big money—but of course, the *really* big mega-yachts owned by billionaires couldn't navigate the relatively shallow depths of Naples Bay. In Naples, a fifty-footer drawing four feet of water put you at the top of the nautical food chain.

Riker came to his *Cassandra*, which, at twenty feet, was one of the smallest vessels docked at the club. He didn't mind; he liked having a sailboat that was large enough to accommodate a few friends on an afternoon sail but small enough so that he could handle her by himself.

In a few minutes he had fired up the auxiliary diesel engine, checked his navigation and safety gear, donned his life preserver, and was slowly motoring south through the bay. The open ocean was nearly four miles away and Riker knew there was no use in hurrying; with the no-wake rules you had to proceed at a speed not much faster than if you were jogging. But it was a beautiful day, with the temperature at seventy-five and a light breeze from the southwest.

In half an hour the *Cassandra* had made the turn west through Gordon Pass and was heading out into the open Gulf. As the seagulls wheeled overhead, Riker raised the sail, killed the engine, and set a course south towards Marco Island, and, just beyond it, the unspoiled beauty of the Ten Thousand Islands and their mysterious mangrove islets.

He was still within sight of Gordon Pass when his phone buzzed. With a sense of irritation, he pulled it from his pocket. How was it that when he needed the damned thing the cellular service was lousy, and now that he was out in the middle of the ocean it suddenly worked perfectly?

The caller ID read, "CDC Atlanta, GA."

The Centers for Disease Control and Prevention—the nation's vanguard against infectious diseases. It was the CDC that had contacted him about the sudden appearance of the smallpox virus at a hospital in New York. The call had triggered a dangerous covert operation that had resulted in Riker's destruction of a terrorist plot.

With a mixed sense of foreboding and excitement Riker tapped the phone.

"Yes—Riker here."

"Martin, it's Jim Gilmore."

Dr. Gilmore had been the person who had first called him on that fateful day almost exactly a year ago. With his heart beating faster, Riker gripped the wheel tightly and lowered his head, away from the blinding sun.

"Jim—what's up?" he asked.

"Martin, we need your help. It's a matter of national security. I need you to meet me in Washington, DC, as soon as possible. I'm on my way there now."

"National security? What is it?"

"Can't tell you—this cell connection isn't secure. But I've been contacted by people at the highest levels of government. You're the only guy who has the right expertise and whom they trust. Like I said, it's a matter of critical importance."

"Jim, I've had my share of excitement. I was lucky to get out of Syria alive. You've got to find someone else."

"No can do, Martin. No one else has your abilities. Let me put it this way—you're a retired military officer. This order comes from the very top of the chain of command."

Riker allowed his gaze to scan the beautiful expanse of rolling waves under the cloud-dotted sky. What the hell—the *Cassandra* would be waiting when he returned. "Okay, Jim, I'm on my way," said Riker. "I'll see you tonight."

Riker spun the wheel and the nimble craft came around. As Riker ducked under the swinging boom, the boat heeled over to the leeward side and the wind again filled her sails.

Chapter 2

* * *

At ten-thirty that night, Martin Riker checked in to The Jefferson. A fifteen-minute walk from the White House, the hotel was a favorite of diplomats, lobbyists, politicians, and wealthy tourists who wanted to be near the center of power. Riker had no personal interest in the hotel, and would have been just as happy at the Sheraton, but this is where Jim Gilmore had texted him to go. Indeed, when Riker arrived he found the clerk had a reservation under his name, and when he pulled out his credit card the clerk smiled and said, "That's all right, Dr. Riker; the room has been taken care of."

The bellhop showed him to his room on the eighth floor. When Riker pulled aside the curtains he was pleased to see that he was on the southern side of the building, facing the White House. In the distance behind it rose the white needle of the Washington Monument.

But he was not here as a tourist. It was for business—the question was, what sort of business?

He released the drape and it fell back into place. Gilmore had told him to wait and he'd be contacted. With a shrug Riker turned away from the window, and, after washing his hands and face in the marble-clad bathroom, descended in the elevator to the lobby. He entered The Quill (every aspect of The Jefferson reflected a colonial-era flavor), the hotel's posh bar that served food until twelve o'clock. It seemed oddly quaint that The Jefferson's food and drink operations ended at midnight. Riker was at one of the finest hotels in the center of the capital city of the most powerful nation on earth—and after midnight the place shut down? Meanwhile, in so many other Washington neighborhoods—Adams Morgan, Georgetown, DuPont Circle—bars stayed open until three o'clock.

Perhaps it was for the better. Riker was here for work, not play.

Taking a seat at one of the small tables, he ordered a Maker's Mark on the rocks, and for dinner the grilled salmon filet with seasonal vegetable medley, salsa verde, and Idaho mashed potatoes.

His phone buzzed.

"Yes?"

"Martin, it's Jim. You're at the hotel, right?"

"Yes—I'm grabbing a bite to eat."

"Good. I'll be there at eight o'clock tomorrow morning. Get some rest. See you then."

As Riker sat at his table, a woman entered the bar and took a seat at a table within his view. As the minutes ticked by, Riker saw out of the corner of his eye that she remained alone, looking at her phone. Riker discreetly glanced directly at her. About thirty years old, she was dressed in a grey business suit that was tailored not to conceal her feminine shape but to reveal it. Her blonde hair fell in a crisp line to her shoulders. Around her smooth neck rested a string of pearls—large enough to be costly but not so large as to be ostentatious. Matching pearls caressed her slender wrist.

The server handed her a menu, which she perused briefly before ordering. Riker got the impression that she had been at The Quill before.

Suddenly she looked up and made eye contact. A faint smile flickered at the corner of her mouth.

After quickly reciprocating with a polite micro-smile, Riker looked away.

As he self-consciously studied a painting of Monticello that hung on the wall next to the bar, his mind pondered the scene. On this, his first night in Washington, at an exclusive bar at the very center of the neighbor-hood of power, a professional woman—a government employee, lobbyist, or lawyer—had flirted with him.

Suddenly all the stories became possible—senators and their aides hooking up in offices and limousines, furtive affairs in the back halls of power, sex used as currency or simply as a celebration of the good life.

Riker dared to glance again in her direction. With her head lowered, she was looking at her phone. Its cool blue light played across her sensual cheekbones.

The server approached the woman.

"Hi, Tina," said the server, "We haven't seen you in awhile."

"I'm only in town for a job interview," the woman replied. "I decided to stay the night before heading home. I'll just have a Martini, dry with a twist of lemon."

"No problem," said the server as she took the menu. "Good luck with your interview."

Riker thought about the fact that the woman—Tina was her name—was a guest at the hotel, and she was traveling alone. Why not have some fun? He put his hands on the edge of his table so that he could push it back and stand up.

When he approached her table, he thought, what would he say to her? If she were willing to initiate a conversation, the opening line wouldn't matter much. Something innocuous like "You look familiar—have we met before?" would work. The rest would unfold effortlessly.

He stopped. It was eleven o'clock. In nine hours, he needed to be alert and ready for whatever was coming. If hooking up in Washington were this easy, he could afford to wait. Business had to come first.

Taking his hands off the table, he sat back in his chair.

As Riker waited for his meal to arrive, with his eyes fixed on the bar across the room, his peripheral vision told him that the woman again glanced in his direction. He saw her coolly take a sip of her Martini and place the glass on the table, her fingers curled around the stem.

The server brought Riker's dinner, which gave him something to do. A moment later, a couple entered the bar and took the table between Riker and the woman. His direct view of her—and hers of him—was now mercifully blocked. There would be no more suggestive glances or awkward avoidance.

After dinner, Riker went back to his room and watched the news for a while. There were no stories about the president, only some routine political stuff, a few worldwide terror alerts, and a mass shooting in Texas. Nothing unusual. He shut off the television and fell asleep.

The next morning Riker went down to the Greenhouse, the hotel's breakfast and lunch restaurant. He quickly scanned the tables for the woman in the grey suit from The Quill. No sign of her.

At exactly eight o'clock, as he was finishing his coffee, Jim Gilmore and Angela Powell entered the room. They spotted him and approached his table.

"Thought we'd find you in here," said Gilmore as he extended his hand. "Thanks for coming on such short notice."

"Did I have a choice?" Riker replied with a smile. "Angela—you're involved in this thing too?"

Angela Powell was a case officer for the Defense Clandestine Service, the arm of the Defense Intelligence Agency that conducts covert espionage activities around the world to fulfill national-level defense objectives for the president, the secretary of defense, and senior government policymakers. Such was the nature of her job that Riker wouldn't have dared state her position in a public setting. She had been of major assistance in his undercover mission to halt the Mideast terrorist plot to disseminate smallpox in the US.

"In this case, I'm acting as a facilitator," she replied. "You'll find out soon enough. Are you ready?"

"Ready?" asked Riker.

"To come with us," replied Gilmore.

"Let's go," said Riker. "But first, let me sign for the bill."

"Put away your card—it's taken care of," replied Powell.

Powell and Gilmore led the way through the lobby and out the front doors. A black Cadillac Escalade idled at the curb. Gilmore opened the back door and ushered Riker inside. Gilmore sat beside him. Powell got in the front seat. The driver, Riker noted, was dressed in a dark grey suit and had the cool look of a Secret Service agent. The doors closed and the Cadillac eased away from the curb.

The driver guided the car south down 16th Street NW. At I Street the driver took a right before heading down 17th Street to State Place.

"We're going to the White House?" asked Riker.

Gilmore nodded.

At the southwest appointment gate the driver stopped. Secret Service agents opened the car doors and checked the identification of the three passengers. Powell spent a few minutes conferring with one of the agents. After a few minutes the car was waved through.

The driver guided the car around the curving driveway to the South Portico of the White House. A Secret Service agent approached the car and opened Riker's door. The group was ushered up the stairs, and after passing through the usual screening devices and being patted down, entered the oval Diplomatic Reception Room, with its walls clad in the spectacular Zuber wallpaper that is, in fact, a continuous panoramic landscape. Titled "Scenes of North America," the wallpaper features eighteenth-century vistas of Boston Harbor, the Natural Bridge in Virginia, West Point, New York, Niagara Falls, and New York Harbor.

Riker had no time to gaze in wonderment at his surroundings. The group walked purposefully through the Diplomatic Reception Room into the Map Room, whose walls during the Second World War were hung with huge maps of the theaters of operations, and where President Roosevelt would come for military briefings. Now it's decorated like a typical ederal period parlor.

They went out into the long Center Hall that runs the length of the building, from east to west. With its low vaulted ceiling, hanging chandeliers, red carpet, and old portraits, to Riker it looked like a fancy subway station.

Powell stopped and pointed to a door opposite. "That door leads to the family elevator, used by the president when he comes down each morning from the upper floor," she said. "He then walks down the Center Hall to the West Wing, where his offices are. And if you turn around, you'll see a door. It's the room adjacent to the Map Room. That's where we're going. It's one of the spaces used by the White House Medical Unit."

"So on his way to work every morning," said Riker, "President Ralston walks right past his doctor's office?"

"Yes," replied Powell. "It gives the medical team a chance to see him—to literally get a look at him and see if he appears healthy."

They entered the office of the Medical Unit. The receptionist got up from her desk and opened another door. After a moment she turned to the group. "The director will see you now."

As they entered the office a woman rose from behind a big mahogany desk. She was dressed in a tailored skirt and blazer over a cream blouse.

"Welcome," she said, "and thank you for coming. Please sit down. I'm Captain Karen Thompson, the director of the Medical Unit and physician to the president."

"Thank you," said Riker. "I must confess that this is my first time inside the White House, and it's a privilege to be here. I'm also looking forward to learning more about *why* I'm here."

"Yes, of course," replied Thompson. "When you hear what I have to say, I'm sure you'll understand why we asked you to leave home and come to Washington on such short notice.

"First, I'd like to familiarize you with our function. We provide care not only to the president but to the vice president, their families, visiting dignitaries, and even tourists who are inside the White House. In this office we have an examination room and trauma center, and there are additional facilities in the West Wing and in the Executive Office Building. In addition, we're responsible for the health of the president when he's traveling, and our teams are placed in advance along his travel route. For example, if the president travels to Tokyo, we will put a team there several days prior to his arrival so that they are fully acclimated and can respond quickly."

"You can't expect jet-lagged doctors to perform at their very best," said Riker.

"That's right," replied Thompson. "Fatigue is one of our major concerns."

"I hope you don't mind if I ask a question," said Riker. "Like all recent directors of the Medical Unit, you're an active-duty officer in the armed forces, and yet you're not in uniform."

Thompson smiled. "Since you're former military, I'd expect you to notice my apparel. The director of the Medical Unit is a military officer not for any mandated reason but simply because civilian physicians cannot afford to close their practices for four or eight years while they serve the president. Like any other officer I'd normally wear my Navy uniform, but it's standard policy in the Medical Unit that members of our staff who are military, myself included, always wear civilian clothes. This is because we work out in the field, and military uniforms draw sniper fire."

"Sniper fire?" asked Riker.

"We need to plan for every contingency," replied Thompson. "This includes the possibility of a planned assault on the president, whether by a lone gunman or a group. Uniforms draw fire. As medical services providers, we need to stay alive. Therefore, no uniforms."

"I'm sure I have a lot to learn about how this office works," said Riker, "but I don't want to make you answer a thousand questions. Let's focus on the question that matters most to me right now: Why have you brought me here?"

"We need your expertise in regards to a situation that is of grave concern to us," said Thompson. "I'm going to be very blunt: President Ralston has AIDS."

Chapter 3

*   *   *

R iker glanced at Powell and Gilmore. Their faces were grim masks. "How long have you known?" asked Riker.

"The confirmation blood tests came back yesterday," said Thompson. "And his CD4 count was below two hundred. There's no doubt."

"Guys, let's back up," said Powell. "I don't know what that means. I'm not a doctor. I don't know any more about AIDS than your average *Washington Post* reader. All I know is that it erupted in the nineteen eighties, it's killed millions of people around the world, and you get it from having sex. And I see public announcements urging people to get tested. Right?"

"You're right on the first two points," said Riker. "But sex is just the major pathway; there are also many less-common possibilities."

Gilmore chimed in, "To get us all on the same page, here it is in a nutshell. AIDS stands for acquired immune deficiency syndrome. You get the disease because your body's immune system has been attacked by a virus called HIV, which is short for human immunodeficiency virus. Oddly enough, you pronounce the disease as the word 'aids,' but you don't pronounce the virus name as 'hiv'; you sound out each letter— 'aitch, eye, vee.'"

"Imagine your body is a castle," continued Riker. "It's defended by soldiers, stationed on the parapets. HIV kills these guys, allowing deadly invaders—cancers, tuberculosis, pneumonia, infections—to ransack the place."

"But HIV is fragile," continued Gilmore. "Outside of blood or bodily fluids, it can't survive long. That's why sexual contact is a very effective transmitting method. But you can also acquire it from blood transfusions, needles shared among intravenous drug users, even an organ transplant. The fetus can get it from the mother.

"Within two to four weeks of infection, it may show itself with symptoms similar to influenza or mononucleosis. But in some individuals it may remain inactive for months or even years."

"Why can't doctors spot an HIV infection right away?" asked Powell.

"This virus is incredibly devious," said Riker. "Its initial symptoms are nonspecific, and often are not recognized as suggesting HIV as the cause. Patients seen by their family doctor or a hospital can be misdiagnosed as having one of several common infectious diseases with similar early symptoms. This is particularly true when the patient is not someone known to have the common risk factors for HIV."

"Such as the president of the United States," said Powell.

"Right," said Gilmore.

"Once it gets inside your body, how does HIV hurt you?" asked Powell.

"It destroys a special type of white blood cells—T-cells—which are crucial to your immune response for fighting infections," said Gilmore. "So you can fall prey to various germs, and you can die."

"Forgive me for asking," said Powell, "but how is it possible that the president's HIV infection wasn't detected earlier? We're talking about the occupant of the White House, not some guy in a rural area with no doctor—no offense intended to present company."

"None taken," said Thompson. "We're all on the same team. When he was serving as governor, his blood got a whole panel of routine tests, including one for HIV. Ditto when he first took office as president. Those HIV tests were negative, or to use the current lingo, 'nonreactive.' So I'm guessing he wasn't infected at that time.

"But I should mention there are a few case reports of people who seem to have spread HIV although their own blood test for the virus was negative—oops, nonreactive. So there's a very slim chance he could have had his infection at the time those earlier blood tests were obtained. I just wouldn't bet on that being the case."

"So why did you test his blood recently for HIV?" asked Powell.

"Frankly, it was a freak accident, or lucky break, depending on how you look at it," replied Thompson. "National HIV testing day was coming up, and the White House press office thought it would be a great photo op if the president could be shown rolling up his sleeve to get his own blood tested. You know, like Princess Diana and Prince Harry both did. The president told me he couldn't understand why previous presidents had never done this. So, with photographers and TV cameras watching, a Navy corpsman drew a tube of blood from his arm.

"Now here's an important item. When Prince Harry had his blood taken, the sample was given some kind of a 'rapid HIV test' right then and there. The result was immediately announced as negative.

"At morning coffee break that day we speculated the palace had the prince's blood tested in advance, 'just in case.' They sure as hell didn't want a positive result popping up on TV right in front of the whole country. And Prince Harry probably would have fainted.

"Well, anyway, our big difference from the Brits was that we didn't want to seem to be ignoring the valuable work done by clinical labs. So we told the press that the sample would be sent off to a government lab, probably Walter Reed.

"What happened was that in all the hubbub, the tube of blood was never sent there; it was carried down to my office and put in the refrigerator. A few weeks later I noticed it, and sent it over with a code number, just to prove I hadn't forgotten the project.

"I nearly fell over when the result came back as positive.

"The test they used was the latest fourth-generation one, so it picks up both the HIV's own antigen and the patient's antibody response.

"Then of course we repeated that test, plus did confirmatory blood tests. Plus, we got viral load and CD4 studies, all with coded blood samples. Yep, high viral load and low CD4 immune cells. So, the explanation for the president's string of infections is that he does have a real HIV infection, and it progressed into AIDS. The diagnosis was confirmed on Monday night—the same night the president was taken to Walter Read with what appeared to be the flu. The next morning, I called Jim Gilmore at the CDC. I needed an expert to lead the investigation. He contacted Martin."

"Sorry to dump all of this on you," said Riker to Powell. "But I know you want to get up to speed on what we're facing."

"Absolutely," replied Powell. "What's the saying? Know thine enemy?"

Riker smiled. "It's from a quote by Sun Tzu, the general in ancient China, 'If you know your enemies and know yourself, you will not be imperiled in a hundred battles.'" He turned to Thompson. "Do you have any idea when the president became infected with HIV?"

"Looks like it happened sometime since he was inaugurated," she replied.

"Any guess on how?"

"That's why you're here," Thompson said. "To find out how."

"How's his overall health?" asked Riker.

"To casual observers and the TV cameras the president appears healthy, and he's lost only a few pounds, but to us there are clear symptoms," said Thompson. "As you may have seen in the news, on Monday he felt very ill and had to cancel an appearance at the Northeast Trade Association luncheon. He was admitted to Walter Reed for tests. That night he came back to the White House. Press secretary Julie Bishop announced that he had the flu, which is what we told her. She doesn't know the truth.

"The reality was much worse. A chest x-ray revealed pneumocystis pneumonia, PCP. No doubt it could take hold because of his weakened immune system. You see this in many AIDS patients.

"On Tuesday, he performed his scheduled duties—a reception with the ambassador from Ireland, meetings with his staff, phone calls, briefings, dinner with his family, and a White House music event in the evening. At eleven o'clock he went upstairs to the family quarters."

"Is that his typical schedule?" asked Riker.

"Except for the concert, yes," replied Thompson. "Although the president rises at dawn, he doesn't come down to the Oval Office until nine thirty. His early morning routine is forty-five minutes in the gym, then breakfast with his family and a skim of the morning's papers. He also reads the Daily Brief, the classified summary of intelligence, news, and developments from around the world. Once he comes downstairs, he generally maintains a busy schedule until six thirty in the evening, when he goes back upstairs for dinner. When he's with his family he remains available for anything that needs his personal attention, but Mrs. Ralston has made it very clear to the staff that unless it's a national emergency, he must be left alone after nine."

"Has he been well otherwise?" asked Riker.

"Basically you'll see a few common colds and recurring bouts with the flu. After the election and his inauguration, I think he was exhausted, and he got the flu that spring. His doctor at that time advised him to cut back on his schedule, which he did, and apparently he felt pretty good for the rest of his first year in office. Over the past year, it's seemed to me that he's been going from one episode to another. We were getting very concerned because these illnesses were beginning to affect his performance. Now that we have the diagnosis of AIDS, we know why."

"Excuse me, Karen," said Riker, "but would you mind clarifying something for me? You said that during his first year in office someone else was his personal physician."

"That's right," she replied. "During that time the director of the Medical Unit and the president's doctor was Lieutenant Commander Ethan Westlake. He had served the previous administration, and agreed to stay an extra year to provide continuity. On January first of this year, I came on board."

"He's back on active duty in the Navy now?"

"Yes. The last I heard, his ship, the *Robert G. Warren*, a guided missile cruiser, had been deployed in the Persian Gulf."

"Okay," said Riker. "Thanks."

"This is not only a medical issue," added Powell, "but a highly charged political issue as well. The past presidential election was brutal. The Democrats accused some of the Southern states of voter fraud, and on

Capitol Hill there are many Democrats who think that Ralston didn't deserve to be elected. The antagonism isn't just rooted in political or policy differences; they personally dislike him. They've amplified the rumors about girlfriends, and they resent the fact that his popularity with the public—his approval rating right now is over fifty percent—allows him leeway for indiscretions that wouldn't be acceptable from anyone else. On the other side, Republicans look at the sniping as nothing more than sour grapes, and say the Democrats will do anything to tear down a popular president."

"Therefore," said Gilmore, "If the public or the press perceived that the president were physically impaired—or if they knew he had AIDS—we might even see calls from Democrats for him to resign. But it's hard to say which way AIDS activists would swing. They might rally around him."

"The political climate is a big factor in how the public views a presidential illness," said Riker. "By the end of his second term, Ronald Reagan had come through a bunch of health challenges, and people knew it, but no one called for him to step down. It began with the assassination attempt in 1981, and a bullet passing near his heart. Then colon polyps, with a polypectomy. One polyp turned out to be cancerous. Next a skin cancer on his nose was removed. Then several more colon polyps. But he carried on well, and people loved him."

With the next presidential election two years away, Riker knew that potential candidates were already jockeying for position. Within six months the campaigns would begin, and political observers assumed that President Ralston would be running for a second term. If he were in anything less than top form by summertime, his campaign would be off to a rocky start.

But even if the disease could be controlled, what should the voters be told?

"By the way," said Thompson, "One of the perks of my job is that no physician ever says 'no' when I ask for a consult. I never say exactly who my patient is, but they understand. I've been here for a year, and I've called lots of other doctors. Never once have I received a bill."

"That's good to know," said Riker. "What do you want me to do?"

"You'll spearhead the effort to find out how the president got AIDS," said Thompson. "You'll work closely with me. I'm sure you're aware that whatever answer you find will have massive political ramifications. If he got it from a prostitute, he can kiss his presidency goodbye. If he got it from something like a contaminated surgical instrument, or from some Russian plot, it may make him appear sympathetic."

"You never know how the public will respond," added Gilmore. "Look at Magic Johnson—in 1991 he was diagnosed as HIV positive. He admitted that it he got it from a sex partner, but it happened before he was married, and today he's the head of a business empire worth seven hundred million dollars. Bush forty-one said, 'For me, Magic is a hero for anyone who loves sports.' It was because Magic came out with the truth, right away."

"This situation is extremely nuanced and the stakes are very high," added Thompson. "Now let's talk about logistics. Martin, you'll be able to come and go from the White House at will, and you can use these offices when you need access to our facilities and records, and also for confidentiality. But in order to minimize gossip and speculation, you can't be seen here every day. We've arranged for you to have an office at 1050 Connecticut Avenue NW. It's a commercial building a half-mile from here—an easy walk. You have suite eight forty. Here's the swipe card." She slid the plastic access card across the desk. "Of course, you'll be living at The Jefferson, which can serve as an additional neutral site for interviews."

"Does the president know that he has AIDS?" asked Riker as he slipped the card into his wallet.

"Yes," said Thompson. "As his doctor, I informed him. Naturally he was shocked. He has promised his full personal cooperation."

"Who else knows?"

Thompson smiled. "As far as I know, no one except us. The lab at Walter Reed was not given a name, only a case number. I believe that the knowledge of the president's condition is confined to this room."

"How about his wife?"

"That's a choice for the president to make, not me. I discussed safe sex techniques with him, which is standard for any doctor and her patient."

Thompson reached for a hard candy from a bowl on her desk. Riker had noticed the bowl but hadn't said anything about it. As she unwrapped the candy she said, "Care for one?"

"They look good, but no thanks," replied Riker.

"I'm trying to quit smoking," Thompson said. "Can you believe it—the personal physician to the president, and I smoke cigarettes? God, if word ever got out, people would throw a fit. It's been three days since I've had one. Pure agony, but I'm determined to do it."

"I wish you the best of luck," said Riker. "I quit thirty years ago, in medical school. It was tough, and even today I sometimes think about how good they tasted. But there's no way I'd ever have one again."

"President Obama struggled with cigarettes," said Gilmore. He did a quick search on his phone. "Here it is. Back in 2009 he told reporters, 'Have I fallen off the wagon sometimes? Yes. Am I a daily smoker, a constant smoker? No.'"

"I guess I'm in good company then," said Thompson.

"How about President Ralston?" asked Riker. "Does he smoke?"

"He told me that he quit five years ago," replied Thompson. "I suspect he may sneak one once in a while. Once on an overseas trip I thought I smelled it on him."

In his mind, Riker made a note to remember that. You never know when a small detail will lead to something important.

"I think we're ready to go to work," said Thompson. "The four of us comprise the core team of the project. Angela, you've agreed to handle the external logistics, while Jim will be assisting Martin with the medical investigation. My job is to get you what you need to find the answers."

"What answer do you want?" asked Riker.

"The truth, wherever it leads," she replied.

Chapter 4

∗　　∗　　∗

S itting in Thompson's office, Riker felt as though a mountain had been placed on his shoulders. While he had conducted many public health investigations during his career, he had never undertaken one under such a stifling shroud of secrecy and where the stakes were so high. One mistake could mean the end of two careers—his and the president's.

Thompson's desk phone buzzed. She picked up the receiver. After listening for a moment, she said, "We'll be right there."

She turned to the group. "We have an appointment with the president. If you will please follow me."

Thompson led the way out of her office and into the Center Hall. It was a short walk to the Palm Room, with its airy latticed walls, and then outside the building along the West Colonnade of the West Wing to the door of the office of the president's secretary. There they were met by the president's chief of staff, Donald Strauss. A friend of Ralston's since the future president had been a lawyer in their hometown of Baltimore, Strauss was known to be as tough and as vulgar as the dockworkers he once represented. He and Brian Conway, the deputy chief of staff, were both cut from the same cloth—guys from the neighborhood who were no strangers to the rough justice of the streets.

Riker, Gilmore, and Powell were introduced to Strauss. Riker noted that his handshake was excessively firm, as if there were a message behind it. While Strauss smiled with his teeth, his eyes were hard with suspicion.

Welcome to the jungle, thought Riker. *The survival of the fittest.*

"The president will see you now," said Strauss tersely. "Please follow me."

He opened a door and they entered the Oval Office. Standing in the center of the presidential seal woven into the beige carpet, President Ralston was shaking hands with two men dressed in business suits.

The men left by the door that would take them into the central corridor.

President Ralston turned to the group. Introductions were made. Riker, who had never before met a president of the United States, noted with curiosity that, in person, Ralston was no taller than he was. Riker recalled from the president's biography that he was six-foot-one. In Riker's imagination, presidents are always taller than you are, and it comes as a surprise when you discover they may not be. Ralston looked very fit— no doubt the result of his daily workouts in the gym—and Riker put his weight at about one hundred ninety pounds, which made him average for recent presidents. He was dressed in a dark blue suit, crisp white shirt, and yellow patterned tie. His brown eyes were clear and he smiled warmly as he greeted his visitors with warm handshakes. From a doctor's perspective, Riker noted nothing about the president that would suggest he was not in the best of health.

Such can be the cruel deception of HIV.

Ralston smiled at Strauss. "Thank you, Don. Now if you'll please excuse us."

With undisguised coolness Strauss made his exit. Without acknowledging the tremor of tension that had emanated from his chief of staff, the president, instead of returning to his chair behind the massive presidential desk—named Resolute because it had been fashioned from the timbers of the British ship by the same name that had once explored the Arctic Ocean—he gestured towards the twin sofas that faced each other in the center of the room. "Please sit down—we'll be more comfortable here."

The five took their seats—Riker, Gilmore, and Powell on one sofa, with the president and Thompson facing them on the other. Between the two sofas was a low table.

"Well, doc, I see you've brought in the big guns," said Ralston to Thompson.

"Your health is priority number one," she replied.

"Martin," said the president, "tell me a little bit about yourself."

"I was born and raised in Stratford, Connecticut," said Riker. "It's about five miles west of New Haven. After graduating from Yale and getting my medical degree at Columbia, I enlisted in the Army. I rose to the rank of lieutenant, and served at the Army Medical Research Institute of Infectious Diseases. After my discharge, I went to work for the CDC. As deputy chief of the Epidemic Intelligence Service, I lived out of a suitcase, chasing deadly diseases across the globe—Ebola, dengue fever, HIV and AIDS, malaria, salmonella, tuberculosis. After twenty years I tried to retire, but lately that particular plan hasn't been working out so well."

President Ralston smiled. "If the Syrian smallpox case wasn't still classified, I'd recommend you for a medal. You did an outstanding job—don't think it went unnoticed by this office."

"Thank you, sir. I appreciate your kind words."

"Now then, as to the business at hand," said the president. "Dr. Thompson has briefed you on my condition?"

"Yes, sir."

"And we all understand that while I like to run a transparent administration, this is something that we need to keep within this room?"

"Yes, sir," said Riker. "I see the national security implications. And as your doctor, I'm obligated to maintain patient confidentiality."

"If anybody here leaks the smallest detail of this investigation, I'll kick their ass," added the president. "What's our public stance?"

"We're not releasing any information to the general public," said Powell. "Those who need to know about Martin's presence here, including the White House staff and the Secret Service, will be informed that the Defense Intelligence Agency is undertaking a threat assessment of possible sources of biological attacks that could be made against the president, and that the research will begin with the current president, who happens to be you.

"The head of the DIA, General Millbrook, has been told that this report is at the request of the White House. And frankly, with more than sixteen thousand people working for him and an organizational budget in the hundreds of millions of dollars, to even the most diligent DIA bean counter our project will be no more than a footnote at the bottom of a thousand-page project inventory. To those with whom we interact, Martin will be the face of the project, assisted by Jim Gilmore. I will be invisible. The budget and operational resources will come from my office at the DCS."

"Sounds good," said the president. "I'll instruct my staff to give Martin their full cooperation. Martin, if you need to see me personally, tell Don. He'll get you in. Okay?"

"Thank you, sir," said Riker. "I hope you'll forgive me, but Karen and I need to ask you a few medical questions. You might prefer that we speak in private."

"No problem," said the president. "Angela and Jim, would you mind stepping outside? Thank you."

Powell and Gilmore got up and left the Oval Office, closing the door behind them.

"Sir, do you have any idea where you might have contracted this disease?" asked Riker.

The president smiled. "Martin, I think you can appreciate the sensitive nature of my position. I'm not exactly a guy who has a long list of girlfriends you can go and interview. I'm a happily married man. I can assure you that I have not gotten the disease through intimate contact. It must have been something else—an accident during a medical procedure, or contact with someone who has AIDS in a public setting. For example, do you know how many people I shake hands with on a daily basis? One day during the election my deputy campaign manager decided to keep an informal count. When he tallied over five hundred people he gave up—and the day was barely half over! When I'm out there on the campaign trail there's no way to know if I'm shaking hands with an infected person who has a cut on their palm or their finger. Of course we use gallons of that hand sanitizing stuff, but who knows how well it really works?"

"So you're saying," said Riker, "that we should look either at some sort of medical mishap or a random infection from a stranger?"

"It could have been after the election," shrugged Ralston. "The business of politics never stops. Why, just last week I was in Detroit, touring a factory that was being reopened. I shook a lot of hands!"

Riker smiled. "Sir, I'll be studying the results of your various blood tests to see if I can get a clue. It's certainly pertinent that some older tests were negative, but the newer ones are positive. In a few people the virus can lay low for a long time. Maybe even ten years. But some patients progress to AIDS faster, maybe in a year or two."

"I've always been a guy who gets things done quickly," smiled the president. "I guess you have to take the good with the bad."

"One more question, if you don't mind," said Riker. "Have you told the First Lady?"

"Not yet, but at the right time I will." The president leaned closer to Riker and looked him hard in the eyes. With his finger he punctuated the air. "Martin, I have three objectives. The first is to avoid panicking the American people. Our nation is facing many challenges, and our citizens don't need the stress of worrying about the health of their president. With the antiviral drugs that Karen has prescribed, I'm confident that I can continue to enjoy good health and serve this great country.

"Second, I'm interested in finding out whether I acquired my disease through some sort of systematic error. In other words, if we can learn something about how to do things better, then it will be worth it.

"Thirdly, we need to rule out a terrorist plot. It may be farfetched, but the possibility has to be examined. If it's a question of national security, then we need to take the appropriate steps, whatever they may be.

"Martin, I hope you understand my position. I'm not looking for scapegoats, just solutions. And if for some reason we never find out the source, then so be it."

The president sat back on the sofa and clapped both hands on his knees. "Martin, are you a man of faith?"

"In my own personal way, yes," replied Riker.

The president nodded. "Fair enough. I personally believe that God has a plan for all of us. In his wisdom, he does not reveal that plan. We never know what it is. We may think we're on the path of our choosing, and then God will set us on another path—the one of *his* choosing. If it's God's will that I should get AIDS, then I would be foolish to question it. It's simply the road he has chosen for me. Martin, I'm a guy who always looks ahead. I try to never look back. Nothing good ever comes of it."

"I understand, sir," said Riker.

There was a knock on the door. Strauss entered. "Mr. President, it's time for your meeting with the secretary of state. She's in the cabinet room."

The president stood up and walked over to the chief of staff. He said something to Strauss, who looked at Riker and nodded. Then the president turned to Riker and Thompson. "Thank you for coming to see me," he said. "Don will show you out."

Riker and Thompson rejoined Gilmore and Powell, who were waiting in the office of the president's secretary.

With the same coolness with which he had brought them in, Strauss escorted the group outside to the West Colonnade. He offered Riker his business card. "I've been asked by the president to give you unfettered access to him," said Strauss as Riker took the card. "I'm sure you appreciate the fact that the president's time is *extremely* valuable."

"Yes, absolutely," replied Riker. "I anticipate that my personal contact with the president will be infrequent at best."

"Thank you," said Strauss. "Enjoy your day." He disappeared back into the building.

As they walked along the West Colonnade, Powell turned to Riker. "I'm going to leave you now," she said. "If you need anything, please let me know. The budget is not a problem. Go where you need to go and get the resources you require. I'll expect weekly reports, but you need to make them in person. We must assume that no communication is entirely secure."

"Okay, thanks," replied Riker.

Powell went on her way, while Riker, Gilmore, and Thompson walked through the Palm Room to Thompson's office, where they sat down.

"The president seems to be taking this remarkably well," said Riker. "However, the message I got from him was very clear: he does not believe he got the disease from a sexual partner."

"You would expect him to tell us if he did?" said Gilmore.

"No, I suppose I wouldn't," replied Riker. "If he's hiding something, it just makes our job more challenging. I appreciate the public relations piece of this—no one wants the president of the United States to have AIDS. At least he appears healthy. That will help keep rumors from starting."

"You should have seen him on Monday afternoon," replied Thompson. "He looked like a refugee from Madame Tussaud's Wax Museum. Thank God he wasn't photographed. If he had gone to that luncheon and gotten sick, it would have made headlines."

"What are his symptoms?" asked Riker.

"On a day-to-day basis," said Thompson, "we're seeing fatigue, the disruption of his natural circadian rhythms, asymptomatic anemia, nausea, and pain in multiple sites from the lower extremities to his oral and abdominal cavities."

"What's his drug regimen?"

"His antiretroviral therapy, which we began this morning, consists of a daily cocktail of HIV medicines. We've got twenty-five to choose from. He's getting five, from three different drug classes. Remember, our patient has to look good, sound good, and feel good in order to fulfill his duties and inspire confidence."

"Can you stabilize him?" asked Riker.

"I hope so, but we won't be able to gauge our progress until a few weeks from now," replied Thompson. "Once a patient starts treatment, their viral load should start to fall and the CD4 cell count should gradually increase. We'll monitor the president's health and adjust his meds as necessary. You'll recall that the elevator he takes to go from the family quarters to the West Wing is directly across the hall from this office. I've asked him to step inside at least once a week. Obviously we don't want to arouse suspicion, but we need to see him regularly. The typical patient has their blood tested every four to six months, but in this early stage of treatment I want to test him every two weeks. He's already receiving a vitamin B-12 shot once a month, so people in the White House are accustomed to seeing him enter this office. A few extra visits shouldn't arouse suspicion."

"He's going to love getting stuck with a needle three times a month," mused Gilmore.

"It'll toughen him up to face the Republican primary season," replied Riker. "Who's been giving him his B-12 shots?"

"One of our nurses handles that," said Thompson. "He started getting them when he was governor. He said they gave him energy. There's a fringe theory that B-12 stimulates the Krebs cycle to work more efficiently and burn off fat. Personally, I think it's a bunch of nonsense, but B-12 isn't toxic. If you take too much, you just piss it away. If the injections have a positive placebo effect, then what's the harm? Here in the White House, for the first year, under Ethan Westlake, Christina Wilkinson did it. She left when Westlake did, and since then Jennet Swift has done it. It's very routine—the president pops in, gets his shot, and he's gone within five minutes."

"Okay, good to know," said Riker.

"Martin, the ball's in your court," said Thompson. "Where do you want to start?"

"I need to know where President Ralston was during every moment of every day for the past two years, and whom he was with."

"You can get a copy of his itinerary from the Office of Scheduling and Advance," replied Thompson. "They're located over in the Executive Office Building, across the street. The director is a woman named Lindsay Baker. She and I work closely together, and you're going to get to know her very well. If we need to dig further back to before the time of the election, then the president's itinerary would be in the hands of the man who was his deputy campaign director, Maxwell Mosely. He's here at the White House—the president gave him the job of assistant director of communications. I don't have to tell you that he has no knowledge of the president's condition, and if he discovers he's out of the loop, he'll be livid."

"Just like Don Strauss," added Riker.

"And let's change '*if* he discovers' to '*when* he discovers,'" added Gilmore. "Unless the president experiences a miraculous cure, eventually this is all going to leak out."

"But not from this office," said Thompson. "All of us are bound by considerations of national security as well as patient confidentiality. The media love to get every detail of a president's health, but there's no legal requirement to provide them anything; and this particular condition carries enormous political ramifications. It's not like having a heart attack or cutting your lip playing basketball. Martin, I think you should go to see Lindsay personally. I'll give her a call and tell her to expect you. Around here, face time is key. You need to build good relationships so that your friends are less likely to stab you in the back."

"Friends?" asked Riker.

"Believe it," replied Thompson. "To paraphrase Aristotle, in Washington your enemies stab you in the front and your friends stab you in the back."

Chapter 5

✳ ✳ ✳

Riker crossed the street to the Executive Office Building, the massive French Empire-style structure that dwarfs its smaller neighbor, the White House. With its nearly two miles of black-and-white tiled corridors and over five hundred rooms, the building Harry Truman called "the greatest monstrosity in America" houses thousands of staffers employed by the Executive Office of the President, including the White House Office, the Office of the Vice President, the Office of Management and Budget, the National Security Council—and the White House Office of Scheduling and Advance.

Passing through the ornate doors, Riker was immediately struck by the scale of the place and its brawny décor. By comparison, the White House seemed cramped and almost quaint; here the bold architecture, immense interior spaces, baroque wall decorations, and lavish use of wrought metals (at the time of construction in the late nineteenth century, to reduce the danger of fire the architects minimized the use of wood) gave the building a decidedly imperial vibe.

After getting lost a few times, Riker made his way to Room 325B, the office of Lindsay Baker. As the door clicked shut behind him he saw the collision of old and new: The archaic and somewhat fussy walls cradled a sleek, hi-tech operation that seemed to hum with improbable precision.

"Yes, may I help you?" said the admin assistant who happened to occupy the desk closest to the door and who therefore, Riker assumed, was the designated greeter.

"My name's Martin Riker. I'm here to see Lindsay Baker. Dr. Thompson called a few minutes ago."

"Oh, yes," said the woman. She made a call and then turned to Riker. "She'll be right with you."

A moment later a woman approached through the forest of cubicles. Tall and slender, with dark hair neatly pulled off her face, she radiated effortless confidence. With a warm smile she offered her hand.

She led Riker through the cubicles to a private office. In the anteroom was a desk manned by another admin assistant. "Sharina, please hold any nonessential calls," Baker said.

They entered Baker's compact but highly functional office. On the windowsill stood a row of pots with flowering plants stunning in their beauty.

"You raise orchids?" asked Riker.

"It's a hobby of mine," replied Baker as she settled into her leather-clad office chair. "They're high maintenance, but worth it." She looked at Riker. "May I get you anything? Coffee?"

"I'm fine, thanks. As Dr. Thompson may have told you, I'm working on a classified project for the DIA, with the full cooperation of the president. It's a threat assessment of possible biological risks faced by the president."

"She only gave me a rough outline," replied Baker. "But I get the gist of it. How may I help you?"

"We're seeking to build a profile of the movements of the president since his election two years ago. We need his complete itinerary."

Baker smiled. "That's a rather tall order. The information exists in several different databases. Do you need overseas travel as well?"

"We especially need overseas travel."

Baker picked up her phone. "Sharina, how soon can you put together a comprehensive itinerary of the president's travel schedule since he's been in office? A *week*? I was thinking more like an hour. Yes, it's a high priority.

Mark it 'For Official Use Only.' Thank you." She hung up the phone and turned to Riker. "We'll email it to you by two o'clock."

"It looks like you know how to get things done around here. Thanks very much."

"By the way," said Baker, "our office only manages the president's movements outside of the White House. If you need to get a minute-by-minute account of his movements inside the White House and while he's at other executive locations such as Camp David, you'll need to go to the Secret Service."

"Okay, thanks."

Baker narrowed her eyes and looked closely at Riker. "Your name seems very familiar to me. Were you the Dr. Riker who uncovered the smallpox terror plot against *The New York Times* last year?"

"Yes, that was me. Officially, however, it never happened."

"Half of what goes on in Washington never officially happened—or at least people wish some things had never happened. I read about the episode in a classified report. You were in Syria?"

"Yes—that's where the plot originated, in a city called Latakia."

"I know the place. It's on the northern coast. It used to be a beautiful area, with lovely beaches and upscale resorts."

"You've been there?"

"Yes, when I was in college. In those days, despite the political repression, Syria was a safe place to visit."

"That's interesting," said Riker. "We'll have to talk about it sometime."

"Yes, we will." Baker's phone rang. With a frown she picked it up and listened. "All right, Sharina, put her through," she said. Covering the phone, she looked at Riker. "I'm sorry, I need to take this call. If I can help you in any way, please don't hesitate to ask."

Riker stood up. "Thank you—I'll keep that in mind."

On the way out Riker stopped at Sharina's desk. "Thanks for taking care of the itinerary," he said.

"I'll get it to you soon as it's ready," she replied with as much of a smile as she could muster.

Riker walked across the street to the White House. As he passed through security he felt a profound amazement that he, Martin Riker, who grew up as an ordinary kid in Stratford, Connecticut, was able to flash his identification and saunter unchallenged into the working residence of the leader of the most powerful nation on earth. It was like an exclusive club that was nearly impossible to get into, and once you were in, you felt different—both exalted and deeply humbled, amazingly free yet carrying tremendous responsibility, immortal yet all too human.

Feeling hungry, and seeing an opportunity to confirm his elite status, Riker went to the Navy Mess. This is the White House staff dining room, located in the basement level of the West Wing, as close as you can get to being directly underneath the Oval Office. (For security reasons, presumably, there's no basement under the Oval Office, only tons of concrete.) Sitting in one of the leather-clad captain's chairs and gazing at the gold-framed paintings of sailing ships on the paneled walls, Riker allowed himself to enjoy the feeling of privilege. To think that it was only forty-eight hours earlier that he had been sitting at his table at the Charter Club in Naples, listening to Howard Fodson spout his conspiracy theories about the Chinese and the Russians. Eventually, Riker knew, he would be back there, facing him again. If the old man were to ask where Riker had been, what could Riker tell him? He'd have to say, "I've been on vacation," or "visiting my family in Connecticut." What about Riker's time spent at the White House, meeting the president, and working within the corridors of the highest levels of power? It never happened. If his mission succeeded, no one would ever know about it.

Whatever political nonsense old man Fodson babbled, Riker would most likely just nod and say, "Hmmm, I see your point, Howard."

Taking advantage of a few minutes of solitude, and the fact that he was sitting with his back to the wall with no other diners immediately near him, he reached into his briefcase and pulled out a legal pad.

On the top sheet he wrote SOURCES OF HIV INFECTIONS. He then drew three vertical columns. He gave each one a header: COMMON, UNCOMMON, AND RARE/THEORETICAL.

Under each heading he listed what he knew, based on his experience while in the Army, and later at the CDC.

Under COMMON, he listed: 1) Unprotected sex (man-to-man and hetero), 2) Intravenous drug use w/shared needles.

Under UNCOMMON, he wrote: 1) Blood transfusions, 2) Organ transplants, 3) Contaminated medical needles and instruments, 4) Infected mother transmitting to her baby during pregnancy, birth, or breast-feeding.

Under RARE/THEORETICAL, he listed: 1) Infected blood transmitted from one person's bloody wound to another's, 2) Sharing contaminated razor, 3) Infected healthcare worker's blood enters a patient, 4) Stepping on an infected needle on the beach or playground, 5) Infected tattoo/piercing equipment, 6) Infected manicure equipment.

He studied the list. The *Rare/Theoretical* section contained examples that were generally not found in practice. So rare they were published as case reports, or just sent out wildly on the Internet. Most experts would consider them to be remote possibilities. But because the president did not fall into any of the categories typical of AIDS patients, even rare circumstances had to be considered. For example, shaking hands. Most people do this only occasionally—maybe once or twice a day—and typically with peers who are presumed to be healthy. Politicians, especially during a campaign, might shake hands a thousand times a day, and have to do it indiscriminately. If a hand is thrust at them, they shake it. If somehow contact were made between two open cuts, could enough of the virus pass from an infected person to the president? Doubtful, but people get hit by lightning, too.

When the server brought his food, Riker quickly slipped the pad back into his briefcase.

It was two o'clock when he got up and walked back to Thompson's office.

"Did you get what you need?" she asked.

"Yes, thanks."

"Lindsay's a good person to know," said Thompson. "She's very focused on getting the job done. No drama, just results."

"Where is she from? Her accent sounds Scandinavian."

"Minnesota, so you're not far off. Her family name is Larssen. They're Norwegian."

"And Baker...?"

"Her former husband's name. They divorced last year, but since Lindsay was already established in her career she kept it."

Riker sat down at a spare desk, logged onto the computer, opened the secure email from Sharina, and downloaded the file. He spent a few minutes studying it before going back to see Thompson.

"You have something?" she asked as she reached for a hard candy and unwrapped it.

"I've made a preliminary inventory of possible external environments where the president could have become infected with the HIV virus," said Riker as he slid a printout across her desk. "He's traveled a lot in the past couple years, so it's a robust list."

"Have you prioritized them?" She wadded up the candy wrapper and tossed it into the metal wastepaper can emblazoned with the logo of the White House.

"Yes."

"Okay. Let's start at the top of the list."

"First, a wild question," said Riker. "Has the president ever received an organ transplant?"

"No," replied Thompson. "Why?"

"In 2010, there was a New York City case reported of HIV apparently transmitted through a transplanted kidney. At the time of surgery, both the donor and recipient were HIV-negative. But, a year later, the recipient was found to have HIV. The donor was retested, and at that point was positive. All other causative factors were ruled out. Conclusion? It came from the donor."

"That's really an oddball," said Thompson. "It sounds like one of those rare cases where somebody is carrying HIV but the blood test comes back negative. However, as far as the president is concerned, the answer is, no transplants."

"Okay, but how about a cornea transplant?"

"Well, he did have one after that softball damaged his cornea in the annual White House softball game, but I don't know I've ever heard that those could transmit HIV."

"I've checked the research on that," said Riker, "and the virus has been found to be present in cornea cells. But so far this is just of academic interest; no clinical case of transmission this way has been reported. So, we'll cross all transplants off our list.

"Now then, the first viable possibility is the accident in Kenya. It was eight months ago, in the spring of this year."

"I remember it well, although I wasn't with the president in Africa; I remained here in the White House. One of our five staff physicians, Norm Gladstone, was with the motorcade in Nairobi." She looked at Riker with a cool, steady gaze. "Are you really sure you want to start with this incident? I can assure you that as long as the president has been under my care, the president has not been exposed to HIV. I mean, of course anything is *possible*, but I've been diligent, and I think that there's a greater likelihood that the president was infected more than a year ago."

"You mean during the time when Ethan Westlake was the director of the Medical Unit."

"It has nothing to do with who happened to be occupying this office," said Thompson with a cool smile, "but rather the likely time frame of infection."

"Of course," replied Riker diplomatically. He consulted his inventory of events. "Here's another possibility. In July of his first year in office, the president attended the Group of Seven summit in Japan. As he was leaving the Nagoya conference center, a protestor threw a plastic baggie of blood at him. A member of his Secret Service detail raised his hand to deflect it, and the baggie hit the agent's hand, splattering its contents. Some of the blood landed on the president's face, neck, and shoulder. The president was hustled into his limo and left without further incident."

Thompson nodded. "The protestor who threw the baggie said it was human blood. The time line is possible. I think this would be a very good place to start."

"Amazing," said Riker. "A few minutes ago, at lunch, I made a quick list of all the ways—both accepted and fanciful—that a person might be able to get AIDS. Getting hit in the face with a baggie of infected blood was not on my list. I don't think it's on anyone's! But I suppose that if enough of the blood entered his nose or eyes, or got into a cut on his face, an infection might result. What happened to the bag? Was it ever tested?"

"I don't know. I'm sure it's in the custody of the Secret Service."

After an hour of making phone calls, asking questions, and then walking from room to room in the vast Executive Office Building looking for Room 1006G, Martin Riker stood in front of the desk of Frank Foster, the Secret Service agent in charge of investigations. Foster leaned back in his chair with his hands clasped behind his head. His dark eyebrows, which in their richness were worthy of a Cossack cavalryman, knitted together, forming a deep V above his eyes.

"Dr. Riker," he said, "the Secret Service employs approximately three thousand two hundred special agents, thirteen hundred uniformed division officers, and more than two thousand other technical, professional, and administrative support personnel."

"I understand that," said Riker. "I'm looking for one of them: the agent who was with the president in Nagoya last year when the protestor threw the bag of blood. I need the incident report and the bag itself, if possible."

"The bag?" said Foster. "Why the bag?"

"The DIA has commissioned a threat assessment of possible sources of biological attacks against the president," said Riker.

Foster's eyes narrowed under his heavy eyebrows. "The DIA is doing this? What for?"

Oh, Christ, thought Riker. *Turf battles.*

"Hey, you know how it is," smiled Riker. "Have budget, will spend."

"You can say that again."

"I'm sure the completed report will be stuffed deep into a filing cabinet in a dusty corner of the Pentagon, never to be seen by human eyes."

Foster laughed. "You sound like a guy who's got Washington figured out." He clicked his mouse and rubbed his chin. "Let's see... that was the fifteenth of July. The G7 conference was held at the Shima Kanko Hotel near Nagoya, Aichi Prefecture. The incident took place at four thirty in the afternoon, local time. I have a list of the special agents who were present. Actually, the incident report wasn't written by the agent who got hit by the bag. It was filed by Roger Winston, the head of the unit that day. Do you want the report?"

"Yes, thank you."

Foster made a few clicks with his mouse. "I just emailed it to you."

"How about the bag of blood?"

Foster shook his head. "Sorry, you'll have to go to Japan for that. Their Public Security Intelligence Agency took it as evidence. As the national intelligence agency of Japan, the PSIA is responsible for internal security and combatting threats to Japanese national security. They're very tough, very aggressive."

Riker walked back to the White House. The sky was overcast, and as a few flurries drifted among the bare trees he pulled the collar of his jacket up around his neck. When he had left Naples the temperature had been in the high seventies. He reminded himself that if he was going to be working in Washington for the next few weeks, he had to buy some winter clothes.

At the security checkpoint going into the White House the Secret Service agent recognized Riker and addressed him by name. When Riker entered Thompson's office, he said, "I seem to be becoming a familiar face around here. I can see your point about keeping a low profile. However, the problem may be temporarily solved: I'm going to Japan."

Thompson nodded. "To investigate the G7 incident?"

"The bag of blood is in the custody of the PSIA. We need to get it and test it for HIV."

"Good idea," said Thompson. "Contact Angela Powell. She'll arrange your flight and hotel. Your travel to Japan will of course be highly confidential. We'll tell the Japanese what we're telling everyone else—that we're doing a threat assessment of possible sources of biological attacks. Take all the time you need."

Chapter 6

$*$ $*$ $*$

To keep interaction with Riker's fellow passengers to a minimum, for the fourteen-hour flight from Washington to Tokyo, Powell had booked him into a first-class seat. That evening, as the big Boeing 777 lifted off and settled into its long cruise over the Great Lakes and Canada, and then over Alaska and down over the barren Kamchatka Peninsula to Japan, Riker was grateful to have a private seat that converted to a comfortable bed, as well as the personal attention of the very agreeable flight attendant who catered to every whim of her sixteen first-class passengers.

Dinner was served—after a respectable shrimp appetizer came a small bowl of lukewarm pea soup, followed by a hunk of overcooked filet mignon placed, for some unknown reason, smack in the middle of a limp salad. At least the champagne was cold. After the smiling flight attendant cleared away the dinner tray and had brought him a double Maker's Mark on the rocks, there was business to attend to. As the clouds, bathed in the golden glow of sunset, rolled beneath his window, Riker brought up the report filed by Ethan Westlake, who was then the director of the Medical Unit and the personal physician to the president:

INCIDENT AT THE G7 SUMMIT MEETING AT THE SHIMA KANKO HOTEL, 15 JULY. 2:30 PM LOCAL TIME.

As he was exiting the hotel and walking to his limousine, the president was splashed by red liquid from a plastic bag thrown by a protestor. The president was not physically injured and walked unaided to his waiting limousine. A member of the president's staff gave the president a towel, with which he wiped his face. In the president's limousine additional towels and wet wipes were provided.

The Medical Unit staff, which according to procedure must be stationed out of harm's way, were on duty in an SUV about fifty yards away from the scene. They were part of the motorcade as the president's limousine drove away from the hotel. Dr. Robert Carson, the senior member of the Medical Unit team covering the president's visit to Japan, was able to examine the president several hours later on board Air Force One as it left Nagoya. The president had no injuries. The president reported that the red liquid had splattered across his face, and that some of it had gone into his nose and on his lips. He said the liquid tasted like blood.

The broken plastic bag was picked up off the ground by an agent of the Japanese PSIA. The PSIA took custody of the bag as evidence in the trial of the accused protestor. The PSIA later confirmed that the baggie contained human blood. The suspect, Tashi Osaki, stated that the blood was his own, which he had drawn himself.

No further details are available.

"Hmm," Riker mused. "Would've been nice if somebody had thought to test the blood for pathogens. But I guess they were distracted by all the excitement."

He opened the duty roster and motorcade personnel list for that day's event. After skimming through the names of the Secret Service agents, sharpshooters, pilots, vehicle drivers, mechanics, cooks, canine security teams, interpreters, the Medical Unit staff, and the rest of the four hundred or so people who accompany the president every time he travels overseas, Riker came to the list that interested him—the core group from the inner circle at the White House.

WHITE HOUSE TRAVELING ROSTER w/POTUS
WEDNESDAY, 16 JULY
NAGOYA

Body man: Stephen Howe
Deputy chief of staff for operations: Brian Conway
Deputy chief of staff for implementation: Wendy Caspar
Deputy chief of staff for policy: Enrique Ismas
Assistant to the president for economic policy: Owen Hauseman
Assistant to the president for economic policy: Janet Long
Assistant to the president for strategy and outreach: David Andrews
Assistant communications director: Maxwell Mosely
Communications officer: Frederick Ng
Special assistants: Fordwell Jones, Anya Robertson, Salvio Salucci.
Personal assistants: Dominic Daoud, Rachel Doucette, Addison
Lanser, Matthew Rourke, Kimberly Schuster.

To Riker, at the moment the list was nothing more than a bunch of names. He knew that if he didn't find the answer to the president's illness, and if he ruled out an accident or medical error, these names would have to become real people, and he'd have to investigate their relationships to the president.

There was one more file: the statement given by Tashi Osaki, the protestor who had thrown the bag of blood. This is what he told the court:

I, Tashi Osaki, freely confess to having struck a mighty blow against the gods of war and the demons of imperialism. To avenge the honor of my venerated ancestors who were savagely cut down by the American war machine, which is today commanded by the notorious criminal President Ralston, I cast upon this *mazuko* who came to our sacred shores the same blood that he has shed of our people, in the hopes that by anointing his foul flesh....

Riker read no more. It was clear that Tashi Osaki was what writers call an "unreliable narrator," meaning that whatever he tells you may have no relationship to the facts. After his conviction, Osaki had been sent not to prison but to Tokyo Metropolitan Matsuzawa Hospital, a big public psychiatric facility.

Riker set aside his research and stretched out on his seat bed. He was amazed that he could fully extend his legs without touching the cocoon of the passenger in front of him. After watching a boring romantic comedy movie, he drifted off to sleep.

When he got off the plane in Tokyo, while his body told him it was nine o'clock in the morning, the dark sky and the bright lights of the airport confirmed to him it was ten o'clock at night. He took a taxi three miles to the reliably antiseptic Radisson Hotel Narita, checked in, and realized that he had better eat dinner before trying to go back to sleep. For Riker, an experienced traveler who in his campaign against bad microbes had visited nearly every continent, the brutal shift in time of over twelve hours when you fly from North America to Asia was something he had never gotten used to, and was one reason why he had been happy to put away his suitcase and make his home on a quiet bay where he could sail his boat.

After dinner he slept for a few hours, woke up groggy and morose, and saw by the clock next to the bed that the time was four o'clock in the morning. He clicked on the television and watched the twenty-four-hour English-language news program. Time crawled by, and eventually the sky glimmered with the dawn. It was Friday, the ninth of December.

His appointment with Shoko Masako, a PSIA supervisory chief investigator, was scheduled for nine thirty that morning. After showering and a breakfast in the Radisson hotel restaurant, Riker took a cab to the PSIA complex located across the moat from the vast grounds of the Imperial Palace, the residence of the emperor and empress and their extended family.

The PSIA headquarters is actually two buildings—a magnificent nineteenth-century structure made of stone with tall arched windows that would not be out of place in Vienna, and, looming over it, a brutal modern box of glass and steel. It was into the modern box that Riker went, and thence to the fifteenth floor—at least the view was impressive—where, after being made to wait for half an hour, he was ushered down a drab grey corridor and into a drab grey office.

A man in a black suit stood to greet him. "Dr. Riker, it is a pleasure to meet you. I'm Shoko Masako." They bowed to each other. "Please—sit down." He gestured towards one of the chairs facing the plain steel desk, on which Riker noticed a small, framed photo of a woman and a young child, taken outdoors by a lake.

"I understand that you have an interest in a piece of evidence that was collected at a crime scene last year," said Masako.

"With all due respect, it's not an ordinary piece of evidence," replied Riker. "The incident was an assault against the president of the United States."

"Yes, of course—a most regrettable act, committed by a deranged individual. We are happy and grateful that the president was not injured. As you probably know, the perpetrator is confined to a mental hospital, and we do not expect him to ever be released."

"So I understand," nodded Riker. "As Angela Powell mentioned in her message to you, we seek the plastic bag that the young man threw at the president. We need to test the blood for the presence of pathogens."

"Is the president ill?"

"Absolutely not," replied Riker. "We're conducting a threat assessment of possible sources of biological attacks that could be made against the president, or indeed any head of state, including the prime minister of Japan."

"We'll appreciate your sharing your findings," replied Masako. "I also appreciate your taking the time and expense to personally come to Tokyo."

"I have been led to believe," replied Riker, "that previous requests for the evidence made through the normal channels—by email—have not been successful. Therefore, it was decided that I should come here in person."

Masako gave Riker a bemused look. "It must be very important, this plastic bag."

Riker gave a casual shrug. "Fortunately, the president has had very few objects thrown at him. For that reason the bag is highly unusual, and worthy of study."

"You want to test it for pathogens? Any in particular?" asked Masako coolly.

"None in particular. We want to examine it for a wide range of contaminants, both chemical and biological."

Masako nodded. "Very well. It may be possible to provide what you ask for. Please call me tomorrow morning."

"Here at your office?" asked Riker. "Isn't tomorrow a Saturday?"

"The bad guys don't care what day of the week it is. We work weekend shifts." He stood up. "Thank you for coming to see me. I hope you enjoy your visit to Tokyo."

Five minutes later, Riker found himself standing on the sidewalk in front of the big ugly box. The temperature had dropped and a cold drizzle dampened his head and shoulders. He took out his phone. The time in Washington, DC, was eleven in the evening.

Karen Thompson answered her phone. "Did you make any progress?" she asked.

"I think so," replied Riker. "You know how the Japanese are. No one ever says 'yes' or 'no.' It's always very vague. But Masako's response was as close to a 'yes' as I've ever heard here. He asked me to call him tomorrow morning."

"All right," said Thompson.

"How's the boss?"

"He was fine today. No problems."

"Glad to hear it."

Riker hung up.

He now had the day to kill. The sky cleared, and for an hour he walked around the East Garden, the public area of the sprawling Imperial Palace compound. As noon approached he began to feel tired—even though he had gotten extra sleep, at home it was well past midnight. He went back to the hotel and took a nap. In the afternoon he had lunch at a restaurant in the neighborhood.

As the hours ticked by, his irritation grew at the Japanese bureaucracy, which seemed as constipated as the American variety.

That night he went to a nightclub, got not quite drunk enough to cause a problem for himself, and fell asleep, alone, on his bed in the hotel.

The next morning at nine o'clock he phoned Masako.

"Ah, Dr. Riker—I have good news for you," said Masako. "The bag is here and will be released to you after you sign the appropriate forms."

"Thanks, I'll be right over."

Riker hurried to the big ugly box and up to Masako's office. There, on his desk, was a clear plastic evidence bag, labeled in Japanese. Inside the evidence bag could be seen another bag, like a common sandwich baggie with a twist tie, crumpled and stained rusty red. Riker signed the forms and Masako handed him the bag.

"It's very unusual for us to surrender evidence in a criminal case to another country," said Masako. "But for our friend President Ralston an exception has been made. We wish you every success with your research."

"Thank you," said Riker as he took the bag from Masako. He put it into his briefcase.

After catching the next plane out of Tokyo, on Saturday at noon, Washington time, Riker landed at Dulles Airport. A feature of flying from Tokyo to Washington is that you land at the same local time as when you took off, as if the intervening twelve hours had never existed. He went immediately to the White House, where Thompson was waiting. He handed her the bag.

She turned it over in her hands. "It's remarkable," she said. "Sealed in this airtight PSIA evidence bag, it appears as though some of the blood in the baggie is still liquid. I'll send it to Walter Reed for tests."

"If I may make a suggestion, it might be better to send it to the CDC," said Riker. "They have no relationship to the president."

"Okay," shrugged Thompson. "That's fine with me."

"We should also send Jim Gilmore home," added Riker. "We're going to be doing a lot of testing, and we need someone who knows the score to keep an eye on the work they're doing."

"I'll tell him," said Thompson. "I think he'll be happy to go back to Atlanta—he misses his wife and his kids. He's not the globetrotting type."

"Good," said Riker. "If we need him to come back to Washington, we can send for him."

"Okay, let's prepare the Japanese baggie sample," said Thompson. "First I'll have to remove the bloody baggie from the evidence bag, which is labeled in Japanese. While I can't read it, it's possible that one of the lab techs at the CDC can. I assume the Japanese labeling has the time, day, and location, which, if the blood tests positive for HIV, could be a cause for gossip and speculation."

She took the bag and went into the clinic room. Riker followed. After donning a pair of gloves and a surgical mask, Thompson carefully opened the Japanese evidence bag, and, with a pair of forceps, extracted the limp and brownish baggie, which she then placed into a fresh evidence bag. Riker noticed that the baggie released two or three drips of liquid blood, which Thompson captured in the new evidence bag. She then sealed the bag and labeled it with the date and a number.

She then took the original Japanese evidence bag, which had blood residue inside, and placed it into another new bag, which she sealed and labeled.

"All set," she said as she removed her gloves and mask. "I'll send the evidence to the CDC, and when their tests are complete we'll either have a viable suspect or we'll be able to cross this off our list."

Chapter 7

∗   ∗   ∗

Riker and Thompson returned to her office.

"What's next on your itinerary?" asked Thompson.

"If we continue with our strategy of tackling the oldest incidents first," said Riker, "which would support the theory that the president's HIV infection was latent for over a year before he began to show symptoms, then we need to look at the emergency dental procedure."

"I've got the report in my files," said Thompson. "Even though at the time of the incident Mr. Ralston was not yet president, as part of his ongoing medical record his physician at the time gave us a copy." She clicked on her computer, and, after locating the file, printed a copy for Riker. She put it into a folder and handed it to him.

"Since today is Saturday, I'm going to knock off and go home," she said. "This might be a good time for you to get settled into your office at the Ten-Fifty."

Riker agreed, and together they left the White House. Under the brooding overcast sky Riker walked the few blocks north up Jackson Place NW, past the looming Executive Office Building and Blair House, also known as the President's Guest House. Then he crossed H Street NW and went up Connecticut Avenue to Farragut Square. After pausing to admire the statue of Admiral Farragut, who during the Civil War became famous for rallying his fleet with the cry, "Damn the torpedoes, full speed ahead!", Riker hurried the last block to his new home base.

At the Ten-Fifty, as everyone called it, Suite 840 was identical to a million other rented offices everywhere throughout the developed world: Grey wall-to-wall carpet, walls painted "eggshell white," overhead fluorescent lights, a plain metal desk, standard reclining vinyl-clad office chair, Dell computer, landline phone, printer, coffee machine, and ficus tree by the window. If "anonymous" is what Thompson and Powell wanted, this space fit the bill.

After inaugurating the coffee machine, which produced a decent cup, Riker opened the folder and took out a stack of papers. According to the report compiled after the fact by the Medical Unit, it had been two years ago, in August, during the presidential campaign and before the election in November, when then-governor Ralston had been in Maine, making a campaign appearance at the Skowhegan State Fair. Governor Ralston was standing next to a horse, holding its bridle, and posing for a photograph. Suddenly the horse jerked its head and the steel bit in its mouth struck the governor on the side of his face. The impact broke the skin, cut the gum inside, and loosened the right maxillary first molar. Profuse bleeding occurred.

The skin wound was covered with a flesh-colored Band-Aid. Because of a tight schedule, the decision was made to rush the governor to the nearest dentist, patch him up, and continue with the campaign. A state fair manager directed the governor and his caravan of tour bus and three SUVs to the office of Dr. Winslow Palmer. The governor was driven to a three-story Victorian house that had once been the private residence of a wealthy lumberyard owner. He was ushered into the waiting room. Fifteen minutes later he was seen by Dr. Palmer. After administering a local anesthetic, the dentist stitched the gum and inserted a temporary bridge to stabilize the loosened tooth. Within an hour of his arrival at the dentist's office, Governor Ralston was back on the road, headed for another appearance in nearby Waterville.

Riker closed the report. It seemed inconsequential—a simple procedure at the dentist's office.

In the spirit of due diligence, Riker researched Dr. Palmer.

What he found was highly disturbing—a newspaper report from eight months earlier.

SKOWHEGAN MORNING SENTINEL
DENTIST SUSPECTED AS AIDS SOURCE
April 24

Skowhegan police and the State Dental Board are investigating a Skowhegan dentist who is suspected of transmitting AIDS to his patients. The investigation began when Josephine D'Arcy, 26, of Skowhegan, told authorities that she had been diagnosed with AIDS despite having never engaged in any behaviors that are associated with the disease.

She stated that the only possible exposure occurred three years ago during a routine dental procedure at the Palmer Family Dental Center in Skowhegan.

The investigation by the State of Maine Board of Dental Examiners revealed that Dr. Palmer failed to properly sanitize equipment between patients and he reused dirty gloves. Hygiene procedures were routinely ignored and equipment was stored in a bathroom.

State health officials are attempting to contact every patient treated by Dr. Palmer during the past decade to ask them to see their physicians, and, if necessary, get tested for blood-borne diseases such as HIV, hepatitis B, and hepatitis C.

Dr. Palmer has been suspended by the SMBDE. Two years ago, he was diagnosed as being HIV positive. He apparently has not exhibited symptoms, and doctors are not sure when or how he contracted the disease, or if he transmitted the HIV virus to any of his patients.

Riker then pulled up the preliminary report from the SMBDE, and scanned it for relevant sections:

THE PROFESSIONAL PRACTICE OF WINSLOW PALMER, D.D.S., AND AIDS EXPOSURE TO PATIENTS: PRELIMINARY REPORT BY THE COMPLIANCE COMMITTEE, SMBDE.

The committee conducted a comprehensive medical survey among 716 individuals who are known to have been patients of Dr. Palmer at his dental office in Skowhegan, Maine. Our survey identified four patients who have been diagnosed with AIDS.

The four infected patients all denied sexual contact with Dr. Palmer, and they did not name each other as sex partners. For the past two years, all of the patients made numerous visits to this dentist for a variety of invasive procedures, including prophylaxis (cleaning), extractions, periodontal scaling, restorative fillings, root planing, and fixed and removable prosthodontics.

Based on the following considerations, this investigation strongly suggests that these four patients were infected with HIV during their dental care. All the patients had invasive procedures personally performed by Dr. Palmer. The DNA sequence analyses of the HIV strains from these four patients indicates a high degree of similarity of these strains to each other and to the strain that had infected the dentist, a finding consistent with previous instances in which cases have been linked epidemiologically.

In addition, the strains found in the four patients (including patient D) and Dr. Palmer are distinct from the HIV strains found in the seven other HIV-infected persons residing in the same geographic area, and from the twenty other North American isolates.

The precise mode of HIV transmission to the four patients remains uncertain. Multiple opportunities existed for Dr. Palmer to sustain needlestick injuries (such as during suturing, administration of local anesthetics, and two-handed needle-recapping procedures) or cuts with a sharp instrument. Although the dentist claimed to use barrier precautions, these techniques were not always consistent or in compliance with recommendations. Furthermore, because barrier precautions do not prevent most sharps injuries such as puncture or cut wounds, the occurrences of puncture or cut wounds during treatment may have allowed the dentist's blood to enter an open wound or contact mucous membranes of a patient directly.

Transmission might also have occurred by the use of instruments or other dental equipment that had been previously contaminated with blood from either the dentist or a patient already infected by the dentist. However, this mode of transmission may be less likely than direct blood-blood transfer during an invasive procedure because HIV is present in blood at low concentrations, does not survive in the environment for extended periods, and is typically destroyed by either heat or commonly used chemical germicides.

Riker closed the file. Because of an emergency treatment by Dr. Palmer, was it possible that the president of the United States could be a fifth patient to be infected by the dentist?

This episode warranted inclusion in the list of suspected sources. But it was only one—there was no reason to believe there couldn't be others. Riker needed to keep digging.

He picked up the phone and called Maxwell Mosely, the president's assistant director of communications.

Mosely answered. Riker introduced himself.

"I'm aware of your project," said Mosely. "Don Strauss sent out a memo yesterday. Something about a threat assessment of possible sources of biological attacks that could be made against the president. Sounds like a good idea—our enemies are always looking for new ways to attack us. And I don't just mean terrorists. I'm talking about the Russians, the North Koreans, and the Chinese."

Perhaps old man Fodson wasn't so far off base, thought Riker.

"Thanks," said Riker. "I'm calling you because in our effort to be thorough we're casting our net beyond the current term of this president to include as many other incidents as we can compile. We're trying to leave no stone unturned and no door unopened. You were Mr. Ralston's deputy campaign manager, weren't you?"

"Yep. I've been with Mr. Ralston since he first ran for governor six years ago."

"I'm gathering information about a dentist that Mr. Ralston visited in Skowhegan, Maine."

"Oh, yeah, that was a freaky day. Mr. Ralston got whacked in the mouth by a horse! We had to find a dentist pronto. The guy's name was—let me remember—Dr. Palmer. He did a good job. Stitched up the governor in no time, and we were on our way."

In his mind, Riker debated whether to tell Mosely about Dr. Palmer's shoddy practice. He decided that Mosely would eventually find out, so transparency was the best choice.

"Wow," said Mosely after Riker had told him what he had learned about the dentist. "I remember thinking that the guy's office was pretty funky, but I thought, 'Hey, we're in Skowhegan, so what do I know? Maybe that's the way things are up here.' I think I even remember he had a cat walking around in the office. Very unusual. The boss wasn't infected with anything, was he?"

"No, we have no evidence of anything bad happening to Mr. Ralston," Riker semi-lied. "What I'd like to get from you is the list of staff who were accompanying him that day."

"Do you suspect somebody of something?" asked Mosely.

"No, not at all," replied Riker. "As a part of our project, we're doing two things. We're documenting actual incidents and we're creating hypothetical scenarios. For each actual incident, we want to paint as complete a picture as possible—everything from the weather that day to what the president was wearing. And, of course, who was with him."

"I get the idea," said Mosely. "While I can't say exactly which blue suit Mr. Ralston was wearing, I can send you the staff list. Hold on a sec.... Okay, I just sent it to you."

"Thanks," said Riker.

"Say, I understand you're new in town—is that right?"

"Yes. I live in Florida. I was called up for this project on Tuesday. I was thrown into it, you might say. I've been to Washington few times over the years, but only as a visitor. This is the first time I expect to actually live here for an extended period of time."

"It's Saturday night!" said Mosely. "What do you expect to do?"

"I hadn't thought about it," replied Riker. "I suppose just take a walk around the neighborhood and then hang out at my hotel."

"Where are you staying?"

"The Jefferson."

"Oh my God, that's like being at the house of your elderly spinster aunt. Tell you what—I'll show you a bit of the town. We'll grab some dinner and hit a few of the hot spots. Okay?"

"Sounds good," said Riker.

"Meet me at eight o'clock at Harry White's. It's at two hundred Seventh Street SW."

Mosely gave Riker a set of complicated instructions for how to get into the bar.

"It sounds like a damned speakeasy," said Riker.

"Exactly," replied Mosely. "That's the concept. The problem is that too many people are finding out about it. To get a table you need to make a reservation, which I'll take care of. I guarantee you that six months from now, nobody will want to go there. It'll be full of tourists."

After they had hung up, Riker checked his email. After clicking on the message from Mosely, he downloaded the file, which he opened.

GOVERNOR PAUL RALSTON
STAFF LIST
14 August
Augusta, Skowhegan, Waterville, Bangor, Maine. Concord, New Hampshire.

Campaign director: Brian Conway
Campaign manager: Wendy Caspar
Deputy campaign manager: Maxwell Mosely
State campaign manager: Enrique Ismas
Volunteer coordinator: Pierce Fredericks
Polling director: Frederick Ng
Special assistants: Fordwell Jones, Halston Railsback, Rachel Doucette, Addison Lanser.

After quickly skimming it and noticing some names that were familiar to him from the Japan trip, Riker saved and closed the file.

Chapter 8

*   *   *

At eight o'clock, Riker, wearing a new overcoat he had bought to ward off the December cold, stood outside 200 Seventh St. SW.

He saw nothing but an unmarked wooden door. Unsure of whether to believe what Mosely had said about there being a popular nightspot at this address, he hesitated.

A cab pulled up and a man got out. Not very tall and rather round, he bounced on his heels. He was wearing a dark coat and a stylish fedora.

"Ah—Dr. Riker, I presume!" he said as he extended his hand. "Maxwell Mosely. I see I've arrived just in time. Shall we go in?"

"Lead the way," said Riker, amused at his host's dapper demeanor.

Mosely pushed open the door. They entered a dingy vestibule that led to a hallway to the left and a set of narrow wooden stairs to the right. Without hesitation Mosely led Riker up the stairs. As they ascended, they passed a man and a woman who were coming down. They both appeared drunk.

After the couple had passed, Riker turned to Mosely. "It looks like we're on the right path."

At the top of the stairs was a landing with another door. A typewritten sign in a thin frame read, "Please knock and we'll open the door." Without hesitation Mosely rapped on the door with his knuckles. The door opened and a man wearing a white shirt and red brocade vest said, "Hello."

"Reservation for Mosely."

The man consulted his list. "Yes, of course. Please come in."

Riker and Mosely followed the man as he led the way through the crowded rooms to a dim paneled chamber with a bar, some booths, and a few tables. One booth was available, and the man gave it to them.

"You really feel like it's the Roaring Twenties and you're in a speak-easy," said Riker as they perused the menu.

"The thing is, the food and the drinks are exceptional," answered Mosely. "Try the seared scallops with garlic jam and fire roasted vegetables. Terrific."

They ordered from the waiter who, like everyone else who worked there, wore a white shirt and red brocade vest. His mark of distinction was that he also sported an immense handlebar moustache with perfectly waxed tips. He told them that his name was Alphonse.

After Alphonse had delivered their drinks—two concoctions named "Rusty Wagon" and "Ice, Ice, Baby" for Riker and Mosely, respectively—Riker said, "How did you get involved with your present-day boss?" He was unsure of under what circumstances White House staffers ever spoke the words "the president" in casual public situations.

"Ah, the boss," said Mosely with a smile. "I first got to know him in Baltimore, when he was a lawyer for the longshoremen. I worked for the city, in community relations. Our paths crossed a number of times, and although the Longshoremen's Association was known to be a pretty rough crowd, I always thought Paul was a straight shooter. He didn't bullshit you. He was upfront about what he wanted from the city. When he announced he was running for governor, I thought, 'Boy, this guy has balls!' I gave him a call, just to wish him good luck. He asked me to join his team. My first reaction was, 'Is he kidding? I'm an openly gay guy. What does he want with me?' But I agreed to meet with him, and before I knew it I was his deputy campaign director. It was more fun than I expected. I'm a numbers guy, and I liked poring over the polls and churning through statistics. Paul's campaign was a long shot, but somehow we pulled it off. I spent the next four years in Annapolis, working as one of his assistant communications managers—writing press releases, setting up press conferences, and updating his website.

"When Paul was two years into his term, he told me that he was thinking about running for president of the United States. I thought, 'Oh boy, here we go again!' We formed an exploratory committee, and by the time summer rolled around he was ready to make his announcement. The only unresolved question was his wife."

"His wife?" asked Riker.

Even though they were in a private booth, Mosely leaned forward and lowered his voice so that Riker could barely hear him over the music.

"Yep. She never saw a bottle of booze or a pill she didn't like. I don't want to be an armchair psychologist, but the story is that when she was a child, her mother rejected her—you know, mom was the icy, non-maternal type. Anyway, Susan has her demons. It's the worst-kept secret in Washington."

"Does she receive treatment?"

"Karen Thompson has tried to counsel her. Not much luck. Susan also has a family doctor she's known for many years. But you gotta understand something—when you're the First Family, everything you do is under the white-hot glare of the media. Your political opponents are waiting for you to fall on your ass. My guess is that Paul tries to keep the simmering pot from boiling over into the public view. He doesn't need another headache. Congress gives him enough of them already."

At that moment Alphonse delivered their food, and the conversation ended.

As they ate, they talked about other matters, such as the Washington Redskins and their ongoing troubles with their name, which the team's owners steadfastly refused to consider changing. "The commissioner of the NFL wants the boss to weigh in on the dispute, but he's not going to touch it with a ten-foot pole," said Mosely. "The Redskins are the third most valuable NFL franchise, after the Cowboys and the Patriots. Public opinion polls about their name are all over the map—you can find some polls that say the team should change the name, and others say the opposite. For the boss, aligning himself with either side would be a losing proposition."

Mosely asked about Riker's career, and mercifully did not insist upon hearing every detail of the Syrian smallpox affair.

Mosely's phone rang. He picked up the call. He looked at Riker. "Sure, sweetheart, come on down. I'm sitting here with Dr. Martin Riker. Join the party." He hung up.

"Who was that, if I may ask?"

"Lindsay Baker," replied Mosely. "You've met her, haven't you? She's the boss's director of scheduling and advance. We hang out together a lot. She's divorced and I'm single."

"No significant other in your life?"

"There was one. His name was William. He was the light of my life. But before I met him—this was many years ago—he led a reckless life. He got AIDS, and after battling it for five years it finally got him. He passed away just before the election. So I buried him in Baltimore and came to Washington."

"I'm very sorry for your loss."

"Thank you."

For Martin Riker, who had lived and worked in some of the worst AIDS-ravaged areas of the world including Swaziland, Botswana, and Lesotho—where nearly one-quarter of all adults are living with HIV, and where he had seen people dying of AIDS in nearly every village and town—every death was still poignant. Every victim was someone's brother, sister, child, parent, or loved one. News of someone dying from a preventable—and now treatable—infectious disease was never easy to accept or understand, and the human pain was always acute.

"Of course," continued Mosely, "as a member of the president's senior staff, I need to keep my personal life very private. There are any number of people who would make it a distraction if they could."

"But it's no secret that you're gay, is it?"

"You're right—it's no secret. But in Washington there's still a difference between someone who's *quietly* gay and someone who's *blatantly* gay.

Especially if you serve the president. It's my job to never be a distraction. I'll give you an example. If I were to attend a Washington social function, and I walked into the event holding hands with a man, it would cause unacceptable headlines. If I walked in holding hands with an attractive young woman, no one would notice."

"A double standard," said Riker.

Mosely shrugged. "Yes, but it could be worse. Heck, in the old days it was *much* worse. Thirty years ago, if I wanted to work in Washington, I'd have to stay so far in the closet that I'd reek of mothballs. At least today I can live like a normal person—that is, if you consider anything about Washington to be normal." He leaned closer to Riker. "One of the first things you learn about the City of Magnificent Intentions—as Charles Dickens christened it—is that everyone has an agenda. Everyone wants to get ahead, and this can only be done by stepping on someone else. People will lie to your face. They'll tell you what a great guy you are and then, the moment your back is turned, they'll try to destroy you."

"Except for you, of course," laughed Riker.

"That's right," said Mosely. "I'm the exception to the rule. And do you know why? Because I could walk away from all of this in a second." He snapped his fingers. "I could go back home to my little bungalow on the banks of the Patapsco River, catch me some blue crabs, and have a nice life. All these other people"—he swept his hand around the crowded room—"want more and more power. They'll do anything to get it."

"Aren't you generalizing?" said Riker. He motioned for Alphonse, who sauntered over. "We'll have two more."

Alphonse nodded as he cleared the empties.

"Yes, I'm generalizing," continued Mosely, "but around here you have no choice but to assume the worst of everyone. It's like what Harry Truman supposedly said: 'If you want a friend in Washington, get a dog.'"

"And yet you and I sit here, acting like friends."

"Sometimes I'm just a naïve fool," laughed Mosely. "I can't help myself—I try to keep myself free of the deadly infection of Washington ambition."

At that moment Riker saw Lindsay Baker making her way through the crowd. Riker waved to her. Seeing him, she smiled and came over to the booth. Mosely slid over to let her sit next to him. "Right here, sweetheart," he said as he patted the banquette.

"It looks like you two have gotten a head start on me," she said.

Alphonse appeared.

"I'll have a Gibson," said Lindsay. She turned to Riker and Mosely. "Have you two been getting to know one another?"

"We were discussing what a dangerous place Washington is," said Riker. "Makes me think I should have brought a can of shark repellent from Florida."

"Oh, you'll get used to it," said Lindsay. "When a shark gets too close, you whack it on its nose, and it swims away to find an easier target."

"You make it sound so simple," said Riker.

"That's Lindsay's great gift," said Mosely. "She makes complicated stuff sound easy. Besides, everyone loves Lindsay. She hasn't got an enemy in the world."

"Except the entire island of Martha's Vineyard," she said. "Yesterday I had to tell the tourism director there that next summer the First Family is taking their annual vacation in Sag Harbor. The way she reacted, you'd think that I had told them we were selling the Vineyard to the Chinese."

"Kids," said Mosely as he drained his glass, "I'm going to leave you now. Yes, I know you're heartbroken. Try to carry on without me."

Lindsay stood to let him slide out of the booth. After giving her a peck on the cheek and shaking Riker's hand, Mosely disappeared into the crowd.

"He's quite a guy," said Riker as Lindsay sat down across from him.

"A ray of sunshine," she smiled.

"Are you alone?" asked Riker.

"I was out with a girlfriend, but her boyfriend called her, so she had to leave. I was ready to go home when I thought I'd call Max. I was only a few blocks away, so I decided to stop in here and say hello."

"Well, hello," said Riker.

"Hello," she laughed, showing her white teeth. She folded her hands on the table. "What do you think of this place?"

"It's fun, if a little bit self-consciously trendy. Max predicted that within six months no one will come here because it'll be full of tourists."

Lindsay nodded. "The owners will sell it and open a new place that's even more difficult to find. It will be the hip place for a year or so, and then the process will repeat itself."

"Eventually, the most obscure location for a bar will be in a cave somewhere."

"A bar in a cave?" said Lindsay. "I like the idea. Except for the bats. They'd have to get rid of the bats."

"Agreed," said Riker, even though he personally liked bats.

"Tell me about yourself," said Lindsay.

Riker was struck by her directness. "What do you want to know?"

"You like to investigate viruses and other microscopic bugs?"

"I guess you could say that. I've always been interested in the complexity of life, and how all life forms are interrelated. Did you know that your body—right now—is home to trillions of bacteria? They outnumber your own cells by ten to one. Their total weight is about three pounds. And they're all different—the bacteria in your upper intestines are not the same as the bacteria in your stomach."

"Oh, my gosh—where do all these bacteria come from?"

"Many of them came from your parents. When babies are first born, their insides—their guts—are sterile. Each time your mother kissed you, she gave you some of her bacteria. Call it a maternal gift."

"Thanks, Mom."

"And here's something else. Many scientists believe that when two people fall in love, it's really because their respective microbiomes—the bacteria living within them—agree with each other. In a sense, you and I are nothing more than repositories for vast populations of bacteria that direct our actions."

At this point, Riker knew, most women who heard this speech would politely excuse themselves and get up from the table. Yet Lindsay stayed, and even appeared to be interested.

In Riker's book, this quality made her exceptional.

"Enough about me," said Riker. "You seem very comfortable in the Washington cage match of egos and intrigue."

She laughed. "I grew up with three brothers—two older and one younger. I quickly learned how to navigate among the guys. When I was in junior high, my mother became ill with crippling arthritis, and couldn't do much of the daily work around the house. With Dad on the road—he was a sales rep for a chemical supplies company—we kids had to step up and do our share of the work. I became a sort of junior mom, making sure that my brothers got their chores done. But don't get me wrong—we had lots of fun, too. We made sure we took care of each other. Mom did her best to help, and I know she appreciated our pitching in. When I was seventeen, Dad left—or I guess it would be more accurate to say he didn't come back. I think that because he was away so much, he just sort of fell into a new relationship."

"Do you see him much?"

"Yes—he and Cheryl, his wife, live in San Diego. I get out there once in a while, for his birthday or some other occasion. What can you do, especially if you're a kid? You try to go along with what the adults are doing. If Dad leaves, you still want him to be your father."

"And your mom?"

"She lives with my brother Donny, in Woodbridge, which is a forty-minute drive from Capitol Hill. But we may move her to an assisted living facility. Donny and his wife both work, and last week when they were out of the house, Mom fell. One of the grandkids found her when they came home from school. Mom didn't break any bones, but it was a wakeup call. She could have been seriously injured."

They talked about their families, and eventually Riker learned that Lindsay was divorced with no kids, and she learned that he was a widower with three kids.

As they talked and the minutes quickly ticked by, Riker became aware of Alphonse hovering nearby, looking at them. With his hand on the table, he leaned closer to Lindsay—close enough to inhale her floral perfume—and said *sotto voce*, "What's up with our waiter? He's standing over there, giving us the evil eye."

Lindsay smiled and lightly touched her fingertips to the back of Riker's hand. The sensation was electric. "Here at Harry White's," she said, matching his conspiratorial tone, "they have a reputation for turning over the tables as fast as they can. They don't want people lingering over drinks for hours, taking up valuable real estate, while they turn away customers at the door. Therefore, to keep ourselves in their good graces, we have two choices—either spend more money on food and booze, or give up our booth."

Riker turned over his hand so that the palm was up. To his immense happiness, she did not remove her fingertips, but allowed them to rest against his. Having understood this subtle signal, he curled his fingers slightly so that his fingertips cradled hers.

"Personally, my ass is getting sore from sitting here," he said. "This banquette is as hard as a church pew."

She laughed. "Then let's leave Alphonse a nice tip, vacate our space, and stretch our legs. I'm in the mood to take a walk. How about you?"

"Sounds good," said Riker.

No sooner had they stood up than Alphonse rushed over to clear the table.

Riker and Lindsay made their way through the crowd to the door. Even though they were jostled, Riker resisted the urge to take her by the hand—it seemed too early for such a move.

They found themselves on the sidewalk. The night was clear and cold. As they began to walk north, Lindsay slipped her arm through his. Riker discovered that Lindsay had grown up in Virginia Beach, and the family had a little summer house on the water with a dock and a couple of Sunfish for the kids to sail around in.

"I've got a twenty-footer in Naples," he offered. "If you're ever in the neighborhood, I'll take you for a sail."

"That would be fun," she replied. They arrived at East Capitol Street NE. A half-mile to the west loomed the majestic dome of the Capitol Building. With a shiver, Lindsay said, "I'd like you to take me home now."

They flagged a black car. "Where to?" said the driver.

"Thirty-six hundred Reservoir Road, in Georgetown," said Lindsay as they climbed into the back seat. As the car pulled away from the curb, she snuggled close to Riker. Fifteen minutes later, the car eased to a stop in front of a brick townhouse.

"Thanks very much," said Lindsay to the driver. She opened her door and got out.

Riker remained in his seat.

Lindsay turned and leaned down so that she could speak to Riker. "Don't you want to come in for a nightcap?"

"Sure I do," replied Riker as he slid across the seat towards the open door. "I just didn't want to—you know—make an assumption."

Lindsay smiled. "In Washington these days, true gentlemen are few and far between."

Chapter 9

*   *   *

On Monday morning the snow came down in big, fast flakes as Riker hurried up the curving walkway to the South Portico of the White House. After passing through security, he entered the office of the Medical Unit. The receptionist—whose name, Riker had learned, was Dorothy—looked up from her computer.

"Has the president passed by yet?" he asked.

"Yes, right on time," replied Dorothy. "He's in the Oval Office."

"How did he look?"

"Fine. Well rested. He spent Saturday and most of Sunday at Camp David. Came back last night. I think getting away for some R&R was helpful."

"Is Dr. Thompson in?"

"Yes, she's waiting for you."

Riker entered Thompson's office. She was behind her desk, peering at a report. Outside the window, in the swirling snow the trees and South Lawn were cloaked in white.

Thompson looked up. "Good morning, Martin. Coffee?"

"No, I'm fine, thanks. I ate breakfast at The Jefferson."

She put down her report and casually swiveled in her chair. "I understand you discovered Harry White's the other night. It's quite an interesting place. Rather dark and mysterious, wouldn't you say?"

Riker narrowed his eyes. "Word sure gets around quickly, doesn't it?"

"This is Washington!" said Thompson with an expansive wave of her hand towards the wintery window. "You can't go anywhere in public without someone seeing you."

"And reporting on you, it seems."

"Now don't get your knickers in a twit," laughed Thompson. "We all live in a fishbowl. As a matter of fact, in this particular case no one was spying on you. I had to call Max this morning, and he mentioned he had taken you there. He's a good guy. Sometimes a bit naïve perhaps, but a good guy."

"Naïve?"

"He's not too fond of Washington power politics. He's still clinging to his youthful idealism. He thinks that human beings are innately good."

"And what do you think?"

"I think that all of us are driven by self-interest. If our personal needs are satisfied, then we can afford to be altruistic. If we feel threatened or deprived, we act to preserve and strengthen ourselves. It's perfectly normal."

"Yes, but some people are *never* satisfied," said Riker. "They feel threatened all the time. Whatever they have, they're convinced someone else wants to steal from them."

"That sounds like some recent candidates for president," replied Thompson. "If you always want more—more power, more money—then Washington is a pretty good place to aim for."

Even though Thompson's attitude was one of casual fun, Riker felt acutely relieved that Max did not see him leave the bar with Lindsay. If he had, everyone in town would know. The less he was the topic of conversation, the better.

Thompson swiveled around and faced Riker directly. "I understand you've had a productive week. Let's review what you've found."

"In a nutshell," said Riker, "I've identified two incidents where Mr. Ralston could have been exposed to HIV in his travels. The first occurred two years ago, during the presidential campaign, when he was treated by Dr. Palmer, the dentist in Skowhegan. A few months after he worked on Mr. Ralston, it was discovered that the dentist had AIDS. On top of that, the hygiene in his office was severely substandard. It looks like at least four of his patients who now are HIV-positive could have gotten it from him."

"It was incredibly stupid to have allowed Mr. Ralston to have been treated by such a dangerous dentist," said Thompson with what to Riker was surprising vehemence.

"Of course," agreed Riker, "but he was on the campaign trail, they wanted to get him treated as quickly as possible for a minor injury, and apparently Dr. Palmer came with good recommendations."

"Who was the governor's physician at the time?"

Riker scrolled through the screen on his phone. "Records indicate it was Dr. Joseph Winneker, who had been the Ralston family physician for many years in Baltimore. He retired when Mr. Ralston was elected president."

"Winneker, huh?" said Thompson. "And now he's retired? My guess is that he's an old-school sawbones who knows nothing about AIDS. He probably never considered the danger."

"I really don't know—" began Riker.

"Okay," interrupted Thompson. "That's a solid possibility. In fact, I'd say it's highly probable that you, Dr. Riker, have solved this case in less than a week. When they said you were the best, they weren't kidding."

"Thank you, but in my opinion we're still a very long way from making a conclusion. There is at least one other instance of the president being at risk—the baggie of blood thrown by the protestor in Japan. There may be others. I haven't yet investigated the accident in Kenya. And once we compile an inventory of every possible source, we'll try to pin down which one caused the president's infection. Hopefully we can perform DNA testing on the strain of HIV present in the president's blood and compare it to the strain of HIV from the suspected source. If we're lucky, we'll get a match, and we'll know the origin."

Thompson frowned. "I'm sorry—I'm not familiar with that new stuff. It's been a while since I learned about AIDS in med school, and I haven't seen a case since. If you don't mind, please get me up to speed."

She reached for the bowl of hard candies. Riker watched as she fished around with her fingertips, and after a moment extracted a red one. "I don't know why I buy the assortment," she said as she unwrapped the nugget. "The cherry flavor is my favorite. I end up throwing away most of the other ones." She expertly wadded and tossed the wrapper into the White House waste can.

"AIDS research has made tremendous strides," said Riker. "I'll give you a thumbnail sketch. HIV is the overall name of the virus, but there are subcategories. You know, like blood cells have types, or resistant and non-resistant strains of staph."

"Right," said Thompson.

"The first subdivision contains the 'types,'" continued Riker. "Globally, there are two, types 1 and 2. The predominant one we deal with is type 1. HIV-2 is found most often in West Africa, and is less infectious.

"HIV-1 can be further classified into four groups: M, N, O, and P. The biggest, M, is responsible for the majority of the AIDS epidemic. The other three are uncommon.

"Drilling down further, within M, there are at least nine genetically distinct subtypes. Subtype B is the dominant one in Europe and the Americas.

"Beyond that, the nine subtypes can also combine to form hybrid viruses, known as CRFs, for 'circulating recombinant forms.' Hundreds of these have been identified. Each time HIV replicates by infecting a new cell, small changes or mutations may occur. This means there are countless different forms of the virus."

Thompson stood up and went to the window. The snow was falling more heavily, and the low shrubs under the trees were now white masses. On the pathway to the southwest appointment gate, a groundskeeper plowed with a tractor.

"So can DNA testing pin down which particular variations of the virus are in a particular patient?" she asked.

"Probably yes. Barring a freak coincidence whereby two strains have the same markers, if the sample from your patient matches one from another person of interest, you've found the pair you're looking for. Remember, though, at that point you won't know which of the two was the donor of the HIV and which one was the recipient."

"How long does it take to sequence the DNA in a sample of HIV?"

"A few days," replied Riker. "The time span is getting shorter and the reliability is getting better."

"We haven't yet sequenced the president's HIV," said Thompson as she returned to her desk. "I'd say that needs to be our first priority."

"I can arrange for it to be done confidentially," said Riker. "I'll need four samples to send to the CDC, each identified only by number. For extra assurance, they'll distribute them to four different testing labs."

"Let's do it," replied Thompson. "We have recent samples of the president's blood securely stored here, in our refrigerator. I'll ensure they're packaged appropriately for transport by courier."

"It would be better if we sent them by FedEx, overnight delivery," replied Riker. "They cannot appear to be anything out of the ordinary. And, if in fact the blood in the Japanese baggie is determined to contain HIV, we'll need it to be sequenced as well. I'm sure the Japanese government didn't do this, because to them the case was cut and dried—Tashi Osaki was a kook who needed to be institutionalized, and the quicker the case was closed, the better."

"Can they do it even though the blood is dried?" asked Thompson.

"My best information is that as long as the sample was not heated or subjected to destructive forces—chemicals or ultraviolet light, for example—the virus can remain intact and its DNA sequenced. It's emerging science. We won't know for sure until the test is performed."

"Okay," said Thompson. "Martin, I'd say you've earned yourself a few days off. After you send the blood samples to the CDC, there's nothing to do but wait for the results. You might as well go home and get some Florida sun. Then, if there's more to be done, you can come back."

Riker was taken aback by Thompson's casual attitude. "That's a very kind offer, but I'm not sure that I agree with you. While it's true that while we've made solid progress, we owe it to ourselves, and to the president, to leave no avenue unexplored. We're just beginning the investigation. We need to produce a comprehensive report. There remains the president's motorcade accident in Kenya earlier this year, and any other incidents that I haven't yet evaluated. In addition, we haven't even opened the subject of direct sexual transmission."

"Martin, are you joking?" said Thompson. With an irritated expression she fished in the candy bowl. Riker watched as her fingertips churned the candies. "Damn," she muttered. "No more cherry. I'll have to settle for orange." Looking up at Riker, as she unwrapped an orange candy she gave him a rueful smile. "Time for a new bag. I'll suffer with orange and lemon, but never grape. I can't stand the grape."

"I'm with you on that—I'm not much of a grape person either," said Riker.

"Saying the president got AIDS from either a bad dentist or a crazy protestor will be acceptable to the voters," continued Thompson. "If his illness becomes public, those causes—neither of which he took a risk for—will make him appear sympathetic. Hell, I even wish we could blame it on a contaminated blood transfusion, except he hasn't received one. He could become an advocate for tighter regulation of the health-care industry, or, if the cause was the protestor, a crusader for improved presidential security when the president is traveling overseas. Either way, he'll win the liberal gay vote at the same time that he wins the conservative evangelical vote."

"Evangelical vote?" asked Riker.

"Sure," said Thompson. "Can't you see the message? President Paul Ralston, infected through happenstance with the demonic disease, steadfastly soldiers on."

"Demonic?" said Riker. "Karen, aren't we scientists? A virus isn't demonic. It's just a virus."

Thompson laughed and slapped her hand on her desk. "Martin, you know as well as I do that in politics, *everything* is political. *Everything* can be assigned a moral context. There are millions of voters who, when they learn that President Ralston has AIDS, will immediately want to know if it's an indicator of hypocritical behavior. Especially sex. You know, portraying himself to the public as a happily married man. This is why there's a huge difference between the happily married president getting AIDS from a crazy protestor or dentist and his getting it from a girlfriend he had on the side!"

"Or boyfriend," said Riker.

"Oh, my God, don't even go there," said Thompson as she rolled her eyes. "Not with the image he's cultivated. Now you're talking about Armageddon. The end of the world as we know it."

Riker smiled to himself. He could imagine the uproar.

"Needless to say," pressed Riker, "We need to clear all of these possibilities from our list. We need to be certain how the president got AIDS. It's a matter of national security."

Riker saw Thompson's back stiffen and her eyes harden. He could tell that he had hit a nerve. For a moment he thought she might throw him out of her office. Riker said nothing more.

After a long second had passed, Thompson's tight face relaxed as her eyes slid away. A slight smile played across her lips. When her eyes returned to Riker's, they were softer, less electric.

"Of course," she said evenly. "Perhaps I was letting my enthusiasm for finding a solution to the puzzle so quickly get the best of me. Therefore, I suggest that we push ahead with the investigation without delay. Do I understand correctly that the next incident on your list—and the most dramatic of them all—was the motorcade accident in Kenya?"

"Yes."

"I think you should go to Kenya and see the scene for yourself. It was a ghastly accident, and several people were killed. It led to a fundamental change in how the president's security team evaluates the routes that the president travels in his motorcade. As you know, I wasn't there; the Medical Unit was represented by Norm Gladstone. He's still with our team. His office is over in the EOB, room 213D. I'll give him a ring—hold on." She picked up her phone and made the call. After a quick conversation she hung up. "He's available now."

As Riker walked through the driving snow to the Executive Office Building, it entered his mind that the first time he had visited the building had been five days earlier, when he had called on Lindsay Baker. The thought made his heart beat a little bit faster. Saturday night had been lovely. Perhaps....

Get a grip, he told himself. *You're not a teenager.*

Having acquired a familiarity with the building, in a few minutes he found room 213D. The assistant at his desk said, "You may find Dr. Gladstone in his office." He motioned with his head. "Through that door."

Riker entered a room that looked as if it were a storage closet for the Museum of Natural History. The shelves groaned under glass jars of fish and other sea creatures suspended in formaldehyde. A tall stuffed ostrich stood in a corner. A glass case held the skull of what looked like a chimpanzee. Into Riker's nostrils came the faint odor of preservatives and dried leather.

"Ah, Dr. Riker, please have a seat," said a wiry man with white hair and a white goatee, like an intellectual version of Colonel Sanders.

"Dr. Gladstone, thanks for seeing me on such short notice," said Riker as he picked up a pile of medical journals that were on the chair and moved them to an open spot on a table that supported a stuffed furry mammal resembling a mouse grown to the size of a football. Riker paused to look at the creature.

"That's a hyrax," offered Dr. Gladstone. "Very common in Africa. I know what you're thinking. Yes, I'm a medical doctor who treats human beings, including presidents. African zoology is a bit of a hobby of mine. I keep many of my specimens here because my wife doesn't want them in our home. She thinks they're creepy."

"Ah, domestic bliss," smiled Riker as he sat down. "What can you do?"

"Indeed, what can you do? Now then, I understand you're working on some sort of threat assessment for the president. Not a bad idea at all. Nowadays, you never know how an enemy, a terrorist, or a crazy guy will try to harm the leader of the free world."

"We're also looking at ways the president could be harmed through an accident or negligence," said Riker. He told Dr. Gladstone about Dr. Palmer. "We can't know whether Dr. Palmer intentionally infected any of his patients. That's probably what happened with that dentist in Florida, Dr. Acer. But Palmer was also unbelievably lazy about maintaining professional standards of hygiene."

"Either way, a very bad guy," said Dr. Gladstone. "But that reminds me of another dentist case, a Dr. Schmidt, as best I can recall. In Louisiana. He was sentenced to fifty years for infecting his mistress by injecting her with blood from an AIDS patient. Of course, in our case, Palmer had no idea the president would be coming in as a patient."

"I'd like to ask you about the accident in Kenya. You were there—correct?"

Dr. Gladstone's eyes narrowed and he shifted his body away from Riker. "Yes, I was there," he said tersely. "It was a mess, with injured people everywhere. A lot of blood splashed around, but once we cleaned up our people, actual injuries weren't that bad. Fortunately, the president escaped with only a cut down his arm, which occurred as he tumbled around inside the rolling car. The wound wasn't that deep, but it was about four inches long, from the right elbow along the underside of the arm."

"Did it bleed much?"

"Yeah, but apparently from just superficial layers. I covered it with a clean dressing and a compression bandage. We changed it daily, and within a week it had healed sufficiently so that covering it was no longer necessary."

"Was the president injured in any other way?"

"A slight cut on his left hand and a bruise on his left shoulder—neither particularly serious."

"Did the president come into contact with any other blood or injured persons?"

"Not that I can recall," he said quickly. Then he looked Riker in the eye. "No, he did not."

"While it was a tragic event," said Riker, "if that's all that happened to him, this incident may not fall within the purview of this project, and we'll be able to cross it off our list. Can you email me a copy of your full report?"

"I'll have to find it," said Dr. Gladstone. "I'll get back to you on that."

"Thank you for your time," said Riker as he stood up. "I'll find my way out."

Chapter 10

$*$ $*$ $*$

In the long ornate hallway outside Dr. Gladstone's office, Riker paused. He pulled out his phone and punched a number.

"Lindsay? Hi. It's Martin. Listen, I'm in the building—I had another appointment. Do you have a minute? Okay, great. I'm on my way."

A few moments later Riker entered room 325B. The admin assistant by the door waved him through. He made his way to Lindsay's office, and, after greeting Sharina, found Lindsay behind her desk.

With her slender hands folded on top of her desk, she gave him a smile that was slightly more generous than professional courtesy required. Her eyes shone.

"Good morning, Dr. Riker," she said brightly.

Her demeanor was everything he had hoped for.

"Good morning, Ms. Baker," he replied.

"How may I help you?"

"I'm looking into the president's trip to Kenya last April."

"Oh yes—the terrible accident with the motorcade. We were very lucky that no one in the president's party was killed."

"Can you give me the staff list for that day?"

"No problem." She found the file on her computer and attached it to an email. "It's in your inbox."

"Can you print one page of it for me now? I don't need all four hundred names—just the White House staff who would be interacting directly with the president."

She made a few clicks. Then she stood up—rather unnecessarily, thought Riker with satisfaction—and walked around the desk to the printer, which was on a table directly behind him. She took the paper from the printer and handed it to him. It was a simple task that he could have easily done himself. Then she brushed by him on the way back to her desk. She was close enough so that Riker could smell her perfume—the same scent she had worn on Saturday night.

While pleased with Lindsay's subtle flirtation, Riker showed no response. With his eyes on the paper, he studied the list, on which he noticed both new names and familiar ones.

"So far, I've seen two of these rosters," said Riker. "The G7 Japan trip and this one. Is there a separate list for the First Lady and her staff?"

"If she accompanied the president, there would be," said Lindsay. "Her entourage would typically consist of an additional twenty people—secretaries, wardrobe people, hairdressers, and so forth. But she generally does not travel with the president on overseas business trips. She'll only go if a state dinner is on the agenda and she has to appear with her counterpart—the wife or spouse of the host country's prime minister or president."

"Why doesn't she go more often?"

Lindsay hesitated.

"I've heard about certain health issues," said Riker.

Lindsay nodded. "I think that's a factor."

Riker folded the list and put it into the inside breast pocket of his jacket. "One more thing—what can you tell me about Stephen Howe?"

"The president's body man? He's been with the president since the beginning of the presidential campaign. He's Mr. Ralston's valet, personal assistant, golf partner, procurer of snacks—you name it, and Stephen's probably done it."

"He's always with the president?"

"You very rarely see the president without Stephen nearby. Obviously, his role is more important when the president travels, and perhaps less demanding when the president is working a routine schedule in the Oval Office."

"Thanks very much." Riker stood up. He noticed that the door to Sharina's office was open, and he could hear her speaking on the phone. Leaning closer to Lindsay's desk, Riker said, "I'm sure I'll be seeing you around."

"I'm sure you will," she smiled.

Riker left the office and hurried through the snow to his office at the Ten-Fifty. With a hot cup of coffee on his desk, he clicked open his email and looked for a message from Dr. Gladstone. There was nothing.

"I guess I'll have to do it the hard way," he said to himself. After searching the Medical Unit database, he found the report and down-loaded it.

WHITE HOUSE MEDICAL UNIT
INCIDENT REPORT
NORMAN GLADSTONE, M.D., PH.D.
THURSDAY, 6 APRIL
NAIROBI, KENYA

POTUS was in Nairobi, Kenya, to attend a two-day conference of the Organization of African States. While in Nairobi, the president's entourage occupied the top two floors of the Nairobi Regal Hotel. The exact location of where the president spent the night—whether at the hotel, on board Air Force One at Jomo Kenyatta International Airport, at the American Embassy, or some other location, remains classified. The Medical Unit, in conformance with standard operating procedure, was quartered nearby at the Fairmont. Due to her mother's illness, the First Lady did not accompany the president on this trip.

On the first day of the conference, the president attended all the scheduled events and a dinner with the president of Kenya in the evening. Aside from a few demonstrators outside the hotel, there were no incidents.

On the second day of the conference, a side trip was scheduled to the Nairobi National Park. The motorcade route had been carefully planned and vetted by the Secret Service. Due to the *kusi* monsoon season, April is the wettest month of the year in Nairobi, and the constant heavy rains often cause river flooding. It had been raining for three days, but overnight the skies had cleared and the air, while humid, was dry. The temperature was seventy degrees Fahrenheit.

At nine-thirty in the morning the president's motorcade, consisting of approximately twenty vehicles, left the Nairobi Regal Hotel. I was riding in an SUV about ten cars behind "The Beast," the president's personal limousine, which, as is customary, had been flown from the US to Kenya by C-17 Globemaster transport plane. To be clear, I do not know exactly which "Beast" was deployed for this trip, as there are several of them. The exact number is classified.

Led by a Kenyan motorcycle police escort, the motorcade drove south along Mombassa Road before taking a right turn at National Park East Gate Road and entering the park.

As we approached the Mokoyeti River, our driver suddenly stopped. I looked ahead and saw through the trees that there seemed to be an accident. We got a radio call that POTUS was down. I got out of the SUV, and along with others in the motorcade, began to run alongside the road, towards the river.

I came around the bend and saw a horrific scene. The bridge had collapsed, and several vehicles had plunged directly into the river, while a few others, including the president's limousine, had slid down the embankment. The president's car had rolled over and was lying on its roof. People—Secret Service agents, Kenyan police, White House staffers— were slipping and sliding on the rocky slope. In the twisted wreckage of the bridge itself, the first members of the motorcade—mostly Kenyan motorcycle police, and the occupants of the lead Secret Service car—were struggling to hold onto parts of the bridge as the strong current pulled at them. A few let go, and we later learned that two people were swept away and drowned.

My primary concern was the president. I slid down the embankment just as the Secret Service got the car doors opened. The president emerged. He appeared to be dazed but not seriously injured. But his right sleeve from the elbow downwards was ripped open and soaked with blood. He stood with his body man, Stephen Howe, next to the car. I also saw Brian Conway, deputy chief of staff for operations. He was sitting on the ground, and appeared to have struck his head. Because Christina Wilkinson, one of our Medical Unit nurses, was attending to him, I did not approach him.

The scene around the bridge was chaotic. At least ten of the motorcade vehicles were either in the water or on the embankment. The occupants of these vehicles, plus the Kenyan police escort victims, totaled roughly fifty people. Of these, at least twenty had head wounds, broken limbs, and cuts from glass. The injured included three Secret Service agents. One of them had been the driver of the president's car, and another was the agent who had been riding in the front passenger seat. One of them was bleeding profusely from a cut on his face, which a member of our team treated. Visually, it seemed a lot of blood had been splashed around inside the car, but volume-wise it probably wasn't that much.

In addition, several local Kenyans who had been standing by the side of the road, waving small American flags as the motorcade passed, had been hit by vehicles as the drivers frantically braked and swerved to avoid plunging into the river. Several of these Kenyan civilian victims had broken limbs and head injuries.

I was able to get close to the president and briefly examine him. He had a bleeding gash down his right arm, but, I saw no serious injuries. He was wearing his customary blue suit, but had taken off the jacket while riding, I suppose because of the humid climate. His white shirt was ripped down the right sleeve, and soaked with blood.

One of the president's assistants, Rachel Doucette, emerged from the SUV that had been following directly behind the president's limousine. She was bleeding profusely from a gash on her head. The president saw her and went to her. He gave her a comforting hug before a member of the Medical Unit assisted her up the embankment.

I saw the president do this with several other members of his staff and even a few of the Kenyans. Despite the strenuous protests of his Secret Service handlers, he approached many who were injured, and either hugged them or took their hands to comfort them.

Not more than two minutes after the crash—the scene was chaotic and fast moving—Don Strauss came down the embankment and spoke to the president. By this time several members of the Secret Service, brandishing automatic weapons, had surrounded the president and isolated him. Strauss told the president that a car was waiting on the road. Together the group started to climb up the embankment. About halfway up, the president slipped and his right arm slammed into a rock. I saw him grimace in pain and hold his elbow. A Secret Service agent grabbed him by the upper arm and helped him the rest of the way up the hill.

I went up the embankment also. On the road, the Secret Service had gotten two or three of the SUVs turned around. They hustled the president into one of the cars. I ran to the Medical Unit SUV and told the driver to follow the others. I knew the destination would be Air Force One at Jomo Kenyatta International Airport, about five miles away.

Within a minute we were on our way, at high speed, led by the four Kenyan motorcycle cops who had been bringing up the rear of the motorcade.

At ten o'clock we arrived at the airport. The motorcade raced through the open gate and across the tarmac to Air Force One, which was parked a quarter-mile away from the terminal. The cars screeched to a stop and we got out. As the attending physician I had full access, so I followed the president up the stairs and into the plane.

I examined him in his private quarters. I asked him how he felt.

"A bit banged up," he replied, "but I guess I fared better than many other people. How's my staff? Anybody seriously injured?"

"Initial reports indicate that two of the Kenyan motorcycle escorts were killed. Others have broken bones, bruises, and lacerations. It was a mess. Sir, may I examine you?"

The president stood up and removed his suit and shirt. I examined him and found a four-inch bleeding cut on his right arm. Not deep. The flesh was tender and bloody. After ensuring it was clean, I applied a sterile dressing and compression bandage.

There was a one-inch cut on the side of the palm of his left hand. The president had used a towel to stop the bleeding. After cleaning the wound with water I chose to close it with a tissue adhesive, which was invisible and would fall off in about a week.

He also had a fresh bruise on his left shoulder. No treatment was required.

He appeared alert and fully responsive. His eyes were clear and his speech was good.

"You're ready to go," I said. "Clean bill of health."

He put on a bathrobe. "Thanks, doc," he said. "As soon as you can, please make a list of my staff and their injuries, if any. I want to know how they're doing."

"Of course, sir."

I then went back to the medical office. I had no further direct contact with the president.

POSTSCRIPT
MONDAY, 2 JULY

An investigation by the FBI, the Army Corps of Engineers, and Kenyan officials determined a combination of environmental causes led to the collapse of the bridge over the Mokoyeti River.

Two weeks before the incident, the southernmost bridge support had been struck by a barge, possibly weakening it with undetected hairline fractures in the concrete foundation. On the morning of the event, the force of the monsoon-engorged river water, combined with the weight of the president's motorcade traveling in tight formation, triggered a partial collapse of the foundation, twisting the steel span, popping the rivets, and leading to total structural failure.

No evidence of terrorism or sabotage was found.

Riker closed the report. As he sipped his coffee he thought about what Dr. Gladstone had told him: that during the two-minute period of the accident and the scene by the river, the president had not come into contact with anyone else's blood. According to the doctor's own written report, this assertion was absurd. The Secret Service driver and the right-seat agent were tumbled inside the car with the president, and one of them got a bloody wound. The doctor had described the president, against the wishes of his Secret Service handlers, hugging and comforting members of his staff and Kenyan civilians who had been injured. He specifically wrote that one of his assistants had emerged from a wrecked SUV with a bleeding head wound, and that the president had hugged her. It was inconceivable that the president hadn't been exposed to other people's blood.

Was Dr. Gladstone hiding something?

Or was he just instinctively responding the way that everyone else in Washington would, which was to cover his ass? Perhaps Dr. Gladstone had heard the recent rumors about the president having AIDS, and wanted to ensure that no one could say that it happened while on his watch.

Chapter 11

*   *   *

Riker picked up his phone and made a call. After a short conversation, he said, "Thanks very much. I'll be right over."

He left his office at the Ten-Fifty. The snow had stopped and the sun had come out, warming the streets. Dodging the pools of soupy slush and mounds of chunky plowed snow, Riker made his way to the White House. At the southwest appointment gate, he cleared security and walked up the curving path to the South Portico.

As he approached the steps it occurred to him that up until a week ago he had never been near the White House, and had, like most Americans, seen it only from a distance, or on television. At this moment, he realized that his attitude about entering the White House had evolved from a sense of wonderment to almost casual familiarity, so much so that when passing through security at the southwest appointment gate he had felt a twinge of irritation when the guards did not simply wave him through while saying, "Dr. Riker? Of course. Go right in. Enjoy your day." They had actually patted him down, as if he were any ordinary pedestrian off the street and not someone who had been given access to the inner sanctum of the Oval Office.

Ah—to ascend to the level where you don't get the patdown from the guard at the gate. Now that would be *real* power!

At that moment Riker heard his mother's voice: "Don't get too full of yourself, mister smarty pants!"

Upon entering the Diplomatic Reception Room, instead of walking through the Map Room and into the Center Hall, and thence to the office of the Medical Unit, Riker went across the Center Hall and entered the office of the White House curator. He found himself in a windowless space surmounted by a low vaulted ceiling and crammed with bookshelves. A man was sitting at a desk piled high with books and papers. He looked up as Riker entered.

"Dr. Riker," he said. "I'm James Mansfield, the curator. Please come in. Stephen Howe told me you were coming. He'll be down in a minute. You can have a seat if you like—just take those books off the chair and put them on the floor."

"Rather cramped quarters here, aren't they?" replied Riker as he dutifully relieved the plain ladder-back chair of its burden of leather-bound tomes.

"Over the years, this space has been through a lot of changes," said Mansfield as he shuffled a stack of papers. "Originally it was part of the White House kitchen, then it became the furnace room. In the twentieth century, it was turned into the servants' dining room, and then the Broadcast Room for the president's radio and television announcements. When the Kennedys came, the space was used as part of the upholstery shop before being made into this office."

Riker had picked up an old book and was perusing it when the door opened and a tall, slender man entered. His grey business suit, white shirt, and narrow blue tie were impeccable yet understated. He walked over to Riker with his hand extended.

"Dr. Riker—I'm Stephen Howe, the president's personal assistant."

Riker stood up. Howe's handshake was firm and confident.

"His 'body man,' as they say?" said Riker.

"It's become the unofficial title," smiled Howe. "I understand you're doing some research?"

"Yes. It's an overview of the risks associated with being the president—not only the obvious ones like people who want to harm him, but accidents as well, with a focus on biological threats, which is my specialty. I'm interested in the suit the president was wearing at the scene of the accident in Kenya."

"A terrible day," said Howe. "Very frightening. It's fortunate that the president's limousine—the Beast—is built like a tank. Even though it rolled over, not even a window was broken. Inside the car, we got tossed around, but we only got some cuts and bruises. Some of the cuts were bloody, but nothing compared to the two Kenyan motorcycle officers who died. It was a real tragedy."

"The president sustained a cut on his arm, correct?"

"Yes. When the car rolled over, one of the drinking glasses fell out of its holder and shattered. I believe a piece of its glass slashed him, and it bled quite a bit until we found a towel. Now then—you wanted to see the suit the president was wearing?"

"Yes, if possible."

Howe turned to Mansfield. "Jim, where did we put that? Isn't it in one of your special boxes?"

"It's over here," said Mansfield as he went to a tall metal cabinet and opened the doors. He pulled out a flat box made of grey cardboard. "Acid-free storage," he said as he put the box on a table and pulled off the lid. After donning a pair of white cotton gloves, he lifted the tissue covering the suit. He then gently lifted the folded jacket out of the box.

The jacket was medium grey lightweight wool, and on its front Riker's trained eye instantly saw stains of what he knew was dried blood.

After laying the jacket on the table, Mansfield took from the box a folded white button-down shirt. It showed massive deep brown stains of dried blood. The right sleeve was ripped open.

"These clothes are a mess," said Riker.

"As soon as the president boarded Air Force One," said Howe, "he went to his private quarters, took off his clothing, and got into the shower.

I knew these pieces were ruined, so I saved them, and when we got back to the White House I asked Jim to hang onto them."

"This is the office of the White House museum, not a presidential archive," added Mansfield, "but we felt that this was an artifact that the family might not want to be kept upstairs in the family quarters."

"In the interest of the completeness of our report," said Riker, "I'd like to have the blood on these items tested. Not that we expect to find anything—we just want to cover all the bases. Stephen, are there any identifying marks or labels on any of the pieces? Monograms, laundry labels?"

"No," replied Howe. "The president doesn't want any of his clothes to have his name on them. He thinks it will discourage what he calls the needless veneration of 'souvenirs,' as he calls them."

"He won't be selling his used handkerchiefs on eBay?" said Riker.

Howe laughed. "Absolutely not."

"I'd like to send the suit and the shirt to the CDC in Atlanta," said Riker. "The testing will take a few days. To be honest, we may not get much from dried blood, but it's worth investigating."

"I don't see a problem with that," said Howe, "as long as the president is not identified as the owner. Do you have an office offsite that you're working out of?"

"Yes," replied Riker, "in the Ten-Fifty."

"Perfect," said Howe. "A courier will bring the suit and shirt there today." He turned to Mansfield. "Thanks very much for your help. I'll have someone pick up the box."

"No problem," replied Mansfield.

"Are you on your way out?" Howe said to Riker.

"Yes."

Howe opened the door to the Center Hall. "Let's take a walk," he said. He led Riker around a corner and down a flight of stairs to the Basement Hall. Directly in front of them was the flower shop, where several staffers were working on cutting and arranging flowers for a reception that afternoon. Walking past the flower shop and a cold storage room, Howe turned another corner, and Riker found himself entering the White House bowling alley.

"We can talk privately here," said Howe as he stood on the parquet floor in front of the two long lanes. "I'm with the president every day, and I'm concerned about his health. There are some days when he seems fine, while there are other days he literally looks like he's ready to throw up. He drags himself out of bed and plods through his schedule. Believe me, I can tell that something isn't right. I've known him since I was a kid—he was a friend of my parents, and he took an interest in my career advancement. I've been with him nearly every day since he announced he was running for president. You're a doctor. I looked you up—you're not just a doctor, you're a microbiologist, and you've traveled the world fighting infectious diseases. And now, suddenly, you're at the White House, working on a special project about possible threats to the health of the president. This is at the same time that the president, in my view, is battling some sort of recurring disease. It's like a bad case of the flu that doesn't go away. It only waxes and wanes."

Riker looked into Howe's brown eyes, which showed genuine concern. What could he say to him? Breaking both the rules of national security and ordinary doctor-patient confidentiality was out of the question. But Riker also knew enough about politics to know that equivocation would be interpreted as tacit acknowledgment.

"You understand that I'm not the president's physician," replied Riker, not quite truthfully.

"If you're working for the Medical Unit, you're part of his medical team, no?"

"I suppose there's some validity to that way of thinking, which would make it even more unethical for me to comment on his health without his permission."

Howe nodded. "I understand. What I'm trying to say is that in the event of an investigation into the state of the president's health, I may be able to help fill in the blanks. Few people outside of his immediate family see him more often than I do, and unlike many others, I tend to see him when he's offstage, so to speak. They see him at meetings and state dinners and news conferences, while I see him in his sweatshirt when he's working out in the gym every morning. I think I could be of help."

"Is there anything you want to tell me now?"

Howe smiled. "We each have our code, Dr. Riker."

At that moment Riker became aware of activity in the hallway outside the bowling alley—voices and footsteps. The door opened and a man in a grey suit entered. He was thirty years old, with a crewcut shaved close to his narrow head, accenting his sharp cheekbones. He looked like a tough nightclub bouncer, which happened to be his job while he was getting his master's degree in political science at Johns Hopkins University. Without hesitation he approached Riker.

"I'm Brian Conway, deputy chief of staff for operations," he said coolly. "And you are—?"

"This is Dr. Martin Riker," interjected Howe. "He's here at the White House on a special assignment for the DIA."

"Dr. Riker," mused Conway. "Your name sounds familiar. I remember seeing it in a briefing paper. Was it the terrorist smallpox attack on The *New York Times?*"

"To be honest, I try to stay out of the headlines," replied Riker. "Especially those of The *New York Times.*"

Conway smiled—more warmly, noted Riker, now that in Conway's eyes Riker had been elevated from Annoying Nobody to Real-Life Tough Guy.

As a doctor, Riker couldn't help noting that Conway had a mild but distinctive case of speech apraxia. He couldn't make the "t" sound, so he substituted a "d" sound instead. Hence "Martin" became "Mardin," and "terrorist" became "derrorizd." The contrast of his speech with his tough-guy reputation was curiously incongruous.

Turning, Conway ushered another man into the bowling alley. He was tall, with a short white beard and glasses. He wore a *docha*, the traditional Himalayan knee-length shirt.

Then came President Ralston.

Startled, Riker stepped back.

The president looked at Howe. "Hey, Stephen—sorry to barge in like this," he said jovially. "Are you guys bowling?"

"No, sir—I'm just showing Dr. Riker around."

"I suppose we're both acting as tour guides, then," said the president. He turned to the tall man with the beard. "Minister Pashtar, this is my personal assistant Stephen Howe." They bowed to each other. "And Dr. Martin Riker." More bowing. Riker was impressed the president remembered his name. "Minister Pashtar is visiting from Nepal," said the president, "where there seems to be a growing interest in bowling. So I thought I'd bring him down here to show him our lanes." The president stopped for a moment, covered his mouth, and coughed—not a little dry-tickle-in-the-throat cough, but a deep volcanic eruption. As minister Pashtar politely looked away, Howe quickly handed the president a handkerchief, which he used to dab his mouth. "Please excuse me," said the president to minister Pashtar. "I seem to have picked up something. A little cold, perhaps."

The minister smiled, and then approached the ball rack. He picked up one of the bowling balls and held it in his hands. "Is there an official weight of a bowling ball?" he asked.

"That's a very good question," said the president.

"Yes—a very good question," added Brian Conway.

"The weight limit is sixteen pounds," offered Riker. "There is no minimum. Typically, a bowling ball used by an adult male weighs between fourteen and sixteen pounds—that's six or seven kilograms. For an adult female, five or six kilograms."

"Martin, you're a font of knowledge," said the president.

"When I was in college, I worked a few summers in a bowling alley," replied Riker.

"And the required circumference?" asked minister Pashtar.

"Roughly twenty-seven inches," replied Riker, "or about sixty-eight centimeters."

"Thank you," replied the minister. He indicated the lane. "May I?"

Brian Conway peered down the alley. "The pins are set up," he said. "Please do."

The minister assumed the correct stance, leaning slightly forward with the ball held at his shoulder. With one graceful move he took two steps forward, bent low at the waist, and released the ball, which arced gracefully down the lane before smacking squarely into the center pin. Pins scattered. A moment later, only two were left standing.

"Not bad!" said the president as he began to applaud. Conway, Riker, Howe, and the man in the *docha* applauded too—not vigorously, but with a polite pattering.

"Let's see if I can finish them off," said the minister. Taking another ball from the rack, he launched it down the alley. With a satisfying "whack" it knocked over the two remaining pins.

"A spare!" said the president. "I can tell you've done this before."

"Not as often as I'd like," said the minister. "This is a very nice bowling alley."

Suddenly the president began to cough, with deep explosions that seemed to wrack his body. He gasped for air and coughed again. Howe hurried to his side with another handkerchief. (Riker realized that Howe must have been carrying a supply with him in his jacket pocket.) The president seemed unsteady on his feet. As Howe tried to take him by the elbow, the president shook him off and bravely stood fully upright. "I apologize," he said to minister Pashtar, who had discreetly stepped back a few steps. "Just a little cough. It must be the weather—we don't often get much snow in December."

"Of course," smiled the minister. "Perhaps you might want to try some hot tea made from the leaves of the peppermint plant. It's an ancient remedy."

"Yes, thank you," said the president as he struggled to get air into his lungs. After a moment he was breathing more freely, and he became more relaxed. Riker noticed a drop of perspiration on his forehead, even though the room was cool.

Brian Conway, who Riker thought was looking increasingly tense, said, "Well, then, now that we've shown minister Pashtar the bowling alley, perhaps we should return to the Green Room, where the rest of his party is waiting."

"Of course," said the president. "Lead the way."

With Conway at the head of the line, the group filed out the door, leaving Riker and Howe behind.

"See what I mean?" said Howe. "The president seems fine, and then bang! He sounds terrible."

"Based on what I saw and heard, I'd say he's got a bad case of bronchitis."

"Can you give him something for it?"

"I think that his physician—Dr. Thompson—has the president on a medication regimen. He's being treated."

"I do see him taking a bunch of pills every day—he started on them a few days ago."

"See? I'm sure that Dr. Thompson is treating him appropriately for whatever condition he may have."

Apparently satisfied, Howe reached for the door, and then paused and turned to Riker. "The bloody suit and shirt—what will you test them for?" he asked.

"Anything out of the ordinary," replied Riker.

"Do you suspect that the president could have been infected with something—some disease?"

Riker was getting the idea that Howe was beginning to sniff out the true direction of the investigation. It was time to put a lid on it.

"Listen," he said. "I'm just a guy doing the job I was asked to do. Nothing is more important than the safety and security of the president of the United States. This means that we examine every possibility, even those that are completely far-fetched. We go down every blind alley. We pursue every crazy theory. It doesn't mean that any of it is actionable. So yes, we want to document everything we can about the blood on the president's clothing. However, it would be a mistake to think that this has any particular significance other than wanting the most complete picture possible."

Howe thought for a moment. Then he said, "Okay. I understand. I guess I just wanted you to know that I was concerned."

He pulled open the door, and they walked out into the hall.

Chapter 12

∗   ∗   ∗

Riker returned to his office in the Ten-Fifty. As Howe had promised, a few minutes later a courier delivered the box with the president's suit and shirt. After examining them, Riker re-packed them. He then took the box to the FedEx office on the next block, where he had it shipped to Jim Gilmore at the CDC in Atlanta.

His next stop was the office of Frank Foster, the Secret Service special agent in charge of investigations. Under a sunny sky and with the slushy snow draining from the streets, Riker walked over to the Executive Office Building and made his way to Room 1006G. He found Foster behind his desk.

"Dr. Riker, how was your quickie trip to Japan?" he asked as he took a bite of the turkey club sandwich that he had picked up from the crumpled wax-paper wrapper on his desk. His Cossack eyebrows scrunched down over his eyes. "Forgive me—I've got back-to-back meetings, and I've got to eat at my desk."

"No problem—sorry to barge in like this."

"The time difference really screws you up, doesn't it?"

"Actually, I wasn't there long enough to adjust. Fourteen hours over, twenty-four hours there, and thirteen hours back. What drove me crazy was sitting on the damn plane for over a day of my life."

"I hear you," said Foster as he took a slurp of his diet soda.

"You shouldn't drink that stuff," said Riker. "It's worse than regular soda. It makes you feel hungrier. Get yourself a glass of whole milk."

"Or a beer," said Foster.

"A beer would be better for you than the poison you're drinking now."

"Yeah, but it's against regulations." He took another bite of his sandwich. "Did you come here to lecture me about nutrition?"

"Nah, I wouldn't do that. It's about the threat assessment project. Agent Masako at the PSIA turned over to me the bloody baggie that the protestor had thrown at the president. It's being sent to the CDC in Atlanta for testing. What I came to see you about is the towel that he used to wipe off his face."

"The towel?" said Foster. His big eyebrows lifted.

"Yes. The report indicates that after the blood was splashed on the president, a member of his staff handed him a towel, which he used to clean his face. Do you have any idea what happened to that towel?"

Foster shook his head. "No. I have no idea."

"He didn't hand it to a Secret Service agent? It would have been the obvious thing to do, since at that moment their detail had surrounded the president and was hustling him to his car."

"Let's settle this right now," said Foster. Putting down his sandwich, he made a few clicks with his mouse. Then he rotated the computer screen so that Riker could see it.

"The scene was videotaped," said Foster. "We shoot video whenever the president is out in public. Here it is."

Riker watched as the president, loosely surrounded by his entourage, walked out of the front door of the Shima Kanko Hotel. It was a sunny day and the sky was blue. As the group made their way down the stairs towards the waiting motorcade, the president paused to answer a question. Suddenly a blurry streak arced from outside the frame towards the president. A Secret Service agent saw the incoming object and raised his hand. The object hit his hand and splattered bright red. The president ducked, and Riker could see that some of the red liquid hit him in the face.

There was a half-second pause as the president stood upright and appeared to smile. His face was quite red. As the agents around him began to react, several of them pulled out their weapons. A Japanese woman who was standing near the president reached into her oversized purse and withdrew a white towel. She handed this to the president just as he was being led to his waiting limousine. As he walked, he put the towel to his face and began to wipe. The group approached the open door of the car, and the president, with the towel still in his hand, ducked inside.

"Who's the Japanese woman who gave the president the towel?" asked Riker.

"Hanako Amari, the deputy minister of state for economic and fiscal policy. A very nice lady. Her husband cultivates bonsai trees."

"What do you think happened to the towel?"

Foster shrugged. "When the president travels in the Beast, or in any of the other officially sanctioned presidential vehicles, there are always at least two people with him: the driver and the lead Secret Service agent. The Beast has room for four additional passengers." He clicked open another list. "On the drive to and from the hotel that day, the occupants of the limo were the president, the driver, lead agent Gerard Slade, body man Stephen Howe, and deputy chief of staff Brian Conway. My guess is that they left the towel in the car. The driver is responsible for keeping the interior of the car clean."

"Who was the driver that day?"

More clicking, and then, "Andrew Santapaola."

"Where can I find him?"

"He's over in the main Secret Service building on H Street NW," said Foster. "You'll find him in the garage. I'll tell him you're on your way."

Riker left the Executive Office Building, grabbed an Uber car, and moments later stepped out onto the sidewalk in front of the sleek modernistic glass wedge nestled against what looked like a nineteenth-century office building that, presumably, had been invisibly reinforced to withstand any assault from firearm, rocket, or bomb.

After passing through security, Riker made his way down to the garage. There he was astounded to see the Beast—the immense black limousine emblazoned with the seal of the president of the United States.

Riker was doubly amazed to see the Beast's identical twin parked directly behind it.

"We've got several of these," said a voice behind him. Riker turned to see a square-jawed man in a black suit and a crew cut. He looked like a Hollywood version of a 1960s G-man. "The exact number is classified." The man stuck out his hand. "Andrew Santapaola."

"Martin Riker." He took Santapaola's hand. It felt like a steel vise.

"You drive these?" said Riker.

"Yep."

"You can do a J-turn in this car? Drive fast in reverse, whip the wheel around while you jam on the brakes, spin the car one hundred eighty degrees, and end up traveling forward in the same direction you were going?"

Santapaola laughed. "Yep. They used to call it a moonshiner's turn, 'cause bootleggers would use it to get away from a roadblock. It's faster than a standard Y-turn."

"How many of these cars do you guys have?"

"Sorry, that's classified. In fact, you're one of the very few civilians who's been down here."

Leaving the cars, they went into a small office that looked more like a break room.

"Did agent Foster tell you why I was coming?" asked Riker as Santapaola poured two cups of coffee from the pot that was resting on the machine.

"Something about the G7 trip to Japan last year—the protestor who threw the bag of blood." Santapaola brought the cups to the table and sat down. He brought his cup to his lips. "Ugh—this stuff tastes like it was made last week."

"Dump some cream and sugar in it," suggested Riker. "I understand you were the driver from the hotel to Air Force One, which was waiting at the airport in Nagoya."

"Yeah. It was a tense ride because anytime there's an incident like that, you get jacked up. You don't know if it was just some stupid moron who threw something or a much more serious attack. You have to assume the worst until proven otherwise."

"At the airport, the president and his entourage got out of the car and went into the plane?"

"Right."

"And you cleaned up the car?"

"Yep."

"The president was given a towel to wipe his face. Did he leave it behind?"

"Yes. It was on the floor of the car. I picked it up and put it into a plastic bag. I didn't know what to do with it because it wasn't exactly trash. It was a nice towel. It also had blood on it. So I saved it."

"What did you do with it?"

"We've got a storage area where we keep stuff like that—things that may have some significance or we think we shouldn't throw way. I gave it to the agent who's in charge of it. Her name is Jennifer Dine."

"Where can I find agent Dine?"

"She's on assignment out of town. I can't tell you where. But she'll be back tomorrow."

"Okay, thanks very much."

Santapaola walked Riker to the door and signed him out.

When he had returned to his office at the Ten-Fifty, Riker called Jim Gilmore, and told him to expect the box with the suit and shirt.

"Okay," said Gilmore. "Let's review where we're at. Here at the CDC we've received four samples of blood from the White House. They are each identified only by a number. Our goal is to sequence the DNA of the HIV present in the blood, which we'll compare to the DNA of any HIV we find in a possible source of infection. If we get a match, then we know how the boss got HIV. Correct?"

"Probably yes," said Riker. "Unless by a one in a million chance two different sources give the same DNA pattern."

"And now you're sending me a man's grey business jacket, trousers, and white shirt. These items have dried blood, and the blood may be from multiple sources—correct?"

"Yes, that's it."

"We need to test each dried blood sample for HIV, and then we have to attempt to sequence it to see if it matches the HIV carried by the boss?"

"Yes, that's it. How about the blood from the Japanese baggie? The same process will apply, right?"

"It would," said Gilmore. "But we haven't received it yet."

"What?" said Riker. "I thought our colleague would have sent it by now."

"Nope. Haven't seen it come in."

"But she sent you the samples from the boss?"

"Yes—I got them yesterday afternoon."

"Okay, thanks." Riker hung up.

Leaving the Ten-Fifty, Riker walked to the White House and entered the office of the Medical Unit.

"Hi Dorothy," he said to Thompson's assistant and receptionist. "How was your weekend?"

"Same-old-same-old," she replied. "My husband watched football while I worked on my paintings."

"Oh—you're an artist?"

She laughed. "I try to be. I paint flowers, mostly. I've been in a few exhibitions. There's one of my pieces." She pointed to a framed watercolor of a vase of tulips that was hanging on the wall over the copy machine.

Riker looked at it. "Wow—pretty good," he said. "Say, is Karen in?"

"She stepped out. I expect her back any minute."

"Maybe you can help me. We were supposed to send a baggie of dried blood to Jim Gilmore at the CDC in Atlanta. You remember—the baggie I brought back from Japan on Saturday."

"I really don't know anything about that," replied Dorothy. "Karen told me that she'd handle it personally."

"And she hasn't sent it yet?"

"Not that I know of."

At that moment the door opened and Thompson entered the office.

Before Riker could say anything, Dorothy said to Thompson, "Hi, Karen—Dr. Riker is wondering about the baggie from the Japanese protestor."

Thompson gave Dorothy an irritated look. "I'm taking care of that." Then she looked at Riker. "Let's go in my office."

Once they were seated, Thompson said, "I'm sorry—I haven't sent it yet. With the president's medications, I've had a very full plate. I'm sure I'll be able to send it tomorrow morning."

"I'd be happy to do it myself," said Riker. "It's no problem. I just FedExed to the CDC the president's suit and shirt from the Kenyan accident. They should be there tomorrow morning."

Thompson gave a tight smile. "I wasn't aware the suit and shirt still existed."

"Yes, they do—Stephen Howe saved them."

"Well, that's fortunate," replied Thompson. "I suppose it's a good idea to test them, just to make sure we've covered all our bases. By the way, as long as we're thinking about Kenya, have you considered infection by mosquito bite?"

"It's far down on my list," replied Riker. "The CDC says there's no evidence of HIV transmission from mosquitoes, even in areas where there are many cases of AIDS and large populations of those bugs. When a mosquito bites a person, it doesn't inject its own blood or the blood of its last meal."

Thompson nodded. "I understand. Still, I've long been puzzled by the so-called 'Belle Glade AIDS epidemic.' Funny enough, it's not too far from your town of Naples. About a sixth of the cases of AIDS had no detectable risk factor for acquiring the infection. Researchers theorized that there must have been traditional risk factors that had escaped notice, but I personally thought there was still a chance mosquitoes could transmit the virus in a few cases."

"You're speculating," said Riker.

"But consider this," said Thompson, warming to her subject. "The Zika virus was thought to be transmitted to people only by mosquitoes.

Now CDC says it can also be sexually transmitted from one human to another, with no mosquito involved. But the first person in that chain got his Zika from a mosquito.

"So, maybe HIV is similar in a few cases. They ought to go back and study that possibility in more detail, what with the Zika revelations. Suppose a mosquito sucks up blood from a guy who has both Zika and HIV in his blood, and then it bites another fellow. Do you mean to tell me the mosquito will then transmit only the Zika and not the HIV? Maybe so, but they'll have to prove it to me.

"And if you claimed you got your AIDS from a mosquito bite, who would believe you? Nobody, no matter how risk-free your life appeared to be."

"Can we get off the speculation?" said Riker. "If we exhaust every other conventional possibility, perhaps we can consider mosquito transmission."

Thompson shrugged. "I'm just putting these ideas out there. My guess is that the president was infected well before the trip to Kenya." She reached for the bowl of hard candies and fished out a yellow one. "I've got to get this thing refilled," she said. She picked up her phone. "Dorothy? Next time you go out, please stop at Eckart's deli on New York Avenue and pick me up a bag of their hard candies. Yes, it's across the street from the National Museum of Women in the Arts. Thanks very much." She hung up.

"Why don't you go on Amazon and order them by the case?" asked Riker.

"That would be admitting that I'm addicted," replied Thompson. "If I buy one bag at a time, I can deny that I'm hooked. Now then, let's talk about your trip to Kenya."

"Actually," said Riker, "I don't think I need to go. I can't imagine what evidence I could find there, or new information I could uncover. We have the president's clothing and the report from Dr. Gladstone—he dragged his heels in sending it to me, so I dug through the files and got it myself."

"He's one of those guys who's leery of anybody looking over his shoulder," said Thompson. "He wants to put in his time and then collect his pension." She sat back in her chair. "I suppose there's not much more to do except wait, is there? We've sent the president's blood to the CDC so that the DNA of his HIV can be sequenced, you've sent the clothing from Kenya, and I'm going to send the baggie of blood from the Japanese protestor. I'd say we've gone as far as we can go at the moment."

Riker was puzzled and intrigued by Thompson's casual attitude. Maybe that's how it was in Washington—you sit behind your desk, do what's necessary to keep your job, and try not to make any waves. From the viewpoint of a bureaucrat, it was understandable, if not laudable. But Riker was both curious by nature, and, by virtue of his work in developing nations, where infectious diseases posed an ongoing threat to entire communities, not inclined to relax until the job was done and every avenue had been explored.

"As long as I'm here in Washington," said Riker, "staying at taxpayer expense at a nice hotel, I think I'll keep poking around."

Thompson shrugged. "Okay—but be sure to keep me fully informed."

It was the end of the day. Riker said goodnight and left for his hotel.

Thompson was alone in her office. From a desk drawer she took out a box that had been sent to her by a colleague at a New York medical clinic. She carefully opened the box and removed a small vial. Holding it up to the light, she confirmed that it contained blood. Smiling, she placed the vial on a table.

She went to the refrigerator and removed the evidence bag containing the bloody baggie from the Japanese protestor. Donning a pair of latex gloves, she carefully extracted the baggie from the evidence bag, and, using forceps, teased it open. Taking the vial, she unscrewed the cap. Cautiously tipping the vial, she allowed a few drops of the contents to fall into the baggie. After gently jiggling the baggie to ensure the contents were intermingled, she put it back into the evidence bag and sealed it.

She then rinsed the vial in the sink. The watery pink liquid circled the drain. After throwing the vial and the box in the secure trash, Thompson cleaned the sink before disposing of her gloves. She packaged the evidence bag into a FedEx box and labeled it for shipment to Gilmore at the CDC.

Chapter 13

*   *   *

E vening had fallen. Snow flurries sparkled as they swirled under the streetlights. As Riker walked through Lafayette Square, on a whim he pulled out his phone and punched a number.

"Hi, Lindsay? Martin here. I just got off work. I thought I'd give you a call and see what you were up to. How about dinner? Okay, sounds good. I'll meet you at eight."

After freshening up in his hotel room, Riker walked up Connecticut Ave. NW to Equinox, a fashionable eatery with big front windows that made you feel like you were practically sitting on the sidewalk while the traffic and pedestrians flowed around you. He found Lindsay waiting for him in one of the trim booths tucked away from the windows, which came as a relief because he didn't think it was a good idea to advertise their relationship.

She greeted him not with a kiss but a professional handshake. He sat down.

"How are your orchids?" he asked as the server handed them their menus.

"You remembered," she said. Her caramel eyes smiled. "As a matter of fact, I got a new one today—an *Ansellia africana*. It looks like a yellow five-pointed star with burgundy splotches. Because of its coloration, they call it the 'leopard orchid.' People also call it the 'trash basket orchid' because it grows high in trees, and its long stringy roots grow upwards in a basket shape to collect falling leaf litter, from which they get nutrients."

"Is this creature in your office?" asked Riker.

She laughed. "No, it's at my apartment—which I think you remember."

"Yes, very well, thank you," said Riker. "A very charming place."

Suddenly Riker felt tremendously awkward. Why was he here? What did he expect was going to happen—not necessarily today or tomorrow, but weeks from now, when he had to return to his home in Florida? Did he anticipate some sort of long-distance relationship with an ambitious woman with a career at the highest levels of government in Washington, DC? Or would this be just a fun tryst that they'd both put behind them when it was time to say goodbye?

For a brief moment Riker felt like he was *programmed* to pursue an attractive woman—that there was some deep primeval instinct, which still, at the age of fifty-eight, compelled him to cultivate a woman with whom a mutual attraction had developed. He could not help himself. He wanted Lindsay *just because*. There was no other reason. He had phoned her and asked to meet her because *that was what you did*.

At these thoughts, his mind rebelled. No! He was not just a simple creature attracted to the light. For Lindsay he had real feelings—sincere feelings—and if they were complicated, well, then, that was life in the adult world.

"A penny for your thoughts," said Lindsay.

Riker smiled. "Funny—I haven't heard that expression in years. My mom used to say that. My thoughts? Oh, I was just thinking about stuff. Getting introspective. After thirty years of marriage, my wife Rebecca died of cancer. It was the last thing I expected. When you're a doctor, you think that diseases are things that happen to your patients, not to your loved ones. When she got sick, it was like a bomb dropped on us. We gave her the very best care in the world, but pancreatic cancer is particularly deadly. Suddenly Rebecca was gone and I was walking around in a big empty house. It was not what I ever expected—not for me or for our kids."

Lindsay squeezed Riker's hand. Their fingers locked together for a moment until, self-consciously, they each pulled away.

"Sorry to be a Debbie Downer," said Riker. "I'm sure you have enough to worry about without hearing my troubles."

"You can tell me your troubles any time," said Lindsay. "After all, what are friends for?" She fingered the stem of her water glass before lifting her eyes to Riker's. "As long as we're baring our souls, I might as well unload mine."

"Okay," said Riker.

"I have a boyfriend," she said. "Well, sort of."

"Sort of?"

"John works for the State Department. For the past three weeks he's been in Germany. Tomorrow he goes from there to Belgium, to consult with them about the problem of terrorism. He'll be there for at least a week. Then he's back here for a few days before going to the Far East."

"How long have you known him?"

"Six months. We met at a reception at the White House." Her eyes moistened. "It's just so hard around here. Everyone's rushing everywhere, frantically climbing the career ladder, never standing still, never stopping to ask what it all means."

"We're living and working at the very center of the most powerful nation on earth," said Riker. "There's going to be a lot of pressure."

"Yeah, well, everyone's killing themselves to get here, and then once you arrive, you wonder if you're at the center of the universe or the seventh circle of hell." She took a swallow of her water. "I could use a *drink*," she said.

"Well, it looks like we're the leaders of the Dismal Society, doesn't it?" said Riker with an exploratory laugh.

Lindsay smiled. "You're right. It could be a lot worse. But I just wanted you to know what was going on, in case I was acting weird. I like you a lot, but I'm conflicted."

"I'd like you to be however you want to be," said Riker. "I'll be all right."

The arrival of the server interrupted their conversation. After ordering—pan-seared sea scallops for Lindsay, grilled yellowfin tuna loin for Riker, with a bottle of champagne—Lindsay leaned in. "I've heard you've had a busy day."

Riker paused.

It was his inclination, whenever he met a new romantic interest, to share with her the details of his life, such as what he did during the day and what he was looking forward to in the future. Lying was against his nature, especially in a personal relationship. Reflecting on his marriage to Rebecca, he could not recall a single time when he had lied to her, except when his buddies had taken him to a strip club in Vegas—but that had been a lie of omission. When Rebecca had asked him about his weekend, he had glossed over the detail of the club and the lap dances. No harm, no foul, and what was the point of getting her upset over nothing? He had kept his pants on, and that was the bottom line.

Looking at Lindsay's trusting face, he forced a smile. He had a greater obligation than his own code of ethics. It was a matter of national security. It was time to give a quick lie before pivoting to another subject.

"Just routine," he said with a shrug. "I'm sure our little report will get filed away in someone's desk drawer, never to be seen again. Or pointlessly marked 'classified,' thus ensuring its permanent demise." He glanced at her eyes. They betrayed no suspicion. "You know," he continued, "it's funny how quickly working in Washington—at the White House, no less—becomes just like working anywhere else. The buildings are smaller and older than many offices in New York, and you see tourists everywhere; and aside from the heightened security, working in the White House seems not much different from working in any other historic house museum. The computers aren't even particularly sophisticated."

"Tell me about it," said Lindsay. "The computer on my desk is ten years old. I'm amazed the damn thing still works. But you have to admit—the palace intrigue in Washington is pretty intense. Money and power are a potent brew. It can get pretty hot."

The server came with the champagne. After he had departed, Riker and Lindsay raised their glasses. "To the Washington pressure cooker," she said.

"May neither of us get boiled alive," added Riker. He took a sip. "What do you think—too dry?"

"No, it's perfect," replied Lindsay.

"I'd like to ask you a professional question," said Riker. "I've taken a close look at the boss's trips to Japan for the G7 summit and to Kenya for the Organization of African States. We've identified some significant risks with both. I also noticed that on a trip to Australia he stopped at the Walter and Eliza Hall Institute, in Melbourne, where he met with the bioscientist, Sir Gustav Nossal. He also visited a koala sanctuary. Can you give me any details?"

"Let me think," said Lindsay. "This was last January. He went there to appear at a United Nations conference on endangered species. He landed, gave the speech, visited the sanctuary, and met with various dignitaries including Sir Gustav. After being on the ground for ten hours, he took off for India. Why do you ask?"

"It just so happens that those cute little koala bears are dying at an alarming rate from various forms of cancer, like leukemia and lymphoma. The cause is a retrovirus."

"What's that?"

"Well, I'll put it like this. You probably know that all viruses invade the cells of living hosts. In most cases, the virus carries its own DNA into the cell. Retroviruses don't carry DNA; instead they carry RNA. HIV, which causes AIDS, is one. So is what's infecting koala bears. It's called the koala retrovirus, or KoRV. It appears to be the agent of koala immune deficiency syndrome, or KIDS, which leaves those cuddly animals more susceptible to infectious disease and cancers."

"Like AIDS does in humans," said Lindsay.

"Exactly. Koala bears happen to have extremely sharp claws, and you have to be very careful when you handle them. While they look cute their claws can rip right through your clothing. It's been theorized that zoo-keepers could become infected with KIDS if they were clawed. If the boss got clawed, there could be a risk."

"Put a number on it," said Lindsay.

"I'd say the odds are about a billion to one," said Riker. "But it's worth noting, if not actively investigating."

"As long as we're on the topic, have you got any other long-shot scenarios?" asked Lindsay.

"Sure," said Riker. "Here's one: has the boss been to anyplace where he might have come into contact with dead bodies—corpses?"

"You mean aside from his meetings with the House leadership?" asked Lindsay with a perfectly straight face.

Riker looked at her, dumbfounded.

Then she burst out laughing. "Hah! I had you going there for a minute. Just a little Capitol Hill humor. As far as I know, the answer is no. The boss has toured disaster areas. Last summer—in August—he went to Corpus Christi, Texas, to see the hurricane damage, but it was just a fly-over. He never got anywhere near the destruction. I suppose that's a good question, because you can get diseases from dead bodies, right?"

"Yes, at one extreme would be embalmers who happened to handle the bodies of people who died from very infectious microbes like smallpox or Ebola. But for something like HIV, it would take direct contact with the bodily fluids of an infected corpse. There are a few cases where that is suspected to have happened."

"I don't think the boss has ever worked as an embalmer," said Lindsay.

"Okay," said Riker, holding up an imaginary notepad, "we'll cross that off our list."

The server arrived with their main courses.

"While my tolerance for down-and-dirty medical talk is pretty high," said Lindsay as she speared a sea scallop, "why don't we talk about something more pleasant while we eat?"

"Fair enough," agreed Riker. "Say, could you do me a favor tomorrow?"

"Depends on what you've got in mind," she said as she cut one of her sea scallops in half and held it up in front of her plate. "Here—you've got to try one of these. The baby leek confit and brown butter hollandaise are out of this world."

Leaning forward, Riker took the scallop between his lips. "Wow, you're right," he said. "Really good." He reciprocated by offering her a bite of yellowfin tuna, which had been served in a lobster bouillabaisse.

"My mother, were she sitting here with us, would be horrified at our behavior," said Lindsay. "She's very old-school. Sharing bites of your dinner is not what nice people do."

"She's probably missed out on some good samples," replied Riker. "Back to my small favor. How many trips outside of Washington has the boss taken in two years?"

"Day trips? Hundreds. Overnighters to international destinations? Five or six a year. Then you've got vacation time—about thirty days in each of his two years. When you add up all of his travel, among modern presidents he's about average."

"Doesn't the boss have a place on Marco Island, in Florida? That's just down the coast from where I live."

"That's the winter retreat," said Lindsay. "The family has a summer place on Deal Island, in Chesapeake Bay. The Secret Service loves it because it's very isolated—there's only one road to the mainland. Easy to defend."

"And there's also Camp David," said Riker.

"It's only seventy miles from the White House," said Lindsay. "A quick helicopter trip."

"Do the same people go with him to these various destinations?"

"There's some overlap, but the lists change. I'd say that Stephen Howe is probably the most consistent name, along with the people from the Medical Unit and certain Secret Service agents."

"Here's the favor I'm asking," said Riker. "Can you put together a bunch of the trip rosters and send them to me?"

"Except for the identities of the Secret Service agents, which is classified information, I can send you every single one of them. Knock yourself out. What are you looking for?"

"I don't know," shrugged Riker. "I just like being thorough." Having finished his dinner, he sat back in his chair. "I could use a little bit of brandy. How about you?"

"Dr. Riker, it's a work night, so if you have any thoughts of getting me tipsy and taking advantage of me, forget it," said Lindsay with a twinkle in her eye.

"Darn," said Riker. "My evil plan has been revealed."

The server appeared.

"I'll have a Grand Marnier and a cup of black coffee," said Lindsay.

"Sounds good—I'll have the same," said Riker.

After the server had cleared the table, Riker said to Lindsay, "Tell me something—how often does the name of the boss's wife appear on these lists?"

"My guess is that for official international trips, maybe half the time. On vacation trips, more often, but they don't always travel together. She has her own schedule of events in Washington and elsewhere, and sometimes she just can't go. Their daughter, Chloe, who attends NYU, joins them on holidays." She lowered her voice. "Also, there's talk of certain health issues that are, shall we say, self-imposed. These health issues often keep her at home."

"Yes, I've heard the same thing," said Riker.

Their drinks and coffees came, and they spent the next few minutes chatting about events around Washington—the upcoming Scottish Christmas Walk Weekend and the prospects for the Washington Redskins, who were closing in on the NFC East Division title for the ninth time in their history.

Lindsay put down her coffee cup and glanced at her watch. "Martin, very shortly I'm going to turn into a pumpkin. Before that happens, I need to get myself home."

"We'll get a car and I'll drop you off," he replied as he gave their server a wave.

They split the bill. A few minutes later they were standing on the sidewalk, and Riker hailed a black car.

At her door, Lindsay turned to Riker and said, "The last time we were in this situation, I said that in Washington, true gentlemen are few and far between. Thanks for again being the exception." After giving him a kiss on the cheek, she opened her door and stepped out onto the sidewalk. Riker watched as she walked through the snow to her door. When she was safely inside, he told the driver to take him to The Jefferson.

Chapter 14

$*$ $*$ $*$

The next morning when Riker went to his office at the Ten-Fifty, a voicemail message was waiting for him. It was from Secret Service agent Jennifer Dine, who asked that he call her back.

"Good morning, Dr. Riker," she said when she picked up. "I heard that you were looking for a towel from the president's G7 trip to Japan. I think I have what you want—it's the one he used to wipe off his face when he was hit by the baggie full of blood. The towel was left in the Beast when we arrived at the airport in Nagoya."

"That's the one," said Riker. "Can I pick it up from you?"

"I'll do you one better," she said. "I'll swing by the Ten-Fifty and pick you up. I have it in my car."

This seemed like an unnecessary extra step—after all, she could have just said that he could take it from her. Curious, Riker put on his coat and went down to the front door.

After waiting no more than a minute in the biting cold—overnight, a cold front had moved in and the temperature had dropped to well below freezing—a black SUV pulled up to the curb. The window powered down. "Dr. Riker," called the woman behind the wheel.

Riker opened the door and got in the passenger seat. Instinctively—or perhaps because he had seen too many gangster movies—he glanced behind him at the rear seats. No one else was in the car.

"Don't worry," said the woman with a smile. "You're not being kidnapped." Riker guessed she was about the same age as his daughter—twenty-five, maybe twenty-six. She was compact, with arms that pushed the seams of her black suit jacket. Her dark hair was pulled back in an efficient bun, revealing a smooth but sturdy neck. Wrap-around sunglasses concealed her eyes.

She looked like she could take care of herself on the streets.

"I'm Jennifer Dine," she said as she pulled into traffic. "The towel is on the seat next to you."

Riker glanced down. Between them on the seat was a plastic bag—not a formal evidence bag, just a food storage bag—with a white towel inside. Riker picked up the bag. The towel was blotched with dark brown stains the color of dried blood.

"Thanks," said Riker. "This will be a big help." He replaced the bag on the seat where it had been. "If you don't mind my asking, where are we going?"

Dine smiled. "We're doing a drive-around," she said.

"A drive-around?"

"In the Secret Service, within our operational area we deploy our assets in a variety of postures—on foot, in cars, in retail stores, visible, invisible. You name it, we might be doing it. This morning, I'm driving around."

"So if you're a bad guy who's hanging around the Capitol, you'll never know where the next Secret Service agent might be," said Riker.

"Exactly," said Dine. "He or she might be the person who sold you your newspaper, or the woman pushing a stroller." The car was now heading south along 17th St. NW. To the left was the Ellipse, covered in a blanket of gleaming snow.

"That's good to know," said Riker, "but if you don't mind my question, why am I here?"

"There are rumors going around," said Dine as she turned left onto Constitution Ave. NW. "Rumors about the health of the president."

"With all due respect, Agent Dine, I'm not going to comment on the president's health. I'm sure you already know that."

"Yes, I know that. I'm not here to *ask* you for information. I thought I might be able to *give* you some information."

"Such as?"

With the car stopped at a light, Dine turned to him. "Let's say, just hypothetically, that the president has a serious disease. We all know that he's got *something*. I first met him when I was assigned to protect him during the campaign. He was given Secret Service protection in March of that year, and I was among the first group covering him. His code name was "Big Bull," because it fit him. He was as tough as they come, and he was never sick. I never even saw him sneeze. Then about six months ago—it was during the summer—he got the flu, or whatever it was. I'm not a doctor, so I can't say exactly. The agents who knew him thought, 'Okay, everyone gets sick now and then, including the president. No big deal.' Then he got sick again, and again. He seems a little bit thinner, too. Of course, we all know that being president is an extremely stressful job—everyone saw how President Obama's hair turned grey in eight years, right? But this is different. President Ralston seems to have a lingering illness that has changed him."

"Okay," said Riker. "I understand you may have that perception. Once again, I cannot make any comment."

"That's fine," said Dine as she headed north on 14th St. NW past the big Ronald Reagan Building, the centerpiece of the massive Federal Triangle complex. "It's hard to imagine," she said as she waved her hand at the formidable government buildings that flanked the street, "but in the nineteenth century this area was full of saloons and brothels. From the front steps of the whorehouses you could see the Capitol Building. During the Civil War, there were nearly five hundred brothels in Washington, and five thousand prostitutes. It was a very public industry."

"It makes the culture of today seem downright puritanical," said Riker.

"If you were a gentleman of the time and your wife was not in the mood, you had to only take a short walk to another neighborhood," said Dine. "Nobody thought twice about it." She stopped the car at a traffic light and turned to Riker. "If you were the president of the United States, of course you couldn't do that."

"No, you couldn't."

"Presidents who are looking for female companionship need to make other arrangements—and where there's a will, there's a way. In the modern era, President Kennedy is said to be the champ. He allegedly had affairs with a bevy of women: Mary Pinchot Meyer, Marilyn Monroe, White House intern Mimi Alford, Judith Campbell Exner, Blaze Starr, and two young White House staff aides known as 'Fiddle' and 'Faddle.'"

"There are many stories about various presidents," said Riker. He was beginning to sense that Dine was leading the discussion to a particular destination.

"They do what they think they gotta do," said Dine. "Or *can* do."

"Let me understand you clearly," said Riker. "You first tell me that this president, who was once the picture of strength and health, has become, in your opinion, chronically ill. Then you open a discussion about men seeking extramarital satisfaction, leading to American presidents who have had girlfriends. Have you seen with your own eyes something specific that I should know about?"

"Since he took office, the president has kept a group of special assistants who seem to have minimal official duties," said Dine. "While mostly women, there are also a few men. They travel with him. As you may already know, the First Lady is an infrequent traveler. It was widely believed that this was because she wanted to stay home with Chloe, but now she's attending NYU. With their daughter away at college, there's less reason for Susan Ralston to stay home, but yet she frequently does. Think about it—if you knew you were going to live a life of power and glamour for four years or maybe eight years, wouldn't you want to grab it while it lasted? If you could fly around the world and meet extraordinary world leaders, wouldn't you do it? You wouldn't sit at home while your husband jetted across the globe."

"So why, in your opinion, does the First Lady stay home so often?"

"The word around town is that she's often too incapacitated to travel, and that her husband doesn't miss her, shall we say, companionship."

"But surely if he were fooling around on the side, he'd need someone to cover for him," said Riker. "There's no way he could manage it alone."

"The Secret Service detail assigned to the president is always in *close proximity*," said Dine, "but not always in *visual contact*. There are plenty of times every day when the president is behind closed doors."

"And who closes the doors?" asked Riker.

"Ninety percent of the time it's either Don Strauss or Brian Conway."

Dine suddenly pulled over to the curb. They were northeast of the White House, near the McPherson Square Metro station. She clicked on her headset. "Car fifty-four, at McPherson Square. Roderick is standing on the corner of I Street and Fifteenth Street. He's carrying his sign. Yeah, the usual thing— 'Ralston's a War Criminal.' He's just standing there, looking like he's freezing. Roger. Out."

Dine turned to Riker. "There's a whole population of local characters who hang around on these streets. Roderick's been active for two years. We've patted him down a bunch of times, and never found any weapons. He's not breaking the law, so we keep an eye on him."

"His sign said 'war criminal,'" said Riker. "What war?"

Dine laughed and shrugged. "Beats me."

"While we're on the subject of extracurricular activities, the Secret Service has hardly been immune," said Riker. "How about the incident in Cartagena? A bunch of agents on the advance team went to a club, picked up prostitutes, and brought them back to their hotel."

"Believe me, we all remember that," said Dine as she headed north on Vermont Ave. NW. "I wasn't on that trip, but trust me, what those guys did was not unheard-of. The only reason they got caught was because one knucklehead refused to pay his hooker the eight hundred bucks she wanted. He only gave her twenty-eight dollars! Can you believe it? What an idiot!"

"Prostitution is legal in Colombia," said Riker.

"But even aside from the moral aspects and the image damage, it's against Secret Service regulations," replied Dine. "It's behavior like that which gives the Service a black eye."

"The girl got her fifteen minutes of tabloid fame," said Riker. "I hope she's found better things to do with her life." He looked out the window at the flurries that were beginning to drift down from the overcast sky. "You mentioned the president seems to have a group of personal assistants with vaguely defined duties. How about Secret Service agents? If a president wanted to find a sex partner, why not look to the people who travel with him wherever he goes?"

"It might be a good strategy if the president were gay," said Dine. "But if he's straight, the numbers are against him, because only ten percent of Secret Service agents are women. That would make a relationship with one of them very difficult. By the way, many people think having more female agents would curb some of the men's bad behavior. In fact, one of the few female agents is Paula Reid, who was in charge of the Miami office at the time of the prostitution scandal. She was in Cartagena, and she's the one who ordered the offending guys home."

Riker's phone rang. He picked up the call. After a moment he hung up. "Would you mind dropping me off at the Ten-Fifty? I've got an appointment."

"No problem," replied Dine. "We're only a few blocks away."

Outside the Ten-Fifty, Riker, with the bag containing the towel in hand, got out of the car. "Thanks for the background," he said to Dine. "If anything comes up that I need to ask you, can I contact you?"

"Sure," she said. "If it's off the record."

Riker hurried to his office and put the bag with the towel in his drawer—he'd box it up to send to the CDC later. After putting on a necktie, he went down to the street and walked to the White House, with the delicate flurries dampening his hair.

As he had been instructed, he entered the South Portico and went through the Diplomatic Reception Room to the Center Hall. Instead of going into the office of the Medical Unit, he stepped across the hall to the family elevator. There he was met by an usher, a young woman of college age, who opened the door and said, "This way, Dr. Riker."

Riker and the usher stepped into the elevator, with its dark wood paneling accented by classical columns topped by carved Corinthian capitals. After the attendant closed the door, the compartment eased upwards. When the door opened, Riker entered a little vestibule that led into the Center Hall.

Riker followed the usher along the Center Hall past the stair landing and into the sunny East Sitting Hall, with its large fanlight window and marine paintings hanging from the cheery butter-yellow walls. The usher continued along a short corridor to the Lincoln Sitting Room, which was adjacent to the Lincoln Bedroom. The ambiance of this compact space was more formal than the East Sitting Hall, with stiff-looking armchairs and sumptuous swagged curtains. A life-sized portrait of a rather dour Mary Todd Lincoln gazed down from the wall.

Riker recalled that this room was the favorite haunt of President Richard Nixon, who would sit in a leather armchair next to the roaring fire, working on his speeches.

"Please make yourself comfortable," said the usher.

Riker chose one of the armchairs and sat down. The usher, who did not seem inclined to conversation, left the room, closing the door behind her.

Chapter 15

∗   ∗   ∗

A few minutes later, the door opened.
Riker stood up.

The First Lady walked over to him and extended her hand. "Dr. Riker, I'm Susan Ralston," she said with an honest smile. Riker shook her hand. Her grip was firm, and she released his hand at precisely the right moment.

She was wearing a half-sleeve dress in pale yellow silk that was beautifully tailored but not ostentatious. A simple gold chain hung around her neck, and pinned to her dress was a delicate gold-and-enamel brooch of a butterfly—a symbol of one of the many conservation programs she supported.

Riker was immediately struck by the fact that Mrs. Ralston was even more attractive than she appeared in photos and on television; perhaps this was because here, in her element, she was more relaxed. But despite her confidence, no doubt honed by years of encounters with perfect strangers in every conceivable situation, in her face Riker's medically trained eye saw the slight furtiveness of someone who is being careful to control their behavior, as if something unexpected and undesirable might happen—a nervous tic or fingers that could slightly shake.

With a full smile, Susan Ralston said, "Please, sit down." She had nice teeth, noted Riker, and they looked like her own.

"Thank you, ma'am," said Riker.

"Would you like some tea or coffee?"

"No thank you, ma'am."

"Well, I could use some."

The usher had entered with the First Lady. Turning to her, Mrs. Ralston said, "Judy, would you please bring us some coffee? Thank you."

The usher left the room, closing the door behind her.

Riker and Mrs. Ralston were alone.

"I asked you to come here today," she said, "because I want to discuss my husband's condition."

"Condition?" replied Riker.

"Yes, he told me last night that he has AIDS."

Riker was stunned at her matter-of-fact tone. It was as if she had said, "My husband told me that he needs reading glasses."

"Yes," said Riker. "It's a very unfortunate diagnosis."

Susan Ralston's mouth turned down and a frown flickered across her face, revealing inward pain. Then, catching herself, she relaxed her face and raised her chin. Her expression once again became one of First Lady dignity. She sat with the posture of a ballet dancer, her knees together and offset to the left, and her hands folded in her lap. You could have photographed her at that moment and gotten a perfect picture.

"I understand you're well-versed in all aspects of the disease," she said evenly.

"The field of AIDS research is evolving very quickly, but I try to keep abreast."

"Yes, of course," she replied.

At that moment the door opened and Judy entered, carrying a silver tray, which she set on the low table between Riker and Mrs. Ralston. On the tray was a silver coffee pot, two cups and saucers, cream and sugar, two silver spoons, and two linen napkins.

"Thank you, Judy," said Mrs. Ralston. "We'll serve ourselves."

Riker accepted a cup of coffee, with cream and sugar, as Mrs. Ralston took hers. He took a polite sip and rested the cup on its saucer, which he held above his lap. Alongside the arm of his chair sat a small table, to which he hoped to exile the cup and saucer as soon as was polite.

Without drama, Mrs. Ralston asked all the usual questions—how long her husband had the disease (anywhere from six months to two years, or even longer, replied Riker), where he got it (unknown), and if he was contagious (only through direct transmission of bodily fluids).

"If HIV is difficult to transmit in everyday circumstances," she said, "then are you saying my husband has been having an affair with an infected woman?"

Riker could see the marital hurricane building in strength. With a calming smile, he said, "Not necessarily. While the two most common methods of transmission are sexual contact and the sharing of infected needles, other methods are not unknown. For example, there are examples of unscrupulous dentists infecting patients with HIV, either by an accidental cut with a needle or by using infected instruments."

"A dentist?" said Mrs. Ralston. Her eyes briefly flashed before returning to their First Lady cool. "Do you mean that guy in Maine?"

"We're looking into every possibility, but have reached no conclusions. Mrs. Ralston, even though your husband, as the president of the United States, lives in what most people would consider to be an airtight bubble, he's an active man who likes to get out and be with people. He's athletic and very sociable. He has also been in his share of risky situations, such as the motorcade accident in Kenya, in which a lot of blood got splashed around."

"Oh," she frowned. "What a terrible day. I wasn't there, and I'm glad I only found out about it when the president called me to say that I'd be hearing about a bad accident, but not to worry because he was uninjured. It looked like a real mess, and some people got killed. Do you think he could have gotten exposed there?"

"Once again, due diligence requires that we look at every possibility, no matter how remote. We have made no conclusions."

"Okay," she smiled. "I understand. I don't want to go fishing for answers that aren't there."

Riker took a sip of his coffee, which in its thin porcelain cup had gotten cold. He discreetly parked the cup and saucer on the little table next to his chair.

"Mrs. Ralston," he said, "as long as we're here and have the opportunity to speak candidly, I need to ask you whether you've been tested for HIV. I realize this is a delicate question, but the sooner we catch it the more effective the treatments can be—"

She held up her hand. "Forgive me for interrupting, but I can assure you that if my husband has been infected at any time during the past two years, I have not been."

"I'm sorry, I don't want to intrude…"

"Are you familiar with the story of Lady Randolph Churchill, the mother of Sir Winston? When she was informed that her husband, Lord Randolph, was suffering from syphilis, and that she needed to take extreme caution, she laughed and said that there was no need to worry because she and her husband had not had 'relations' for many years. While I'm not sure if my marriage has been in the same condition for as long, the effect is no different. For political purposes the president and I maintain the outward appearance of a loving husband and wife, and in fact we do have a certain level of comfort with each other; but we've not been intimate for quite a while and have no plans to turn back the clock to our younger days. So, to answer your original question, you're free to test me, but I can assure you that the test will be negative."

"I understand, Mrs. Ralston," said Riker. As a physician he was accustomed to being privy to the private details of the lives of his patients, but her bluntness coupled with her position as the First Lady of the United States jolted him. What any tabloid newspaper, crummy rumor-mongering website, or salacious supermarket magazine would have paid a fortune to learn, Susan Ralston had told him, plainly and without reservation. He could see the screaming headline: "INSIDE THE RALSTON'S MARRIAGE OF CONVENIENCE." There would be the split shot, with the president, glowering, on one side of a jagged divide, and his wife, crying (surely a photo of Susan Ralston in tears could be found *somewhere*) on the other side.

It was almost as if the First Lady were yearning for a reason to speak the truth, and she had finally found one.

She could have just as easily said, "Of course I'll have my blood tested." The test would have come back negative, everyone would have breathed a sigh of relief, and no one would have the wiser. Instead, she had chosen to entrust Riker with potent information.

"I really need something a bit more than coffee," said Mrs. Ralston suddenly. She took out her phone and tapped a number. "Hello, Judy? Please bring in two brandies. The Courvoisier will be fine. And some ice. Thank you."

It was not yet noon. Riker, who in his lifetime had done his share of drinking, was again taken aback. This was indeed a day of surprises!

"Where are you staying while you're in Washington?" asked Mrs. Ralston, as if the conversation about AIDS had never happened.

"At The Jefferson," replied Riker. "It's very convenient to the White House."

"I recall that Mr. Ralston and I stayed there when he was governor— we were attending one of the inaugural balls. Little did I imagine that just two years later we'd be attending his inauguration! It's a lovely hotel, very steeped in history."

This harmless discussion continued until Judy appeared with another silver tray, this one with a bottle of Courvoisier, two snifters, and a bucket of ice. Judy expertly slid the new tray onto the table while taking up the previous tray. Without a word she left the room.

"A lot of brandy snobs say you shouldn't drink cognac on ice," said Mrs. Ralston as she prepared the drinks. "I say, let 'em drink it the way they want, and I'll drink it the way I want."

"Is anyone on your staff inclined to write a tell-all book?" asked Riker as he accepted his glass.

"Oh, God, I hope not!" she laughed. "But everyone who works here has to sign a non-disclosure agreement. If anyone on the White House staff wrote a book, we'd come down on them like a ton of bricks."

Mrs. Ralston knocked back a slug of cognac. She then let out a little sigh and nodded her head as if agreeing with herself. She then placed her glass on the tray.

"Now then, as for your investigation," she said in a matter-of-fact tone. "I hope that what I told you will be useful in providing, or suggesting, a direction to go. There are a few things that I want to tell you now that may help you. As you have said, my husband is a vigorous, healthy man—or at least he was before he became ill."

"With treatment, he can probably remain vigorous and healthy for many years to come," interjected Riker.

"Yes, we can hope so," said Mrs. Ralston. "But my point is that with no intimacy at home, one would hardly be surprised if he sought it elsewhere. Without going into endless details, I'd like to give you two names."

"Two names?"

"Yes. While I'm sure you will, as you say, proceed with every bit of due diligence and leave no stone unturned, I think that I can throw a spotlight on two young ladies that, for various reasons, may be likely candidates for outside intimacy. Of course I have no idea if either of them has AIDS or any other sexually transmitted disease, and it's absolutely not my intention to slander them; but I have good reason to believe that my husband has had relations with one or both."

"And who are these two women?" Lifting his glass, Riker took a swallow of his cognac. It seemed like the appropriate thing to do.

"The first is Kimberly Schuster. She came to the White House after she graduated from Boston University. This was in May of my husband's first term. Her father, Boswell Schuster, owns a software company in Boston and was a big donor to my husband's campaign. She's a good-looking girl, and she very quickly became a member of the traveling staff."

"I remember seeing her name somewhere," said Riker. "Oh yes—it was on the roster of the trip to Nagoya for the G7 Summit."

"Funny you should mention that," said Mrs. Ralston in a tone that suggested there was nothing funny about it. "When my husband goes on a trip, Stephen Howe generally takes care of my husband's personal suitcase, which contains things like his shaver and pajamas. When the president returned from the Nagoya trip, for some reason Stephen wasn't around, so I unpacked the suitcase myself. I still do a few wifely chores! Anyway, in the suitcase I found some blue pills with the name 'Pfizer' on the side. Going online, I quickly discovered they were Viagra."

"What did you do?"

She shrugged her shoulders, and for the first time since their conversation had begun Riker thought she might burst into tears. After taking another slug of cognac, she breathed deeply.

"I didn't do a damn thing," she said. "Our marriage was already lacking in intimacy. What difference did it make? I thought that I'd play the part of the devoted wife and First Lady, and after he left office—after four or eight years—I'd think about divorcing him. Or maybe I wouldn't. Who knows? By that time maybe I wouldn't care."

"Is Ms. Schuster still on the staff?"

"No. After working for a year and a half, she left in August to go back to grad school. Stanford, I think."

"And who is the other name?"

"Rachel Doucette. Another little hottie. She's the daughter of the campaign chair in New Hampshire. She came on board when Schuster did, shortly after the election. She was also on the traveling team. God only knows what was happening on those twelve-hour flights on Air Force One, or during those midweek getaways to Camp David! Doucette isn't here anymore. I got rid of her."

"You got rid of her?"

"Yes. It was this past September. I went down to the Oval Office to see my husband about Chloe. She was having some trouble at NYU—she had skipped some classes and the Secret Service was concerned that she was trying to ditch them. I really wanted my husband to give her a fatherly talking-to. So I marched right past Don Strauss, who tried to keep me out—"

"I'm sorry to interrupt, but what exactly did Don Strauss say?"

"Something stupid like, 'The president is in a high-level meeting.' I didn't care—I was a mother on a mission. I went into the Oval Office. It was empty. Next to the Oval Office is a private bathroom, for the use of the president. Suddenly the door to the bathroom opened, and my husband walked out. Before he could close the door, I caught a glimpse of Rachel Doucette. She had been in the bathroom with him! My husband tried to steer me away, but I went to the bathroom door and yanked it open. Doucette was trying to zip up her dress. I said nothing to her. After she had arranged herself, I watched as she left. I turned to my husband

and said, 'I want that slut out of here *now*.' Then I told him that he needed to straighten out our daughter. I was so furious that I took a paperweight and threw it on the floor. The damned thing just bounced off the carpet. I'm glad it didn't set off some sort of alarm."

"I'm sorry—it must have been a difficult experience," said Riker.

She shrugged and took another sip of cognac. "Men will be men," she said, as if the words were bitter drops on her tongue. Then she glanced at Riker. "To present company, no offense intended. Are you married, Dr. Riker?"

"I was, for thirty years. My wife passed away. Cancer."

"I'm so very sorry." The pain crept back into her voice. "It's that kind of unfortunate event that makes you stop and think about the person you've chosen to spend your life with. When you're the First Lady, you have no choice but to accept the fact that your husband, despite the protective bubble in which he lives, is in a high-risk occupation. I guarantee you that every new First Lady who walks through the doors of the White House for the first time has one thing on her mind: that photo of Jackie Kennedy wearing her black veil at her husband's funeral. You think, 'Will I be the one to wear the black veil? If it happens, how will I bear it?' That's why I've said nothing. I want to get through these four or eight years, and then sort out where we want to go."

She put her nearly-empty brandy snifter on the table. Suddenly she seemed tired, like a balloon that had lost some of its air. Her eyes lost their focus and her eyelids seemed heavy. Then, as Riker had seen before, she took a breath, sat up straight, and was once more the picture-perfect First Lady. After a moment in which nothing was said, she stood up, extended her hand, and said, "Dr. Riker, it has been a pleasure to meet you."

Riker stood up and shook her hand.

"I hope the information I've given you will be helpful in your investigation," she said.

"I'm sure it will be, and I assure you of the utmost discretion," replied Riker.

"Of course," said the First Lady. "If I can be of any further assistance, you can reach me through Judy."

She turned and left the room.

Chapter 16

* * *

After descending in the family elevator to the lower level of the White House, Riker went into the Medical Unit office. He found Thompson behind her desk.

"I've just come from interviewing the First Lady," he said as he sat down across from her.

Thompson's face showed a tremor of irritation before her eyes narrowed and her mouth curled up in a smile. "Oh? You're moving fast, Martin. Did you reach out to her?"

"No, her assistant, Judy, called me this morning. I was summoned to the Lincoln Sitting Room."

"And what did you find out?" she said as she reached into her candy bowl and selected a cherry lozenge. Apparently, noted Riker to himself, the supply had been replenished.

"A few things," he replied. "First, Mrs. Ralston has assured us that we need not give her a blood test because it is impossible for her to have contracted AIDS."

"Impossible?" asked Thompson as she balled up the cellophane wrapper and tossed it into the wastepaper basket.

"She was very specific that there has been no physical contact with her husband for, as she said, 'many years.'"

Like two birds, Thompson's eyebrows lifted. "Oh. I see." Then her face relaxed. "Now that we've got that particular issue out of the way, what else did you learn?"

"The First Lady gave me the names of two young women who, she asserts, probably had precisely the type of intimate contact with the president that she has not had."

"Only two?" replied Thompson. "The rumor mills have long claimed there have been more. But perhaps the wife knows best. Who are these lucky ladies?"

"Kimberly Schuster and Rachel Doucette."

"The names are familiar," said Thompson.

"They often travel with the president—for example, both of them were with the group that accompanied the president on his trip to the G7 summit in Nagoya last year. Schuster left the White House in August of this year to go to grad school at Stanford. Doucette left the following month. Mrs. Ralston had a specific story about Doucette. She told me she caught her husband and Doucette in the private bathroom of the Oval Office. She implied that Don Strauss was guarding the door, so to speak, and that he insisted to her that the president was in a high-level meeting."

"High level indeed," said Thompson.

"When the First Lady discovered her husband with Doucette, there was a nasty scene. She told Doucette to clear out. An hour later Doucette submitted her resignation, claiming that she had to attend to her invalid mother in New Hampshire. Don Strauss gave her a nice letter of recommendation."

"These two girls definitely sound like people we need to check out," said Thompson.

"By any chance do we have current blood samples for either of them?" asked Riker.

Thompson went to her computer. "Our database says 'yes' for Schuster, 'no' for Doucette. Let's see... Schuster had blood drawn in July, a month before she left the White House. She thought she might have contracted malaria from a mosquito bite in Africa."

"The president's trip to Kenya was in April of this year," said Riker. "The incubation period for malaria is typically seven to thirty days, but it can be as long as a year. Did she show any symptoms?"

"No," replied Thompson. She peered at the screen. "We're in luck. We ran our usual battery of tests on her blood, not just the one for malaria. The HIV test, both antigen and antibody, was nonreactive. By the way, most people don't even know we routinely include that test, so we don't broadcast it. Too much gossip, you know."

"Okay," said Riker. "I recommend we put Schuster on the back burner. If we come up empty everywhere else, we can revisit her. As for Doucette—there's nothing?"

"No, nothing in our system."

"We need to change that," said Riker.

"How?" said Thompson. "After that ugly scene in the Oval Office, there's no way she'd come into our office willingly."

"Leave it to me," said Riker. "I'll be in touch."

Riker left the White House and walked to The Jefferson. That morning, a seasonal snowstorm sweeping up the East Coast had hit the Washington area, and Riker found himself leaning into a fierce wind and driving snow. More than once he had to dodge an impatient motorist who either didn't see him crossing the street or didn't much care about the human being walking in the path of their three-thousand-pound car. With his mind echoing with images of sunny Naples and his sailboat riding the breeze past swaying palm trees, Riker plowed his way to the hotel.

Once in his room, having shed his soggy overcoat, Riker picked up his phone.

"Angela?" he said. "Riker here. I need your help with a job that's come up. I'd say it will take two days, max. I need one person. Up in Portsmouth, New Hampshire. Our target is a twenty-five-year-old woman, and I need a woman to interface with her. It's got to be clean—I don't want our target to be aware of anything invasive or threatening. When? The sooner the better. Okay, I'm leaving this afternoon. Thanks."

Riker hung up. He went to the closet and pulled out his medical kit. After checking its contents, he packed an overnight bag. After buying a plane ticket online, he went downstairs to get a cab to the airport.

At a few minutes before eight o'clock that evening, having endured an hour's wait on the tarmac at Reagan National while the plane was repeatedly de-iced, and having driven in the snow from Manchester, New Hampshire—a fifty-mile trip that took an extra hour behind the plow trucks—Martin Riker sat at a table at the Garden Grille & Bar of the Hilton Garden Inn, watching the snow fall on downtown Portsmouth. The hotel was a curious place, thought Riker—given the name "Garden Inn," he expected to see some evidence of flora, either living or perhaps only in the inanimate décor, such as printed on the wallpaper. Yet as he had scanned the public areas of the hotel, and now the Garden Grille & Bar, the sterile businesslike design of walls, windows, and furnishings betrayed not one living plant, either in reality or represented. There wasn't even a lowly ficus tree or forlorn fern tucked into a corner. Not a speck of green could be seen anywhere—only corporate shades of espresso grey, slate grey, and cool grey.

Perhaps the word "garden" referred to something more representational, like the blooming of great business deals, or the cultivation of valuable contacts, and not actual plants.

From the efficient server in her grey shirt and black slacks, Riker ordered the ubiquitous New England staple dinner of clam chowder, "local caught" baked haddock with lemon butter crumbs, and a salad of iceberg lettuce and cherry tomatoes. He complemented his meal with a local Redhook beer.

At the front door, within Riker's field of vision, a woman appeared. She was in her mid-twenties, slender, and wearing a tweed blazer over a white blouse and pressed blue jeans. Her shoulder-length brown hair was just a little bit messy. With her oversized tortoiseshell eyeglasses, she looked like a novelist with a few bestsellers under her belt.

Riker glanced at his watch. Eight o'clock on the dot. He smiled. Angela's people were pros.

The hostess led the woman to Riker's table.

Riker stood up and offered his hand. "Martin Riker," he said.

"Meryl Madson," said the woman as they shook hands. She sat down opposite Riker.

While waiting for the server they chatted about ordinary things. Madson had driven up from Boston, where she had been on another assignment, working surveillance on a terrorism job. The highway—Interstate 95—had been a mess, with cars spinning out onto the snowy shoulders. "Do you notice that it's always the guys in pickup trucks who drive the fastest in snow?" asked Madson. "They get in the left lane and fly! Don't they realize that rear-wheel-drive pickup trucks are the *worst* vehicles to drive in the snow? I saw one guy in a pickup start to fishtail—and then he somehow regained control and just kept going as if nothing had happened!"

Riker remembered that Madson's profile, which he had seen on the classified DIA intranet, stated that she was a trained driver who had passed the Secret Service driving program. She knew how to keep a car on the road.

From their server, Madson ordered shrimp scampi and a glass of sparking water.

The server left, and after glancing around the restaurant, Madson said, "Let's discuss the job. There aren't many people here tonight. I suppose we can talk about generalities without any problem."

Riker nodded. "For various reasons, which unfortunately I cannot reveal, you and I need to get a blood sample from a woman named Rachel Doucette."

"But she can't be aware of what's been done to her—right?" said Madson.

"Correct."

"She's a former White House staffer?"

"Yes. For about two years she was a special assistant to the president. It's not as exalted a position as it sounds—the special assistants are often not much more than glorified gofers. Doucette got the job because her father was the party campaign chair here in New Hampshire, a state that Ralston won. She was fresh out of college, and having a White House job on her resume would be a huge advantage."

"And yet she has left the White House."

"Yes, and what I'm going to say to you will show you why this is a very sensitive issue. Doucette left the White House because Mrs. Ralston caught Doucette and her husband in the private bathroom of the Oval Office."

Madson nodded her head and smiled. "I get it. Say no more."

Riker glanced at Madson's clothing. "I must admit, you definitely look like an author who's writing a tell-all book about the White House. I have a hunch that Rachel Doucette will be more than happy to meet with you in private."

"When do I contact her?"

"As soon as we finish our dinner."

A half hour later, they got up from the table. Riker glanced out the window. "Thank God the snow has stopped," he said. "The last thing we want is to get stuck here for days because we've gotten snowed in." He glanced at Madson. "I'm not saying that would be terrible in every way, it's just that we both have things to do—"

"No need to explain," laughed Madson.

They went up to Riker's room, with its carpet and chair fabrics done in vivid geometric patterns that suggested anything but a garden.

"Before you call Ms. Doucette, let's get to know her," said Riker. A quick Internet search revealed several photographs of an attractive, if somewhat plain, blonde-haired woman. Her address was 3245 Surfside Avenue, Unit 7, which Google maps revealed to be a modest apartment building on Marcy Street, a block from the Piscataqua River, which flowed into the Atlantic Ocean.

"She's obviously not living with her parents," said Madson.

"You're right," replied Riker. "Mr. and Mrs. Joseph Doucette live in York Harbor, a much more upscale neighborhood about ten miles up the coast. That's where Rachel grew up; she graduated from York Country Day School, an expensive private school located in the town. She then attended Plymouth State College in New Hampshire—a state school, not exactly top tier. Her major was political science, which is typically a catch-all for any kid who doesn't know what they want to do. She graduated with a mediocre average of two point eight. She went straight from college to the White House. Ah, I see there was one slight detour along the way—an arrest for drunk driving. This was when she was a junior in college. The judge let her off with probation and deferred adjudication, which meant that once she successfully completed her six-month probation, her record was struck clean."

"Is she working now?" asked Madson.

"I don't see anything to suggest that she's employed," replied Riker.

"Good—then she'll be tempted by a fat payday. Okay, I'll give her a call." Madson took out a prepaid cell phone and tapped a number.

A moment later she said, "Rachel? Hi. My name is Cynthia Rawling. I'm a writer, and I'm working on a new book about the White House. I'm taking a sort of 'Downton Abbey' approach where I focus on the support staff that surrounds the president. I understand you were a special assistant for nearly two years. I'd love to talk to you about your experiences! I'm sure you could give me some key insights. I may even decide to feature you in the book—that is, if you would like that. I'm only in town for one more day, so I'd like to see you as soon as possible."

Madson listened for a moment.

"Oh… you're thinking about writing your own book?"

She shot Riker a glance that said, *We need to shift gears.* Riker nodded.

"You want to tell your own story—what a marvelous idea!" gushed Madson into the phone. "Do you have a literary agent? No? Do you have connections with book publishers? No? Honey, I really would love to talk to you. Girl-to-girl. The publishing world is full of sharks, and they'll chew you up in a second. I don't want any money—like I said, I'm only in town for another day, and I think we should meet and get to know each other. I can hook you up with a top publisher in New York. Yes, the Big Four—Simon & Schuster, HarperCollins, Penguin Random House, and Hachette. I know them all. I think you could have a blockbuster. Imagine it—'Behind the Scenes at the White House—One Woman's Story.' Here's what I want you to do. I'm at the Hilton Garden Inn. You know where that is? On Garden Way, off Market Street. Suite 3301. But I tell you what—I'll meet you in the lobby. At eleven o'clock tomorrow morning? Perfect! Let's plan on spending a couple of hours, okay? Make a day of it. Great! I really think this is going to change your life. See you tomorrow."

Madson hung up.

"We have a date," she said.

"All right," said Riker. He looked at his watch. "It's only ten o'clock. We have over twelve hours to kill. Perhaps you'd like to go out for a drink."

"I appreciate the thought," said Madson. "But I'm really rather tired. It's been a long day and I'm going to turn in. And besides, it would be better if we were not seen together."

"Sure," said Riker. "Good idea."

She left his room. Riker watched a movie before falling asleep.

Chapter 17

*   *   *

The next morning, at ten minutes before eleven, Riker was ready, waiting in his room. He had eaten breakfast alone at a restaurant down the street. He had felt good getting outside in the fresh air, and from the hotel the ocean was close enough to smell its salty aroma. The sky was a clear brilliant blue, and the piles of newly plowed snow lay in gleaming heaps. On the way back from the restaurant he had stopped at a Dollar store and bought a cheap hat with a wide brim.

In the lobby, Madson waited, reading a magazine. At ten o'clock she had called Doucette to confirm, and the girl said she was looking forward to their meeting. Madson was wearing an outfit similar to what she had worn the day before—jeans, a cream-colored blouse, and the tweed jacket. Her brown hair, cut in bangs, hung loosely around her big tortoiseshell glasses.

Eleven o'clock came and went. Riker, in his room, texted Madson. She replied that she was still waiting.

At fifteen minutes past eleven, Madson saw a woman enter the lobby. The woman, who was wearing a green goose-down parka, paused and removed her wraparound sunglasses. Madson recognized her, and setting aside her magazine, approached her.

"Rachel Doucette?" inquired Madson. "I'm Cynthia Rawling."

Doucette smiled and offered her hand. "Hi," she said.

"What a pleasure to meet you," gushed Madson, taking Doucette's cool hand in both of hers to warm it up. "Have you had breakfast?"

"I could use a cup of coffee and a muffin," said Doucette.

"They have a self-service area next to the restaurant," said Madson. Taking her new charge by the arm, she led Doucette to the Garden Bistro, where Madson bought them each a coffee and muffin.

"I can't *wait* to talk to you," said Madson as Doucette lingered at one of the stand-up tables. "What do you say we go upstairs? We'll be much more comfortable and have some privacy."

Doucette agreed. They went to the elevator and up to the third floor. Using her card, Madson opened the door to her suite and they went inside.

"Wow," said Doucette. "This is a nice place. How many rooms do you have?"

"A bedroom, living room, bathroom, and a kitchenette," said Madson. "Make yourself comfortable."

They sat down at the table that Madson had moved close to the window. In the distance, over the rooftops of the neighboring buildings, loomed the green steel towers of the Memorial Bridge, whose center section could be lifted to permit the passage of ships.

"Cynthia, are you from the South?" asked Doucette. "I love your accent."

"Honey, I'm Georgia born and raised," said Madson.

After setting her coffee and muffin on the table, Doucette took off her parka and tossed it on the bed. She was wearing black jeans and a pale turquoise V-neck sweater. Her plain blonde hair framed her oval face. Madson noted that her eyebrows had been too aggressively plucked, her eye shadow was too blue, and her lipstick a shade too red, suggesting a girl who had some issues with self-esteem.

Doucette sat down and picked at her muffin. "I only like the top," she said. "The inside part is too fattening."

"It's a trend," said Madson as she sat down. "There are places where you can buy just the tops. They must bake them in special pans. So, tell me—you want to write a book about your experiences in the White House?"

"Yes," said Doucette. "Remember the book by Kate Anderson Brower? It was called *The Residence*. She made a lot of money spilling the secrets of the White House."

"But she covered several First Families, from the Kennedys to the Clintons," said Madson. "You were at the White House for less than two years. Honey, unless you've got a bombshell of a story, you're going to need more than just your personal experiences."

"I've got a bombshell," replied Doucette.

"What is it?"

Doucette smiled. "I was the president's lover."

"You're kidding!" said Madson with feigned astonishment. "Really? You did it with President Ralston? Where?"

"In his private bathroom, in the White House theatre, in Air Force One."

"Oh my God, honey, you've got a gold mine," said Madson. "But you need someone to protect you and guide you. Let me tell you, when we publish this book, you're going to wake up in a shitstorm. I don't know of any other way to say it. You'll be the most notorious woman in America. You'll be on every news show and tabloid cover. Some people will hate you and other people will see you as a victim. Your life will be white-hot. Honey, you need to be prepared."

"You said when 'we' publish the book," said Doucette with a tone of suspicion.

"Honey, have you ever written a book?"

"No."

"Published a book?"

"No."

"Well, I have," said Madson. "Plenty of them. I know the business backwards and forwards."

"Can I Google you?"

"Sure—I'll give you my list of pen names. I don't publish under my own name."

"Oh," said Doucette, uncertainly.

"I like my privacy," explained Madson. "But in your case, using a pen name is not possible. It has to be your story, from you."

"What can you do for me?" asked Doucette.

"I can help you write your book, find a literary agent—I know all the top agents in New York—and get your book published. Trust me, the book business is a sea of sharks. They'll eat you alive."

"Okay," said Doucette with more conviction.

Madson got up from the table. "Rachel, let's celebrate your future." She went to the refrigerator and took out a bottle of champagne. Two champagne flutes waited on the counter. She popped open the bottle and poured two glasses. Leaving the bottle on the counter, she carried the glasses to the table. She handed one to Doucette.

"To your success!" said Madson as she raised her glass.

"Yes—to success," said Doucette with a smile. She drank half the glass. "This is pretty good stuff," she said.

"Get used to it," replied Madson. "You're going to be drinking plenty of champagne as our book climbs the bestseller lists and you make the talk show circuit—Kimmel, Colbert, Fallon, all of them. They'll all want you. Of course, I'll be out of sight. Like I said, I enjoy my anonymity. I'm a strictly behind-the-scenes type of person. You're the star."

Doucette drained her glass.

"Let's talk about you," said Madson as she deftly removed Doucette's glass and carried it to the counter, where the bottle was waiting. "Why did you leave the White House?"

"Mrs. Ralston caught us," said Doucette without a trace of embarrassment. "We were in his private bathroom. The president didn't know she had entered in the Oval Office. Don Strauss was supposed to keep people out. When Paul was finished, he opened the door, and there she was."

"Was Strauss actively helping the president to hook up with you?" asked Madson. "Wow—that would be an explosive angle to the story!" She walked back to the table and handed Doucette her champagne flute, which she had refilled.

"I'm sure Don knew," replied Doucette as she accepted the glass. She took a swallow. "The president would buzz Don and say that he was in a meeting and that no one could come in. Or he would ask Don to watch the door of the movie theatre while we did it. How could he not know?"

"Indeed—how could he not know?" Madson took a tiny sip of her champagne. "Let's talk about you for a moment. Are you working now?"

"Um, not at the moment," replied Doucette. "I've applied to some jobs in Washington and New York, but nothing yet."

"How are you surviving?"

"My parents are giving me some money until I get another job."

"Do they know why you left the White House?" asked Madson.

Doucette shook her head. "No." Her voice was tinged with sadness. "I told them the White House rotates the assistants, and it's normal to serve only two years. But I suppose I'll have to tell them the truth, won't I?"

"If you're going to write a tell-all book, they need to know before the rest of the world does," said Madson. Suddenly Madson felt touched by this young woman's predicament, and how her appetite for excitement had almost certainly ruined her life. And her parents—how were they going to feel about what her daughter had done and was planning to broadcast to the greedy world?

"I'm not feeling well," said Doucette. She rubbed her forehead with her hand. "I feel kind of dizzy."

"Oh, I think we've had too much bubbly in the middle of the day!" said Madson cheerily. She went to the kitchenette and returned a moment later with a glass of sparkling water with ice. "Here—drink this."

Doucette took a long sip before clumsily putting the glass on the table. "It tastes funny," she said.

"That's because it's mineral water. It's good for you."

"I really feel dizzy," said Doucette. Her speech was slurred and her eyes half-closed.

"Honey, you just need to lie down for a minute," said Madson soothingly. She helped Doucette to her feet. Unsteadily Doucette walked into the bedroom. Madson gently turned her around and sat her on the bed.

"Now you just lie back and close your eyes," said Madson as she eased her down. "There you go. Just put your feet up and relax. I'm sure you'll feel better in no time."

Within moments, Doucette was unconscious. Madson gently lifted one of her eyelids. The pupil did not respond to the light.

Madson took out her spare phone and tapped a number. "We're ready for you," she said.

Then she went to her travel bag and pulled out a pair of latex gloves. With a towel she began to wipe every surface of the room that she had touched.

The hotel security cameras, which the police viewed later that day, showed a man approach the door to suite 3301. The time was eleven thirty in the morning, which corresponded to when Rachel Doucette said she had passed out. But the tape told the police nothing useful. The man was wearing a shapeless overcoat and a big hat, and he kept his head down, never looking up. He carried a small suitcase or travel bag. The man knocked on the door, and a moment later the door opened. The man went inside.

Exactly fifteen minutes later the door opened. The man stepped out, followed by the woman. The man, still wearing his hat, kept his head down. The woman made no attempt to hide her identity; the desk clerk quickly identified her as Cynthia Rawling.

The couple were seen on camera going down the elevator to the lobby. They casually walked through the lobby and out into the street.

Had the police reviewed the lobby security tape that captured the scene fifteen minutes later, they would have seen, among the other routine foot traffic, Dr. Martin Riker, the resident of room 2650, walk into the lobby carrying a small suitcase. He took the elevator up to his room. Twenty minutes later—at twelve twenty in the afternoon—he checked out of the hotel.

It was at two o'clock when the third-floor security camera showed the door to suite 3301 swing open again. A young woman stumbled out. At first glance, she appeared to be drunk. A housekeeper saw her and asked if she were all right. The woman's speech was slurred, and the housekeeper, thinking she might be having a medical emergency, called security.

At two thirty, Rachel Doucette was sitting in the office of the hotel manager, being interviewed by a Portsmouth police detective. She told a story of having come to the hotel to meet with a woman named Cynthia Rawling. They were to discuss a book project. Rawling took her to suite 3301, where they had champagne. Doucette remembered feeling woozy and lying down on the bed. Two hours later, she woke up. It took her a few minutes to remember where she was. Finding the suite empty, she went into the hallway, where she was discovered by the housekeeper.

A search of suite 3301 revealed no champagne bottle, no flutes, no fingerprints, and no personal items. It was as if the suite had never been occupied.

A search for a woman named Cynthia Rawling turned up nothing. Her photo from the security camera was circulated, but she was never found. She had paid for her room with a generic pre-paid credit card.

Rachel Doucette was taken to the hospital for an examination. Her clothing was intact. There were no signs of an assault. The only anomaly was a small puncture wound on the top of her left foot. Doucette had no idea how it got there.

When Riker had left the hotel at twelve twenty, he went to his rented car. On his way to the Manchester airport he made a stop at the Portsmouth FedEx office. There he placed a small box into a larger padded box, which he addressed to Jim Gilmore at the CDC, overnight delivery.

At the airport, Riker passed through security and walked to the gate for his flight to Washington. On the way, he passed another gate, where people were waiting for a flight to New York. He paused and scanned the passengers. Recognizing one of them, he approached her.

The woman had short strawberry blonde hair. She was not wearing glasses, and she was dressed in a blue North Face parka, black slacks, and slip-on boots. She looked like a soccer mom coming home from a ski trip.

When she saw Riker, she smiled and stood up.

"Martin Riker, fancy meeting you here," she said.

"Meryl Madson, what a surprise," replied Riker. "What brought you to Portsmouth?"

"Visiting a friend," she replied. "And you?"

"I was seeing a patient."

"And how is your patient?"

"No prognosis yet. We're running some tests. We'll know in a day or two."

"I hope you get the results you want."

The boarding call came for Madson's flight.

"It was nice seeing you," she said as she picked up her carryon.

"You too," replied Riker as he shook her hand. "Please give my best regards to Angela."

Riker turned and made his way through the crowd to his gate.

Chapter 18

*   *   *

I t was nearly seven o'clock in the evening when Riker tossed his suitcase onto his bed at The Jefferson, kicked off his shoes, and turned on the television. On the political scene, there was not much going on; at a ceremony in the Oval Office, President Ralston had signed a trade agreement with the European Union. On television he looked perfectly normal, and he smiled as he shook hands with the members of Congress and trade officials who had backed the bill. Then he had gone to the East Room to greet the members of the World Series winning team before leaving for two days at Camp David.

Anyone seeing him would have no way of knowing that he was battling a deadly disease.

Riker's phone rang. He picked it up.

"Hey Martin," said Maxwell Mosely. "Glad I caught you. Are you free for dinner?"

Riker was hungry and he liked Mosely, so he said that he'd be happy to meet him.

A half-hour later Riker scanned the room of Casa Antonio, a Mexican restaurant on Vermont Ave. NW, a few blocks from the hotel. He saw Mosely sitting in a booth.

"Try the house margarita," said Mosely as Riker slid onto the banquette. "They make it strictly in the classic style—Don Julio tequila, triple sec, and lime juice, shaken with ice. Personally, I skip the salt."

"Okay, I'll follow your advice," agreed Riker.

"And on the menu, try the pan seared salmon with roasted corn salsa. Incredible!"

"Going out with you is easy," smiled Riker. "All I have to do is show up and eat."

After they had ordered, and Mosely had extolled the virtues of the Casa Antonio house tortilla chips and fresh salsa, which the server had brought, Mosely leaned forward.

"So, how's the project coming along?" he asked. "The one whose goal is to identify any biological threats to the boss?"

"It's coming along just fine," replied Riker. After weighing how much his question might tip his hand, he said, "By the way, I've seen on the staff lists that you were on at least two trips—Skowhegan and Nagoya—in which the boss's entourage also included an assistant named Rachel Doucette. What do you know about her?"

Like a hound dog whose supersensitive nose detects the faintest whiff of a possum, Mosely became alert. His keen blue eyes stared through Riker, as if he were seeing a plump partridge in the distance. Then a smile emerged on his face.

"Ah, Rachel," he said. "One of BB's babes."

"BB?"

"Big Bull, the boss's Secret Service handle."

"Babes—plural?"

"Yes," replied Mosely. He paused to take a sip of his margarita. "You can really taste the superior tequila," he said as he placed the glass on the table. "Rachel was one of the most attractive, I have to say. She may have been a particular favorite."

"Have you got any more names for me?"

"Kimberly Schuster."

"We know about her."

"Gwen Peterson."

"I don't know her."

"She's a media consultant who lives in Georgetown. I use the term 'media consultant' very loosely, because her company, GP Associates, seems to have no clients other than the Committee to Re-Elect President Ralston. She's on the committee's payroll, but what she does is anyone's guess. She comes and goes at the White House, and occasionally pops up when we're on the road, even though she doesn't travel with us. She's so well-known that the Secret Service has a handle for her—Candy Cane."

"Candy Cane, huh? Thanks. I'll have to look into her."

"You don't suspect her of carrying some sort of biological weapon that might harm the boss?"

"Not exactly. But thanks, Max, for the info. I appreciate it."

"Aren't you overlooking something?" asked Mosely with a sly smile.

"What?" replied Riker with a trace of irritation.

"Why limit your search to one gender?"

"What do you mean?"

Mosely shrugged. "What law says that BB's babes need to be only women? Might there be a BB's boy?"

"There's no law that says there couldn't be a BB's boy," replied Riker. "It's just that—"

"I know, I know," said Mosely. "The notion of a straight president having a girlfriend or two is almost acceptable. No one really cares, as long as he doesn't get caught and is forced to lie about it. But a boyfriend? Oh my God, now *there* would be a firestorm! There are people who would wink at a good Christian having a *girl* on the side but who would be ready to storm the White House with pitchforks if he had a *boy* on the side. Whoa, the stakes would be infinitely higher. Republican or Democrat—it wouldn't matter."

"Max, you're making innuendoes but I'm not hearing any substantive evidence."

"Okay, I'll give you evidence."

At that moment the server appeared with their entrees. Riker waited patiently as the two seared salmon plates were put on the table.

"May I get you anything else?" asked the server.

"No, no, that's fine for now," said Riker. "Thank you."

With excruciating slowness, the server moved away from their booth.

"Okay, Max, let's have it," said Riker.

"I'd actually rather *show* you than *tell* you," replied Mosely. He took out his phone and quickly sent a text. Within seconds he smiled. "I've gotten the answer I wanted." He put away his phone and said, "After we finish our delicious dinners, you and I are going to take a ride."

Riker, feeling helpless, took a bite of his salmon. "Wow, Max, you were right—this is really good."

"I'm always right," he laughed. "Now then, Martin, let's have a frank discussion. I've been thinking about this project of yours. On its face, it sounds like a typical government undertaking, designed to generate a report, and, in the event that something bad happens, to cover someone's ass. Biological threats to the president are possible, and should be prepared for. This is especially true when he's out in public, like at the G7 event in Nagoya when that crazy nut threw a bag of blood at him. Who knows what could have been in that bag?"

"Exactly," said Riker.

"But like I said, I've been thinking about what's been going on inside the big house, and my intuition tells me that if the boss contracted some sort of ordinary social disease—you know what I'm talking about—which could be treated with antibiotics, then he wouldn't be getting sick so often and you wouldn't be camped out in the Medical Unit. Therefore, I've concluded that it's something more serious, and it's something that can't be resolved quickly. It's also something that no one wants to talk about, and it's linked to his proclivity for, shall we say, extracurricular activities."

"And?" said Riker.

Mosely lowered his voice to barely a whisper. "Having been around the block a few times, I know the signs. I think the boss has AIDS."

"Max, you know I can't say anything about that."

"Which makes the possibility of a BB boy even more significant—although, as we both know, gay men have no monopoly on the disease."

"Very true," said Riker.

"What if the boss had AIDS?" said Mosely. "And then consider this: What if he chose to make it public?"

"Max, are you completely insane?" said Riker.

"Think about the possibilities," continued Mosely. "Think about the huge impact that Magic Johnson had when he announced he had AIDS. He was a heterosexual male. His openness forced people to reconsider what they thought about the disease! He single-handedly reduced the shame and stigma of AIDS. Now think what would happen if the boss did the same thing! Think about the amazing impact it would have, and how millions of people who are at risk would get themselves tested and treated. He could save millions of lives!"

"Max, really—" said Riker.

"And just think what it would mean to the Office of National AIDS Policy. The director, Uma Davis, was appointed last year by the president. They coordinate the government's efforts to reduce the number of HIV infections and expand access to care and treatment, here and in other countries. And they sponsor all kinds of education initiatives."

"Okay, Max, settle down," said Riker. "I understand what you're saying. But I need to tell you that it's never going to happen. If—and I mean strictly theoretically—the boss somehow got AIDS, it likely would not be broadcast to the world. And do you know why? Because in America, the majority of new cases of AIDS are acquired either by unprotected man-to-man sex or by sharing dirty needles. If the boss got it one of those ways, he's not going to admit it. It would be political suicide. So forget it."

"All right," said Mosely reluctantly. "You win round one. But I'm not throwing in the towel."

The server came and removed their plates. Mosely glanced at his watch. "I still need to show you something," he said. "We have a few minutes to get where we need to be."

After paying the bill, they went outside. Mosely's car was parked a block away. The weather was cold and clear, and through the city glare a few of the brightest stars glimmered overhead. Mosely got behind the wheel, and when they were both buckled in he pulled away from the curb.

Ten minutes later Mosely parked on Rhode Island Ave. NW and they walked a block to a big Victorian building on the corner. A small sign by the bronze and glass door said simply OPAL.

They went inside and found themselves in a lavishly decorated room with a mirrored bar and dining area with white tablecloths. Judging by the ratio of men to women, Riker immediately knew that he was in a nightclub catering to gay men.

"There are three levels here," said Mosely as they made their way up the curving staircase with its ornate banister and red carpet. "The street level is the restaurant. On the second floor is the bar and lounge, with pool tables and things like that. The third floor is the dance club, where they have DJs and drag shows."

On the second floor, they entered the crowded lounge and made their way to the marble-topped bar with its old-fashioned globe lights and mirrored back wall.

"I feel like I'm in the Folies-Bergère," shouted Riker over the din of the music.

"That's the idea," replied Mosely. "Opal is a favorite among Washington politicians and bureaucrats, because while it's lavishly decorated it's actually a very low-key place. They don't advertise and the tourists don't know about it. They also have a back door that's covered by an awning. If you're a politician who's still not out of the closet, you can have your car pull up to the awning and you can duck inside without being seen."

"Are there many closeted Washington politicians?" asked Riker.

"Keep your eyes open—you'll be amazed!" laughed Mosely.

As Riker nursed his bourbon on the rocks, he was indeed surprised to see more than one face that he knew from watching the political news channels.

"See that guy over there?" said Mosely. "The one standing next to that painting that looks like a Renoir?"

"Oh yeah," replied Riker. "He looks familiar."

"He's a congressman from a district in the Bible Belt," said Mosely. "If his constituents knew he was here, they'd freak out. He's been their representative for nearly twenty years!"

"And no one knows?"

"Deep in their hearts they may know, but he's very careful to keep his private life private. He doesn't talk about it, and his constituents return the favor by not asking about it. To keep up appearances, every once in a while the congressman will show up at a public event with an attractive woman on his arm. Everyone sees the picture they want to see."

"Why doesn't he come out?"

"Because his district isn't ready to have an openly gay representative. Maybe someday they will be, but they aren't there yet."

They stood at the bar for a while, watching the crowd.

"Okay, Max, this is fascinating," said Riker after a few minutes. "But where's the big surprise? I've known plenty of gay guys in my life. This is nothing new."

"Be patient," said Mosely as he looked at his watch. Then he peered at the door. "Good timing. Our surprise just walked in. When I texted him, he told me he'd be here now."

"Who?" asked Riker.

"Look," said Mosely as he nodded toward the door.

Riker directed his eyes to the entrance to the lounge.

There stood Stephen Howe.

Riker watched as Howe chatted briefly before easing his way towards the bar. Moving towards the door, Mosely intercepted him, and they spoke for a moment. Mosely nodded towards Riker, and then motioned for Riker to join them.

"Mr. Howe, it's good to see you again," said Riker as they shook hands.

"Please call me Stephen," he said.

"You two have met?" asked Mosely.

"Yes," said Riker. "A few days ago we had a nice chat in the bowling alley. Stephen was concerned about the boss's health."

"Yes, that's a topic of considerable concern," said Mosely. He turned to Howe. "You won't get anything out of Martin. National security, doctor-patient confidentiality—you know how that goes. But I've told him my own personal theory—that the boss has AIDS."

"I've had the same concerns," said Howe. He leaned over the bar to order a gin and tonic.

"I was telling Martin at dinner," said Mosely, "that I thought if the boss were so unfortunate as to have contracted AIDS, it would be amazing if he went public, like Magic Johnson did. Think of the good he could do and the awareness he could raise."

"But the public opinion outcome could be positive," said Riker, "only if he were shown to have somehow gotten it without using a dirty needle or having sex with a girlfriend while he was married. And I'm not even going to consider man-to-man sex."

With drinks in hand, the three found an empty booth in a far corner of the room, where it was quieter and they could speak more freely.

"I can tell you unequivocally that the boss is not an IV drug user," said Howe.

"And?" asked Riker.

"And what?" replied Howe.

"Another one of the possibilities," said Riker. "Can you tell me unequivocally that he has not engaged in man-to-man sex?"

"Not to my personal knowledge," replied Howe.

Riker was thunderstruck. The man who spent more time with the president than anyone else, and who himself was gay, had given an answer that seemed carefully legalistic.

His reply opened up a new world of possibilities.

"Hey, the boss wouldn't be the first occupant of the Oval Office to take a walk on the wild side," said Mosely. "Read your history books. Consider James Buchanan. He was president just before the Civil War—from 1857 to 1861. A lifelong bachelor, he never married. During his lifetime, it was commonly accepted that he had a very close relationship with a man named William Rufus King. For ten years—from 1834 until King was appointed minister to France in 1844—they lived together in a Washington boardinghouse. King referred to their relationship as a 'communion,' and the two often attended social functions together. Andrew Jackson called them 'Miss Nancy' and 'Aunt Fancy.'"

"What happened to King?" asked Howe.

"He actually served as our nation's vice president under Franklin Pierce," replied Mosely. "Unfortunately, he got tuberculosis and died a month into his term."

"He was our nation's shortest-serving vice president," said Riker, "and he may very well have been our first gay vice president."

"Moving up a century," said Mosely, "Who can forget JFK's pal, Lem Billings? They first met in prep school, and became inseparable. Billings served as an usher at Kennedy's wedding and helped him run his presidential campaign. After the election, Kennedy gave him his own bedroom on the third floor of the White House. Everyone knew Billings was gay, but nobody ever thought that JFK was involved with him."

"And how about Lyndon Johnson?" said Riker. With a few drinks under his belt, he was warming to the conversation. "In 1939, when he was a congressman from Texas, a guy named Walter Jenkins began working for him. They were inseparable, and Jenkins followed Johnson as he rose to become a senator, vice president under Kennedy, and finally president. But a few weeks before the 1964 presidential election, Jenkins was busted in a restroom at the YMCA here in Washington. He and another guy were charged with disorderly conduct. Then it was revealed that he had been arrested in 1959 for the same thing. In October, a month before the election, he resigned and went back to Texas."

"Did Goldwater use it against Johnson in the campaign?" asked Howe.

"Surprisingly, not much," replied Riker. "I guess it was a different era back then—more polite. The Goldwater campaign made bumper stickers that read, 'ALL THE WAY WITH LBJ—BUT DON'T GO NEAR THE YMCA.' That was about as near as they got."

The men sat for a moment, pondering the tides of history.

"Stephen," said Riker, "I really need to ask you, very specifically, whether to your knowledge there's any possibility that the boss could have engaged in man-to-man behavior that put him at risk for AIDS?"

Howe thought for a moment. He put down his drink and said, "To my knowledge, the boss has never engaged in man-to-man behavior that could have put him at risk."

"Well, I guess that settles it," said Mosely.

"I suppose so," said Riker. "Just one more question, and then I'll stop pestering you. Can you give me any names of men who *might* have had a relationship with the boss?"

Howe shook his head. "I can't, because I don't want to out anyone who isn't publicly gay. That would include me, by the way. As far as I'm concerned, you never saw me here. I've heard what people say about me in the gossip columns, but unless someone can prove something, no one can touch me."

"Martin, you're looking at two cowards," laughed Mosely. "Our closet doors are firmly shut."

"People from all walks of life have secrets they hide," shrugged Riker. "It's often a decision born out of pragmatism."

"I suppose you're right," said Howe as he drained his glass. "You do what you have to do."

Riker looked at his watch. "Gentlemen, it's been a long day. I'm going to call it a night."

"I could use one more drink," replied Mosely as he waved for a waiter.

"Then I'll grab a cab," said Riker. He turned to Howe. "If you want to add anything to what you've told me, please let me know."

"Will do," said Howe.

Riker got up from the booth and made his way through the crowd to the door.

Chapter 19

*   *   *

I n his office at the Ten-Fifty on Thursday morning, Riker logged onto a secure video conference call with Jim Gilmore at the CDC.

"Good morning, Martin," said Gilmore from his desk. "Let's review the case to date. You've identified a variety of scenarios whereby the subject could have been exposed to AIDS. You've sent us some blood samples, some in a tube and some as residual blood on a cloth item. Our first step is to determine whether the samples show evidence of an HIV infection, either antibodies or antigen. If we get positive results, then we verify, through DNA tests, if the particular strain of HIV matches the one in our subject.

"Let's go through the cases one by one.

"First, the dentist in Skowhegan. We only have the fact that the boss was treated by this individual who had AIDS at the time of contact. We need to determine if his strain of HIV matches the boss's. This takes a few days. We'll have results by the weekend.

"Second, we have the baggie from Japan. Our tests have shown that the baggie's blood is infected with HIV."

"Are you sure?" said Riker.

"Well, the sample is a bit old, but we're pretty confident."

"That makes sense," said Riker. "By the way, the baggie had both liquid blood and dried blood. Was there any difference between them?"

"Dried blood spot analysis is useful in controlled settings, where the blood has been spotted on a special filter paper," replied Gilmore. "It's not as reliable if the dried blood was on a piece of plastic baggie. But whatever, our blood typing tests suggest that the baggie contained blood from two individuals. Our initial virus testing suggests that the dried blood does *not* contain HIV."

"Okay," said Riker. "So far, we have one infected dentist and one infected baggie. That's two possible sources. What's next?"

"The third case is the accident in Kenya," said Gilmore. "We have the subject's bloody clothing. Through blood typing we identified blood from the boss and three other individuals."

"And?"

"One of those three was positive for HIV antigens. We're conducting DNA tests now."

"Okay," said Riker. "How about number four?"

"Number four, which we received early this morning, is the adult female. This sample has tested positive for HIV antigens and antibodies. This individual has HIV, and, unless she gets treatment, will eventually develop AIDS."

"Four scenarios," said Riker, "and four possible sources of HIV that could have infected our subject. Jim, you've handed me a real headache."

"I wish it could be simpler," said Gilmore, "but the tests say what they say."

"What are the odds of a false positive?" asked Riker.

"You know I never say 'never,' but it's damned unlikely. We used the latest fourth-generation tests, and even repeated them. So you've got four samples reactive one way or another."

"Thanks, Jim," said Riker. "I'll stay in touch."

After ending the call, he tapped another number.

"Angela? Riker here. I have a favor to ask. I need to know the name of the primary care doctor for Rachel Doucette." He gave her Doucette's address. "Yes, I know you have to do a little bit of digging. I'll wait." A few moments passed. "You've got it? Doucette is covered by the Neighborhood

Health Plan, and her doc is Edna Redford, in Portsmouth. Roger that. Thanks."

From his desk drawer he took out a throwaway cell phone. He tapped the number of Dr. Redford's office. After staying on hold for a few minutes, listening to a ghastly 1970s soft rock song played over and over again, he got the receptionist, who put him on hold again. After another few minutes a voice came on the line.

"This is Dr. Redford. How may I help you?"

"Dr. Redford, I'm a friend of one of your patients, Rachel Doucette. She needs to be tested for HIV as soon as possible."

"Rachel Doucette?" repeated Dr. Redford.

"Yes—is she a patient of yours?"

"I can't comment on that."

"I understand. But if she is your patient, she needs to be tested for HIV. Thank you for your time."

He hung up. There was nothing more that he could do.

Riker reviewed his notes. Four possible sources of HIV! Now he had to wait for the second round of tests, which could hopefully match one of the four possible sources to the RNA in the president's strain of HIV.

At that moment he heard a knock on his door.

Who the hell could that be? Riker couldn't think of anyone who would visit him at the Ten-Fifty.

He went to the door. "Yes, who is it?" he asked without opening it.

"Special agent Sam Flood," said a man's voice. "I'm with the FBI. May I come in?"

Riker opened the door to admit the man, who was wearing a grey business suit, white shirt, and blue necktie. His hair was neatly brushed back. His face was a blank mask.

"Dr. Riker?" asked Flood as he showed his identification.

"Yes, that's me."

"May I sit down?"

"Sure. What's this all about?"

Agent Flood sat in the chair in front of Riker's desk. "Angela Powell has informed us," he said as he took a tablet out of his black leather attaché case, "that you're doing some research on the president's inner circle, with a particular focus on possible biological threats to the president."

"Yes, I am," said Riker.

"In the course of another investigation, we've identified a person of interest. Her name is Gwen Peterson."

"I've heard of her," said Riker. "She lives in Georgetown, and has a media company called GP Associates. The Committee to Re-Elect President Ralston is her primary client."

"Right," said Flood.

"You said you identified her through another investigation."

"Here's what we know," said Flood. He propped up his tablet on the desk so Riker could see the screen. A man's face appeared. "This is Leon Sakharov. He was assigned to the Russian Embassy in Washington. While his nominal title was attaché, he was a member of the Foreign Intelligence Service of the Russian Federation, or SVR RF, which is Russia's external intelligence agency for civilian and political affairs. In short, he was a spy.

"This is all perfectly normal; we have our spies in Moscow, they have their spies here, and as long as people behave themselves, no one gets too upset about any of it. The last big blow-up between the United States and Russia was in 1991, when we kicked out fifty of their diplomats in connection with the Robert Hanssen spy case. In response, the Russians kicked out fifty of our guys. So it goes. Two years ago, Sakharov met Peterson at a diplomatic reception. She had wrangled an invitation through her White House connections, and attended the reception with a guy named Rory Timmons, who's basically a professional beard."

"You go to an event with Timmons, and he doesn't care if he leaves alone," said Riker.

"Exactly."

"Why did she go to the reception in the first place?" asked Riker.

Flood shrugged. "Thrill seeker. Social climber. Like Michaele and Tareq Salahi, the couple who wormed their way into a state dinner at the White House. The world is full of them. After the reception, Timmons went home alone. Peterson accompanied Sakharov to his apartment on

Benton Street NW, which is a few blocks south of the embassy complex on Wisconsin Ave. NW. She left his place at nine o'clock the next morning."

"You say that Sakharov *was* a spy," said Riker. "What happened?"

"I'll get to that," replied Flood. "Off and on during the following year, Peterson and Sakharov were observed having a relationship. They'd enter the same hotel a few minutes apart, and then leave a few hours later; or Peterson would be seen going to his apartment in the evening and spending the night. They rarely appeared in public together, and always at group events, such as receptions, where they could be seen talking to each other without any eyebrows being raised."

"Do you think Sakharov wanted sex or information—or both?" asked Riker.

"Both," replied Flood. "He compensated her very generously. Not with cash, though—only with gifts. For example, Sakharov was observed going to the Tiffany store in Chevy Chase, where he purchased a necklace with a pendant in the shape of a flower with a yellow diamond in the center. It cost eight thousand dollars. A week later, she went to see him at his apartment. When she left the next morning, she was wearing the necklace."

"Clearly, she was getting what she wanted," said Riker. "A taste of exciting international intrigue, social status, and some expensive bling. Do you think she passed along any sensitive information?"

"Being a consultant to the White House gave her a vantage point that most people don't have," replied Flood. "For the Russians, cultivating her was worthwhile, because while she didn't have access to classified material, she was privy to things like the president's schedule and who was at the White House. Her information, probably divulged naïvely, added to the mosaic that the Russians could create."

"Every little piece of the puzzle helps," said Riker. "So how does the story end?"

"About six months ago, Sakharov was suddenly recalled to Moscow. For two weeks we heard nothing. Then we received a report from one of our sources inside the Kremlin. I can't reveal the details, but here's the gist.

"We learned that while he was here in Washington, Sakharov was suddenly taken ill with what appeared to be a bad case of the flu. Because he hadn't been home in a year, the Russian Ministry of Foreign Affairs decided to bring him back to Moscow. When he arrived, he was given the usual tests. They couldn't figure out what was making him sick, so they ordered additional screenings. One of them was a rapid test for HIV. They probably administered it just so they could check it off the list.

"It was cheap and gave fast results. Supposed to turn positive within three months after infection. If you get a reaction, you need to go to confirmatory tests. Sakharov's was positive, but his docs thought it was a false positive—after all, Russian spies are not supposed to get AIDS! So, a bunch of other tests were done. They also all came up positive. It eventually dawned on them that their spy really had AIDS."

"Poor guy," said Riker. "If you get AIDS, Russia is not the place you want to be. The state's attitude is very harsh. Every year, their government makes a big announcement about its commitment to fight the disease, but because of the toxic attitude toward those who have the virus, nothing happens. The afflicted are shunned and treated like outcasts.

"The Russians see AIDS as a disease that affects drug addicts, and they're treated as criminals who should be locked up rather than sick people who need help. People who suspect they may have HIV feel stigmatized and are afraid to go to the hospital. By the time they get into the medical system, many of them are very sick.

"Concepts like educating the public about HIV and how it's transmitted are foreign to Russian society. The government's policy toward sex and drugs is to ignore them and clamp down hard on anyone who engages in what they see as deviant behavior, which means that those afflicted by HIV get exiled to the margins of society."

"Exactly," said Flood. "Sakharov has fallen off the face of the earth. He may have been shipped off to his family home in Omsk, where his sister and cousins live."

"That's in Siberia," noted Riker. "Over a thousand miles from Moscow."

"Yep," nodded Flood. "Out of sight, out of mind."

"I'm sorry that our Russian spy has met a bad end," said Riker. "But do you have a link to Peterson, other than the fact that they were lovers?"

"Yes, which is why I've come you," said Flood. "We have reason to believe that she gave Sakharov the disease."

"What's the evidence?"

"In connection with another case, we happen to be monitoring a website called Notify.org, an online service operated by the Internet Sexual Health Consortium, or ISHC. It's something like another website in Washington, inSPOT. Just Google the DC Health Department—you'll find it."

Flood took out his phone and brought up the Notify.org website to show Riker. It was a very simple landing page, with just some text and a few bullet points.

"It's common knowledge that if you've been diagnosed with any STD including AIDS, you should tell your sexual partners so that they can get tested. But many people are too ashamed or too busy to do this personally, so the service does it for you. You go to the site and open an account. Then type in the email addresses of every sex partner you've had. You can either create a personal message or use the pre-written 'card' they offer. Then hit 'send.' Each addressee receives an email 'card' saying that they need to see their doctor. You can send your message anonymously or sign it. The service urges you to sign, because when the recipient knows who the sender is, they're more likely to respond and go to the doctor."

"And you're saying that Peterson was involved with Notify.org?"

"Yes," said Flood. "As part of another investigation, we were monitoring the site."

"Do you mean contact scraping? Building lists of email addresses that had been entered into the system?"

"Well, I'm not sure how our IT guys do it, but they get it done."

"Isn't the service supposed to be confidential?" asked Riker.

"Yes, and there are legal restrictions on what we can do with the information. But those discussions are above my pay grade. Here's the bottom line: At about the same time that Peterson began hooking up with Sakharov, a man signed onto the website. He sent a message that he had been diagnosed as HIV-positive. He did not specify how this happened, although the contacts he entered into the system included both men and women. One of the email addresses he entered belonged to Gwen Peterson."

"Strictly speaking," said Riker, "this man could not be certain if Gwen Peterson *got* HIV from him, or if she *gave* it to him."

"I suppose not," agreed Flood. "Anyway, we decided to reach out to you because we know that Gwen Peterson has frequent access to the White House."

"Thanks—I appreciate the tip," said Riker.

Flood gathered his papers and stood up. "If you have any further questions, don't hesitate to contact me," he said as he handed Riker his card. "It's been a pleasure to meet you. I'll see myself out."

Riker sat for a moment, pondering this new information. His list of possible sources of the president's HIV infection had increased from four to five.

He also had to figure out a way to get a blood sample from Gwen Peterson.

Chapter 20

*   *   *

Riker glanced at his watch. In twenty minutes, President Ralston was due to visit the Medical Unit to have his blood drawn and to receive his B-12 shot. Thompson had also texted Riker that their patient wanted a brief consultation with an update.

Hurrying over the slushy streets and snow-dusted sidewalks, Riker arrived at the White House and found Thompson behind her desk. He told her about the visit of FBI agent Sam Flood, and the indications that Gwen Peterson may be carrying HIV.

"The list of possible sources is growing longer," said Thompson. "To help narrow it down, we should soon be getting the results of the DNA sequencing of our three blood samples—the Japanese baggie, the president's suit from Kenya, and Rachel Doucette. However, I do have something tangible to report: We've got the DNA sequencing of the HIV that infected Palmer, the dentist. His strain of HIV is not the same as the one that infected the president."

"Okay, we can cross Dr. Palmer off our list," replied Riker. "The Skowhegan event is the oldest, and the only one that predates Paul Ralston becoming president. On the timeline, the next event is the protest at the G7 in Nagoya."

"Unless there was a sexual encounter with Rachel Doucette—or possibly Gwen Peterson—before that time," interjected Thompson. "Both had access to the president since the time he took office."

"Right."

At that moment Dorothy opened the door to say the president had entered the Medical Unit. Thompson and Riker immediately went to greet him. In a private examination room, he had taken off his grey suit jacket and rolled up his sleeve. The nurse, Jennet Swift, was preparing his arm for the blood draw.

"Mr. President, how are you feeling?" asked Thompson.

"All things considered, not so bad," he replied with a smile. "I was a little bit nauseated this morning after breakfast, but it passed. My appetite is good."

"We'll put you on the scale," replied Thompson as Swift expertly drew a vial of the president's blood. "But offhand I'd say you don't appear to have lost any weight. You're taking your meds?"

"Absolutely!" replied the president. "By the way, am I still getting a B-12 shot? Do I need it?"

"It's your choice," replied Thompson. "As you recall, you started receiving them when you were governor because you felt they gave you more energy. Frankly, there's not a medical indication that you need them. Your blood tests don't indicate a B-12 deficiency. So your shots are excess, and with this vitamin being water soluble, that overage is passed out in your urine. My advice is that the shots aren't necessary, particularly now that your AIDS meds include a multivitamin."

"I started getting the shots after I read that lots of movie stars get them," said the president as he rolled down his sleeve. "But maybe you could call my feeling they help a placebo effect."

"Very likely," said Thompson.

"Then let's stop them," said the president. He turned to nurse Swift. "No offense intended regarding your skill with the needle," he said. "You're really an expert. When you slip it under my skin, I hardly feel a thing."

"Thank you, Mr. President," said Swift.

"Not like your predecessor," he continued as he put on his jacket. "What was her name?"

"Christina Wilkinson, I believe," said Thompson.

"Yes, Wilkinson," said the president. "I hate to speak ill of people who aren't present, but I'm telling you, when she jabbed that needle in my arm it was like she was St. George slaying the dragon! It really made me jump to attention."

"We all try our very best," said Thompson diplomatically. "We're happy to have someone as qualified and as caring as nurse Swift."

The president smiled and gave Swift an up-and-down glance. Riker instantly picked up on the unspoken vibe: *If I didn't have this damned AIDS, I'd be happy to recruit you to be one of BB's babes.* But those days were over—or so Riker hoped.

"Mr. President, if you would care to step into my office, we can give you a quick update on your case," said Thompson. "Or would you rather do it in the Oval Office?"

"Let's go to my office," replied the president. "I can give you ten minutes."

Riker and Thompson followed the president out into the Center Hall, where a few staffers were waiting, including Don Strauss. Without delay the entourage made its way through the Palm Room, across the West Colonnade, and into the West Wing. In a moment Riker and Thompson were seated on one of the twin sofas in the Oval Office.

The president sat opposite. Don Strauss, who had cleared the room of other staff before closing the doors, joined them.

"I've told Don and Brian about my condition," said the president. "Brian isn't in the office at the moment; otherwise he'd be joining us."

"I completely understand—whom you tell is your personal decision," said Thompson.

"How about Stephen Howe?" asked Riker. "He's your body man. He spends more time with you than anyone else."

"I may tell him," replied the president. "I'm just trying to limit the knowledge to those who absolutely need to know."

"And Uma Davis at the Office of National AIDS Policy?" pressed Riker.

"No," said the president. "We are not going public."

"Let's review," said Thompson. "To my knowledge there are eleven people inside the circle. They are you, your wife, Don Strauss, Brian Conway, me, Dr. Gilmore, Dr. Riker, Angela Powell, my assistant Dorothy, and two nurses in the Medical Unit—Jennet Swift and John Daughtry."

"All right," said the president. "Let's make sure we keep the circle very tight. Martin, what have you got for me?"

"Our list of possible sources of the infection has been narrowed to four," said Riker.

"My God—*four*?" replied President Ralston. "That many?"

"You're not a shrinking violet, Mr. President," said Thompson. "Despite precautions, the world manages to find you."

"Until today, we had five possibilities," said Riker. "By DNA analysis, we've been able to eliminate the dentist in Skowhegan. That leaves four. Two are what you might call environmental in nature. A variety of HIV tests have revealed infected blood in the baggie thrown by the Japanese protestor and on the shirt you were wearing on the day of the accident in Kenya. Those were incidents that were clearly beyond your control."

"How could I have gotten infected in Kenya?" asked the president.

"It's a long shot, but you had that bleeding gash on your arm," said Riker. "In your car other people were also cut, and you all tumbled about together. Also, at the accident site you comforted many of the injured, and more than one person bled on you. If an infected person's blood entered your arm wound, possibly enough virus could have been transferred to infect you."

"All right," said the president. "Go on."

"The other two possible sources are somewhat more sensitive in nature," said Riker. "Both are young women with White House connections. They are Rachel Doucette and Gwen Peterson."

After a moment of silence, the president said, "They're both infected?"

"We're certain that Doucette is infected," replied Riker. "We suspect that Peterson may be as well. Mr. President, has the director of the FBI contacted you about Peterson?"

"No," said the president.

"You have a phone call scheduled with him in an hour," said Strauss. "He requested the call this morning."

Riker paused to consider whether he should deliver the news or give the FBI director the privilege. He decided to forge ahead. "Sir, this morning I was visited by an FBI agent, who revealed to me that Gwen Peterson was having an affair with a Russian attaché named Leon Sakharov, who was also a spy working for the SVR."

"Oh, Christ," said the president.

"Sir, did you ever say anything to her—?" asked Strauss.

"No, absolutely not," replied the president. "I mean, if she wanted to go running to the Russians with our plans to defeat the Republicans in the next election, I suppose that could be interesting to them. But we never talked about the business of the nation."

"I'm sure we all appreciate the extreme potency of this story in the national political arena," said Strauss. "JFK had girlfriends, and one of them was cozy with a Mafia don at the same time she was seeing him. But Russian spies? Jesus, no!"

"I'm sure we all understand the political ramifications of my indiscretion," said the president. "We can handle it, right, Don?"

Strauss nodded.

"The FBI agent told me that Sakharov was recalled to Moscow," continued Riker, "where he was diagnosed as HIV-positive. He's been retired and sent away, probably to his family in Omsk. While we don't know for sure, it's possible that Peterson also has HIV, and if so, she may have transmitted it to you."

"Wow," said the president. "I always assumed that people got AIDS from using dirty needles and having casual gay sex."

"Those may be the leading causes in the US," said Riker, "but other avenues exist. And, in some other cultures, the equation is very different. For example, in certain parts of Africa, particularly Botswana, rates of HIV infection are high among heterosexuals. And most don't use drugs."

"How can that be?" asked the president. "Why are so many straight people getting infected?"

"If you'll forgive me for venturing into delicate territory—" said Riker.

"Delicate, shmelicate," retorted the president. "Just tell me the facts."

"Well, in Botswana, researchers believe the high heterosexual transmission is explained by the local custom of men having two or more long-term sexual partners."

"They have multiple long-term casual relationships?" asked the president.

"Yes," replied Riker. "Seems a guy in Botswana may have a wife at home, a girlfriend in town, and another girlfriend somewhere else. These relationships can last for years, and as a sign of trust they don't use condoms. Having unprotected sex repeatedly with the same infected person over a long period of time greatly increases the chances of transmission. So, in places like Botswana, men tend not to get HIV from prostitutes or other one-time encounters, but from their steady girlfriends. These women also pass their virus along to their other long-term boyfriends."

"Oh—so the girlfriends are doing the same thing as the guys," said the president.

"Just like Rachel Doucette and Gwen Peterson," said Riker. "Both of them had other steady partners. We know that Peterson was informed by one of her partners that she was at risk for HIV."

"What did she do about it?" asked the president.

"As far as we can tell, nothing," replied Riker.

"My God," said the president. "How long ago was this?"

"About a year."

"So she's known all this time?"

"Let's just say that she's chosen to ignore it," said Riker. "Think about it, sir. She's a social climber who has gotten into an intimate relationship with the president of the United States. In a twisted way, she's at the pinnacle of prestige, at least in the sad world of mistresses. She knows that if she were found to have HIV, her fairytale romance would come to a screeching halt."

"But you say you're not certain if she has AIDS," said the president.

"Correct," replied Riker. "We know that Sakharov is infected, and we know that another man has informed Peterson that he's infected;

presumably this second man notified her because they've had a sexual or needle-sharing relationship. But it's possible that Peterson could be free of the disease. Just one or two sexual encounters with an infected person may not lead to acquiring the virus. It can take more 'meetings' than that."

"Which leads us to an important question," said Thompson. "As your doctor, I need to get a clear picture of your recent sexual history. I know of three names: Kimberly Schuster, Rachel Doucette, and Gwen Peterson."

"Kimberly?" interjected the president. "Has she—?"

"Ms. Schuster had a blood test performed in July of this year, shortly before she left the White House to attend Stanford," said Thompson. "The test was nonreactive. Because of this, for the time being we're putting her aside."

"Okay," said the president.

"How often would you say you had sexual encounters with Doucette and Peterson?"

"Doucette was about once every two weeks," replied the president. "She was part of the traveling staff, so sometimes it was more often. Peterson was the same—about once every two weeks."

"Anyone else?" asked Thompson.

"No."

"You're certain?"

"Is this since I've become president?" he asked. "There were a few when I was governor."

"Who were they?"

"Jessica Young was an intern at the State House. Regina—gosh, I forget her last name—was a former Miss Maryland."

"That would be Regina Quentin," interjected Strauss.

"Yes, you're right—Quentin was her name," said the president. "And Amy Gold. She was a fundraiser."

"That's all?" asked Thompson.

"Are we counting everyone, including the girls who only gave me oral sex?" asked the president.

"No, we'll let them pass for now," said Thompson wearily.

"How about condoms?" asked Riker.

For the first time, the president looked embarrassed. "Sorry, if I try to use one of those things I can't, you know...." He shook his head. "I know doctors say to use one for protection. But I was the guy who needed to perform. Besides, I didn't think there'd be any risk with these ladies. I mean, just looking at them, would you be suspicious?"

"This is all absolutely confidential, correct?" interjected Strauss.

"Don, you don't have to ask such a question," said Thompson. "For God's sake, you know everything we hear is confidential, both for national security reasons and patient confidentiality."

"And you too, Dr. Riker?" asked Strauss.

"Yes, me too," replied Riker.

Thompson let out an exasperated sigh.

"What's our next step?" said the president.

"While we wait for test results, we need to get a blood sample from Gwen Peterson," said Riker.

The president turned to Strauss. "Don, get her on the phone."

"Yes, sir," replied Strauss. Picking up a phone that was resting on a table, he dialed a number. After listening for a moment, he said, "Gwen? Don. The boss wants to talk to you. Hold on." He passed the phone to the president.

"Gwen, it's me. I'm fine, thank you. I have a doctor here with me. Her name is Karen Thompson. I'm going to put her on the line. I want you to do what she says. Okay? You'll do what she wants? Good. Here she is." He handed the phone to Thompson.

"Ms. Peterson, this is Dr. Thompson. I need to get a blood sample from you. Why? It's for national security purposes. That's all I can say. Yes, combatting terrorism. Good—I knew you'd be happy to cooperate. I want you to go to the office of Dr. Henry Donaldson on Dumbarton St. NW. It will only take five minutes and won't hurt a bit. I'll call him now and they'll be expecting you. Yes, go there now. Okay? Thank you. I appreciate your cooperation."

She hung up and dialed Dr. Donaldson's number. She asked the nurse to take Peterson's blood and send it to Riker's office at the Ten-Fifty. Then she put the receiver back on its cradle.

"All set," she said.

"Mr. President, it's time for your meeting with the senior staff," said Strauss.

The president stood up. "Karen and Martin, thank you, and please keep me informed."

Don Strauss opened the door and ushered them out. But instead of going back into the Oval Office, he stood outside with them in the corridor.

"May I have a word with you please?" he said. "My office is at the end of the hall."

The Oval Office occupied the southwest corner of the West Wing. Strauss led them along the corridor to the office of the chief of staff on the southeast corner. He closed the door behind him.

Riker found himself in a space that was nearly as spacious as the Oval Office, with tall windows on two sides. With its long sofa, coffee table, and easy chairs, it looked more like a living room than an office. Strauss's desk and a small conference table provided the requisite flavor of a place of business.

Strauss remained standing.

"I'm due back in the senior staff meeting," he said, "but I wanted to convey something to you that concerns me. This morning Max Mosely called me. I like Max, but he can be a loose cannon. He asked me if the rumors about the president were true. I said, what rumors? He said, the rumors that the president has AIDS. I was floored. I was under the impression that this knowledge was confined to a very tight circle. Hell, the vice president doesn't even know! The joint chiefs don't know. The secretary of Homeland Security doesn't know. How can the assistant director of communications know?"

"I have no idea," said Thompson.

"No clue," said Riker. "But in all fairness, as you say, Max is a gossipy kind of guy, and he may be putting two and two together. He may be observing the president's health and making an educated guess."

"Of course I denied it," said Strauss. "But then he started to say to me that if it were true, what a golden opportunity it could be to raise awareness about a terrible disease! He told me that President Ralston could advance the cause of AIDS acceptance and promote common sense measures to control the disease."

"What did you say to that?" said Riker.

"I told him he was completely out of his mind, that what he was talking about would never happen, that the president doesn't have AIDS, and that he, Mosely, needed to zip it."

"Sounds pretty clear," said Thompson.

Strauss took a slow deep breath. "You're doctors," he said evenly. "Tell me something: Will the pills the president is now taking make him healthy? Will he able to keep to his schedule, or will he keep getting sick?"

"With today's treatments," said Thompson, "most AIDS patients can live full, happy, and productive lives. There are men who have been living with AIDS for thirty years. But life expectancy is influenced by the strain of HIV. Some are more virulent and drug-resistant than others. The president is not even two weeks into his drug therapy. He seems to be responding well, but only time will tell."

"All right," said Strauss. "If you'll excuse me, I need to get to the meeting." He ushered Riker and Thompson to the door before hurrying to the Oval Office.

Chapter 21

*   *   *

"Next step?" said Thompson as she and Riker walked back to the Medical Unit.

"We wait for Peterson's blood sample," replied Riker. "Meanwhile, I need to talk to Max Mosely."

After calling to make sure he was in, Riker went across the street to Mosely's office in the EOB. He found Mosely behind his desk, which was a scene of riotous untidiness, with papers and files piled high, framing an open space in the middle for his computer and keyboard. Riker got the feeling that if Mosely sneezed, fifty pounds of paper would come flying off his desk and scatter across the non-government-approved Persian carpet.

"Martin, what a pleasure to see you," said Mosely. "Come in, sit down. I'm glad I happened to be here. How can I help you?"

Riker told him what Strauss had said. As he listened, Mosely nodded. When Riker was finished, Mosely leaned forward so that his round stomach was pressed against the edge of the desk.

"Between you and me," he said, "Don Strauss has a poker up his ass. He's the most uptight, rigid human being I've ever known. He has no imagination. No vision. His only mission is to keep people away from the president—that is, unless the person is young, female, and has the look of availability in her eye."

"Are you saying that Strauss facilitates the president's dalliances?"

"My friend, don't be naïve," said Mosely. "Every minute of every day of the president's life is meticulously scheduled. Lots of people want to speak with him, meet him, shake his hand, twist his arm, lobby him, and get photographed with him. It's the job of the chief of staff to control this flow of contacts.

"Without the active participation of the chief of staff, two things would be impossible. First, it would be impossible for the president to be guaranteed the privacy he needs to have sex, whether that's in the Oval Office, the White House bowling alley, Air Force One, or Camp David— it doesn't matter. The president needs a guy to guard the door while he and his galpal get it on. Second, the girlfriend needs to get through the filter. Not just anybody can walk up to the president, even people in the White House. There has to be a plausible reason why the woman is near the president. The chief of staff is the gatekeeper, the bouncer at the exclusive nightclub who sees a pretty girl and raises the red velvet rope for her."

"All right," said Riker. "Don Strauss is a combination guard dog and pimp. I get that."

"And perhaps he gets the leftovers," said Mosely with a devious glint in his eye.

"You mean like the lead singer in a rock band passes his extra groupies to the bass player?"

"It seems that way. In unguarded moments, I've heard both Don and Brian laugh about 'getting a pretty good perk last night,' or words to that effect. There's definitely something going on there."

"Do you mean with the president's girlfriends?" asked Riker.

"Possibly, but more likely with girls whom the president doesn't want, or just doesn't have time for. I mean, the man has a country to run!"

"Okay, that's all very interesting," said Riker. "What I want to talk to you about is your suggestion to Strauss that the president has AIDS."

"He does, doesn't he?" replied Mosely with his bushy eyebrows raised.

"What makes you so sure?"

"I have my own eyes, and I have confirmation."

"Confirmation?"

"My own version of 'Deep Throat.'"

"You're referring to the person who fed inside information about the Watergate scandal to Woodward and Bernstein."

"Yes," replied Mosely.

"Do you care to reveal who this person might be?"

"Not really."

"Well, whoever's told you anything, whether it's true or false, is guilty for blabbing about national security and patient confidentiality."

"Yeah, I understand that," said Mosely. He stood up from his desk and went to the window, where he fussed with the blinds. Riker figured he was killing time while he pondered what to say. He let Mosely have his moment.

"I hope you understand," said Mosely as he turned away from the window and sat down behind his desk, "what it would mean to millions of AIDS sufferers if the president of the United States were to come out and say, 'I am one of you.' It would be transformative! It would be like a bright beacon of hope shining out across the stormy sea. Such a revelation would demonstrate that there's no shame in having AIDS, and that if you get treatment, you can live a full and productive life."

"That's a nice theory," said Riker, "but I want you to think about the reality. Yes, the virus itself is neutral. But if it turns out the president acquired it from intravenous drug abuse or visiting prostitutes, there's not likely going to be a lot of public sympathy for him.

"Nobody will object to his getting treatment. But he won't get many votes. Maybe it should be different. But I'm just trying to get you to face reality for America.

"On the other hand, the public in this country has gotten a lot more accepting to HIV acquired through sex other than commercial sex. More open-minded. Gay rights are now part of our landscape.

"But internationally, the picture is very different. In Russia, the government makes HIV carriers hide by promoting laws that punish homosexuality. How do you suppose a US president with AIDS would be viewed in the Kremlin?"

"Not very well, I suppose," acknowledged Mosely.

"In many countries," continued Riker, "public policies openly discriminate against HIV-positive people. AIDS is seen almost entirely as a moral issue, and leaders assert that only people whom they consider to be of low virtue—drug users and gays—get the disease.

"So if, and I emphasize *if*, the president had the disease, deciding whether to publicly reveal it couldn't be made hastily, and would involve some very difficult calculations."

Mosely impatiently tapped his desk with a pen. "I think we should end the discussion," he said at length. "I think you're a good guy, and clearly we have some differences. So let's not let this spoil our day."

"I agree," said Riker. "But please promise me you won't say anything."

"I'll think about it," said Mosely.

"Please do." Riker got up and went to the door. Then he turned to Mosely. "Let's have dinner sometime. No politics, just a few laughs."

"Sounds good," said Mosely.

While he was in the EOB, on a whim Riker took out his phone and called Lindsay Baker. She picked up.

"Hey, how about some lunch?" asked Riker.

"Sure—you're in the building now? By the time you get here I'll be ready."

Riker made his way through the labyrinthine halls of the EOB to room 325B.

"Hi, Sharina," he said as he closed the door behind him. "Lindsay is expecting me."

Before Sharina replied, Lindsay came around the corner. "All set," she said cheerily.

"Where to?" he asked as they walked to the elevator.

"I'm sick of the same old boring places," she said as the doors slid shut. "I've got an idea. Let's take a walk to the Hay-Adams Hotel. They've got a cute bar there called Off the Record. It's supposed to have a good lunch menu. Max was telling me about it the other day."

"Is there any watering hole in Washington that Max doesn't know about?" laughed Riker.

They walked to the hotel with its immense portico supported by majestic columns. Inside the bar they found a table for two by the long wall. Lindsay slid onto the quilted red banquette, while Riker sat opposite her in a matching red-upholstered wingback chair. With its low plasterwork ceiling, arched roof supports between the big square columns, and red walls punctuated by wall sconces with little antique lampshades, the place reminded Riker of an expensive Victorian bordello.

"They could use some of your orchids in here," said Riker as he picked up a menu. "They'd fit right into the décor."

"Do you know why restaurants are often decorated in red?" asked Lindsay. "It's because red excites you. When you first enter, the red environment makes you feel hungry. It's a good feeling. But after you've eaten, all that red becomes irritating. You want to relax, not get excited. So you get up and leave."

"Ah," said Riker. "It stimulates you to eat more, and then it encourages you to turn over the table more quickly."

"It's a particularly effective tactic during the busy lunch hour," smiled Lindsay. She glanced at her watch. "It's going to succeed today—I have to be back at the office in forty minutes."

"No two Martinis?"

"Not even one," she laughed. "We'll save that kind of thing for the evening."

Their conversation was interrupted by the server. When she had departed, Lindsay asked Riker how his project was coming.

"It's going well," he fudged. Then he gave a disarming laugh. "Do you know what Max Mosely told me a few minutes ago? He's convinced the boss has AIDS. This is the problem with Washington. It's such a small town, and people are hypervigilant when it comes to the slightest tremor coming from the White House. I can understand it—we're in the center of power of the richest nation on earth, so what happens in the White House can have a huge impact on people's' lives."

"Well, does he?" asked Lindsay.

"Does he what?"

"Have AIDS. To be honest, I've heard the rumors too."

Riker put down his wine glass. "What have you heard?"

Lindsay picked up a breadstick and pointed it at Riker. "C'mon, Martin, let's not forget that I'm the director of scheduling." She took a bite out of the breadstick. "I know where the boss goes and who goes with him. I know who the players are. When I repeatedly see the names of the same young ladies on the travel rosters that Don or Brian send to me, I can put two and two together. I know the personal assistants who travel with him. I know who Candy Cane is, and why she needs to be at Camp David when the boss is there. The only consulting she's doing is between the sheets."

"And?" said Riker.

"And, despite having access to the world's finest healthcare, the boss has a knack for getting the flu. Did you know that he's logged more visits to Walter Reed than any president since Reagan, and he's twenty years younger than the Gipper was when he was in his first term?" With a shrug she reached for the butter. "Back in the good old days of JFK, we didn't have AIDS. If you got a 'social disease,' a shot or two of penicillin would make you as good as new. Not anymore. Am I right?"

Riker felt a drop of sweat trickle down the back of his neck. "You're a pretty sharp girl," he said.

"Not really," she replied. Then she smiled. "Of course I'm a sharp girl. What I meant was this: You don't need to be a rocket scientist to figure out what's probably going on with the boss. Anyone who can put two and two together can see it. I'm just a little bit closer to the action than most. I have a front-row seat."

"I can't keep you or anyone else from speculating," said Riker. "All I can say to you is that I can't comment on the president's health. You know, national security, medical confidentiality; all that stuff."

"Oh—okay," said Lindsay. "I got carried away. Sorry. I shouldn't have asked."

They talked about other things, including Lindsay's plans for the holidays, which would include a visit to her brother and mother in Woodbridge, followed by a jaunt to the south for some sun.

"If you're in Naples, look me up," said Riker.

"I'd love to," she replied. "Do you think you'll be finished with your project by then?"

"Today's the eighth of December," he replied. "We have two weeks until Christmas. I sure hope I'm done by then. I'm supposed to be getting together with my sister and my daughter."

"And your boys?" asked Lindsay.

"They may go to their in-laws," he replied. "They alternate years—one year with me, and then one with the families of their wives. They were both in Naples last year."

The time passed quickly until Lindsay glanced at her watch. "Omigod," she said. "I'm supposed to be in my office for a conference call in exactly four minutes. I've got to run."

"You go," said Riker. "I'll get the bill."

"Thanks—you're a sweetheart," she said as he helped her with her coat. Picking up her purse, she gave him a kiss on the cheek before hurrying out the door.

Riker watched her leave before sitting down. While he waited for the check he pondered what Lindsay and Mosely had said, and how they both suspected the president had AIDS. Unless the president's health began to improve soon, the sparks of idle gossip would grow into a firestorm of speculation and tabloid headlines.

Chapter 22

*   *   *

By the end of the afternoon, as twilight was beginning to descend on the city, Riker was in his office at the Ten-Fifty. The question of who had talked to Mosely gnawed at him. As he reviewed the list of people who might have known the president had AIDS, an unfamiliar name presented itself: John Daughtry. He was one of the two nurses in the Medical Unit who were privy to the president's condition, and he had occasionally given the president his B-12 shot when Jennet Swift had been absent.

A quick social media search for Daughtry revealed that while he never explicitly said he was gay, he belonged to the Metropole Health Club, which, if you were a gay guy working or living in the area of the Capitol, was the preferred gym to join.

Max Mosely also belonged to the Metropole.

Riker reached for the phone to call Karen Thompson. As Daughtry's boss, she should be in the loop.

He paused. Perhaps it was better to approach the issue more informally.

He emailed Dorothy and asked her about Daughtry's schedule. A moment later she replied that he had gotten off work a few minutes earlier. You might catch him at the gym, she added.

Did she have his personal phone number? asked Riker.

Yes, Dorothy replied. She included it in her message.

Riker threw on his coat and walked a few blocks east to Vermont Ave. NW. The Metropole Health Club occupied a former book publishing building erected at the end of the nineteenth century with a cast-iron frame under stone cladding, tall windows, and ornate cornices. Passing through the grand bronze revolving door, Riker found himself in a sleekly remodeled industrial space with exposed beams and massive overhead heating ducts. Beyond the reception desk were tall-ceiling rooms punctuated by slender cast-iron columns and filled with the modern tools of physical fitness: elliptical trainers, treadmills, stair climbers, stationary bikes, rowers, weight lifting sets, racks of free weights, benches. All around him, young men—mostly fit-looking, but with a smattering of softies and a few burly bears—worked out or socialized. Some were focused intently on their fitness machine of choice, while others were clearly determined to do as little exercising as possible.

Riker instantly realized that there was a slim chance of finding Daughtry in the crowd. He pulled out his phone and punched the number Dorothy had given him. After three rings a man answered. After introducing himself, Riker asked if Daughtry were in the club. He was—up on the second floor, at one of the juice bars. Riker said he'd be right up.

At the top of the old cast-iron staircase Riker looked around and spotted the juice bar. Daughtry was sitting at its end with two other men. Riker approached them, said hello, and asked if John would mind having a few words.

"Sure, no problem," replied Daughtry. "Let's go to the squash courts. It's quiet in there now."

They walked through a maze of rowing machines and stationary bikes to a door that led onto a glassed-in balcony overlooking the squash courts. Daughtry was right; the area was deserted. Down on the court only two guys were playing, and no one was watching from the balcony.

"What's up?" asked Daughtry. He was a handsome kid, with dark curly hair and big brown eyes. He took a sip of his mango and wheatgrass smoothie.

"I'm here because you're one of the nurses at the Medical Unit," replied Riker.

Daughtry nodded.

"And as I understand it," said Riker, "you have direct knowledge of the boss's state of health."

"The boss?" replied Daughtry.

"Big Bull."

"Oh, yes. Sorry. Yes, I suppose I do." He gave Riker a suspicious look. "Why do you ask?"

"You're quite right to be cautious. We've seen each other at the office. I'm working with Dr. Thompson on a project." Riker showed Daughtry his White House pass.

"Of course," Daughtry nodded. "Sorry I didn't recognize you right away."

"I see that we're in an interesting situation," said Riker. "Because we're meeting for the first time and we're away from the office, I'm not sure what I can say to you, and you're not sure what you can say to me. There are issues of patient confidentiality and national security at play."

"Yes, that's true."

"Even though we're both members of the boss's healthcare team," said Riker, "I'm going to skirt around the question. I'm going to ask you if you believe the boss has a serious disease. Not if you *know* for a fact, but if you *believe*."

"Um, yes, I do," said Daughtry.

"And do you believe that the disease is AIDS?"

"Yes."

"Do you have any idea about where he might have gotten this disease?"

"Everyone knows he has lots of girlfriends," said Daughtry. "It's probably the worst-kept secret in Washington. I'm amazed that the Republicans in Congress haven't picked up on it. If they knew, they'd have a field day."

"Yes—more investigations and more hearings," replied Riker. "But tell me—what's your attitude about it, assuming it to be true? Should the boss go public? Should he make like Magic Johnson and lay it out there for everyone? Or should he keep it quiet?"

"He should keep it quiet."

"Why?"

"Because unless it impacts his ability to do his job, it's nobody's business," said Daughtry. "Think about it. If a United States senator had AIDS and it was under control, should he or she be required to make it public? How about a representative in Congress? Or a state rep, or a small-town mayor? At what point does a person stop being a public figure and can live a private life? Should *anybody* be forced to reveal they have a disease, including AIDS?"

"For most people," said Riker, "the answer to your last question is 'no.' They should not, and cannot, be compelled. But if you have AIDS you're technically not entitled to complete and absolute privacy in all circumstances. There are certain people you may be required to tell. Across the country you'll find a patchwork of state laws addressing disclosure. Many states require persons who are aware that they have HIV to disclose their status to sexual partners, and some require disclosure to needle-sharing partners."

"That raises some sticky questions," said Daughtry. "Just suppose, hypothetically, that the boss had AIDS. Would he be legally obligated to inform all of his sexual partners—his wife and girlfriends? Wow! Imagine the possibilities if one of the girlfriends decided to call the tabloids and sell her story."

"Here's the catch," said Riker. "State laws that criminalize sexual activity by someone who knows they are HIV positive aren't retroactive. There's no law that says when a person learns they are HIV positive they must inform *past* sexual partners. Let's say, God forbid, a guy gives you HIV. Tests confirm it. You may have been infected a month ago or a year ago. While the testing laboratory is required to maintain a record of your test result, you are not required to inform your past partners. In most states, you're only required to inform a *future partner*—the person with whom you will have sex after you've gained the knowledge of your condition. And in Washington, DC, you don't even have to do this."

"Here in the nation's capital we have no laws penalizing someone with HIV who willfully spreads the disease?" asked Daughtry.

"Nope," replied Riker. "If you have HIV, you're not required to tell the person with whom you're going to have sex."

"That's scary," said Daughtry.

"In the case of the boss, because he lives in Washington, he'd have no obligation to inform. But let's say you argued that he's still a legal resident of Maryland. In that case, he would be obligated to tell a person with whom he intends to have sex in the future, whether it's his wife or a girlfriend. But I doubt a president would be impeached just for 'failure to notify.'"

"So, no more girlfriends for the boss," said Daughtry. "Not unless he wanted to tell the lucky lady that she was playing Russian roulette when he banged her."

"That's a crude way of putting it," said Riker. "Let me ask you something else. Do you have any reason to believe that the boss has had a man-to-man relationship?"

Daughtry paused. He put his smoothie on the narrow ledge in front of their chairs. For a moment he watched the two guys playing squash on the court below. Then he turned to Riker.

"From my direct experience, no. But there's been talk."

"Talk?" said Riker. "Do you mean the crazy late-night radio personalities who assert the president is secretly a communist, or talk among responsible people around town?"

"There's a guy I know," said Daughtry. "He's an usher at the White House. He's told people that he's made it with the boss."

"You've got to be kidding me," said Riker. "Who is this Romeo?"

"His name is Jerome Sydney. He often comes to this gym after work. In fact, I can see if he's here now." Daughtry tapped his phone. "Hey Jerome," he said. "What's up? I'm at the gym. Are you here now? Cool. Listen, I have a guy who wants to talk to you. No, it's not like that—he's straight. It's something about business. We're sitting up in the balcony overlooking the squash courts. Good. See you soon."

A few minutes later a man came up the stairs. He was in his mid-twenties. The physical feature that Riker first noticed were his large ears that stuck out from his round head like two wings. With his fluffy brown hair, he looked like a woodland rodent.

Riker turned to Daughtry.

"John, would you please excuse us for a moment?" he said. "Stick around. I'll call you when we're done."

Daughtry got up and went down the stairs.

"Mr. Sydney, please have a seat," said Riker with a smile.

"Sure," said Sydney. "Call me Jerome. You work at the White House too?"

"Yes. My name's Martin Riker. I'm working on a classified project for the DIA. You know what the DIA is, right?"

"Yeah," nodded Sydney. "The Defense Intelligence Agency."

"Right," said Riker. "Dudes you don't want to mess with."

"I know." Sydney shifted in his chair. His eyes darted to the guys playing squash and then back to Riker. "So what's up?"

Riker leaned forward. "I've heard through the grapevine that you've seen some action with the president of the United States."

Sydney tilted his head back and looked at Riker through lowered eyelids. "I may have said that."

Riker put his face inches from Sydney's. "I want places and dates."

"Uh, I can't remember exactly. It was upstairs in the family quarters."

"Upstairs in the family quarters?" hissed Riker. "Listen to me, Jerome. This is no game. There are implications for national security. Once again—I want places and dates. Upstairs? Where? In the president's bedroom that he shares with the First Lady? When? In the evening, when he joined his wife and daughter at dinner? Or at bedtime?"

"Okay, okay," said Sydney with his hands raised. "I'm sorry. I told a few stories around the gym to impress other guys. I never made it with the president. Never. It was all a fantasy. But because I'm an usher at the White House, a lot of guys would ask me, you know, what's he really like? They're like groupies. Presidential groupies. It's the power and the prestige that turns them on. So I made up a few stories to impress some guys. It made me a rock star, at least in their eyes. I mean, come on, Martin, look at me. I'm not exactly Rock Hudson! I need all the help I can get."

Riker sat back in his chair, relieved to have gotten the truth. "Jerome, what you've done could have caused very serious problems," he said. "You should be fired."

Sydney hung his head. Riker thought he might start crying.

"I'm sorry," he mumbled.

"Pull yourself together," said Riker firmly. "Sit up straight. You're a White House usher, for God's sake. In your own small way, you represent the most powerful institution on earth. Have some pride!"

Sydney managed to straighten his spine. He took a deep breath and gave Riker a timid smile.

"This nonsense stops now," said Riker. "If I have to come back here and talk to you again, your ass is toast. Got it? And by the way—when was the last time you were screened for HIV?"

"Two months ago," said Sydney.

"Good for you," said Riker. "Where?"

"At the clinic in the Band Building, on Massachusetts Ave. NW. Not far from the Mayflower Hotel."

"What's that?"

"It's a confidential clinic operated by the federal government, for federal employees only. There are so many of us in Washington, you know. And frankly, most of them consider themselves middle class, so they wouldn't be caught dead going to the District's public health clinic, where the patients are mostly street people or poor ones. And God, in there you feel like you're on public view.

"You can go to the Band office and not be noticed in the crowd of office workers coming and going. It's very low profile. There isn't even a sign on the door, just a room number. You have to know about it. And it's located in a big busy building, so you don't draw attention to yourself. You could be there for any reason.

"You can also use them for partner notification."

"Like the website Notify.org?" asked Riker.

"Yes, but the Band Building clinic promises confidentiality. So does Notify.org, but with a website, who knows? Everything can be hacked."

Riker chose not to mention what FBI agent Flood had told him about the agency monitoring the Notify.org site.

"I assume your HIV test was negative?" asked Riker.

"Yes," said Sydney. "I get tested every six months. Always clean. I'm a big believer in safe sex."

"Good for you," said Riker. "Keep it that way. And no more tall tales, or you'll find yourself living under a bridge in New Jersey. Got it?"

"Yes," nodded Sydney. He got up. "Thanks, Martin, for not busting me." He went downstairs.

Believe me, thought Riker, *I've got bigger fish to fry.* He pulled out his phone and called Daughtry.

"How did that go?" asked Daughtry when he had taken his seat again.

"Good," said Riker. "False alarm. Jerome was just blowing hot air to impress potential partners."

"Figures," shrugged Daughtry.

"Have you ever heard of a clinic in the Band Building?" asked Riker.

"Yes," replied Daughtry. "It's on Massachusetts Avenue. The fed civil service runs it. It's supposed to be confidential."

"Have you ever gone there?"

"Sure. A lot of government workers have."

"You've been tested for HIV?"

"Yes, and I'm clean."

"Okay. One more question. How much do you know about Gwen Peterson?"

"The one they call Candy Cane? No more than what everybody else in the White House knows—that's she's a consultant who never seems to produce any work. She's a bimbo. Just like the others."

"But how can this bevy of beauties be managed?" asked Riker. "I understand that there's a certain level of what you might call 'buzz' about the boss's activities, but no one ever sees anything."

"Don Strauss is the traffic cop," said Daughtry. "He does a good job of shuttling the girls in and out under some pretext, and then raising the drawbridge so that nosey people don't get in."

A thought occurred to Riker. He dismissed it—John Daughtry was not the person to ask. He'd save it for someone higher in the food chain.

"Thanks for your time, John," said Riker as he stood up. "Have a pleasant evening."

Chapter 23

∗   ∗   ∗

Having received a text that Thompson had some urgent news for him, Riker walked to the office of the Medical Unit. Night had fallen; in mid-December, the sun set in Washington well before five o'clock. The air was cold and damp, with more snow predicted.

He walked into Thompson's office to find her behind her desk. Even before she spoke, Riker saw that her mood was ebullient. Her face radiated cheer as she took another cherry candy from the bowl, unwrapped it, and expertly lofted the ball of crumpled cellophane into the wastebasket.

"We have our DNA analysis results from the CDC," said Thompson as if she were announcing the winner of the Kentucky Derby.

"Okay, let's hear it," said Riker.

"First, the Kenya accident," said Thompson. "No match. It's not where he was infected. Some of the blood on the president's coat and shirt was HIV positive. But its DNA did not match the president's HIV. Therefore, someone with HIV got his or her blood on the president, but it wasn't the blood that infected him."

"Rachel Doucette was at the scene," said Riker. "Has her HIV been typed yet?"

"Not yet," replied Thompson. "But it's irrelevant, and I'll tell you why. The culprit is the baggie of blood that struck the president in Nagoya.

DNA analysis indicates that the HIV in the blood from Nagoya matches the strain of HIV that has infected him. We have our smoking gun."

"That's amazing," said Riker. "I don't know what to say."

It was true—he really didn't know what to say. It seemed so easy: Get blood samples, analyze blood samples, find HIV in both, match the DNA of the two strains of HIV, and bingo! You have a winner.

"Case closed," said Thompson. "We can chalk this up to a freak accident. The protestor loaded his baggie with human blood, which he may or may not have known was infected with HIV. I'm sure the Japanese authorities will be questioning him on that point. He threw the baggie at the president. It splattered on his face, and enough of the infected blood must have entered his mouth and nasal passages to find its way into his bloodstream."

"It's an extremely unlikely way to get HIV," said Riker, "but I suppose that if the DNA matches, then it matches. It's inconceivable that the protestor, who was ten thousand miles from Washington, DC, could have possibly procured infected blood from one of the president's girlfriends. He must have gotten it from an HIV-positive volunteer or a blood testing lab in Japan."

"Right," said Thompson.

There was a moment of silence.

Then Thompson said, "I'll write up the report. It's too bad this happened on Ethan Westlake's watch. Of course there was nothing that *he* could have done to prevent the incident—that was the job of the Secret Service—but perhaps a more aggressive medical investigation, including testing the blood in the baggie for HIV, would have been warranted. But that's all water under the bridge." She gave him a broad smile. "Martin, it has been a pleasure to get to know you. You've been an invaluable part of this investigation. If you hadn't gone to Japan to retrieve the baggie, we may never have solved the case. I'm sure that before you return to Naples, the president will want to thank you personally."

"Return to Naples?" asked Riker.

"Well of course!" smiled Thompson. "I'm sure you'll want to hurry home for the holidays. I must admit I envy you. It's been a brutal winter here in Washington—it seems like the snow has never stopped. It's grim and depressing. I'm sure Naples is sunny and warm, and you can walk around without worrying about falling on your ass on the ice. You're a sailor, aren't you?"

"Yes, I have a little boat."

"No one is doing any sailing on the Potomac in this weather," she said. "I hope you can go home, get some sun, go for a nice sail, and be with your family over the holidays." She glanced at her computer. "Ah—I see that Don has responded to my email. The president is going to stop by this office as he makes his way to the family quarters. He'll be here in five minutes. Excellent! He can thank you personally and you can be on your way."

Riker was stunned. Was it possible? Could he be flying home tomorrow?

The next few minutes passed by in a blur.

The door opened and President Ralston strode into the office. He was smiling as he extended his hand to Riker. "Dr. Riker, I can't thank you enough," he said. "It's a huge load off my mind to know how I got this terrible disease. From a protestor! Who could have imagined? Even though I can't thank you publicly, rest assured that I'll never forget your tremendous service to me and to our nation. Thank you." After pumping Riker's hand, he turned to Thompson. "Nice job, Karen. I knew I could count on you. I'll stick to my meds and we'll lick this thing!"

"Yes sir, Mr. President," said Thompson. "You're going to live a long and productive life."

The president turned, and in a moment he was gone.

"Martin, thanks again," said Thompson. "I hope our paths will cross again, only in less stressful circumstances."

"I hope so too," said Riker.

For Riker, there was nothing more to do except take his last walk out of the White House. He went out into the Center Hall, and, after taking a lingering look at the corridor of executive power, entered the Diplomatic Reception Room, with its warm glowing chandeliers. From there he stepped out the door onto the South Portico.

The air had turned biting cold, and Riker could see his breath. Well, he thought, it would be nice to get back to Florida and feel the sun on his face, hear the gently lapping waves against the hull of his boat, and see the warm breeze filling its sail.

After passing through the familiar southwest appointment gate, with his collar turned up against the frigid wind, Riker strolled along the snow-dusted streets to The Jefferson Hotel. Once in his room, he sat on the edge of the bed, took out his phone, and pulled up airline flights to Ft. Myers. He could depart the next day at eight in the morning and be home by lunchtime.

He paused.

Before leaving Washington, why not first tie up any loose ends? Not that Riker doubted the test results—the CDC's labs were as good as anyplace else in the world—but Riker's scientific mind liked first-hand confirmation.

He tapped the number for Jim Gilmore.

"Hey, Jim," he said when Gilmore answered. "Thompson gave me the good news. You made a match between the Nagoya sample and the boss."

"We did," replied Gilmore. "But is that all she said?"

"Yes—why?"

"It's not quite as simple as that. It's true that the DNA of the HIV found in the baggie matched that of the boss. However, by blood typing we think the baggie contained blood from two different people. The problem is that one of those people happens to be the boss."

"So you're saying that the HIV that matched the boss's may have come from the same source—the boss himself?"

"Yes, it's possible. It's going to be extremely difficult to determine a precise answer. If there were two blood samples in the baggie, they became intermixed. There are a few areas of dried blood from various nooks and crannies in the baggie, which we assume must date from the day of the attack. We're trying to get samples that are large enough to test, but there are no guarantees."

"Thanks, Jim. Listen, I've been officially released from this project, and Thompson assumes I'm flying home tomorrow. I think I'll stick around for a few days to see what I can uncover."

"Good luck, and be careful," said Gilmore. "Your continued presence in Washington may no longer be welcome."

After he ended the call, Riker checked the time. In Tokyo, it was seven thirty in the morning. He recalled Masako mentioning that he was usually in his office at dawn. He tapped his number.

"Dr. Martin Riker here," he said when Masako picked up. "I'm glad I caught you. Yes, I've been well, thank you. May I ask you a question?"

"Yes, of course," replied Masako.

"The guy who threw the bag of blood at the president last year—his name was Tashi Osaki. Was he ever interviewed about how he prepared for his attack? Specifically, where he got the blood, and how he put it into the baggie?"

"No," replied Masako. "He was judged to be mentally incompetent and sent to Tokyo Metropolitan Matsuzawa Hospital."

"Would it be possible for me to ask him a few questions?" asked Riker. "All I would need would be for someone to bring him to a place where there was a laptop or even a phone with a videoconferencing app. It will take about five minutes. I just want to ask him a few questions."

"I'll contact the hospital," said Masako. "If the doctors say he's competent to answer questions, I'm sure it can be arranged. I'll get back to you."

Not a minute after the call had ended, Riker's phone rang. The caller ID showed it was Max Mosely. With a feeling of apprehension, Riker answered.

"I heard the news," said Mosely.

"What news?" replied Riker.

"C'mon, Martin, you know what I'm talking about! The unpleasant surprise the boss got in Nagoya. A terrible thing to have happened, but in a way it's a godsend."

"Max, no matter what your viewpoint, it is *not* a godsend. And how the hell did you find out?"

"Hey, I'm the assistant communications director, and I communicate! So Martin, what's he going to do?"

"What do you mean, 'what's he going to do?'"

"He can't just go along and pretend nothing has happened! Martin, this is a huge milestone in our nation's history. He's the first president to have AIDS—and he got it through no fault of his own."

"Max, I hope to hell your office door is closed, and no one can hear you," said Riker. "Listen to me. I'm not commenting on the health of my patient. If someone who has a particular disease wants to make a public announcement, that's their decision alone. Not mine and not yours. Got it? My advice is to forget what you think you've heard. It never happened. The president is healthy and fit for office. End of story."

"Martin, you're not seeing the big picture," replied Mosely. His tone was serious. "There are broad implications. What the boss does could impact millions of lives. I'm sure you know that in the United States alone over a million people are living with HIV, and the CDC estimates that one in eight don't know they're infected. What's worse is that these people who are infected with HIV but are undiagnosed account for almost one-third of transmissions and have the highest transmission rate."

"I've seen all the statistics," replied Riker.

"Why don't these victims know they have HIV?" asked Mosely. "Maybe some of them are truly naïve. Maybe a few just don't give a damn. But I'll bet it's because most of them are scared. They're afraid to go and get tested, for fear of being discovered. I know people here in Washington who are scared to get tested."

"Why don't you tell them to go to the clinic at the Band Building?"

Mosely burst out laughing. "Martin, you sure are new to Washington! Here's what I want you to do. Go to the Band Building and stand in front of room 606, which is the door to the clinic. Then look to your right, down the hall, and smile and wave to the camera."

"Camera?"

"Yep. I've heard the FBI has had a camera there since the clinic opened. The story goes that when they got wind of the plan to open a confidential VD clinic there, they sent some guys in painters' coveralls to join the crew of the contractor refurbishing the office for the changeover. To get a record of whoever came and went, they installed some video cameras in the hallway and inside the clinic itself. And of course, they may be backing up the effort by hacking the computers where the patient records are kept. They must think we're all a bunch of idiots. That's why a lot of people won't go there. All the folks I know of go to docs or clinics out in the suburbs, in Virginia or Maryland."

"It probably was triggered by a Cold War mentality," said Riker. "I doubt they're interested in the average John or Jane. Probably the FBI worries that anyone with access to desirable government information, and who also has a lifestyle they wouldn't want publicized, would be at risk for being blackmailed by the Soviets or similar. So, they probably check the clinic names against their list of security clearances.

"And let's not forget J. Edgar himself."

"Ah, good ol' J. Edgar Hoover!" exclaimed Mosely. "Now there's a fascinating case. During his lifetime, he waged a public vendetta against homosexuals, and kept secret files on the sex lives of congressmen and presidents. But by most accounts, our first FBI director was actually deep in the closet himself. Lived as a bachelor with his mother until he was forty. Had a long relationship --forty years--with Clyde Tolson, his associate director. Real togetherness—riding to work, daily lunch at the Mayflower, and travel for business and vacation. Sometimes they even wore matching suits. When he died in 1972, he left Tolson most of his estate. You tell me which team Hoover was playing on!

"By the way, did you know that the clinic room number, 606, is the same as the first arsenic compound found effective for treating syphilis, back around 1900? Is that a coincidence, or maybe not?"

"Max, that's fascinating, but let's get back to business," said Riker. "The bottom line is that if you spread speculation about the health of the president, you're going to get fired. Please, think about the direction you're headed. Consider national security, or at least his medical privacy."

"But he's not like you or me," replied Mosely. "He's the highest public official in the land. His life needs to be transparent. If he has a serious disease, even one that is treatable, the public has a right to know."

"Max, I'll say it again—don't do it. Okay? I have to go now, so I'm going to hang up. Let's have dinner sometime, but only under the condition that we don't talk about this subject."

"All right," replied Mosely.

As Riker ended the call, he saw an email pop up on the screen of his computer. It was from a Dr. Han Yamata in Tokyo, asking Riker to respond to an invitation for a Skype call. He opened Skype and accepted the call.

On the screen he saw a middle-aged man wearing a white coat and rimless spectacles. He was sitting in what looked like a doctor's office, with books on a shelf in the background.

"Hello, Dr. Riker," said the man. "I'm Dr. Han Yamata. I have Tashi Osaki here with me. He's available to talk to you for a few minutes. I'll translate if needed."

"Great," replied Riker. "Thanks very much. Please put him on."

Dr. Yamata got up from the chair he was sitting in and for a moment the room appeared empty. Then a young man took the doctor's place on the seat. Wearing a plain green collarless hospital shirt, he looked about twenty-five, with a thin angular face and a shock of black hair closely cropped on the sides. He stared intently at the screen.

"Tashi," said Riker, "my name is Martin Riker. I'm an American doctor. I'd like to ask you a few questions."

Osaki listened, nodded, and quickly said, "Okay." He nervously ran his hand through his hair before rubbing the back of his head. His eyes stayed fixed on the screen in front of him.

"Tashi, do you remember the bag that you threw at the president of the United States last year? It was in Nagoya."

"Yes, I remember."

"What was in the bag?"

"It was blood," said Osaki. "I wanted to avenge the honor of my venerated ancestors who were savagely cut down by the American war machine, which is today commanded by the notorious criminal President Ralston." Glowering, he sat back with his arms folded across his chest.

"I understand how you felt," said Riker. "What I want to know is, did you fill the bag yourself?"

Osaki frowned, leaned forward, and ran his hand through his hair again. "Yes, of course I did. No one did it but me."

"Where did you get the blood?"

"It's mine."

"Yours? But how did you collect it?"

"I know how to do it," replied Osaki as if the question were the stupidest one he had ever heard. "You just draw it and collect it in a jar. I kept the jar in the refrigerator. It took me two times to get enough to fill the bag. I did this a week before I went to the hotel. I wanted to make sure I had time to become strong again. When the president walked out of the hotel, I shouted that I was taking revenge, and I threw the bag."

"I understand," said Riker. "So you're saying that all the blood in the bag was yours? You didn't mix it with anybody else's?"

"No," Osaki replied sharply. "Why would I want someone else's blood mixed with mine? No. It was all mine."

"Tashi, do you by any chance have HIV?"

Osaki looked confused. He spoke to someone off camera. Then he leaned to one side to make room for a woman's head and shoulders to be seen on the screen. She was dressed in a nurse's uniform.

"I'm Ona Suzuki," said the woman. "I'm on the staff here at the hospital. Tashi didn't understand the question. No, he does not have HIV."

"Thanks," said Riker.

At that moment Osaki got up and went out of view.

"Dr. Riker, do you want to ask him any more questions?" said Suzuki, who slid onto the seat so that she was now center screen.

"No, but I have one for you. Tashi said that he drew his own blood. Is he capable of doing that?"

"Yes," nodded Suzuki. "He studied phlebotomy at a community college in Nagoya. He knows how to do it. When he arrived here last year, he had two healing puncture wounds on his arm. These were consistent with having blood drawn. When the police searched his apartment they found phlebotomy equipment—needles and tourniquets—as well as a bloody jar in the refrigerator. The conclusion was that he had acted alone."

"Thanks very much," said Riker. "You've been very helpful."

After signing off, Riker stood up and went to his office window. Tiny flurries of snow drifted under the heavy grey sky. So! Tashi's blood in Japan would have been HIV-negative, yet the sample of it Karen Thompson had sent to CDC tested HIV-positive, and was even the same virus strain as the president's. Plus, the sample of blood in the bag contained some red cells of the same blood group as the president's.

It suddenly dawned on Riker what must have occurred. Thompson had tampered with the Japanese blood baggie before sending it to the CDC for testing. She'd added some of the president's blood to it!

It was a classic bureaucratic cover-my-ass move. By that maneuver, she had managed to both close the case and keep her own reputation spotless—it would look like the infection had occurred before she came on board. While the previous doctor couldn't be directly blamed for the president getting infected with HIV, Thompson had made it much more uncomfortable for Ethan Westlake, who, conveniently, was six thousand miles away on a ship in the Persian Gulf.

As far as Thompson was concerned, everyone except Westlake would came out a winner. The president was happy that he had gotten AIDS not from cheating on his wife but from a terrorist attack in Japan. Don Strauss was happy because the private life of the president could remain private. Likewise for Susan Ralston. Thompson was happy because the Medical Office under her direction was blameless. And, had they been privy to the facts of the investigation, the girlfriends would have been happy, too, that they had been kept out of the headlines.

But what should Riker do?

He had the testimony of Tashi Osaki. It was clear and unambiguous. But Riker knew how things worked in politics. If he said anything, and referenced Osaki's testimony, he knew that Thompson would simply reply that Osaki was confined to a mental hospital for a very good reason—he was crazy! Whatever he said had no credibility. He might very well have gotten blood from more than one source, and then lied about it for purposes of self-aggrandizement.

Riker went to his desk, reached down, and pulled open the bottom drawer. He took out the plastic bag containing the towel that special agent Jennifer Dine had given him. Holding it in his hand, he saw the deep brown stains. After putting the bag in a shipping box, he printed a label addressed to Jim Gilmore at the CDC.

Picking up his phone, he tapped Gilmore's number. "Hello, Jim? Martin here. I'm sending you another piece of evidence. It's the towel that the boss used to wipe his face in Nagoya. I got it from the Secret Service. I'm sending it to you for testing. Please keep this out of the official workflow. Because the results may contradict the official line, send them only to me. Thanks very much."

Riker glanced at his watch. If he hurried, he could walk the box to the FedEx office before it closed, and Gilmore could have the towel by tomorrow morning. He put on his coat, grabbed the box, and headed out the door.

Chapter 24

*   *   *

Having delivered his box with the Nagoya towel into the hands of FedEx, Riker walked back to The Jefferson. It had been a long day, and while he was tired, he felt strangely invigorated. The assignment that he had been happy to accept—to find out how the president of the United States had been infected with HIV—had taken a new and dangerous twist. The politics of power in Washington, which had remained out of sight during the initial investigation, was now showing itself, like a virus that lives quietly in the body only to suddenly erupt on the skin with toxic lesions. Having rigged the evidence, Thompson had declared the case closed, and had practically offered to drive Riker to the airport and put him on a plane for home. But underneath the self-satisfied congratulations lurked a sinister vibe. The unspoken message was, *Don't mess with us. We love our power and we'll fight to keep it.*

Of his situation, Riker was of two minds. They both demanded his attention.

The Naples sailor in him said, *Who cares? It's the Washington cesspool. Let them do what they want. Go home and see your kids for the holidays.*

The career epidemiologist inside him said, *The truth matters! You have the opportunity to make a difference. Don't be a coward!*

As he walked in the cold night air, he knew in his heart that between the two emotions there was no contest. He wasn't going anywhere until he had uncovered the truth.

He pulled out his phone and tapped the number for Angela Powell.

"Martin," she said. "I heard the good news from Karen Thompson. Congratulations! I suppose you're on your way back to Florida?"

"No, I'm not," replied Riker. "I have reason to believe that Thompson fabricated the evidence. The boss was not infected with HIV in Nagoya. I don't know exactly how he got it, but I'm certain it wasn't at the G7 conference. I know this for two reasons. First, Jim Gilmore told me that the baggie contained the blood of two people, not one. Second, the crazy terrorist, Tashi Osaki, told me a few minutes ago that he had used only his own blood to fill the bag originally. And his nurse told me he was HIV-negative.

"When I came back from Japan I turned the bag over to Thompson. She held onto it for a day before sending it to the CDC. I believe she added some of the boss's HIV-positive blood to the original stuff that was in the bag. That's why the samples that were supposedly straight from Tokyo were positive for HIV, and it matched the boss's."

"This is incredible!" exclaimed Powell. "But if not the Nagoya baggie, then what's the source of the boss's HIV?"

"Our possibilities are dwindling," replied Riker. "The dentist has been disqualified. Likewise the Kenya auto accident. One girlfriend, Rachel Doucette, has HIV, but her virus is not a genetic match for the boss's. Another girlfriend, Kimberly Schuster, recently underwent a rapid test and she's clean."

"Aren't those rapid tests inconclusive?" asked Powell. "Shouldn't she be retested?"

"Yes to both questions," said Riker. "We'll be studying her more. We can't forget that on very rare occasions a few people with proven HIV stay negative in the tests for antibodies.

"Another source possibility is Gwen Peterson, the media consultant who lives in Georgetown. While she was seeing the boss, she was also having an affair with a Russian spy named Sakharov. He's been recalled to Russia and has disappeared."

"Tough break for him."

"There's one more avenue I want to investigate," said Riker. "The federal civil service maintains a confidential STD clinic in the Band Building on Massachusetts Avenue. It's designed so their employees can go there and get tested in confidence. It's a nice idea, but apparently it's an open secret that the FBI has the place under surveillance. The Bureau's rationale is probably that a federal employee who has a security clearance and an STD like AIDS or HIV could be compromised or blackmailed by some adversary, like the Russians."

"Or the Chinese, or the North Koreans," added Powell.

"I need to ask my FBI contact if I can cross-reference our list of candidates with their list of people patronizing the clinic."

"Weren't you supposed to be big on medical confidentiality?" asked Powell. "I can practically see the transgression from here."

"When in Rome, do as the Romans do," replied Riker.

"How about Thompson?" asked Powell. "What are you going to do with her?"

"I'm going to let her enjoy her moment of triumph until I get back some more test results from Gilmore at the CDC."

"Okay," said Powell. "What can I do for you?"

"Get ready to pull me out of here when the shit hits the fan."

Riker had arrived at The Jefferson. He took the elevator to his room. As soon as he had closed the door he pulled out his phone and tapped a number.

"Flood here," said the voice on the other end.

Riker explained what he wanted.

There was a moment of silence.

"Dr. Riker, I'm not confirming the existence of any program conducted by the Bureau," said Flood. "However, I can send you a subset of a certain list, which will include only names of employees of the executive branch. It will be on plain paper, no letterhead. It's just a collection of names and dates. You didn't get it from me. Okay?"

"Yes, thank you," said Riker.

Sure enough, a few moments later a file arrived in Riker's email box. He opened it.

There were three columns. The first column contained names. There were about three hundred, with some repeats. The second contained dates. The dates covered the period of the Ralston presidency. The most recent date was a week earlier. The third column listed the time of day.

Riker carefully scanned the list. None of the initial names looked familiar. He kept looking.

Suddenly one name jumped out.

Amy Gold.

The president had given Riker the same name, saying she was a fundraiser. He had implied that he hadn't seen her since he had taken office, and yet Gold had visited the clinic on the fourth of April, three months after the inauguration.

Another name caught his eye.

Christina Wilkinson. She had visited that same year, in May. Could she be the same person as the former Medical Unit nurse?

Possibly.

Riker realized that he could not be sure if these individuals were the same people who worked for the president. After all, these were not unique names.

A check of the Washington, DC, white pages directory confirmed that in the metro area there were currently four women named Amy Gold and three named Christina Wilkinson.

Riker knew he would need more information to make a match.

He picked up his phone and called Sam Flood.

"Yes?" said Flood with a trace of irritation. "I'm just leaving the office."

"I received the list of names," said Riker. "Thank you very much. I need to ask you, does the information go any deeper? These names do not correspond to unique individuals."

"What you have is raw data," replied Flood. "It hasn't been analyzed. But give me an example."

"I have two. Amy Gold and Christina Wilkinson. In the metro area there are several women with these names."

"Those names refer to individuals who were employees of the executive branch at the time," replied Flood. "A more detailed identification could only be made by matching up video records with the names and dates. That will take some time."

Riker pleaded, "Isn't there anything else you can do?"

"Well," Flood said, "Maybe we could go the computer route. I've got two ideas for you. First, in the District, like just about everywhere else, it's a requirement that docs report any HIV-positive patient to the health department, with the name and address! Same for labs when they find a positive HIV test. The department keeps what they call The Registry. Supposedly it's all confidential, but, hell, we've had a friend on their IT staff for years. So, he can probably run the gals' names against the big list of AIDS and HIV, and see if they turn up. Only problem is, what with federal employees being so sensitive about their reputations, they beg their docs to send in the clinical reports or blood test samples under a phony name. So I'm pretty sure that if either, or both, of these ladies have AIDS, or HIV, their info is in there somewhere—but maybe not under their real names.

"But we may have an ace up our sleeve. Some people I know are doing a beta test here in metro Washington on a new computer search program that uses a clever strategy to identify and find people who have HIV. But are you sure this is totally, completely off the record?"

Riker assured him it was.

"In New York City there has been a program where state Medicaid cooperates with an insurance company called Amigo," continued Flood. "Their motivation seems to be very idealistic and commendable; they want to keep HIV-positive patients taking their anti-retrovirus medications so the illness will stay in check and not progress. They call it 'adherence.'

"But some patients aren't motivated and stop taking the pills, or are too deep into drugs, alcohol, or homelessness to stick to their regimen.

So the goal of this program is to find these guys and get them back on their daily requirement of pills. This would help preserve the patients' health and save the taxpayers big bucks downstream by avoiding hospital care of AIDS complications.

"But how to find out which HIV patients have stopped? I mean, there are thousands in New York who are supposed to be taking these meds every day. Most adhere. How do you find among them the ones who have stopped?

"Well, somebody had a brainstorm. The patients who are no longer taking their pills have stopped refilling their prescriptions for them. So, the trick is to find these non-refillers, contact them, and convince them to get back on their pills.

"So you work with the insurance companies who process the pharmacy payments. Or you could work with the drugstore companies themselves; I'm not sure which they do up in New York. But anyway, here's the method. You have their big computer pull out all the names of patients on retroviral drugs. Basically, this gives you everybody in metro New York with AIDS or HIV. I mean, nobody else is taking anti-retrovirals, right? So now you know who's infected.

"From that list, you print out just those people who have not refilled their prescription. Every prescription has the name and address of the patient it belongs to. Bingo! Exactly the folks you're looking for.

"Then, the way it works up there, they first try any phone number in the record. If that doesn't work, or there isn't one, they send out a gumshoe to the last known address, and he tries to track down the patient. Sometimes they can get them back on the pills.

"Certain people here have gotten access to a big database covering metro DC that has all the prescription info. I don't know if it's at a drugstore chain, an insurance payer, or at Medicaid-Medicare. And please don't ask me how they got access; I don't even want to know that.

"But one of those guys owes me a couple favors, so I'll meet him for a drink tonight and see if he can somehow run those two names that interest you. If they're in there, you'll get their address. Can't promise anything of course. But hey, it's another net in the water, right?"

"This is really incredible," said Riker. "I had no idea something like this was going on."

"You still don't know it," replied Flood.

"Yeah, don't worry, I'm clear on that."

Riker thanked Flood and hung up.

Two steps forward, one step back. But as he mulled what he had just been told, he had mixed feelings. If the computer search of DC prescriptions could actually be pulled off, it might really narrow down, or even pinpoint, the specific Amy Gold or Christina Wilkinson he was looking for. No wasting time checking out irrelevant ones; just give him the one, or maybe two, taking anti-retrovirals.

But his fetish about patient privacy bubbled up. Damn! An enemy agent, or blackmailer, or even a political operative, could access these prescription files. Use a hacker or bribe a technician. Even get your own guy on their IT payroll. If you knew what medicines people were taking, you knew a lot about them. Meds for HIV would infer a lot. Nobody would be taking insulin unless they had diabetes. Or digitalis unless they had heart failure. Or drugs which point to depression and schizophrenia? Seemed like the New Yorkers had already breached these privacy walls, though with the most innocent intentions. So would these computer tactics turn out to be some kind of Frankenstein? He parked these thoughts in his mind's storage unit.

Riker realized that he was hungry. He glanced at his watch. It was nearly seven o'clock. Suddenly he felt very alone. He didn't look forward to the idea of spending the evening eating by himself and then sitting in his room watching a movie. The prospect of hitting the bar scene and picking up a new female friend was even less appealing.

He called Lindsay. She answered.

"I'd be happy to have dinner with you tonight," she said, "but there's one slight problem."

"What's that?"

"I'm in Boston, doing some advance work for the boss's visit next month. I'm taking the nine o'clock flight to Washington and won't get home until after eleven. Then I'm going to have a glass of wine and go straight to bed. But I'll take a rain check—maybe tomorrow night? It will be Friday, and I won't have to worry about going to sleep early."

"I'll put you on my calendar," said Riker. "Friday night it is. Have a safe flight home."

Riker sat on the edge of his bed. Who else could he call?

Oh yes. Good ol' Max.

For a moment Riker thought, *Lindsay and Max? What kind of loser knows only two people in town to call to have dinner with?*

He shrugged. He had been in Washington for only ten days, and he had been busy. What could you expect? Instant social popularity?

He called Mosely.

"Martin!" said the cheery voice. Riker could tell that he was someplace noisy. "What's up?"

"Just wondering what you're doing for dinner," said Riker.

"I'm all yours," replied Mosely. "My friend, if we keep this up, people are going to start talking!"

"Yeah, well, let 'em," said Riker. "Where are you?"

"I'm at the Dog Pound on M Street," said Mosely.

"It's called the Dog Pound? Max, I don't want to know what that is. Maybe I should make other plans."

"Oh, don't worry," said Mosely. "Don't let the name fool you—it's just a neighborhood bar. It's not even a gay bar. I just stopped here to say hello to a friend. I'm on my way to the best Thai restaurant in town, Bangkok Palace. It's up on Corcoran St. NW. Meet me there and we'll have some fantastic *pad thai.*"

"Okay," said Riker. "I'm on my way."

Riker grabbed a taxi and within a few minutes walked through the doors of a modest storefront restaurant that didn't look like much on the outside. He found Mosely at a quiet booth near the back, underneath a big framed portrait of King Bhumibol.

"See that guy hanging over our heads?" said Mosely of the portrait. "He's been the king of Thailand since 1946, which makes him the world's longest serving head of state. Can you imagine if we, in the United States, still had Harry Truman as our head of state?"

"In all fairness," said Riker as he slid onto the hard leather banquette, "Bhumibol was a mere lad of nineteen when he assumed the throne. Truman was sixty-one when he became president. He'd be over a hundred and thirty years old by now."

"Wouldn't that be a sight?" laughed Mosely. "A president of the United States who was one hundred thirty years old."

Mosely gave Riker his opinion of the menu. Since getting to know him, Riker had learned that there was nothing under the sun about which Mosely hadn't formed a clear and unambiguous opinion.

"Try the spicy tilapia in basil sauce," announced Mosely, "or the *gaeng sapparod* shrimp with red curry and coconut. I'd avoid the duck tamarind—they put something in there that tastes like dirty socks."

"I don't want dirty socks," said Riker. "How about the chicken *rama* with broccoli and peanut sauce?"

"Good choice," smiled Mosely. "With Thai beer, of course."

"I'll take a Singha," concurred Riker.

Having put in their orders, Riker and Mosely settled back in their seats.

"This is an exciting time!" exclaimed Mosely.

"Do you mean this exact moment, or in general?" asked Riker.

"Both. As we sit here, at this minute, the fact that the boss has AIDS will transform the fight against this terrible disease. For too long, people have been fearful of getting tested and fearful of dying a horrible early death. A door is opening, Martin. Mark my words. A new era of understanding and progress is dawning, and our president will be leading the way."

Riker leaned forward. "Max!" he hissed. "Are you completely insane? You've got to come back to reality. The boss isn't going to say a damn thing about AIDS, and neither will his doctors. Trust me. I beg you to take this out of your mind. It's history. Case closed. It *never happened*. By talking this way, you're going to get fired. You'll never work in Washington again."

"Relax, Martin," said Mosely with a smile. "I know what I'm doing. I have a parachute ready to deploy. There are plenty of people who are ready to hire me."

Riker felt the blood drain from his face. "Max, you're not talking about this in public, are you?"

"Just laying the foundation," Mosely shrugged. "Very discreetly."

"Max, you know better than I do that in Washington there's no such thing as 'discreetly.' You give someone a golden nugget of information, and faster than a lobbyist can sell his own mother, it's all over town. Whom exactly have you told?"

Mosely held up his palms. "Just a few very well-connected people whom I trust. I only gave them a heads-up hint."

"Oh, my God," said Riker. He shook his head. "Well, I've given you my opinion. All I can say is that you'd better be leaving my name out of it."

"Absolutely," nodded Mosely. "You are never mentioned. I guarantee you that. By the way, it's not as if the boss was a complete stranger to efforts to draw attention to the AIDS epidemic."

"What do you mean?"

"As I'm sure you know," said Mosely, "The twenty-seventh of June is National HIV Testing Day. It's a way to publicize the continuing threat of AIDS and motivate people to get tested. The boss did a photo op in the Medical Unit. Karen Thompson was there, as well as Uma Davis, the head of the Office of National AIDS Policy. As the cameras clicked and whirred, the boss rolled up his sleeve and John Daughtry took his blood sample. Everyone congratulated everyone else, the video was released, and the message to the American people delivered. I heard that it actually had an effect, and that the number of people having HIV tests jumped that week." Mosely stopped and took a sip of his Singha. He smiled. "Gee, I wonder what happened to those blood samples?"

"I wouldn't know," replied Riker quickly.

In reality, he knew full well. The samples had been placed into a refrigerator, but forgotten, until the president had become very ill and had been tested for HIV at Walter Reed. Remembering the samples taken five months earlier, Thompson had them tested as well. They were found to be positive. If they had been tested at the time, the president's disease could have been treated earlier.

The server arrived with their food, ending the conversation.

As they dined, to avoid getting heartburn Riker did not revive the topic of the president's health; and he was happy when Mosely entered into a lengthy discussion of his recent trip to Bangkok, followed by a week at a four-star resort in Ko Lanta, on the Andaman Sea. "Just gorgeous," Mosely gushed. "Beautiful people and amazing hospitality, and the best part is that most of the island is still undeveloped. Hardly a soul goes there. Very few annoying tourists. The sunsets over the water are among the most spectacular I've ever seen."

Riker, too, had been to Thailand, but his experience had been very different. While working for the CDC he had spent a month in the remote highlands researching Japanese encephalitis, a virus related to dengue, yellow fever, and West Nile viruses, and which is spread by mosquitoes. It's the main cause of viral encephalitis in many countries of Asia, and there's no cure. While it's rarely fatal, survivors can suffer permanent intellectual, behavioral, or neurological problems such as paralysis, recurrent seizures, or the inability to speak.

As Mosely had promised, Riker's dinner was delicious, and as the meal drew to a close he more deeply appreciated Mosely's cheerful companionship. It wasn't that Mosely was a shallow or glib person; he was, in fact, terrifically focused on his work, and few events on the political scene escaped his notice. But he had a remarkable ability to take setbacks in stride, put failures behind him, and set his course on a positive future. It was this quality, thought Riker, which propelled his seizing upon the president's illness as a golden opportunity to do good—a vision that Riker was certain was not shared in the halls of the White House.

After lingering over dishes of ginger ice cream, they decided to call it a night. "I've got to get up for a meeting at seven thirty tomorrow morning," said Mosely as he slid out of the booth. "I'm telling you, Martin, I could never be president. My brain doesn't begin to function until nine or ten o'clock in the morning. If I got one of those national security phone calls at three a.m., I'd say, 'Look, can you call me back after breakfast?'"

"I'm sure the Joint Chiefs would be reassured by that," laughed Riker. "They'd have to say to the Russians, 'Please don't attack us in the middle of the night. Our president needs his sleep.'"

"You've got that right," said Mosely.

They made their way to the door. "Can I give you a lift?" asked Mosely. "My car is parked down the block."

"Thanks, Max," replied Riker, "but I think I'll walk back to the hotel. It's only a half mile away, and I could use the exercise."

Mosely patted his broad stomach. "I should do the same! I always say I'll start exercising—*tomorrow*."

"But you belong to the Metropole Club, don't you?" said Riker as he pushed open the door to the street. The cold air felt refreshing on his face.

"Sure, and whenever I go there, I end up talking to my friends," laughed Mosely. "I haven't touched one those machines in months."

"Max, you're too damned popular." Riker extended his hand. "If I don't see you, have a good weekend. And stay out of trouble."

"Sure," said Mosely as they shook hands. "You too."

Riker turned away and began to walk west towards 16th Street. The sky had cleared, and a few of the brightest stars were barely visible through the glare of the streetlights. The sight made Riker think of when he would take his boat, *Cassandra*, for a motor cruise at night, heading down past Gordon Pass and into the inland Dollar Bay, where there weren't any houses or streetlights. On clear moonless nights you could see the Milky Way with its billions of tiny stars, like a sparkling river of light.

Suddenly from behind him Riker heard a pop. Then two more in rapid succession. His military ear told him instantly that the sounds came from a handgun.

Instinctively ducking low, he whirled around. He heard the sound of a car accelerating, going the other direction. Peering down the sidewalk, he saw nothing except the blur of a dark vehicle. It turned a corner and was gone.

Riker sprinted back in the direction of the restaurant. As he passed the door to Bangkok Palace a few people came out and looked up and down the street. One of them pointed down the block. "It came from over there," she said. Running farther, Riker saw a figure lying on the sidewalk.

Without understanding how or why, a sick feeling in his gut told him it was Max Mosely.

Panting, out of breath, Riker came to Mosely, who was lying face down. A set of car keys lay nearby. Riker saw a puddle of blood seeping out from under his chest. Gently, Riker rolled him over. He pulled open Mosely's overcoat and suit jacket. There were three entrance wounds in his chest. One was over his heart.

"Max!" he shouted as he placed his hand on Mosely's chest. "Max!" There was no response. Riker checked for a pulse on his neck. Nothing. No pulse at his wrist, either. Mosely's eyes were open and glassy. A thin trickle of blood appeared at the corner of his mouth.

A bystander appeared, and then another.

"Call 911," commanded Riker as he began CPR by pressing rhythmically on Mosely's chest.

"Did you see what happened?" someone said.

"Some guy robbed him, is what it looked like to me," said a man.

"A car pulled up and a man jumped out," said a woman. "He walked over and shot the guy. Just like that. Then he got back in the car."

"Poor guy," said someone. "Are you a doctor? Is he going to make it?"

"Yes, I'm a doctor," said Riker without looking up. "Has someone called 911?"

"Yes, they're on their way."

"C'mon Max, give me something!" said Riker. But the body was inert, the open eyes unseeing.

The faint wail of sirens became louder. A moment later a police car pulled up, and then an EMT bus.

"What happened here?" said the EMT as he crouched over the body.

"Multiple gunshot wounds to the chest," replied Riker as he wiped his bloody hands on his coat. "I'm a doctor. I've been doing CPR. He's nonresponsive."

"Did anybody get a license plate?" asked the cop.

"No—but I think it was a Toyota. Dark grey," said a man.

"It looked like a Ford to me," said another. "It turned south on 16th Street."

Riker stood and watched as his friend, Max Mosely, was loaded onto a stretcher and put into the EMT bus.

He knew he wouldn't be seeing Mosely alive again.

Chapter 25

*   *   *

A s the bus pulled away in a flurry of flashing lights and the wail of the siren, a police detective slouched towards Riker.

"You saw what happened?" asked the detective. He had the inquisitive eyes of a hound dog.

"I was walking down the street at the other end of the block," said Riker. "Max and I had just had dinner together at Bangkok Palace. He was walking to his car. I had decided to walk back to my hotel. I heard three shots. They sounded like a handgun—maybe a nine millimeter. I came running back and found him on the sidewalk. I administered CPR but he was nonresponsive."

"You had dinner with him? Anybody else?"

"No, just the two of us. Max works at the White House."

"The victim works for the president?" said the detective.

"Assistant communications director."

"And you?"

"I'm a consultant with the DIA. For the past ten days I've been working at the White House too." Riker took out his wallet and showed the detective his pass.

"Christ, that brings this thing up to a whole 'nother level," said the detective. "It's gonna be a damned national security issue."

"Instead of a typical mugging of an ordinary taxpayer?" asked Riker.

The detective gave Riker a hard look. "Hey, I don't make the rules. Anytime someone from Capitol Hill gets knocked off, it's big news. Any idea who might want to shoot him?"

"You don't think it was an attempted robbery?" asked Riker. He put his wallet back into the hip pocket of his pants.

"Could go either way," shrugged the detective. "The shots were quick and clean. Deliberate. But we didn't find a wallet on the body. Did he have one at dinner?"

"Yes," said Riker. "We each paid separately. Max used his American Express card."

"All right," said the detective wearily. "Dr. Riker, don't leave town, okay? We might want to talk to you again."

Riker handed the detective his business card, which included his cell number. "No problem," he said to the detective. "In fact, I want you to call me if you find something. Anytime, day or night."

"Seeing as you're with the DIA, I suppose I could bring you in," said the detective. "My name's Mark Forsythe. I'm with the Second District, on Idaho Ave. NW. Where are you?"

"I'm staying at The Jefferson," said Riker.

"Do you want a lift there? One of the uniformed officers can drive you."

For a moment Riker was inclined to refuse. It wasn't a long walk, and there was no reason to use a car. But he glanced down the long lonely sidewalk and the rows of parked cars. Suddenly an instinct gripped him. He knew that Mosely hadn't been gunned down by a random mugger who sped away in a car. He had been targeted. Walking alone at night back to the hotel would leave Riker vulnerable.

"Thanks, I appreciate the offer," said Riker.

Detective Forsythe grabbed a uniformed officer, who took Riker to his cruiser. The officer offered him the front seat, saying, "If I put you in the back seat, it would send a message that wouldn't be accurate."

A few minutes later, the car pulled up in front of The Jefferson. After thanking the officer, Riker went up to his room. He showered and changed into clean clothes. It was not yet midnight, so he went down to The Quill for a double bourbon on the rocks. Half an hour later he returned to his room, alone. Before going to sleep, he shut off his phone.

At seven thirty the next morning he woke up and turned on his phone. He had fifteen new messages. Ignoring them, he turned on the news. As he expected, the news shows were giving the story top priority. As Riker watched, he got the sense that the official line was that Mosely's death was a robbery gone bad and just another terrible example of the out-of-control crime rate in Washington, DC, where even a street a mile from the White House was not safe. Dan Haldridge, the White House communications director and Mosely's immediate superior, made a statement expressing his deep sorrow at the loss of a good friend and valued colleague, and offering his hope that the very capable Washington, DC, police detectives would bring the perpetrator to justice.

Riker wanted to reach out to someone, but to whom? Officially, he had no reason to call anyone at the White House. He was off the case and presumed to be bound for Florida.

He tapped the number for Angela Powell. She asked him to come to her office as soon as possible.

After showering and grabbing a quick breakfast at the Greenhouse, Riker hired a black car to take him south across the Anacostia River to the sprawling headquarters of the Defense Intelligence Agency. After passing through security he made his way to Room 5671. There was no name on the door, but Riker had been there once before, a few days before he had left for Syria to smash the terrorist plot to launch an attack using smallpox virus in *The New York Times*' printing ink.

He found Powell at her desk. Behind her, the big window provided a view of the Ronald Reagan Washington National Airport just across the Potomac River, and, to the north, the downtown skyline, with the gleaming white Capitol building at center stage.

"Martin, thanks for coming," she said. "Given the sensitivity and gravity of the situation, I thought it better that we meet in person. Can I get you anything? Coffee?"

"Actually, coffee would be good," said Riker.

Powell picked up her phone and asked her assistant to bring some. After she hung up she turned to Riker and said, "I'm always conflicted when I have to ask Jenny to perform menial tasks. I really need to get a coffee machine installed in here. Now then—what's your opinion about the Mosely shooting?"

"I'm sure it wasn't a robbery. I think Max was targeted. It looked like an execution. The killer took his wallet, but I think that was just a diversion."

"Why would someone want to kill him? Was it a terrorist attack?"

"I don't think it was a terrorist," said Riker. "I think Mosely was killed because he had figured out the president has AIDS and was determined to release the news to the public."

"But why would he want to do that?" asked Powell.

"He sincerely believed that the president could be a global champion of AIDS awareness, much like Magic Johnson."

"I take it the folks in the West Wing would not have endorsed such a plan?"

"No. My information suggests that the president and his inner circle regard his illness as a private matter, and as long as he receives treatment, can fulfill his duties, and appears healthy to the voters, knowledge of his condition would be a huge liability, or at least a major diversion."

"Enough of a liability to shoot someone who threatened to disclose it?"

"Possibly. Stranger things have happened."

At that moment Jenny came in the office carrying a tray with two cups of coffee, sugar packets, and half & half, which she put on the table next to Powell's desk.

"Thanks very much," said Powell as Jenny excused herself. Powell stood up and went to the table, and as she tore open a sugar packet she said to Riker, "Any suspects?"

As he stood up to get his coffee, Riker shrugged. "In a word, no. As for the actual perpetrators—the shooter and the driver—whoever did it knew that Max was going to be at the restaurant. They probably followed us there. Thank God I didn't accept a ride home from him. Had I done so, I'm sure that I would have been taken out as collateral damage. My decision to walk home probably saved my life."

Powell nodded. "Lucky break. Martin, do you have a sidearm?"

"No, I didn't bring one because I knew they'd never let me into the White House with one, and the job didn't seem dangerous—I was hired to find out how the president got AIDS, not go head-to-head with terrorists or killers."

"Because you're going to be continuing your investigation, I think we need to give you some personal protection," replied Powell as she sat down at her desk. "The people who shot Mosely may be afraid that you're equally dangerous to them. Before you leave, stop at the armory in the basement. Pick up something you can conceal-carry. If I were you, I'd wear it whenever I was walking the streets. And keep your eyes open."

"Thanks, I will."

"What's the next step?" asked Powell.

"Now we have two investigations," replied Riker. "Our new challenge is that we have to find out who killed Max Mosely. I assume the DC police will pursue the robbery angle, while we need to look at the White House. We also have to take care of our original mission, which was to uncover how the president got AIDS. Our possibilities are narrowing. I'm waiting for Jim Gilmore at the CDC to confirm my suspicion that the bloody towel from Nagoya does not contain any evidence of HIV infection. This would mean that Thompson added the president's infected blood to the baggie before sending to the CDC for testing."

Powell took a sip of her coffee. "Speaking of Thompson, do you think that a medical doctor—someone who is professionally dedicated to healing—would arrange for a perceived enemy to be shot?"

"At this point, I would believe anything," replied Riker. "In Washington, the rules of normal behavior are broken every day by somebody. The virus of ambition and greed is a formidable force to which few are immune." He got up and put his coffee cup on the table. "I need to start talking to people. Thanks for the coffee. I'll stop by the armory on the way out."

Twenty minutes later, with a 9mm Glock comfortably nestled in its shoulder holster under his jacket, Riker took his car back to the Ten-Fifty. On the way, he scrolled through the voicemail messages that had been piling up on his phone.

One was from Lindsay Baker. "Hey, Martin, it's me, Lindsay," the recording said. "I heard about Max. It's a terrible, terrible thing. I heard you were with him last night at the restaurant. I'm just calling to see if you're okay. Give me a call when you can. Okay. Bye."

Another call was from Karen Thompson. "Hi Martin. An awful thing about Max. To think that someone could be attacked like that, right on the sidewalk. It makes you afraid to go anywhere at night! I'm sure the DC police will make every effort to get the guy. I suppose you're on your way to Florida. It must be much safer in Naples."

After saving the message, Riker tapped the number for Jim Gilmore at the CDC.

"Give me some news, Jim," he said.

"I was just about to call you," replied Gilmore. "We got the towel this morning and rushed the tests. Our preliminary results indicate no presence of HIV anywhere on the towel. The blood appears to be from one individual of Asian descent."

"Thanks, Jim," replied Riker. "You've been a big help."

"What's the story with the Max Mosely murder?" asked Gilmore. "It's all over the news—a top White House staffer gunned down on the street last night. They say it was a robbery. People are freaking out because they think they're not safe, even near the Capitol."

"I don't think it was random," said Riker. "But I'll get back to you on that. Thanks for the fast work on the towel. It means a new set of headaches, but that's just the way the ball bounces."

"Are you going to confront Karen?"

"Not yet," replied Riker. "When I do, it could create a firestorm. I need to choose the right time and place."

After thanking Gilmore, Riker hung up.

While it was good to have confirmation that Thompson had falsified the evidence in the baggie, there was no reason to blow the whistle now. Thompson—and the president—could remain in the dark about Riker's newfound knowledge.

The investigation into how the president got HIV had to continue. Riker had two more names on his list: Amy Gold and Christina Wilkinson. Both of them had visited the supposedly confidential clinic in the Band Building, and their visits had been dutifully recorded by the FBI.

Amy Gold had been a fundraiser for the president. Riker needed to talk to her.

He picked up his phone and called Lindsay Baker.

"Martin!" she answered. "Thank God you're all right. This thing with Max is horrible, just horrible. Were you there? Did you see it happen?"

Riker told her about his dinner with Max, walking out the door of the restaurant, hearing the shots, seeing the car drive away, and finding Mosely lying on the pavement.

"If it's any consolation, I think he died instantly," he said. "One of the bullets appeared to have struck his heart. When I got to him, he showed no signs of life."

"Was it a robbery, like the police are saying?"

Riker hesitated. Since Mosely's death, Lindsay was the first person he found himself talking to who was outside of the narrow investigative team of Powell, Riker, and Gilmore. To his knowledge, she didn't know that the president had AIDS. She didn't know that Mosely had wanted to make the president's illness public. And while Riker felt emotionally close to Lindsay, and wanted desperately to be able to talk to her openly and honestly, he knew he couldn't reveal the secrets of the case. Besides, her hearing these could possibly endanger her, too.

"I suppose it looks that way," he said.

"Wow. It makes you worry about doing the normal stuff you do, like go out to dinner at night."

Riker wanted to say to her that no, it wasn't a mugging, it had nothing to do with unsafe streets in the nation's capital, the cops had it all wrong—but he couldn't.

"Well," he offered, "No matter where you are, you need to be careful."

"Do you still want to have dinner tonight?" she asked. "I'd understand if you were too upset or too busy—"

"On the contrary," he replied. "There's nothing that I'd rather do than have a nice quiet evening with you."

"Okay," she said. "But I want to relax. I'm afraid that if we were at a restaurant I'd be too nervous. Let's have dinner at my place."

"Oh, no, I couldn't possibly ask you to go to all that trouble. Really, I insist–"

"No, I'm the one who must insist," she interjected. "Your job is to bring a nice bottle of wine and your cooking ability. We'll make dinner together. Okay?"

"Okay—I surrender," said Riker. Secretly, it was a battle that he was delighted to lose. "Before I hang up," he said, "I have a question. Have you ever heard of a professional fundraiser named Amy Gold?"

"The name rings a bell," replied Lindsay. "She's with Liberty Associates, a company that works with national and statewide candidates. From time to time, the president has used them to fundraise; they handle direct mail campaigns, email blasts, and so on. We also interface with them if the president is attending one of their political events. This past June they put together an evening with Mandy Summer, the singer. It was a two-thousand-dollar-a-plate affair at Mandy's estate in East Hampton. Three hundred guests were invited, and they held the event in a big tent on her front lawn. The money they raised went for statewide races."

"Was Amy Gold there?"

"Yes. She handles all the celebrity fundraisers."

"Okay, thanks," said Riker. "I'll see you at seven o'clock, along with a bottle of wine and my culinary skills."

Interesting, thought Riker. The president had implied that he hadn't seen Amy Gold after he had taken office, yet by all appearances they had the opportunity for contact. Out of curiosity, Riker Googled Mandy Summer's East Hampton estate. The aerial view showed a typical East Hampton layout. The property consisted of a three- or four-acre lot, shaped like a skinny rectangle, with its narrow side fronting the beach; from there the lot extended a thousand feet inland to the other narrow side, which faced the charmingly named Lily Pond Lane. All of the lots in the neighborhood were shaped thusly; the effect was like seeing a fleet of long ships berthed side by side, with each of the great houses placed near the prow, where a ship's bridge would be, overlooking the ocean. If your head chef wanted to borrow a cup of sugar, he had only to walk a few steps to your neighbor's mansion.

On the Summer estate, the long lawn had room for a tennis court and a small pond. No helipad could be seen; in recent years, noisy private helicopters had become a sore subject among the East Hampton elite. From the road, a tree-lined driveway snaked to a circular turnaround on the inland side of the big rectangular main house with its two smaller wings flanking the driveway. Tiny toy-like cars parked in the driveway gave a sense of scale; Riker estimated that if the western wing of the house were the garage, you could park ten cars side by side within it, with room to spare.

From the terrace of the main house a set of curving stairs led down to a big kidney-shaped pool. From the pool house, another set of stairs led down to the private beach.

Riker didn't envy the rich folk and their huge houses. Not for him were the headaches and responsibilities of a big, expensive household, with its army of servants and gardeners and pool boys. He liked living lean; his compact house in Naples and his twenty-foot sailboat were just the right size for a man who didn't want to spend time or money worrying about the stuff he owned.

He went to the website of Liberty Associates. The home page showed a banner photo of the US Capitol Building. Under the photo the text read,

"Liberty Associates, LLC provides a full range of campaign fundraising and financial management services. So that we may give each campaign the best service possible, we maintain a small client roster. We also partner with corporations as well as consult with political action committees. With our fifteen years of experience in fundraising, our team has built relationships across the most influential sectors in Washington including business, energy, financial services, agriculture, pharmaceutical, technology, transportation, labor, and health care industries."

Riker clicked on the "Meet Our Team" button. Scanning down the staff list—there were about a dozen—he quickly found Amy Gold. The photo showed an attractive woman with short dark hair and large almond eyes that gave her the appearance of being surprised. She was smiling broadly, showing perfect white teeth. Next to her photo, the text read, "Amy Gold, Associate, is a graduate of the University of Maryland, where she earned a bachelor of arts in political science. Amy served as the congressional scheduler and director of operations for former congressman William Sharpe. Prior to coming to Capitol Hill, she worked on two Maryland statewide campaigns, serving first as the scheduler for Amanda Cartwright's US Senate campaign, and then as finance coordinator for Paul Ralston in his campaign for governor."

Riker downloaded the photo and attached it to an email to Lindsay. "Have you ever seen her around the president?" he asked.

A moment later came the reply: "Yes. The last time was at the Mandy Summer event. Haven't seen her since."

Riker asked Lindsay if the president had been out of sight at any time during the Mandy Summer party.

She messaged back that yes, the president had gone into the house a few times. It was not a scripted event and the president had the freedom to move about.

Riker thanked her and signed off.

The Mandy Summer fundraising bash had been in June. There had been plenty of high-roller events since then; Riker wondered why Lindsay hadn't seen Amy Gold at any of them.

Riker remembered what Susan Ralston had told him when he had interviewed her in the Lincoln Sitting Room. When asked about her husband's affairs, she had given up two names: Kimberly Schuster and Rachel Doucette. The former had voluntarily left the White House in the fall to go to grad school; the latter had been caught *in flagrante delicto* by Susan Ralston and sent packing. The First Lady hadn't mentioned Amy Gold. Perhaps she didn't know about her.

Chapter 26

* * *

As he was pondering the emergence of Amy Gold as yet another possible presidential girlfriend, Riker's phone rang. He glanced at the caller ID. Stephen Howe. Riker picked it up.

"Stephen—what a pleasant surprise," said Riker.

"Have you got a moment?" said the president's body man.

"Sure, go ahead."

"Are you still in Washington?"

"As a matter of fact, yes," replied Riker. "I have some unfinished business. I'll be in town for a few days. Why do you ask?"

"I wanted to talk to you about Max. Can you meet me at the White House, in the bowling alley?"

"When?"

"As soon as possible. The boss and the First Lady are visiting a grade school in Washington Highlands, a poor neighborhood on the southeast side of town. I'm off until three o'clock."

Riker was amazed that, after being convinced that his tour of duty at the White House was over, he'd be returning so soon. No matter—now was the time to respond, not analyze.

Leaving his Glock in his desk drawer—there was no point in carrying it because he'd have to surrender it at the southeast appointment gate—Riker hurried to the White House. The afternoon sky was a brilliant blue, and, like most people in Washington, Riker was grateful to have a respite from the seemingly endless waves of snowstorms that since the beginning of the month had rolled up the East Coast.

With a familiar sense of excitement Riker strode up the curving driveway toward the South Portico. He remarked to himself that it looked just the same as when he had last seen it—which had been less than twenty-four hours earlier. Riker had to laugh at himself. The exterior of the White House hadn't changed in nearly two hundred years! Why would it change overnight?

Entering the Diplomatic Reception Room, Riker went to the Center Hall, crossed it, and descended the stairs to the Basement Hall. Passing the flower shop and the cold storage room, he entered the bowling alley.

He was alone.

It was odd, he thought, to be *anywhere* in the White House and be alone. Generally, the place was a beehive of activity, and sometimes even felt over-crowded, such as when the president and his entourage were walking through the relatively narrow Center Hall, or when the press was crammed into the briefing room when the president made a personal appearance there.

Riker paused. He could hear nothing except the sound of the heating system. He picked up a bowling ball from the ball return rack. He felt its hard, smooth weight in his hands.

He heard the door open, and as he replaced the ball in the rack, Stephen Howe entered.

"Sorry to keep you waiting," said Howe as he extended his hand. "It's good to see you."

"I'm happy to help any way I can," replied Riker.

"You were with Max when he got shot, weren't you?" asked Howe.

"Yes. We had just had dinner at Bangkok Palace. Max had recommended we go there. It was not more than a minute after I left him and started walking home than he was attacked."

"Do you think he was targeted because he was gay?" asked Howe with sincere and deep concern in his voice.

"No." For the second time that day, Riker felt pressure to reveal the truth about the entire case, including the illness of the president; and he knew that as the days passed and the police investigation stalled, the pressure that he felt would increase.

"To be honest," continued Howe, "A hate crime was the first thing that I thought of. Maybe I'm being paranoid, but we live in an environment where we're all targets. Some nutjob who can't get close to the president might move down the list and go after a White House staffer who's accessible. If the assassin has an anti-gay bias, his drive to attack might intensify. Does that make sense?"

"It might," conceded Riker. He looked into Howe's brown eyes; and as he saw Howe's clear sincerity, Riker's mind turned a corner. It was like bringing his boat around in the wind, watching the boom sweep across the deck, and feeling the boat heel over to the opposite side, plowing through the waves on a new course.

He had to broach the subject of the president's illness.

"I have my own ideas about what happened to Max," said Riker.

"What do you mean?"

Riker chose his words carefully. "Let's just suppose—hypothetically—that the president, by some unfortunate accident, contracted HIV that developed into AIDS." For Riker, this was the first time in his professional career that he had pushed the boundary of doctor-patient confidentiality. As he said the words, he felt his stomach tighten.

"What are you saying?" said Howe. His voice was almost a whisper, as if he did not want to be overheard in the empty bowling alley.

"I'm saying what I said. Strictly as an example, let's say the president has AIDS. And let's say that Max Mosely became convinced of this."

Howe lowered his head in thought. Then he took Riker's arm and looked him in the eye. "Oh my God—that would explain everything! It would explain the president's recurring illnesses, and his visits to the Medical Unit, and his pills that he tries to hide from me. It would explain why Don Strauss would close the door to the Oval Office and stand outside of it, like a guard at a harem. It would explain—sadly—why the

president and the First Lady behave more like brother and sister than husband and wife."

"You're drawing the same conclusions that Max Mosely did," said
Riker. "All without confirmation from me."

"But what does this have to do with Max being shot in the street?"
asked Howe.

"That's the sinister part," replied Riker. "Over the past week, Max—
who had come to believe the president has AIDS—had expressed to me
his desire to publicly announce that the president had AIDS. He thought
this would raise awareness in the same way that Magic Johnson did. I
strenuously objected. I told him that the president—who as the patient
has the ultimate authority to make such information public—would never
consent. I repeatedly urged him to put this notion out of his mind. He put
me off, and the impression I got was that he was going forward. He had
even told some other people of his plan."

"Who?" said Howe.

"I don't know," replied Riker. "He didn't specify. He said this to me
at dinner at Bangkok Palace. I told him—in so many words—that he was
crazy. I told him to leave my name out of any discussions. He assured me
that he would. Twenty minutes later, he was dead. It's my gut feeling that
this was not a botched robbery. I believe Max was targeted, and the reason
he was targeted was because the wrong people had gotten wind of his plan
to make President Ralston's alleged AIDS a national cause célèbre. There
are many powerful people who would be horrified at the notion that the
president's illness should be made public."

"Are you saying that President Ralston is involved?" whispered Howe.

"My instinct says no," replied Riker. "Personally, I think he's the kind
of guy who, if he learned of Max's ideas, would pick up the phone and
say, 'Max, shut the hell up!' Do you know what I mean? The president is a
very gutsy, straight-shooting guy. He would believe that he could influence
someone like Max. He would believe in the power of his persuasion. And
I think that if the president had been given the opportunity to personally
tell Max that he, the patient, was flatly opposed to publicizing his illness,

Max would have respected that. Think about it—Max was a guy who kept his own sexual orientation out of the headlines. If you asked him if he were gay, he would have said yes; but on the other hand, he wasn't marching in the Gay Pride Week parade. He was sensitive to the realities of high public office. He knew enough not to remind Mr. and Mrs. Bible Belt that there are some LGBT folks serving at the highest levels of government."

"I know it too," nodded Howe. "But to Max, the possibilities for education and enlightenment presented by the president of the United States having AIDS probably seemed too good to pass up."

"Yes," agreed Riker. "He thought it was a golden opportunity. But as I said, I'm sure that if the president had gotten on the phone with him, he could have convinced Max to back off."

"Which means," said Howe, "in all likelihood, the president never knew about Max's idea and was never informed. Someone acted unilaterally to remove him—quickly and brutally. But was that person someone within the White House?"

Riker shrugged. "Max knew a lot of people, and many them could have had their reasons for wanting Max to keep quiet. Even a pro-gay-rights extremist could have a rationale."

"How do you figure that?" said Howe. "It sounds counterintuitive."

"People on the fringes of any movement often take positions that are at odds with its mainstream. The fact that the president is a straight man—at least, all the evidence points that way—and that he allegedly has AIDS, which he therefore did *not* get from man-to-man sex, could be seen by an LGBT extremist as being a huge distraction from the main AIDS challenge in the United States. Namely, that AIDS mainly strikes gay, bisexual, and other men who have sex with men, and in particular young African American and Hispanic men in those categories."

"I see what you mean," said Howe. "I have some LGBT friends who are, shall we say, rather militant in their beliefs, and who are constantly pestering me to come out of the closet and proclaim to the world that the president's body man is gay. But I come from a family where sexuality is not something that you discuss in public. My sister is straight, and she would never dream of being like Kim Kardashian and broadcasting her intimate life to the world. Our parents are very conservative. They didn't raise us to do that."

"Have you ever been threatened or blackmailed?"

"Do you mean by the far right or the far left?" laughed Howe. "No, not yet." He leaned down and rapped on the wooden frame of the ball rack. "Knock on wood." He stood upright and ran his hand through his short-cropped black hair. "I try to avoid contact with extremists of any variety. I have to be mindful of my job."

"I understand," said Riker. "You can't exactly live a wild and crazy life."

"That's right. When I took this job, I resigned myself to living for four years like a monk. No cruising for me, thank you. After all, how many people get to serve in the White House? I figured that after four years—or maybe even eight years—I could rejoin the human race and have some fun."

"And yet there are some members of the president's inner circle who have not taken the vow of bodily purity," said Riker. "To the contrary, they're hitting the groupie buffet table hard."

"Are we gossiping now, or investigating?" said Howe.

"A little bit of both," replied Riker. "It's part of my job to develop the fullest possible picture of any biological threats that could threaten the president. These include diseases like AIDS, which can be spread among sexual partners. The risk of heterosexual infection is low, but it still exists."

"Among the men, you might look at Don Strauss and Brian Conway," replied Howe. "Also Owen Hauseman, the assistant to the president for economic policy, and David Andrews, the assistant to the president for strategy and outreach. And there's a special assistant named Fordwell Jones, but he got married, so I think he's off the gravy train."

"My God," said Riker, "It sounds like a college frat house."

"If you're a young guy with a healthy libido, it's like a being a kid who gets a summer job in a damned candy factory! You know you're not supposed to sample the product, but it's incredibly hard to resist. You're at the center of political power in the richest nation on earth, and you're surrounded by smart, sexy women—and men—who will do just about anything to gain admission into that center of power, and to feel the adrenaline rush of walking in the footsteps of the president, of being in the same room as the president, and maybe even exchanging a word with him."

"Or getting behind closed doors with him," said Riker.

"Or the next best thing—pressing the flesh with one of his deputies." Howe glanced at his watch. "If you'll excuse me, I have to go—the president will be arriving shortly."

"Stay in touch," said Riker.

Howe left the bowling alley first. So that they wouldn't be seen together, Riker lingered for a moment before making his way up the stairs to the Center Hall. As he walked he pondered how his vision of the White House had been transformed over the past ten days. The public image of the White House and life within its walls was a carefully constructed narrative, composed of fleeting images, stage-managed speeches, and orchestrated events that reflected and radiated solid American family values. None of this was bad, and one could not hope or ever expect anything different from any president. Yet behind the scrubbed white façade, real people worked. These living, breathing people were complex, imperfect souls, who, as Howe had suggested, more often than not labored mightily to resist temptation and—at least in the case of Susan Ralston—strove to maintain an appearance of genteel chivalry and strength. His new vision of the White House was not necessarily more tawdry or unseemly than before—after all, Riker was a doctor who had traveled the world and had seen human beings in every situation imaginable—but richer and more complex, populated by real, fallible human beings.

Occupied by his thoughts, as Riker stepped into the Center Hall he glanced up and saw Karen Thompson emerging from the Medical Unit.

As she closed the door behind her, her eyes met his.

He knew this was the time, even if he was only ninety-five percent certain.

Chapter 27

∗   ∗   ∗

A t the entrance to the Medical Unit, Thompson stopped. An awkward smile pulled at her face.

"Martin," she said as he crossed the hall towards her. "This is a surprise. I thought you'd be in Florida by now, sailing your boat."

"I had hoped so too," said Riker. "But I'm still here, tying up some loose ends."

"Loose ends?" said Thompson. "What could those be?"

At this moment, with the murder of Max Mosely staining the air, the last thing that Riker wanted to do was dive into the problem of Karen Thompson and her criminal deception. But their sudden meeting—which Riker regretted not having taken greater pains to avoid—had shoved the issue into his face.

"Karen, why don't we go back into your office and talk about it?"

"Talk about what?" she said. "Really, Martin, I have to ask why you're still in the White House. I assumed you were going back to Florida, so I didn't revoke your credentials. But perhaps it will be necessary to do that."

Riker glanced around the Center Hall. Like most public places in the White House, there were staffers walking from one place to another, or quietly talking in doorways. Here, no conversation could be entirely private.

"I think that we need to go to your office and discuss the test results from the Nagoya baggie," he said.

"What about them?" she replied testily.

"You know all about them," said Riker. He nodded towards the door of the Medical Unit. "Let's go."

With a haughty shake of her head, Thompson turned and opened the door to the Medical Unit.

"Hi Dorothy," said Riker as he passed the receptionist's desk. Startled, Dorothy looked up from her computer. "Uh, hi, Dr. Riker," she managed to say as he walked by.

Once in Thompson's office, Riker closed the door. He remained standing. "Karen, why did you do it?"

"Do what?" she replied as she put her fingers in the candy bowl and fished around for a cherry lozenge. There were none. "Damn," she muttered as she reluctantly found an orange one.

"Karen, please," said Riker. "You dosed the baggie from Nagoya with the president's own blood, which was infected with HIV. The tests from the CDC confirm it. Furthermore, tests on the towel confirm the fact that in Nagoya, the protestor's baggie contained blood from only one source, and it was not HIV positive."

"Towel?" frowned Thompson as she unwrapped the orange candy. "What towel?"

"After the president was struck by the baggie, a Japanese diplomat handed him a cotton towel. He cleaned his face with it. The towel was put into the Beast, and then transported back to the United States. The Secret Service had it. They gave it to me, and I sent it to the CDC."

"Without telling me?" said Thompson.

"I had no choice," said Riker. "I'm sorry, Karen, but my suspicions, combined with the CDC findings that the baggie contained the blood from two individuals—one of them being the president—left me no alternative. The question is, what are we going to do about it?"

Like a deflated balloon, Thompson sunk into her chair. Her eyes slid from left to right. The wadded up cellophane candy wrapper, which she still held in her hand, she flicked towards the waste paper basket. Bouncing off the rim, it landed on the carpet.

"I suppose this is the end," she whispered.

"Yes, but in the interest of avoiding embarrassment to the president, and headlines screaming about corruption and criminal behavior in the Ralston White House, I suggest that you take the bull by the horns and take action. Get on the phone. Ask to see the president now. Tell him the truth. He's your patient, and you owe him that much. Go ahead. Do it."

Listlessly, like a marionette controlled by a sleepy handler, Thompson reached for her phone. She tapped the number for Don Strauss.

"Don," she said, "I need to see the president now. It's a health emergency. It cannot wait. All right, thank you. I'll be right there."

As she stood up, she looked at Riker. "I got lucky, if you can call it that. The president will be in the Oval Office for the next fifteen minutes. Let's go."

Together they walked out of the Medical Unit, through the Palm Room, and into the office of the president's secretary. After waiting a moment, Brian Conway, who came out and told them that Don Strauss was tied up in a meeting elsewhere in the West Wing, ushered them into the Oval Office.

The president, who was seated behind his desk, rose to greet them. "Karen—Martin—please have a seat," he said as he gestured towards the sofa. "What's the important medical news?"

Riker noticed that Brian Conway was still in the room.

The president, seeing Riker's hesitation, said, "If this meeting is about my having AIDS, Brian, as I'm sure you recall, is fully aware of the situation."

Riker knew what they had to say was more explosive than a simple discussion of the president's condition, but one does not quibble with the president. "Sir, Karen has something she needs to tell you," said Riker.

"Karen, what's so important that it couldn't wait?" smiled the president. "I'm not going to drop dead, am I?"

"No sir, you are not going to drop dead," replied Thompson. After fidgeting for a moment, she took a deep breath, straightened her back, and said, "Sir, what I told you about the source of your HIV infection was not true."

"What do you mean?" asked the president.

Thompson lowered her head and stared at the floor. Riker was afraid that she was losing her nerve, and that he would have to step in. But then she looked up.

"Sir, I falsified the blood sample that was sent to the CDC for analysis. I obtained a sample of your blood and mixed it with the blood that was already in the baggie. You did not contract HIV from the protestor in Nagoya."

"Karen, this is very distressing news," said the president. "Why did you do it?"

"To close the case and give you an answer," she said. "Also because I thought it would reflect poorly on me if you had gotten the disease on my watch."

"So how did I get this disease?" demanded the president.

"Sir, we still don't know," replied Thompson.

"Martin, were *you* involved in this deception?" asked the president.

"No sir," said Riker. "In Tokyo, I received the baggie from agent Shoko Masako of the PSIA. I immediately boarded a flight for Washington. Upon arrival in Washington, I proceeded directly to the White House, where I delivered the baggie to Dr. Thompson. I invite investigators to check the time line. I had neither the desire nor the opportunity to tamper with the baggie or its contents."

"Sir, he's right," said Thompson. "Riker had nothing to do with it."

"Karen," said the president, "this is extremely disappointing. Of course you'll be submitting your resignation. We'll issue a press release saying that you're leaving for personal reasons. Who's your commanding officer?"

"Rear Admiral Ronny Jones," she replied.

"I know him," replied the president. "He's a good man. Karen, the fact that this entire affair needs to remain confidential will work in your favor. Just as my having AIDS is something that officially doesn't exist, likewise your deception will never officially exist. You'll return to active duty in the Navy, and you will never speak of this again. I thank you for your service. In the interim, Norm Gladstone will head the Medical Unit. Brian, would you please contact him?"

"Yes, sir," said Conway.

"While Dr. Gladstone will become my personal physician and take over my treatment for AIDS," continued the president, "I would like Martin to stay on as the lead investigator of the AIDS problem. I want honest answers. You will report to me directly. Will you do that?"

"Yes, sir," answered Riker.

Brian Conway approached the president and told him that in five minutes he was due to be in the Situation Room for a phone call with the German chancellor. Nodding, the president stood up.

"Sir, one more quick question if I might," said Riker.

"Shoot," said the president.

"Did Max Mosely ever contact your office about your condition?"

President Ralston frowned. The question seemed brazen. "Not to my knowledge," he replied. "Why would he?"

"On more than one occasion he said to me that he suspected you had AIDS. This was based on his observation of your appearance and his knowledge that you had been hospitalized. It was pure conjecture, which I flatly denied."

"You say he thought I had AIDS?"

"Yes, sir," replied Riker. "In fact, he proposed to me that you make this information public. He thought it would help the fight against the disease. Again, I told him in no uncertain terms that I had no comment about the health of any of my patients, including the president, and that he had better put this idea out of his mind."

The president turned to his deputy chief of staff. "Brian, have you heard any of this?"

"No sir," replied Conway. "I have not spoken to Max Mosely in over two weeks. I have not heard anything about his view that your condition should be made public."

The president turned back to Riker. "Do you think that others have come to the same conclusion, based on my appearance and their familiarity with the disease?"

"It's possible," replied Riker. "But now that the disease is being properly treated, your improved health and renewed stamina should make any idle gossip subside. We think that, like most other people with AIDS, with continued medication you'll be able to live a long and healthy life. As president, you can go back to a happier time when your biggest headaches were provided by your political opponents in Congress."

The president laughed. "It would indeed be a blessing if that were my biggest worry in life! Martin, thank you. Now if you'll please excuse me."

The president left the Oval Office. Brian Conway ushered Riker and Thompson to the door. "Karen," said Conway, "I understand your motive. I'm sorry it had to end this way. A Secret Service agent will escort you to your office where you may collect your personal belongings before being seen safely out of the White House. You may remain at the Medical Unit office in the EOB until the Navy has arranged transport for you." He turned to Riker. "Martin, if anyone else approaches you and asserts that the president has AIDS, please notify me immediately. We need to aggressively tamp down any rumors."

Accompanied by a Secret Service agent, Riker and Thompson returned to the office of the Medical Unit. Within a few minutes, Thompson was gone. Riker wished her good luck, but he was not as warm as Conway had been—as far as he was concerned, Thompson was lucky to have kept her license to practice medicine. The necessity for secrecy had worked in her favor. Her departure from the White House would be marked only by a bland press release noting that for personal reasons Capt. Karen Thompson had chosen to return to active duty in the Navy, and that her dedicated service to the president was greatly appreciated.

Dr. Gladstone, having walked over from the EOB, arrived at the Medical Unit. Standing in Thompson's office, he looked around. "Not much space in here for my specimens," he said wistfully. "I suppose I'll have to keep most of them across the street." He turned to Riker. "How's the investigation going—the biological threats?"

"Norm, sit down," said Riker. "I need to brief you on what's going on." He handed Gladstone the president's file, which never left the director's office. "You'll find everything in there. Briefly, though, the president has been diagnosed with AIDS."

"Oh my God," exclaimed Gladstone.

"That's why I'm here. My job is to find out how he got it."

"This is beginning to make sense," said Gladstone as he pored over the file. "For the past few months I've thought something strange was going on. The president has looked like he's got something more serious than food poisoning or the flu. I thought he lost some weight, too. I'm glad that he's gotten a proper diagnosis and is receiving treatment. Who else in this office knows?"

"Dorothy and two nurses—Jennet Swift and John Daughtry," replied Riker.

"A tight group," said Gladstone. "How's your investigation coming? Is there a source?"

Riker reviewed the list of possibilities. The dentist, the trip to Nagoya, and the accident in Kenya had been ruled out.

"Even though he was exposed to HIV by the dentist and in Kenya, he didn't catch the disease from either?" asked Gladstone. With one hand he stroked his white goatee.

"Correct," said Riker. "The investigation has progressed, and we're narrowing our focus to a group of people in the president's inner circle—specifically his girlfriends."

"Girlfriends—plural?"

"Yes."

"So the stories are true," said Gladstone.

Riker smiled. "I can't vouch for which stories you've heard, but yes. The president has led, shall we say, a very active social life behind closed doors."

After studying the file for a few minutes, Gladstone asked, "Who are your top suspects?"

"Our original list of presidential girlfriends contained six names," said Riker. "Rachel Doucette, Gwen Peterson, Kimberly Schuster, Amy Gold,

Regina Quentin, and Jessica Young. Doucette and Schuster have been eliminated. We have Peterson's blood and are awaiting the results. I haven't located Gold yet. As for Quentin and Young, the president said that he's had no contact with them since he left Maryland."

"Any man-to-man sex?" Gladstone asked.

"None that I could turn up from anybody."

"How about casual one-nighters when he's on the road—like in Kenya or Japan?"

"Ditto."

"Okay," said Gladstone. "I'll keep the president healthy. You find out how he got sick."

Riker went into a spare office and sat down at the desk, where he logged onto the secure White House intranet. In a moment he found what he was looking for: the Secret Service security clearance background check on Amy Gold.

The report said that Gold was twenty-seven years old. Her parents were Lionel and Emma Gold, and she had been born in Ocean City, Maryland, where her parents still lived. She had a sister named Wanda and a brother, Frederick. In the report another family name came up—her paternal grandfather was Upton Gold, who had been a Maryland state representative in the nineteen sixties. He was married to the former Penelope Willow.

Armed with this information, Riker logged onto Lineage.com, an Internet service that provided its customers with their ancestry, or as much of it as could be unearthed in a digital search lasting five seconds. Perhaps it would be enough.

Riker opened an account, paid the Globetrotter Level fee of two hundred dollars, and plugged in Amy Gold's family information. A few seconds later, he saw what he wanted.

Closing the page, he picked up his phone.

He called Liberty Associates and asked the receptionist for Amy Gold.

After a pause a voice said, "This is Amy." The cheery voice matched her photo. Riker could practically see her smiling.

Riker introduced himself and said that he was calling from the Medical Unit of the White House.

"Gosh," said Gold. "How can I help you?"

"While I'm calling from the White House," said Riker, "I'm connected with the Centers for Disease Control and Prevention—the CDC, in Atlanta. You've heard of us, I suppose?"

"Yes, I have."

"Good. In partnership with the White House, we're conducting a research project on a very rare genetic disorder that alters the CLP1 gene. Affected children may suffer from seizures, intellectual disability, and delayed or absent mental and motor development. Brain imaging studies of these children show atrophy of the cerebral cortex, cerebellum, and the brain stem."

"That's terrible," said Gold with new concern in her voice. "Are you suggesting that I could be affected by this?"

"No, not at all," said Riker in a reassuring tone. He meant what he said—the odds of Amy Gold having the mutation and passing it along to her unborn children were millions to one.

"I'll tell you why I'm calling you," he continued. "Researchers have uncovered the source of the mutation. Amazingly, this rare brain disorder has its roots in a single mutation in one individual born during the Ottoman Empire in Turkey about sixteen generations ago. Isn't that incredible?"

"But I still don't understand how I'm related to this problem," said Amy with impatience.

"I apologize for not being more clear," said Riker. "Perhaps you're not fully aware of your lineage. The family name of your great-great maternal grandfather was Aydan, a Turkish name common in the modern town in Anatolia. You're at least one-sixteenth Turkish, and possibly more."

"I didn't know that," said Amy.

"Because you're uniquely qualified, I'm hoping that you will agree to come to the White House and help me—and the president—with this vital research project."

"The president is involved?"

"Not directly, of course, but he's keenly interested in the outcome. I believe you've met him, haven't you?"

"Um, yes, I have," said Gold.

"Your company—Liberty Associates—has done fundraising for the president, if I'm not mistaken."

"Yes, we have."

"I remember now," said Riker. "You guys created that amazing event at the estate of Mandy Summer in East Hampton. The president still talks about it. The evening made a favorable impression on him."

Riker did not mention his own detective work: the reason the evening was memorable for the president was that he and Amy Gold had sex in one of the upstairs bedrooms.

"He really remembers it?" said Gold. "I'm so happy to hear that. So— what do you want me to do? How can I help?"

"Oh, it's such a small thing," said Riker smoothly. "I'm sure it seems inconsequential, but it would be very important to our efforts here in the White House."

"Yes—what would it be?"

"We need you to come to the White House, to the office of the Medical Unit, and provide a small blood sample for our research."

There was a pause. Riker held his breath.

"A blood sample?" said Gold. "Sure, I suppose I could do that. Will the president be there?"

"Well, you never know," Riker said cheerily. "He's such a workaholic! I wouldn't be surprised if we ran into him in the hallway."

"When do you want me to come?"

"Our best shot at bumping into the president will be tomorrow morning," said Riker. "How about ten o'clock? Is that good for you?"

"Yes, that would be fine," said Gold.

"Say—have you ever been inside the White House?"

"No, I never have, unless you count a tour I took in elementary school."

"Well then, I'll have to show you around," said Riker. "I'll bet your school tour didn't include the private bowling alley."

"No, it didn't," said Gold. "So you're saying that all I have to do is give a blood sample?"

"Yes, for genetic typing," said Riker. "Strictly for our research into mapping the gene dispersion from the time of your ancestors in Turkey. The president will be very grateful."

Riker told Gold to go to the southwest appointment gate, where he would personally meet her and escort her into the White House. After jotting down her cell phone number, he bade her good evening and ended the call.

Chapter 28

∗   ∗   ∗

As he was getting ready to leave the office, Riker's phone rang. The call was from Gilmore at the CDC.

"Yes, Jim," said Riker.

"We've got the preliminary test results for Gwen Peterson. She has HIV. She doesn't have AIDS yet; she's still in clinical latency. But she could have been carrying the virus for many years."

"She's a media consultant who had access to the White House," said Riker. "The boss told me they had sex once every two weeks. How soon can you do the DNA testing to determine if she's the one who gave it to him?"

"We're putting a rush on it," replied Gilmore. "I'll get back to you over the weekend."

Riker hung up. Gwen Peterson was still on the short list of people who could have given the president AIDS.

The others included Amy Gold, Regina Quentin, Jessica Young, and possibly a girl named Christina Wilkinson.

Riker glanced at his watch. He was due to be at Lindsay's at seven, and he still had to stop for a bottle of wine. He closed up the office, said goodnight to Dorothy, and left the White House.

Outside, the sky had turned heavy and damp. It felt like Washington's brief interlude of clear weather was going to be smothered by more snow. Meanwhile, Riker noted on his weather app, in Naples it was seventy degrees and clear.

After stopping at the liquor store and picking up a bottle of Chardonnay, Riker directed his taxi driver to take him to thirty-six hundred Reservoir Road, in Georgetown.

In the public vestibule of the brick townhouse, next to the oak door that led inside the building, Lindsay's bell was the uppermost of three—apartment C. He pressed the metal button.

"Hello?" came the familiar voice through the scratchy intercom.

"Hey Lindsay, it's me, Martin."

The door buzzed and Riker pushed it open. He found himself in the familiar black-and-white tiled foyer. In front of him was the steep staircase with its ornate carved newel post on the banister. The stairs were covered by the red runner, held in place by brass rods. Overhead was the cast-iron lantern.

He had seen these things before, when Lindsay had invited him upstairs on that first Saturday night. But it had been late, and they had practically run up to her apartment and into her bedroom. In his memory, that visit was a pleasant blur of hurried passionate intimacy and awkward goodbyes. Now he could linger and savor the space of her life.

He went up the stairs to the second floor, and then to the third. There was one door, with a gold "C" painted in the center. He knocked.

Lindsay opened the door. She had changed from her usual grey or blue business skirt and jacket into a pair of jeans and a cotton shirt. Her hair hung loose at her shoulders. "C'mon in," she smiled.

Riker stepped into a spacious living room that smelled like a Caribbean island.

"Is that wonderful aroma from the orchids?" he asked as he tossed his coat on the sofa.

"Yes," replied Lindsay. "Some of them have no scent, but others are quite fragrant."

With his first visit here like a fuzzy dream, Riker didn't remember if he would step into a jungle-like space that had been filled by a compulsive collector, with plants everywhere. Not as bad as someone who owned fifty cats, but still annoying and even creepy. To his relief, the plants—about which Riker knew just a little, mainly a few names and that they came in various colors and shapes—were tucked away in corners or hanging by the front window that overlooked the street. They were lovely but not obtrusive.

"I don't think you saw much of the place last time you were here," said Lindsay as she set the bottle of wine on the low glass coffee table. "Come, I'll give you the official tour." She showed him the kitchen and the dining room before taking him up the cast-iron spiral staircase to the upper floor, which had a bedroom and her office. In the bedroom, with its inviting antique four-poster bed—which was the one aspect of the apartment he remembered vividly—he noted several framed photos of her family, including Lindsay with her three brothers and their mother, who Riker could see was disfigured with crippling arthritis.

There was another photo of an older man with another woman.

"That's my dad and his wife," said Lindsay. "I took that photo last year when I visited them in San Diego."

Riker noticed one more photo, of Lindsay with a man. He was a handsome guy, with dark wavy hair and a square jaw, and they were standing on a boat. To Riker it looked like a forty-foot sailboat.

"You and John, I assume," said Riker. No sense in being coy or beating around the bush.

"Yes," replied Lindsay easily as she picked up the picture in its sleek Lucite frame. "That was last summer, in Bermuda. We went for a week. A friend took us for a ride on his sailboat. We felt like members of the leisure class. Then it was back to reality."

"He's due back soon from—where was it again—Belgium?"

"I thought so," said Lindsay as she replaced the photo on the dressing table. "But with the terrorist bombing this week, he has to stay longer. Another week at least."

"Sorry to hear that."

Lindsay shrugged. "That's the way it is. I thought about flying over there to see him, but I couldn't get away."

Riker thought it was time for the house tour to move along. Perhaps later in the evening the bedroom could be revisited.

"You have a nice place here," he said as they spiraled their way down to the living room. "Just the right size—not too big, not too small."

"Let's head to the kitchen and make some dinner," said Lindsay.

"What have you planned?"

"Very easy preparation—poached salmon, pasta pesto, fresh asparagus, and a salad."

Riker's job was to chop the pickles for the tartar sauce. The work was easy enough—Riker enjoyed cooking—and the glasses of Chardonnay made the task even more pleasant. Riker found himself stealing glances at Lindsay when she was looking elsewhere, and allowing himself to be drawn in by her easy confidence and relaxed demeanor. She was clearly a woman who was comfortable in her own skin, engaged and interested in what Riker had to say, and happy to indulge the occasional rubbing of shoulders or the unforced laying of hand on arm.

Riker glanced out the window.

"Looks like the snow has started," he said.

"Ugh," said Lindsay as she lowered the salmon steaks into the pan of hot lemony water. "It's not even Christmas yet, and I'm sick of winter! This has been a miserable month—at least from the standpoint of the weather."

But as they were making dinner, and Lindsay maintained her cheerful chatter about the weather and orchids and the new exhibit at the National Gallery, Riker suddenly felt crushingly and overwhelmingly alone.

He felt cut off because he could not share with Lindsay the most important thing in his life at that moment, which was his mission to find out how the president had gotten AIDS. Not only that, but he had to actively *lie* about it. She had asked him, as she was cutting the salmon steak into two pieces to slide into the sauté pan, how his investigation into possible biological threats was going. He had replied, blandly, that it was on track, before changing the subject and asking Lindsay about whether she liked the other tenants in her building.

Anything to keep the conversation away from what he really wanted to talk about.

When dinner was ready, instead of carrying their plates into the dining room, Lindsay suggested they eat in the living room, sitting on the carpet, using the low coffee table. They were facing the fireplace, where a log crackled on the andirons.

As they enjoyed their dinner in front of the fire, Riker felt in his gut that Lindsay could be a valuable asset in the investigation. He believed that having only a small circle of people in the White House knowing the truth—the president, the First Lady, Strauss, Conway, Gladstone, the nurses at the Medical Unit—crippled an effective inquiry. The duplicity of Thompson proved it, because the only things that had tripped her up were the statement by Tashi Osaki and the bloody towel, both of which he alone had uncovered. Riker knew that he had gotten lucky on that one, and it probably wouldn't happen again. He needed another set of eyes and ears working for him.

But for Lindsay to be an asset, she had to know what was being investigated, and why. But could he take that step? In a city where everyone was ready to stab the other guy in the back, he had to know that he could trust her.

As dinner was drawing to a close—and the potentially awkward moment of what to do next approached—Riker turned to Lindsay, and, putting his hand lightly on her shoulder, said, "There's something I want to tell you."

"Martin, what is it?" she replied in a concerned tone.

"No—please—it's nothing to worry about," he said as they stood up to carry the dishes into the kitchen. "It's about me. About my work."

"What about your work?" she asked.

Reaching the kitchen, they put the dishes on the counter next to the sink.

"I haven't been straight with you," he said.

"Do I need another glass of wine?" asked Lindsay.

Riker smiled. "I think we're both due for a refill." He took the bottle and topped off their glasses. "I was brought to Washington for a very specific reason. It isn't to do an assessment of biological threats. Lindsay, the president has AIDS."

"You're kidding."

"No, I'm not. I was asked to come to the White House to find out how he got it."

Lindsay sat on one of the bar stools at the counter on the island in the kitchen. "Are you sure? I mean, I suppose that's a really stupid question."

"Not at all. He's had a series of tests. It's confirmed. Last week he began taking medication."

"But how can you find out how he got it? Doesn't AIDS have, like, an incubation period of up to ten years? What was the president doing back then?"

"In most cases, that's true. But roughly five percent of people who get HIV develop AIDS within one or two years. Our evidence indicates that he got infected after he became president."

"But he doesn't engage in—what's the term? Man-to-man sex? And he's surely not shooting up dope in the Oval Office!"

"No, he's not. We did inquire into all possibilities, but those common causes are not on our radar screen now. But there are other ways to get AIDS."

"Who else knows?"

"Very few people. The president has chosen not to release the information. If his medications control his condition, there's no reason why anyone who sees him or interacts with him would recognize his illness. He looks perfectly normal."

"Did the Russians or Chinese give it to him?"

Riker shrugged. "It's possible. We'll know more after we find out how he got it." Riker put his hand on Lindsay's shoulder. "So there you go, kiddo. That's why I'm here. The biological threat project was just a cover. I'm sorry I couldn't tell you."

She placed her hand over his. Her touch was cool and calming. "That's all right. This is Washington. I know you have to do what you have to do." She thought for a moment. "You know something? Max called me a few days ago. He was being very cagey. He asked me if I knew anything about the president's health. I told him what everybody knew—that the president had been sick a lot. Believe me, I notice when the president gets sick, because it makes my job much more difficult. I have to scramble and call a thousand people and reshuffle appointments. Max asked me if I thought the president had AIDS. I said, are you crazy? Then he said that if the president *did* have AIDS, it would be a golden opportunity for public education. I told him he was out of his mind—in a friendly way, of course." Lindsay, with her hand still on Riker's, grew pensive. "Good ol' Max. I'm going to miss him. It's such a tragedy, getting shot in the middle of the sidewalk by some crazy robber."

Riker paused. He had come to another fork in the road of truth.

Riker believed that Mosely had been deliberately assassinated by someone who didn't want him publicizing the president's illness.

But it was just a conjecture. Riker had no proof. The Washington, DC, police were investigating. There was a chance that it really had been a robbery gone bad.

"Yeah, it's a terrible thing," said Riker as he gently moved his hand from Lindsay's shoulder and took hers. She did not pull away.

"Hey, it's been a crazy week," he said. "Why don't we go relax in the living room and find a movie on TV?"

"That sound like a very good idea," she replied as she stood up. Together they went to the big comfy sofa and sat down with their glasses of wine on the low table. Lindsay picked up the remote, turned on the television, and scrolled through the channels. *"Alien Invasion VII,"* she said. "We witness giant spiders attacking Tokyo. No, thank you. *Mob Boss Murder Spree.* Nope. *Jeffrey Dahmer: The Untold Story.* God, no! Oh, here's a good one. *"Nobody But You.* A lighthearted rom-com where two opposites find true love. What do you think?"

"I suppose it's better than giant spiders," smiled Riker. If he were to be completely honest, as long as Lindsay were next to him, he couldn't care less what they watched.

As the opening credits rolled, Riker and Lindsay settled into the cozy embrace of the sofa. They watched as the two protagonists—the young man, a stiff Wall Street type, and the young woman, a free-spirited artist with a tiny studio in Brooklyn—accidentally bumped into each other on the subway.

By the time the screen couple had their first argument, Lindsay had settled her head on Riker's shoulder and was playing with the fingers of his hand.

A few scenes later, when the screen couple kissed, so did Riker and Lindsay.

Long before the screen couple found themselves in her bedroom, Riker and Lindsay had already made their move upstairs.

Later, with the snow continuing to fall outside the bedroom window, as Lindsay lay next to Riker in the messy pile of covers and pillows, she asked, "What do you think happened in the movie?"

"I suppose they both lived happily ever after," said Riker as he gave her a kiss on the forehead. "If you want, we can go online and read the plot summary."

"No, I'd rather not know," she said. "I'll imagine the ending I want."

Riker glanced at the clock next to Lindsay's bed. Ten forty-five. He had assumed the time was much later. It was nice to be comfortable, with hours ahead to relax and put aside the cares of the crazy world. With his arm around Lindsay, inhaling the aroma of her hair, Riker closed his eyes.

Chapter 29

*   *   *

Lying comfortably next to Lindsay, Riker heard his phone ring. It was on the carpeted floor, next to the bed.

Trying not to jostle her, he shifted near the side of the bed and looked down.

The caller ID said that it was the Washington, DC, police.

What the hell? Why were they calling him?

"What is it?" mumbled Lindsay in her sleepiness.

"I'm sure it's nothing," replied Riker as he reached down and picked up the phone.

"Riker here."

"This is Detective Forsythe. You asked me to call you if anything came up in the Mosely murder investigation. Well, something's come up. I want you to go to the MedStar Hospital on Irving Street."

"What's going on?" said Riker.

"We've got a guy who's talking, but he may not last long. Come to intensive care and ask for me."

He hung up.

Riker turned to Lindsay. "Sweetheart," he said tenderly, "that was the detective working Max's case. He wants me to go to the hospital right now. I'm really sorry. I've got to go."

Lindsay sat up. "It's about Max?"

"Yes," replied Riker. "I asked Detective Forsythe to call me if anything broke. He wants me to go to MedStar."

"I'll drive you," said Lindsay as she wrapped the sheet around her torso and swung her legs over the edge of the bed.

"No, really, I'll get a car—"

"Martin, don't be silly. It may be a very long night. I'm happy to do it. Don't argue. Just give me a minute to wash my face and brush my teeth."

Riker sat on the bed and watched her dart into the bathroom.

I'll bet she'll be in there for twenty minutes, he thought. *Why did I agree to this?*

To his amazement she reappeared not more than a moment later.

"It's your turn," she said as she pulled on her jeans. "Come on, what are you waiting for?"

After splashing some water on his face, Riker quickly dressed.

Together they hurried down the stairs and out the front door.

The snow was swirling in the streetlights as Lindsay drove south down Wisconsin Ave. NW, east across K St. NW, and back north up 6th St. NW. "It's lovely that all roads around the Capitol lead to the White House," she said as she beat a yellow light. "But it makes going across town a chore."

She pulled up at the entrance to the emergency room. "You go in and find the detective. I'll park the car. Don't worry about me. Call me when you're done."

Riker bolted from the car and hurried into the hospital. He soon found Detective Forsythe in the hallway outside of a room on the intensive care floor.

"Dr. Riker, thanks for coming on such short notice," said Forsythe. "Our guy may not last long."

"Who is he?" said Riker as Forsythe opened the door to the room.

"Name's Tommy Bardwell. For a couple of years, we've suspected him of being a hired gun. We've linked him to three other shootings. The victims all had some involvement with gang activity."

Riker saw a man in his twenties lying on the bed. From the web of intravenous lines, feeding tubes, nasogastric tubes, suction pumps, drains, and catheters jammed into his body, Riker knew he was in very bad shape. His eyes were closed and his breathing was labored. Riker glanced at the cardiac monitor. At least the guy's heart was still beating.

"What happened?" asked Riker.

"We found him lying on the sidewalk, drilled full of holes, just like Max Mosely. The difference is that under his jacket Mr. Bardwell was wearing a soft Kevlar vest. It stopped most of the bullets. But he was shot at close range with an AR-15. No soft vest is going to save you from that kind of punishment—you need ballistic plates in it. The doctors say Bardwell's gonna become a ghost any minute."

"Has he said anything?"

"Nothing that makes any sense."

"So why did you call me?"

"I'll tell you why. I was investigating the Mosely case. We discovered that a bystander had taken a cell phone video. The license plate of the car was captured in the video. We traced the vehicle to a guy named Rudy Rostum. He's a known associate of Bardwell. We were too late to grab Rostum. Early this evening we found him shot to death in his car. As we expected, Bardwell's prints were inside the car, on the passenger side. We were looking for Bardwell when we got the call of a shooting in Columbia Heights."

"The finger of death found him first," said Riker.

"We rushed him here but it doesn't look good."

"Let me talk to him," said Riker.

"Sure. Maybe you can figure out what he's mumbling."

Under the watchful eye of the attending nurse, Riker and Forsythe approached the bed.

"Tommy Bardwell, my name's Martin Riker. I'm a doctor."

Bardwell's eyes flickered open. Under heavy lids, he turned them in Riker's direction.

"So?" he whispered.

"I work at the White House. I know you shot Max Mosely."

Bardwell's eyebrow gave a little shrug.

"I think the same people who hired you and Rudy for the Mosely job wanted to get rid of you. They got Rudy. He's dead. They didn't get rid of you. At least not yet. You can pay them back, but only if you talk to me. Tell me who hired you to kill Max Mosely."

"I dunno," muttered Bardwell.

"You never saw him?"

"We spoke on the phone. The money was sent to me by FedEx. Cash."

"He never told you who he was?"

"No."

"What did he say exactly?" asked Riker.

"He said, 'Dommy, I heard you can do difficult work. I've got some for you.'" Bardwell smiled, which made him wince. He coughed and struggled to breathe. "The guy sounded like he was punch drunk. Kept calling me 'Dommy.'"

"How did he shoot you? How did it happen?"

"He was supposed to pay me the balance. He called and said he wanted to do it in person. He pulled up, got out of his car, and started shooting. That's all I remember."

"You didn't see his face?"

"Nah. It was dark."

"The car?"

"Just an ordinary black sedan."

Bardwell coughed again, and gasped for air. The nurse said, "You'll have to leave," as she set up a ventilator.

Riker and Forsythe went out into the hallway.

"The man you want to investigate is named Brian Conway," said Riker.

"Who's that?"

"He's the deputy chief of staff of the president of the United States."

"Are you crazy?"

"Bardwell's description of the speech pattern of the guy who hired him matches Conway's exactly. He can't pronounce the 't' sound, so he makes it a 'd' sound instead. When he said 'Tommy,' it came out as 'Dommy.' Conway also happens to be a very tough guy who will do anything to protect the president, even if his efforts are tragically misguided."

"Protect the president from what?"

"An imagined threat. Tomorrow, get an arrest warrant. We're going to his house to pick him up. He lives in Georgetown."

Riker left Forsythe and went down to the central waiting room. There he found Lindsay, sitting and reading a dog-eared copy of *People* magazine.

"What happened?" she said as she put aside the magazine.

"We shouldn't discuss it here," replied Riker. "Let's go to the car."

They walked to the garage, and a few minutes later Lindsay pulled out onto Irving St. NW. She turned on her wipers to clear the flakes of snow as they fell.

"I just talked to the guy who killed Max," said Riker. "Tommy Bardwell was hired by a man he saw only once, a few hours ago, when the guy shot him. But the guy talked to Bardwell on the phone several times. Based on the description of the guy's voice, it had to be Brian Conway."

"Oh, my God," said Lindsay. "Why?"

"I think Conway took it upon himself to silence Max. Conway was being hypervigilant. He believed that if Max publicized the president's illness, the response would be totally negative and might even bring down his presidency."

"I've often worried about some of the people that the president has surrounded himself with," said Lindsay. "He brought some of these guys, like Don and Brian, with him from Baltimore. Just between you and me, they're basically just hoodlums who cleaned themselves up and started wearing more expensive suits and ties. But in their hearts they're still on the street corners and the docks, cracking heads. I can believe that Brian would do something like this. He always hated Max, and I think he figured it was time to take action."

"Hated him because he was gay?"

"No. Brian hated Max because Max enjoyed life. He was always the life of the party. Wherever he went, people loved him. Brian's a miserable human being. Angry. Ready to lash out. I never got along very well with him. I suppose the president keeps him around because he's unflinching and decisive, which can be very good qualities to have."

"Until you unflinchingly decide to do something terrible," said Riker.

They arrived at Lindsay's apartment. As she parked the car, she turned to Riker. "I'm sorry—I wasn't thinking. Perhaps you wanted to go back to your hotel? I know it's late and maybe you just want to be in your own place."

"Are you saying that I would choose a cold and impersonal hotel room over your lovely and comfortable apartment?"

"I suppose not—"

"Are you inviting me in?"

"Yes, I am. But no monkey business. I have to get up early tomorrow."

"Yes, ma'am," said Riker. "Absolutely no business, monkey or otherwise. To be honest, I'm exhausted. I'm not going to be good for much else other than going to sleep. And tomorrow is going to be a very eventful day."

They got out of the car and went upstairs. Intermingled with the scent of orchids, Lindsay's apartment had the delicious lingering aroma of the dinner they had cooked. Riker glanced at the kitchen clock. It was after midnight.

His phone rang. It was Detective Forsythe.

"Bardwell just died," he said. "Based on his dying declaration, we're getting a warrant for the arrest of Brian Conway. We're going to pick him up tomorrow afternoon. I'll let you know the exact time."

"Okay, thanks," said Riker.

Riker and Lindsay went upstairs to bed. Snuggled under the covers, with the snow swirling outside and Lindsay's head resting on his shoulder, Riker was more awake than he thought he'd be.

"Are you *sure* about no monkey business?" he whispered. He gave her bare back a gentle rub.

"Go to sleep," she said. "Tomorrow's another day."

Chapter 30

*   *   *

R iker and Lindsay awoke at dawn, although they wouldn't have known it by looking outside. The overcast sky blotted out the low-lying sun, and flurries danced in the air. It was a grey, dull morning.

Hot coffee, scrambled eggs, and toast with raspberry jam cheered them. Lindsay told Riker that she had to drive out to Woodbridge to visit an assisted living facility. Her mother, who required increasing amounts of care, couldn't live with her brother Donny for much longer, and they had to face the facts that it was time for Mom to move.

Riker had his own appointment, at the White House, with Amy Gold.

"I'll drop you off," Lindsay volunteered.

Saturday morning traffic was light, and Lindsay pulled up to the southwest appointment gate at fifteen minutes before ten. "Take care of yourself," she said as she kissed him.

"You too," he replied. "Drive carefully."

After reminding the Secret Service agent at the gate that he was expecting Amy Gold at ten, Riker entered the White House and went to the office of the Medical Unit. After reading some files for a few minutes, he got the buzz from the Secret Service at the gate. Amy Gold had arrived.

Riker left the office and went back out to the Diplomatic Reception room. He waited by the outside door. A moment later a Secret Service agent walked up the steps. He was accompanied by a woman. They came to the door.

"Dr. Riker," said the agent, "this is Amy Gold."

"Thanks—I'll take her from here," said Riker.

The agent turned and walked back through the drifting flurries to the gate.

"Thanks for coming," said Riker to Gold. "Please come in."

Gold stepped across the threshold. She was slender, with short dark hair framing her strikingly pale face. The contrast was heightened by her red lipstick and the heavy eyeliner circling her almond eyes, giving her the appearance of an actress appearing as Sally Bowles in a production of *Cabaret*.

"Is this your first time here?" asked Riker.

"In this part of the house, yes," she said as she gazed in wonderment at the "Views of North America" wallpaper that had been installed in 1961 by Jacqueline Kennedy. "I was here about a year ago for a concert in the East Room that my company helped to produce. But I couldn't go anywhere else—I, and the people I was with, were restricted to the East Room. We couldn't wander beyond the approved area."

"Did you happen to see the president at the event?" asked Riker.

"Yes," she replied. "I saw him enter and sit with Mrs. Ralston, but of course I didn't speak with them."

"Didn't you guys produce the big Mandy Summer benefit event this past June?" asked Riker casually.

"Yes, that was one of ours," said Gold. "But I didn't see the president," she added quickly. "I was working too hard, supervising the catering and the entertainment."

"Yes, of course," replied Riker. "I'm sure it was a very busy night."

Riker steered her into the Medical Unit. "This is where the president receives his medical care," said Riker as he led her into an examination room. "We also provide services to the White House staff and visitors."

"So if a guest at an East Room event twisted their ankle or got ill, you guys would take care of them?"

"That's right," said Riker. "Now if you'll just roll up your sleeve, we'll get the business part of your visit concluded and you can have your private tour."

"Oh—okay," said Gold uncertainly. "I hope it won't hurt."

"It'll be over before you know it," replied Riker.

After asking her to lie down on the reclining couch, Riker applied the tourniquet, swabbed her arm, and expertly inserted the needle into her median cubital vein. After filling three small vials he released the tourniquet and removed the needle.

He placed a piece of gauze over the site and asked Gold to hold it firmly in place. Then he taped it.

"All done," he said. "Wasn't that easy?"

While Gold arranged the sleeve of her blouse, Riker picked up the phone and called the chief usher of the White House, who had his office in what was called the Clock Room, on the mezzanine level adjacent to the Entrance Hall on the north side of the building.

"We're ready," said Riker. Hanging up, he turned to Gold. "Your personal guide will be here in a moment."

"Oh," said Gold. "I thought you were giving me my tour."

Riker smiled. "You don't want me! You want someone who really knows the building. Trust me, it will be a treat."

A moment later Jerome Sydney came into the office. After introducing himself to Gold, they turned to leave.

"Be sure to show her the old swimming pool under the Press Briefing Room," said Riker.

Sydney nodded. The swimming pool had been built in 1933 for President Roosevelt; in 1970 President Nixon covered it with a wooden top, which formed the floor of the new Press Briefing Room. If you've seen the old swimming pool, you can say that you've gotten a real insider's tour of the White House.

With Gold on her way, Riker packaged her blood samples and arranged for them to be FedExed to the CDC.

He called Gilmore.

"I'm sending you another sample," said Riker. "The name is Amy Gold."

"I'll look for it," said Gilmore. "You called at a good time. I have some results for you. Gwen Peterson is not the person who gave the president AIDS. Our DNA tests have confirmed it. You can cross her off your list."

"Okay, thanks," said Riker.

He sat down at his desk. His list of possible sources was getting smaller.

1. Amy Gold, the fundraiser. Her blood was on its way to the CDC for analysis.

2. Regina Quentin, the former Miss Maryland.

3. Jessica Young, the Maryland State House intern.

4. And possibly someone named Christina Wilkinson.

Riker went to Wikipedia and pulled up the page about the Miss Maryland competition, which was affiliated with the Miss America scholarship pageant. Every winner since 1933 was listed. Riker found Regina Quentin. Her hometown was Madison and she had been Miss Allegheny County. For the talent portion of the competition she had sung "A Change in Me" from the musical *Beauty and the Beast*. Riker clicked on her name. The link took him to a page that said, "Wikipedia does not have an article with this exact name."

After not winning the Miss America pageant, it seemed that Regina Quentin had done nothing to warrant having her own Wikipedia page.

Riker learned that her hometown of Madison was an unincorporated community in Dorchester County, at the south end of Madison Bay, an arm of the Little Choptank River and part of the Chesapeake Bay estuary system.

In the most recent census, the population was two hundred and four souls.

Not exactly a place where someone could hide.

He did an image search for Regina Quentin, Miss Maryland. In a few minutes he had pulled up a page of photos of a tall blonde wearing a variety of outfits—a formal evening gown in jade green, a red dress, and a yellow dress. Most of the photos, however, showed her posing in a hot pink bikini and four-inch heels. She had won the swimsuit portion of the Miss America contest. Riker supposed that having won the swimsuit title, to lose the grand prize she must have been a lousy singer, or she had botched her "how I'd save the world" question.

Riker found photos of Quentin in what looked like a series of low-budget movies that had been made during the two years after the Miss America pageant. Quentin had gotten a few roles, all of which had capitalized on her physical assets: the sexy lifeguard, the sexy babysitter, the sexy schoolteacher. Riker had never heard of any of the movies; they had all gone straight to cable.

Riker picked up the phone and called an old friend of his who worked at the Screen Actors Guild. In a few minutes he had learned that Regina Quentin had let her union membership lapse. Her current address was in the file—2351 West Orange Street in Annapolis.

Another search revealed this was the home of Regina and Garner Hosbrook. He was an executive with a firm called Ascendant Technologies that supplied radar technology to the Navy. They had two children.

It appeared that Regina Quentin had chosen to step away from her career in the spotlight and devote herself to her family.

Could she have HIV?

Possibly. She might still be in clinical latency. The speed with which HIV progressed to full-blown AIDS depended as much upon the victim as the strain of the virus.

This was because in the presence of any infective agent, the body can respond in two fundamental ways: it can either *tolerate* the pathogen or actively *resist* it.

Riker always thought it strange that if the body *tolerates* the pathogen—in essence, lives with it instead of mounting an all-out attack against it—the disease it causes tends to progress very slowly. Sort of a biological détente, or *modus vivendi*—he loved those terms.

By contrast, in people with low disease tolerance, the body is resisting. It's in a constant state of high alert, churning out antibodies and defensive T-cells, including CD4 T-cells, in response to the pathogen. This counterattack by the body, instead of helping, can actually cause the infection to get worse, faster.

Riker made a note that Regina Quentin was still on the list of possible candidates.

Next was Jessica Young, the intern at the Maryland State House while Paul Ralston was governor.

A quick search revealed a photo of a visit to the State House by the Fredericksburg Chamber of Commerce. A bunch of politicians were posing with members of the visiting group, and the caption included, "Jessica Young, intern." The photo showed a college-aged woman with a heap of dark curly hair, pronounced cheekbones, and a confident smile. More searching revealed that while an intern, Young had been pursuing her graduate degree in political science at Loyola University. Had she gone on to a career in politics? Indeed she had, because the very same Jessica Young had recently become a member of the Maryland House of Delegates from a district in Prince George's County. She lived in Piscataway, only a short distance from Andrews Air Force Base and no more than twenty miles south of Capitol Hill.

Further digging revealed that Jessica Young had co-sponsored a bill into the Maryland House requiring health insurers to offer fertility treatments as a benefit, regardless of a person's sexual orientation. The governor had neither signed nor vetoed the bill, and it had become law.

Her home address was a condominium at 965 Wedgewood Drive. A quick search of the Prince George's County real estate records indicated the condo had been bought a few years earlier by Dawn Slattery and Jessica Young.

Dawn Slattery was a physical education instructor at a local gym. She was also a blogger who wrote about LGBT issues.

Was Jessica Young a lesbian, and therefore a highly unlikely partner for Paul Ralston?

Or was she bisexual?

And could she have HIV?

The answers to the last two questions were both "possibly." There was simply no way for Riker to be certain.

A knock on the door interrupted his research. Jerome Sydney and Amy Gold had returned from her tour. With as little chitchat as possible—Gold floated the idea of her staying for lunch at the Navy Mess, which Riker politely deflected—Riker escorted Gold to the door of the Diplomatic Reception Room, where he handed her off to the Secret Service agent.

As he was walking back to his office, his phone buzzed. It was Forsythe. He picked up the call.

"Riker, we're ready to serve our arrest warrant. The address is 1099 Dumbarton St. NW in Georgetown. We're assembling at the Second District Station in half an hour."

Chapter 31

*　　*　　*

Riker turned around and hurried to the southwest gate. He flagged a taxi to take him to The Jefferson Hotel. While the cab waited he went to his room and strapped on his Glock. Then he returned to the cab and told the driver to take him to the police station on Idaho Ave. NW.

In the squad room, he found a handful of officers milling about. Then Detective Forsythe entered. In his rumpled suit and with his mop of uncombed hair, he looked like he had just rolled out of bed. But his eyes were sharp and he spoke quickly and confidently to the uniformed officer who had accompanied him into the room.

Forsythe called the group to order. He announced the name and address of the person named in the arrest warrant. "The suspect is married with no children," said Forsythe. "We don't know the present location of the wife."

An officer raised his hand. "Is this the same Brian Conway who is the deputy chief of staff to the president?"

"It is," replied Forsythe.

"Sir," said another officer, "wouldn't a high profile individual such as this normally arrange with his lawyer to turn himself in?"

"Normally, yes," replied Forsythe. "But Mr. Conway is accused of a double homicide and of ordering the execution of a third. Therefore, he's considered armed and dangerous. He has not yet been informed of the charges against him."

Not unless someone from the court or the police department tipped him off, thought Riker.

After a review of the street where Conway lived and a look at the Google photo of the front of Conway's house, the group moved out.

Riker rode with Forsythe.

Ten minutes later, five police cars silently pulled up in front of 1099 Dumbarton St. NW. Unlike many of the residences on the street, which were connected wood-frame townhouses, number 1099 was a free-standing house of brick, painted pale grey. At the street level, on the right side, was a door, painted black. To its left, in the center of the façade, was a window. On the far left was another door, painted the same buttery white as the house trim; but this door was blocked by the low cast-iron fence. Riker surmised this had once been a two-family house with two entrances, which had then been combined into one.

Above the street level was a second floor, with three windows across. There was a third floor, with a row of three smaller, square windows. Above these windows was an ornate cornice. The roof, like most in the neighborhood, appeared to be either flat or with a shallow slope.

A car was parked in front of the house. Forsythe nodded in its direction. "That's Mr. Conway's car. He's at home."

To the right of the house was an alley paved in brick, just wide enough for a compact car to drive through. At the end of the alley, as if it had pulled around the corner of the house, Riker could see the tail end of a sports car.

Forsythe sent two uniformed officers down the alley to cover the back of the house.

The house appeared to be quiet. The blinds on the first two floors were drawn, but that was normal for a house on a narrow residential street.

With uniformed officers backing them up on the street, Forsythe and Riker approached the front door. Forsythe knocked. "Mr. Conway! Metro police! Open the door!"

The house was silent.

"Brian Conway!" called Forsythe as he knocked again.

Suddenly a gunshot rang out from inside the house. The clerestory window over the front door shattered, showering them with shards of glass.

"Get back!" shouted Forsythe. "He's shooting!"

Riker and Forsythe retreated behind a cruiser.

Hunkered on the pavement, Forsythe got on his radio.

"Active shooter. Ten ninety-nine Dumbarton Street Northwest. Suspect's name is Brian Conway. He's inside his house."

"Is there anyone else in the house?" asked the dispatcher.

"We don't know," replied Forsythe.

Seconds passed. There was no sound except the faint wail of sirens, which grew steadily louder as cops swarmed towards the scene.

Minutes passed. There had been no further shooting from the house. The blinds were still drawn. The bits of glass on the front steps glinted in the sun, like an offering to the gods of violence. Riker and Forsythe waited, kneeling in the street behind the cruiser. Civilians—the curious, the concerned, and those hoping to see someone get shot—were beginning to crowd the barricades that had been set up by the police at the end of the block. Officers had gone into the neighboring buildings and evacuated the residents.

"We need to get this guy on the phone," said Riker.

"We're working on it," replied Forsythe.

The sky, which had been low and heavy all morning, was now pelting them with sharp, stinging flakes. The street was beginning to glisten and snow was collecting in the empty window boxes of the pale grey house.

Forsythe's phone rang. He answered it and listened. Handing the phone to Riker, he said, "Conway wants to talk to you."

Riker took the phone. He held it far enough away from his head so that Forsythe could hear what Conway said.

"Brian, this is Martin Riker. Are you all right?"

"Yes," came the sullen voice.

"Is anyone in the house with you?"

"Yes."

A chill went up Riker's spine. It was bad enough having a desperate, armed man holed up in his own house. If he had a hostage, it would compound the problem and jack up the level of risk.

"Who's in the house?" asked Riker.

"My wife."

"Can I talk to her? I just want to make sure she's okay."

Riker heard Conway say, "Tell them you're all right."

A woman in the distance said, "I'm fine. I'm fine."

"Mrs. Conway?" asked Riker.

Conway came back on the phone. "I told you, she's fine."

Riker turned to Forsythe and whispered, "What's the wife's first name?"

After making a quick call, Forsythe replied, "Linda."

"Brian, you haven't hurt anyone yet," said Riker. "The shot you fired didn't hit anyone. We can resolve this peacefully. Please let Linda come out. I'm sure she doesn't want to be a part of this. Let her come out and we can talk about how we can help you."

"No," replied Conway. "She's my insurance. If I let her go, you guys will terminate me in a second. I know how it works."

"How what works, Brian?" asked Riker. "We're just a group of people who want this problem to be peacefully resolved."

There was a period of silence, during which muffled voices could be heard on the other end of the line. Riker strained to hear what was going on. It sounded like Conway was talking to Linda.

"I want to talk to the president," said Conway suddenly.

"The president?" replied Riker. "How do you think the president will be able to help you?"

"I want to tell him why I did what I did. I *had* to do it."

"Do what, Brian?"

"Don't jerk me around, Riker. You know what I'm talking about."

Suddenly Riker knew he had a complicated problem on his hands. Brian Conway knew the president had AIDS. The reason Conway had hired Bardwell and Rostum to kill Mosely was to keep Mosely from publicizing the president's illness. Then Conway had killed Bardwell and Rostum to ensure they would never turn on him.

And now Conway was cornered in his own house, with his wife as hostage.

Would he start confessing why he had committed his crimes?

Would he announce—deliberately or inadvertently—that the president had AIDS?

"What's Conway talking about?" whispered Forsythe. "What does he mean?"

Riker turned to Forsythe. "Conway thinks that there's a plot against the president. It's a sad delusion."

"Are you there, Riker?" demanded Conway.

"Yes, I'm here," replied Riker. "Brian, I'm sure the president will be happy to see you once this situation is resolved. You and he have a long history, don't you? Didn't you start working for Mr. Ralston before he was elected governor?"

"Sure, we go way back," muttered Conway. "We banged a lot of chicks together, he and I."

"What the hell did he just say?" asked Forsythe. "Something about banging chicks?"

Riker waved Forsythe away. "I don't know what he's talking about," he whispered.

"I guess the chickens have come home to roost," continued Conway. "All that crazy stuff caught up with him. Hey, maybe I should get tested? Maybe *all* of us should get tested."

"Listen to me, Brian," said Riker. "Let's stay focused on how we're going to resolve this situation, okay? All that other stuff can come later. Like I said, I'm sure the president will be happy to speak to you after you let Linda come out, and after you put down your weapon. Doesn't that sound fair? What do you say?"

"No way," replied Conway. "I know how these things end. You're not going to let me get out of here. Not alive, anyway."

"Brian, that's not true," said Riker. "We don't want anyone to get hurt, including you."

"Say, are we on television?" asked Conway.

"No," replied Riker. "You know as well as I do that we're well within the Air Defense Identification Zone around the capital. There will be no news helicopters streaming live video of this situation. This is just between us."

Suddenly Conway said, "I'll call you back." He hung up.

"Damn!" said Riker.

"What was Conway getting at?" asked Forsythe. "Was he revealing his motive? What was he saying about getting tested?"

"I think he was just ranting," replied Riker. "He's obviously mentally unstable."

As the snow swirled around them, they waited.

"I think we need to send in a team to get him," said Forsythe. "The longer this drags on, the greater chance of Conway harming his wife."

"What's your plan?"

"Our infrared cameras are giving us indications of the heat from two individuals in a room on the second floor in the rear. It's probably a bedroom or an office. We can fire a stun grenade through the window and rush the house."

"You may kill Linda Conway in the process," replied Riker.

Forsythe's phone rang. He answered it. "He's back," he said as he handed Riker the phone.

"Brian—what happened?" asked Riker.

"Just taking a break," replied Conway. "Have you talked to the president?"

"I'm surprised you can't just call him yourself," answered Riker. "You're his deputy chief of staff! I'm sure you've got his direct number, right?"

"When he's in the White House, he doesn't carry a phone," said Conway. "I need you to make the connection."

"Like I said, I'm sure he'll be happy to meet with you after this has been resolved," said Riker.

"I think you're just jerking me around!" shouted Conway. "The president hasn't said a damn thing to you!"

"Brian, really—" said Riker.

The phone went dead.

"We need to move in," said Forsythe. "I'll tell the SWAT team to get ready to throw in a stun grenade and tear gas."

As his command filtered through the ranks, the street became eerily quiet. The only sound was the soft pitter of snowflakes hitting the hood of the police cruiser.

From within the house came the pop of a single gunshot.

It was followed by a woman's scream.

"Get in!" shouted Forsythe. "Get in now!"

The muffled blast of a stun grenade was followed by the splintering sound of a battering ram smashing into the front door.

Riker took his time following the SWAT team into the house. He knew what they were going to find.

Linda Conway, dazed but uninjured, was led out of the house by the victim recovery team.

In the second floor office, the body of Brian Conway lay sprawled on the desk. A crimson pool oozed across the green baize blotter. On the floor next to him was a thirty-eight-caliber revolver. He had died from a single gunshot wound to the head.

Chapter 32

* * *

From the street in front of the house, Riker called Don Strauss and told him the news.

"The president is attending a luncheon meeting with members of the Organization of American States," said Strauss. "I'll update him when he returns to the Oval Office. He was planning on going to Camp David for the rest of the weekend, but he may have to scratch that. This is a very tough situation. We need to work with the press office to formulate our response. Martin, to your knowledge did Brian make a statement before he died?"

"Only some inferences that could be interpreted as the utterances of a man who had cracked under pressure. Nothing specific."

"Why did you and the Metro police go to his house?"

"We wanted to question him about the deaths of Max Mosely and the two guys who the police suspect killed Max. When we knocked on his door, he fired a shot through the window at us. During the negotiating process, he put the pistol to his head. His wife saw him do it."

"Did the police fire their weapons?"

"Not a single shot. They acted with great restraint."

"Okay, thanks. I'll be in touch."

As Forsythe approached him, Riker put away his phone. "Can I give you a lift?" said the detective.

"If you're going past the Ten-Fifty, I'd be happy to get a ride."

"No problem," replied Forsythe.

Twenty minutes later, Riker sat at his desk. It was Saturday, and the building was quiet. Soon the Conway story would be exploding across the electronic media, and Riker was curious to see how the White House would spin it.

Riker turned on his television. Sure enough, CNN had a camera crew at Dumbarton St. NW, at the end of the block, a few houses down from the Conway residence. The reporter was announcing the mysterious suicide of Brian Conway, deputy chief of staff to the president of the United States, which had happened shortly after the Metro police had knocked on his door to conduct what was described as a "routine" interview about the murder of White House staffer Max Mosely.

Riker smiled as the CNN reporter dutifully reported that White House sources had told CNN that Mr. Conway had been having "mental health issues."

The White House spin machine was swinging into action.

Riker glanced at his phone. He had missed a call. He scrolled to the list. The call had come during the standoff. It was from Norm Gladstone.

I wonder what he wants. mused Riker as he tapped the return call icon.

Gladstone answered. "Martin, thanks for calling me back," he said.

Riker asked if he had called about Brian Conway.

"No," replied Gladstone, "but I'm aware of what happened. I'm following it on the news. I heard the rumors about Brian being unstable. I hope to God the folks in the West Wing don't ask me to say anything about that."

"Because he wasn't unstable?"

"Overzealous, yes; unstable, no. But that's not why I called you. I ran across an issue here in the Medical Office that I thought you should be aware of. As part of my review of the operations the Medical Unit—after all, I'm the guy in charge now—I'm looking at our drug procurement policies and procedures. I want to make sure I follow office protocol and don't screw up. I've noticed that during the president's first year in office, we requisitioned a steady supply of Percocet. We were getting five-milligram tablets at the rate of fifty a week. The problem is that I can't find any record of them being dispensed to any patient. And I've looked high and low, and can't find them in our locked med cabinet or anywhere else."

"No pills, no trace?"

"None."

"Has the ordering of Percocet stopped?"

"Yes. It stopped when Karen Thompson came in."

"Do you mean when Westlake left?"

"You could put it that way. I know what you're thinking. I know Ethan personally. The guy's stone cold sober. Doesn't drink, doesn't smoke. I've never seen him at anything less than top form. If someone was skimming dope from the Medical Unit, it wasn't him. Fifty pills a week is a significant addiction."

"If it were one person," said Riker. "But someone could have been selling them."

"A pill pusher working out of the White House? Can you imagine the media sinking their fangs into a story like that?"

"No, I don't want to imagine it," said Riker. "Thanks for the information, Norm. I'll look into it. Have a good day."

Riker ended the call and sat back in his chair. This pill-stealing caper wasn't really his concern, and whoever was doing it had probably left the White House with Westlake. Riker had bigger problems to worry about, particularly his number one priority, which was finding out how the president had gotten AIDS.

Still, it was worth a few minutes of his time. More out of curiosity than anything else, he pulled up the roster of the Medical Unit during the president's first year in office. He scanned the names.

One name was familiar: Christina Wilkinson. She had been the nurse who had given the president his B-12 shots. The president had remembered her as someone who had stuck him with the needle as if she were St. George slaying the dragon.

There had also been a Christina Wilkinson who had visited the clinic in the Band Building.

Riker reviewed his list of suspects.

Amy Gold, the fundraiser. Her blood was on its way to the CDC for analysis.

Regina Quentin, the former Miss Maryland, and Jessica Young, the Maryland State House intern. They were unknowns.

Christina Wilkinson was not someone who had been identified as having sex with President Ralston, either before or after he came to the White House. But could she have been the same Christina Wilkinson who had visited the clinic?

Riker saw on his staff list that John Daughtry had served in the Medical Unit during the president's first term. He picked up his phone.

Half an hour later, Riker walked into a Three Guys Burger restaurant on Virginia Ave. NW. He found Daughtry sitting in a booth in a corner, away from the entrance.

"Thanks for agreeing to have lunch," said Riker as he sat down. "I hope you can help me with something."

"Is it about Max?" asked Daughtry.

"Actually, no."

"I've heard talk that Brian went rogue," said Daughtry. "He was the guy who set up Max. Is that right?"

"That's one very strong theory," said Riker carefully.

"The stupid bastard," replied Daughtry. "It's amazing what people will do when confronted with something unknown. They immediately classify it as a threat. They shoot first and ask questions later. It's a sad business. I'm sorry that he took his own life, but he did a terrible thing."

They paused while the server took their orders—a Chili Burger Supreme for Daughtry and Mexican Cheddar Burger for Riker.

After the server had returned with two beers and then left them alone again, Daughtry said, "You said you didn't come here to talk about Max."

"That's right. I'd like to ask you about some of the boss's girlfriends. Do you know anything about Regina Quentin?"

"Miss Maryland? She was before my time."

"Jessica Young?"

"Likewise. By the time I got to the Medical Unit, they were both history. I heard their names from Stephen Howe, but I never met them."

"Christina Wilkinson?"

"Yeah—everyone called her Tina," said Daughtry. "She came to the Medical Unit when I did, at the beginning of the boss's first term. She lasted a year. When Thompson came in, she left."

"Did Thompson get rid of her?"

Daughtry thought for a moment. "Come to think of it, Tina left while Ethan Westlake was still in charge. I was on vacation. It was over New Year's, and I went to Cancun with some friends. I was there for two weeks. I came back sometime around the tenth of January. When I walked into the Medical Office, she wasn't there, and Ethan was looking to hire a replacement. I asked him what had happened, but he just said that she was no longer employed there. So I asked around and got the story. It seems that her boyfriend had tried to visit her at the White House, and was stopped by the Secret Service. He made some sort of disturbance out at the gate, and then he tried to jump the fence. The stupid idiot is lucky he didn't get shot."

"But Christina was involved?"

"I guess he had called her on her cell phone. During the ruckus she went outside and stood on the South Portico. Then she went back inside. Within the hour, she was gone. Ethan had fired her on the spot."

"I don't blame him," said Riker. "The last thing a guy like Ethan Westlake wants is unprofessional behavior on his watch."

After lunch, Riker returned to the Ten-Fifty. He called Frank Foster.

"There was an incident last year at the gate," said Riker. "First week of January. A man claiming to be the boyfriend of a White House nurse tried to force his way in?"

"I remember that guy," replied Foster. "His name was Benny something... Benny Sparks. He came to the southwest appointment gate and said he needed to see someone in the Medical Office. He seemed agitated and unstable. He was frisked but no weapon was found. The agent on duty told him that there was no admittance to the White House. Sparks insisted that he had to see this person—one of the nurses. He said he was her boyfriend. The agent told him that it didn't matter, he wasn't getting inside. The guy turned and left.

"Five minutes later we get a report of a fence jumper. The Uniformed Division rushed assets to the North Lawn and within seconds we grabbed the guy. It was Benny Sparks! We hauled his ass off to jail."

"He's still incarcerated?"

"I think so. He was charged with unlawfully entering the grounds of the White House and convicted. He was sent to the fed prison at Cumberland, Maryland. He should still be there."

"Thanks, Frank."

Three hours later, Riker pulled his rented car through the gates of FCI Cumberland. He went inside, and, after passing through security, took a seat in the inmate visiting area.

A man came through the door. He was about thirty, angular, with bony hands and sunken eyes. He moved with a loping gait, like a mechanical toy that had some loose parts.

Riker stood up. "Mr. Sparks, my name is Martin Riker. I'm a federal investigator. I'd like to ask you a few questions about the incident at the White House."

As Sparks sat down he gave Riker a sneer with the left half of his mouth. The right half didn't move. "What do you want to know?" he said in a raspy voice. "If I was some kind of terrorist?"

"I'm sure you're not," replied Riker. "I just want you to tell me why you tried to enter the White House."

Sparks shrugged his bony shoulders. "I just needed to see Tina."

"You mean Christina Wilkinson?"

"Yeah. My girlfriend. She had pissed me off. I needed to straighten some things out."

"You came with a knife in your pocket," said Riker.

"A man's got a right to protect himself."

Riker looked at Sparks. "Are you getting treatment? Are you clean?"

"Yeah, I'm clean. It's tough getting dope in here. They run the place pretty tight. So now I'm clean and sober. Hallelujah." He tilted his hatchet-like head, like a bird searching for a worm. "Have you seen Tina?"

"No," replied Riker. "How did you meet her?"

"Mutual friend introduced us. We hit it off, and started using together. This was back when I had a job and money in the bank."

"She was working at the White House?"

"Yeah. I thought that was pretty funny, y'know? She's a nurse at the White House and she's shooting up on the side!"

"What were you guys doing?"

"Whatever we could get our hands on. Mostly heroin and oxycodone."

"Percocets?"

"Oh yeah, Tina liked those. She smashed them, and dissolved the pieces."

"One more question," said Riker. "Mr. Sparks, have you been tested for HIV?"

Sparks glanced sideways, and twisted his hands together.

"Yeah. They did it here in the prison."

Riker was gratified to hear him say that. He knew the CDC's HIV guidance for correctional facilities recommended testing inmates when they entered.

"Would you be willing to tell me the results?" asked Riker.

"Why?" replied Sparks with suspicion.

"Because I'm a doctor, and I'm concerned about stopping the disease from spreading. I'm particularly concerned about Tina."

"Why?" replied Sparks. "You don't think—?"

"Anything's possible. I want you to step up and do the right thing."

Sparks took a deep breath and drew down the corners of his mouth. "Yes. I'm HIV-positive. They found it when I came in. They have me on treatment pills."

"Are your partners men or women?"

"Both."

"Did you notify any of them? How about Tina?"

Sparks shook his head.

"Why the hell not?" said Riker hotly.

"I dunno," he said, cringing. "I was embarrassed. I didn't want anyone to hate me. Especially Tina. I mean, how would you feel if some girlfriend called you up and said, 'Hey, honeybear, guess what? I have AIDS and you might have it too.' That would pretty much kill the romance, right?"

"Maybe so, but if you actually *cared* about someone, you'd *tell* them!" said Riker.

"Okay, okay," said Sparks. He looked at Riker. "Are *you* going to tell her?"

"All I can do is urge her to get tested," said Riker. "No one knows if she's infected. Did you guys share needles?"

Sparks shrugged. "We may have. Things got fuzzy sometimes, y'know?"

Riker shook his head. Among intravenous drug users, AIDS education had a long way to go.

"Thank you for your time, Mr. Sparks," said Riker as he stood up. "By the way, has Christina visited you here?"

"She came once or twice when I was first incarcerated," he replied. "But I haven't seen her in several months. I guess she's moved on. I can't say I blame her."

On his way out of the prison, Riker stopped at the visitors office.

After identifying himself as a federal agent, Riker asked if the prison kept contact information on visitors.

"Absolutely," replied the officer. "Anyone who wants to visit an inmate is required by the Bureau of Prisons to fill out a visitor information form. The inmate sends it to them, and they send it back to us. Let's see... Benny Sparks got one for Christina Wilkinson. Twenty-eight Station Road, Chesapeake Beach, Maryland. Nice little seaside town—my uncle used to work there in one of the hotels."

Chapter 33

*   *   *

Sunday morning traffic was light as Riker drove out of Washington along the Suitland Parkway, heading southeast towards the coast. The unseasonably warm weather was accelerating the snowmelt, and for the first time since arriving in Washington ten days earlier Riker didn't feel as though he had been sent to a city of perpetual gloom and dirty slush.

Because Lindsay had been at her brother's in Woodbridge, on Saturday night Riker had been left to his own devices. Rather than choosing a course requiring action, such as hitting the bar scene and maybe trying to meet a girl, he had dined alone before going to see a boring movie. After the horrifying violence of the day, it was nice to let his mind settle into a mode not unlike autopilot, where his actions and decisions flowed from one to the next without a conscious plan.

It was possible, too, that his affection for Lindsay had blunted his drive to meet other women, even though she was technically still involved with another man. Riker wondered what was going to happen with her absent boyfriend, John. He had been far away, in Belgium, when she and Riker had been in bed together. It had been her choice to have a relationship with him, so strictly speaking it was none of his business what transpired between her and her boyfriend. Still, Riker liked his life to be neat and organized. He disliked intrigue and drama—at least when it came to girlfriends.

It was just before noon when Riker turned onto Station Road, which ran from Bayside Road towards the sea, in a section called Roosevelt Cliffs. Riker had seen from the Google satellite view that Station Road, which meandered through the trees, was home to only a handful of big houses on big lots. It was a wealthy neighborhood. Number twenty-eight consisted of a rectangular main house with a chimney at each corner, and smaller wings projecting from each side of the house. There was an attached garage on the north side, and some sort of formal garden connecting the house to an outdoor swimming pool. The house and pool were shaded by tall trees—Riker guessed the satellite photo had been taken in early spring, because the tree limbs were lightly spotted with pale green as if daubed by an artist with a sponge. A path led from the house down to the beach, where the tiny stick of a dock jutted into Chesapeake Bay.

Riker followed the curving driveway to the turnaround in front of the house, which was every bit as grand as the aerial image had suggested. A nineteen-twenties Tudor, its chimneys and turrets loomed majestically as if it were from another time—a time of Stutz Bearcat automobiles, servants in starched dresses, and men who wore tuxedos and smoked Cuban cigars.

With his medical bag in his hand, he rang the bell. Chimes sounded within.

A woman answered the door. Her plain cotton dress and sensible shoes suggested to Riker that she was one of the help.

"Hello, my name is Dr. Martin Riker," he said. "Is this the home of Christina Wilkinson?"

The woman frowned. "Just a minute," she said as she closed the door in his face.

After a moment of silence, the door opened again. Riker faced another woman. About sixty years old, with perfectly cut grey hair, she was wearing beige slacks and a silk blouse, over which she had thrown a yellow sweater with the sleeves tied loosely in the front.

"May I help you?" said the woman.

"Yes. My name is Martin Riker. I'm a doctor working for the White House. I'd like to speak with Christina."

"I'm her mother. What can I do for you?"

"Mrs. Wilkinson, is your daughter at home? I'm a doctor and I have some information for her." He showed his White House card.

After a pause, Mrs. Wilkinson stepped away from the threshold. "Please come in," she said as she opened the door wider.

Riker stepped into a marble-floored entrance hall. With its dark wood paneling and ornate wall sconces it was gloomy, almost medieval. A tall grandfather clock stood against one wall, tick-tocking quietly. In front of Riker the master staircase, its treads covered in a faded red carpet, ascended to the second floor.

Riker followed the lady of the house into the library, with its thick carpet and shelves full of books.

"Please make yourself comfortable," said Mrs. Wilkinson.

Putting his bag on the floor, Riker sat in a leather wingback chair that was next to an old-fashioned globe supported by a wooden stand. Mrs. Wilkinson took her place on a small and very stiff-looking sofa with spindly legs. "Reba, please bring us some tea," she said to the housekeeper, who nodded before retreating through a different door than the one through which they had entered.

"Normally," said Mrs. Wilkinson in a cool voice, "we'd be in church this morning, but Christina is not feeling well, so I decided to stay home with her."

"I hope it's nothing serious," replied Riker.

"Just a touch of the flu," replied Mrs. Wilkinson with a tight smile. "It's going around. Now then—you have some information to impart to my daughter?"

"Mrs. Wilkinson, if it's all right with you, I'd like to speak with her personally. It's a question of her well-being."

"Christina has always been in *perfect* health," replied Mrs. Wilkinson. She drew her shoulders back so that she was sitting ramrod straight. "Is there some general health advisory to be aware of?"

"No, not exactly." Riker decided to back off and attack from another angle. "Mrs. Wilkinson," he said, "your daughter was a nurse in the White House Medical Unit, wasn't she?"

"Yes, for one year. She left to pursue other career opportunities."

"She wanted to be a nurse elsewhere? I'm surprised—it seems to me that the opportunity to work at the White House would be a dream job for anyone in health care. Didn't she have personal interaction with the president himself?"

"She did," said Mrs. Wilkinson. "But as a place to work, the White House is apparently no different from any other. People are abusive. It was not a pleasant environment for Christina."

"Is that what she told you?"

"Yes. She came home one day, very upset. She said her boss—someone named Westlake—had treated her quite harshly, and for no reason. She said she couldn't go back. I asked her if we should file some sort of complaint, or call someone. She insisted no, and that taking any action would be a bad idea. She intimated that the Secret Service was in the habit of 'getting people' who were troublesome. Naturally this was quite horrifying to me, especially since I had voted for President Ralston. I think his wife Susan is a lovely woman. I wish that he let people see more of her. She seems to always be hidden away."

"This is what she said—that Westlake had been abusive, and that's why she had quit?"

"Yes, that's exactly what she said. Why?"

"Mrs. Wilkinson, does the name Benny Sparks mean anything to you?"

"Benny Sparks? No, of course not. Why should it?"

"She never mentioned him?"

"Again, no!" she insisted.

Clearly, Mrs. Wilkinson was a woman who was not accustomed to being contradicted, let alone questioned.

"How did your daughter manage to get a job at the White House?" asked Riker. "I can imagine the process is very competitive."

"Christina is a very capable young lady," replied Mrs. Wilkinson. "Her father, Wilbur, passed away five years ago. Gave her every advantage. She attended Babson Prep and then went to Greenvale College, where she majored in public health and graduated with honors. Then she enrolled in the nursing program at Maryland State. There she met the son of Floyd Perkins, our US senator. They got along very nicely, and I had high hopes for a relationship. I'm sorry that they drifted apart, but Senator Perkins was nice enough to introduce her to Lieutenant Commander Westlake. He's the one who hired her."

"And then the job soured."

"You can't always tell," said Mrs. Wilkinson with a shrug. "People seem pleasant on the outside, but inside they have issues."

"That's so true," nodded Riker. "Is she working now?"

"No. She goes to Washington for interviews, but you know how difficult it can be. She wants to transition away from practical nursing and get into public policy." Mrs. Wilkinson sipped her tea and then regarded Riker with dissatisfaction. "Dr. Riker, this has been a lovely chat, but I'm still not sure why you're here."

"Mrs. Wilkinson," said Riker, "The man I asked you about, Benny Sparks, was apparently Christina's boyfriend during the time she worked at the White House. One day, he came to the White House and caused a disturbance. He tried to enter the White House and the Secret Service asked him to leave. He then tried to jump the fence, and he was arrested. He's now in the federal prison in Cumberland."

"That's ridiculous!" spat Mrs. Wilkinson. "Dr. Riker, I think you should leave."

"Ma'am, I found your address because it's on file at the prison. Christina visited Sparks there several times. Not recently, though— she went there shortly after he was sentenced, but then she stopped coming."

"Okay, so what?" she retorted. "Maybe she had a fling with this man Sparks. Everyone's entitled to make a mistake."

"Benny Sparks is a drug addict. And Christina needs to get herself tested for AIDS."

"AIDS? Are you serious?"

"Absolutely."

Grasping his medical bag, Riker stood up. "Mrs. Wilkinson, we need to talk to your daughter. Is she upstairs?"

"Yes, but—"

"Show me the way."

Mrs. Wilkinson, still on the sofa, slapped the armrest with her hand. "Dr. Riker, I don't—"

"We're going to talk to Christina." Riker walked to the door of the library.

He paused. Mrs. Wilkinson remained on the sofa.

Riker went into the entrance hall and ascended the stairs.

"Christina?" he called.

Hearing someone on the stairs behind him, he turned to see the housekeeper.

"I'll show you to her room," said Reba as she reached the landing. She turned to Riker. "She's a troubled child. Always has been." Reba led Riker to a door at the end of the hall. She knocked. "Christina?"

"What is it?" said a weak voice from within.

"There's a doctor who wants to see you," said the housekeeper.

"Go away," said the voice.

Riker put his hand on the housekeeper's shoulder. "Thank you," he said as he turned the knob and pushed open the door.

He entered a bedroom that looked like any other young woman's, with a canopied bed, white French bureau with an attached mirror, and posters on the walls—mostly celebrities, with a few travel posters mixed in. Putting his bag on the floor, Riker approached the woman lying under the covers.

"Christina?" he said. "My name is Martin Riker. I'm a doctor."

The girl turned her head to look at him.

Riker felt a wave of astonishment. Her face was familiar.

"Didn't I see you last week in The Quill at The Jefferson Hotel?" he asked. "It was about midnight, last Tuesday night. The server addressed you as Tina."

"Yeah, so what?" she replied. "I was in town interviewing for a job."

"Oh? How did it go?"

"Like all the rest. They said, 'Thank you. We'll call if we need you to come in again.' Of course they never call."

"Why don't they?"

Christina frowned. "Maybe they don't want to hire a damned dope addict."

"Just like Benny Sparks, huh?" asked Riker.

"Benny." Christina rolled her eyes. "He's a piece of work. He got me started on the stuff. Before I met Benny I was a happy girl. Nothing bothered me. Then he said, 'Try these. You'll like them.' He handed me a couple of pills. I thought, why not? They're just pills. It's not like shooting dope. So I took them. They made me feel good. I asked him what they were. He told me they were percs, a pill docs give you for pain."

"Was this when you were working at the White House?"

"A few months before."

"And you got hooked."

"Yeah, I guess you could say that."

Hearing a step at the door, Riker turned around. Mrs. Wilkinson had entered the room.

"What are you asking my daughter?" she demanded. "You can see that she's not feeling well. I must ask you to leave."

"I need a few more minutes," replied Riker. He turned back to Christina. "Let me see your arm."

Christina frowned. "Why?"

"You know why. Let me see it."

Reluctantly, Christina held out her left arm. Riker grasped her wrist and gently twisted her arm so that the palm was up.

"You've been shooting up," he said as he let go of her arm. "Heroin?"

"No," she replied.

Mrs. Wilkinson came to her daughter's bedside. "Christina!" she shouted. "What's the meaning of this? Have you been abusing yourself? How *could* you?"

"Mrs. Wilkinson, please," said Riker. "Now is not the time. I need you to stand back."

Glaring at Riker, Mrs. Wilkinson backed away from the bed.

"Did you and Benny ever share a needle?" Riker asked Christina.

"Yeah, I guess so," she replied. "You know how it is. You want to get high and you just do what you have to do. If you've only got one stick, then you share it."

Suddenly Christina's body was wracked by a deep cough and she gasped for air. Riker put his hand on her forehead.

"I think you've got a fever," he said. "Have you seen a doctor?"

"Christina doesn't need a doctor," interjected Mrs. Wilkinson. "She needs to be left alone."

Ignoring Mrs. Wilkinson, Riker turned to Christina. "When you were working at the Medical Unit, you placed orders for Percocet, which you ground up and injected. Tell me the truth: yes or no?"

Christina looked at her mother, and then at Riker. Slowly nodding, she whispered, "Yes."

"And while you were working there, you were the nurse who gave the president his B-12 shots. Yes or no?"

"Yes."

"Now I want you to think carefully," said Riker. "Was there ever an occasion where you used the same needle to inject the president that you had used on yourself?"

Christina sat up in bed, holding the covers over her nightgown. She sat for a moment, thinking. Then she looked at Riker.

"There may have been," she shrugged, as if it were nothing of consequence.

"Tell me exactly what happened, and when."

"It was last winter, when the snow was still on the ground. I had gotten to work around nine o'clock that morning. I needed a hit, so I did my usual thing—I ground up a Percocet, dissolved it, and injected it. It hit me hard! I was feeling really good, and then suddenly I heard commotion in the office. Before I knew what was happening, Ethan came in and told me to get ready to give the president his B-12 shot. He said, 'Right now—he's on a tight schedule.' Then Ethan left the room. I could hear the president talking to him outside the door. I was new on the job and I guess I panicked. I grabbed the syringe I had just used and loaded it with B-12. The door opened and the president walked in. He said, 'Hi Christina! Good—I can see you're ready.' He rolled up his sleeve. Like a robot, I swabbed his arm and gave him his injection. In less than a minute he was gone."

"So you injected the president using the needle you had just used on yourself?"

"I guess you could say that. I'm really sorry. I didn't mean to do it."

"Did you use that needle again, or did you dispose of it?"

"After I injected the president, I threw it away."

"What does this mean?" asked Mrs. Wilkinson. "Is the president sick?"

"The president is fine," replied Riker without hesitation. "We're just gathering all the facts."

Riker went to his bag and took out a small carton, which he opened. "This is a rapid test for HIV," he said. "It's not conclusive, but it's the best way to get a first result." He removed an oral swab from the package. "Open up," he said to Christina.

She obediently opened her mouth and Riker took a saliva sample. He then inserted the swab into a plastic tube filled with solution.

"Now we wait for a few minutes," he said.

Mrs. Wilkinson sat down in a chair. "I'm absolutely shocked," she said to the floor. "Devastated." Raising her head, she glared at her daughter. "How could you do this to us? To the memory of your father?"

"Mommy, please," said Christina. Tears gathered in her eyes.

"But you've ruined our family!" insisted Mrs. Wilkinson. "How will I ever be able to show myself in public again? What will our friends think?"

Riker turned to Mrs. Wilkinson. "Stop!" he said. "This isn't about you. It's about your daughter. She has an addiction problem and she may be very ill. She needs help, not accusations."

With a stunned expression, Mrs. Wilkinson folded her hands in her lap and stared out the window.

Riker checked the tube of the rapid test. He went and sat down on Christina's bed. "Christina," he said gently, "the result is positive. It means that you're probably infected with HIV. And the illness you've got may be

AIDS. We need to get you to a hospital for more tests and treatment. We have to act very quickly."

He turned to Mrs. Wilkinson. "Who's your family doctor?"

"Dr. Anderson, at the Chesapeake Beach Medical Center."

"Call the medical center right now. Get an emergency referral. Christina needs to be hospitalized as quickly as possible."

Slowly, Mrs. Wilkinson stood up and went to the phone at her daughter's bedside.

From his bag Riker took a blood sample kit.

"What's that for?" asked Christina.

"I'm going to take a small sample of your blood," said Riker. "You'll hardly feel a thing. I'm going to send the sample to a lab to have it analyzed. It's all part of the diagnosis and treatment. Please give me your hand."

Riker did not tell her that her sample would be rushed to the CDC for DNA analysis to determine if she had given the president AIDS.

If the results were positive, there was a good chance that Christina Wilkinson would never be told of her ignominious place in history.

Chapter 34

*   *   *

On Monday morning, Riker was at his desk at the Ten-Fifty. The weather, which had been warm the day before, had turned cold again, and the forecast was for a blizzard to come roaring in from the southwest. Riker didn't care; he still had plenty of work to do.

With the blood sample from Christina Wilkinson safely in the hands of Jim Gilmore at the CDC, Riker's list of the four suspects had changed.

Blood samples from Amy Gold, the fundraiser, and Christina Wilkinson, the nurse, were undergoing testing.

Regina Quentin, the former Miss Maryland, was married to Garner Hosbrook. They lived in Annapolis.

Jessica Young, the intern at the Maryland State House while Paul Ralston was governor, lived in a condo in Piscataway with Dawn Slattery, a phys ed instructor at a local gym.

As Riker was pondering his next move, his phone rang. Seeing the caller ID, he picked it up.

"Hey, Lindsay," he said. "How's your mom doing?"

"Thanks for asking," she said. "We made some progress. She's going into an assisted living facility next year. Anyway, I'm back in the office. I heard about Brian Conway. What a terrible thing, to take your own life. I hope this closes this ghastly episode. Is there any other news about your investigation?"

"Actually, yes, there is," replied Riker.

"Why don't we meet for lunch?" suggested Lindsay. "How does one o'clock sound? At Equinox?"

"Perfect. I'll meet you there."

With a warm feeling in his heart, Riker turned his attention back to his shrinking list of suspects.

A moment later his phone rang. The call was from Jim Gilmore.

"Martin," he said. "Pack your bags. You're going home."

"What's going on?" asked Riker.

"We've got results for you. Amy Gold has been cleared. She has no HIV and she's not the source of the president's infection."

"Okay, go on."

"Confirming the results of the rapid test you gave her, Christina Wilkinson has HIV. Her CD4 count is below two hundred, indicating she has AIDS. Here's the result that matters most to you: DNA tests confirm that the strains of HIV that infected the president and Christina Wilkinson are one in the same. They are identical. Given the circumstances under which you say the president and Wilkinson have had physical contact— that is, they never had sexual relations and their only contact was when she gave him his B-12 shots—the only possible conclusion is that Christina Wilkinson transmitted her HIV to the president by using a dirty needle."

"Thanks, Jim," said Riker. "I'll tell the president."

An hour later, Riker, Norm Gladstone, Don Strauss, and the president were together in the Oval Office. They were joined a moment later by the First Lady.

"Martin, Don tells me that you've got some big news for me," said the president as he sat down next to his wife on one of the twin sofas in the center of the room. He took her hand in his. "Susan wanted to be here when you told me. Whatever the news might bring, she wanted to be at my side. I agreed."

"Yes, sir," replied Riker. He glanced at the First Lady. Her face showed quiet dignity. It must take great strength, thought Riker, to be ready to accept what could be a humiliating revelation.

"To get right to it," said Riker, "we've identified the source of your HIV. DNA tests have confirmed that you were infected by a contaminated needle used to inject you with vitamin B-12."

For a moment the president's face showed no expression.

"What did you say?" he whispered.

"You were infected by a dirty needle. This happened in February of your first year in office. Since your time is valuable, and I know you've rearranged your schedule for this meeting, I'll spare you the details of my investigation. The research and my full findings are in this report." He placed a fat file folder on the low table between the sofas. "The bottom line is that a nurse named Christina Wilkinson gave you a B-12 shot using a needle she had just used to inject herself with a solution of Percocet. When you walked into the Medical Office abruptly, she panicked, and instead of taking a moment to get a fresh needle she used the same one she had just used on herself. She had HIV, and enough of her virus was in the needle to infect you. It was a violation of one of the most fundamental and basic protocols of medicine—or, for that matter, of intravenous drug use. No one should *ever* reuse a needle."

"Where is Christina now?" asked the president.

"Rotting in hell, I hope," interjected Strauss.

The president held up his hand. "Let Martin answer."

"She's at the home of her parents," said Riker. "At the time she injected you, she didn't know she was infected. Now she knows she has HIV, and she's getting treatment."

"Can we arrest her for making an attempt on the life of the president?" asked Strauss. "She ought to be locked up in jail, not relaxing at home."

"I'm not a lawyer," replied Riker. "You'll have to ask your legal team."

"We're not going to arrest anybody," said Susan Ralston quietly.

After a moment of silence, the president turned to his wife. "What did you say, dear?"

She straightened her back and looked her husband in the eye. In a clear voice she said, "We're not going to arrest anybody. The girl didn't know what she was doing. She needs help, not incarceration."

"But someone needs to pay the price," replied Strauss. "It was an attack on the president. Anyway, I agree with Dr. Riker. The Secret Service can decide what charges to file. The good news is that the president is healthy, the case has been solved, and we can get on with the business of the nation."

"Do you mean proceed as if this never happened?" asked Riker.

"Absolutely," replied Strauss. "There's no way this can become public. It would be a disaster if the world knew the president of the United States had AIDS, even if he got it through a mistake made by a nurse."

"How would it be a disaster, Don?" asked Susan Ralston.

"Because the president is the leader of the most powerful nation on earth, and in different parts of the world attitudes towards AIDS are not what they are in the United States. I'm sure that some national leaders would refuse to shake the hand of the president, or even meet with him. Our powerful adversaries might believe the president is chronically ill and therefore weak and vulnerable. In his campaign for re-election, the opposition will paint the president as an invalid. I'm telling you, nothing good can come of allowing this to leak out. It will be a nightmare for this administration."

For a moment the room was silent.

"I beg to differ with you," said Mrs. Ralston. "I fully support making a public announcement of my husband's illness. This is for two reasons. The first is that I believe in transparency. We all know that rumors will fly. We've seen four mysterious and violent deaths in the past week, and speculation is rampant, not just among our political opponents but among our friends as well. People have seen the president become ill in public. Some may have heard rumors about Max Mosely wanting to reveal something. This girl Christina may decide to tell her story. The rumors and insinuations will pile up until they bury the White House like a huge snowdrift.

"The second reason is that my husband has the opportunity to educate people and to encourage people to both be safe and get tested. He controls the biggest pulpit on earth! Can you imagine the response if Paul were to stand up and say, 'I have AIDS, and it's going to be okay because I'm getting treatment'? Think of all the good he could do to open up the discussion and make people understand that there's no shame in the fact that a particular little nasty thing—a microbe or virus—has found its way into your body. Think of the lives that could be saved if my husband led a national crusade against not only AIDS but other preventable infectious diseases."

Don Strauss glanced at his phone. Standing up, he said, "Sir, the delegation from the Organization of South Pacific States has arrived. They're in the Diplomatic Reception Room."

The president rose to his feet, as did the rest of the group.

"Martin, thank you for everything you've done," he said as he extended his hand. "I'll never forget it."

"It was my pleasure, sir," replied Riker as they shook hands.

The group moved out of the Oval Office.

A few minutes later, Riker, having said goodbye to Norm Gladstone, was making his way down the path toward the southeast appointment gate. Now all that was left was to check out of his hotel, meet Lindsay for lunch, and then catch a late afternoon flight to Florida.

By dinnertime, he could be home.

At Equinox, he found Lindsay in a booth in the back.

Seeing her was both a great pleasure and a source of anxiety. She looked radiant, and Riker found himself torn between his desire to go home and an equally powerful desire to stay in Washington because she was there. During his two weeks on the assignment, Lindsay had been a bright light, offering stimulating conversation, good advice, and tender love. She would be hard to leave behind.

Perhaps she would be willing to come to Naples for a visit?

At this suggestion she smiled and put aside her wine glass. "Martin, I need to tell you something."

Martin felt his breath stop.

"John's coming back to Washington tomorrow," she said. "We've talked on the phone quite a bit. I think he's going to ask me to marry him."

"And if he does?" said Riker.

She smiled and blushed. "I think I would say 'yes.' He wants to have kids, and so do I, and you know how it is…"

"Say no more," said Riker as he took his wine glass and raised it. "I want you to be happy. I wish nothing but the best for you and John—and, hopefully, your family that's yet to come."

A tear gathered in her eye. "This wasn't easy to say. I really do care for you." She took her glass and gently clinked it against his. "You're a wonderful guy. Thank you."

The time passed quickly, and when Lindsay looked at her watch she said, "Oh my gosh—it's already three o'clock! I need to get back to the office."

Having split the bill, they got up from the table. Riker felt good; for him, resolution, even an outcome he wouldn't have chosen, was always better than indecision. He had never been one to look back with regret. He always looked forward.

As he and Lindsay were passing the bar on the way out, Riker glanced at the television screen. He put his hand on Lindsay's arm. "Look," he said. "The president is making an announcement."

The screen showed President Ralston and the First Lady together before the fireplace in the Lincoln Sitting Room.

"How odd," said Lindsay. "I wasn't notified of an announcement. I wonder what's going on."

They moved closer to the bar so they could hear.

The announcer said, "And now, the President and Mrs. Paul Ralston."

The camera eased closer. The president's chair was drawn up close to that of his wife, and he was holding her hand. She wore the usual benign First Lady smile that was customary at every public appearance. Riker could read nothing into it.

The president leaned forward, looked into the camera lens, and said, "My fellow Americans, I would like to take a moment to tell you something that Susan and I believe you have a right to know.

"The president has AIDS."

* * *

ABOUT THE AUTHOR

Dr. Leslie Norins brings decades of medical research and medical publishing experience to *"The President Has AIDS,"* his fictional mystery about finding the source of an HIV infection in the occupant of the White House

After training with a Nobel Prize winner in immunology, he directed the Venereal Disease Research Laboratory at the US Centers for Disease Control in Atlanta, Georgia.

Then, as a medical publisher, for over thirty years he created and grew more than eighty medical newsletters, providing news and advice for hundreds of thousands of healthcare professionals in specialized niches throughout the US and the world. Trade publications have called him "legendary" and "the dean of medical newsletters."

Dr. Norins received his BA from Johns Hopkins University and his MD from Duke University School of Medicine. His PhD is from the University of Melbourne, where he was a postdoctoral fellow of Sir Macfarlane Burnet, Nobel Laureate, at the Walter and Eliza Hall Institute of Medical Research. He was elected a Fellow of the Infectious Disease Society of America, and has served on committees of the National Institutes of Health and the World Health Organization.

Dr. Norins also authored, with contributions from Thomas Hauck, the thriller, *Deadly Pages*. In it, Mideast terrorists plot to attack the US with smallpox, spread by adding the lethal virus to the printing ink of *The New York Times* to infect readers as they touch their morning newspaper.

A native of Baltimore, Dr. Norins resides with his wife in Naples, Florida.

APPENDIX

Excerpts from Policies for Collection of HIV/AIDS
Personal Identification Data in Selected Jurisdictions

DISTRICT OF COLUMBIA

DISTRICT OF COLUMBIA HIV/AIDS REPORTING REQUIRE-
MENTS (effective November 17, 2006) 22 DCMR § 206 HUMAN IM-
MUNODEFICIENCY VIRUS (HIV) INFECTION

206.1 All Human Immunodeficiency Virus (HIV) infection cases
(including Acquired Immune Deficiency Syndrome (AIDS) shall be reported to the Director of the Department of Health or his or her designee.

206.2 Physicians licensed to practice in the District under the District
of Columbia Health Occupations Revision Act of 1985 (D.C. Official
Code § 3-1201.1 et seq.) shall report all diagnosed cases of HIV and AIDS
to the Director within forty-eight (48) hours of diagnosis and furnish information the Director deems necessary to complete a confidential case
report. Additionally, any provider, laboratory, blood bank, or other entity
or facility that provides HIV testing shall report all cases of HIV infection
to the Director or his or her designee.

206.3 The reports required by section 206.2 shall include the patient's
name, address of residence, including city, state, and zip code, gender, race

or ethnicity, mode of exposure, place or country of birth, date of birth, date of diagnosis of HIV or AIDS and opportunistic infections, the name and telephone number of the person making the report, and the name of the entity providing health or medical services.

206.4 Upon receiving a report of the existence of an HIV infection or potential AIDS case, the Director or his or her designee shall make any investigation that he or she may deem necessary for the purpose of determining the source of the infection and the nature of the treatment. To facilitate the investigation, any entity providing health/medical services shall make medical records and histories available to the Director for inspection.

211.4 Whenever a test made in a public or private laboratory is positive for HIV or is indicative of an HIV diagnosis, including CD4 and viral load tests, the person responsible for the operation of the laboratory shall report the positive test to the Director or an agent of the Director or his or her designee, in writing, within forty-eight (48) hours, giving the following information:

(a) The name of the subject of the test;
(b) The name and address of the physician or provider requesting the test;
(c) The patient's medical record number; and
(d) All other information required under this section.

211.8 Whenever, in the course of its operations, a blood bank determines that a specimen is positive for HIV, the physician or provider in charge of the blood bank shall report the positive test in writing to the Director or his/her designee within forty-eight (48) hours.
DISTRICT OF COLUMBIA S.E. SEXUALLY TRANSMITTED DISEASE CLINIC

SE STD Clinic: "...we will begin asking for insurance information starting on May 1, 2015. Registration staff will photocopy your photo ID and insurance card for your medical chart and provide you with a copy of our HIPAA Notice of Privacy Practices.

Disease Intervention Specialists (DIS)... The DIS in Washington, DC, provide counseling for all patients at the SE STD Clinic who are diagnosed with a reportable disease. **They conduct field investigations on all syphilis and HIV cases in Washington, DC and provide partner notification services.** (*Emphasis supplied.*) ...

...You can also anonymously inform your partners that they have been exposed to an STD by visiting www.inspot.org... Utilizing the electronic greeting card option persons can send an anonymous card informing their partners of exposure to the infection along with information on where to obtain testing services. For more information on inSPOT, visit their website at www.inspot.org.

* * *

MARYLAND
§ 18-337 Positive test results

(a) "Health care provider" defined. -- In this section, "health care provider" means a physician, a physician's designee, or a designee of a health care facility licensed or otherwise authorized to provide health care services.

(b) Notice to others by health care providers. -- If an individual informed of the individual's HIV positive status under § 18-336 of this subtitle refuses to notify the individual's sexual and needle-sharing partners, the individual's physician may inform the local health officer and/or the individual's sexual and needle-sharing partners of:
(1) The individual's identity; and
(2) The circumstances giving rise to the notification.

(c) Enforcement of §§ 18-208 through 18-213.1 of this title. -- When the local health officer is notified, the health officer shall enforce the provisions of §§ 18-208 through 18-213.1 of this title:

(1) Within a reasonable time; and

(2) To the extent feasible.

(d) Referrals to appropriate services. -- Each local health officer shall refer the infected individual and any known sexual or needle-sharing partners of the individual to appropriate services for the care, support, and treatment for HIV infected individual.

§ 18201.1 Article – Health – General

(a) A physician who has diagnosed a patient under the physician's care with human immunodeficiency virus or acquired immuno-deficiency syndrome according to the current definition published in the morbidity and mortality weekly report by the Centers for Disease Control and Prevention of the Department of Health and Human Services shall submit immediately a report to the health officer for the county where the physician cares for that patient.

(b) The report shall:

(1) Be on the form that the Secretary provides;

(2) Identify the disease;

(3) State the name, age, race, sex, and residence address of the patient; and

(4) Be signed by the physician.

NOTICE TO PHYSICIANS FROM MEDICAL SOCIETY OF MARYLAND
The Maryland HIV/AIDS Reporting Act of 2007, Health General Article 18201.1 went into effect on April 24, 2007. The new law:

* Requires physicians to **report HIV cases, by name,** to the health department. This is in addition to the previous requirement for physicians to report AIDS cases by name.

* Changes the requirements for reporting by laboratory directors to the health department from reporting HIV positive and CD4<200

test results by unique identifier **to reporting HIV positive and
<u>all CD4 test results</u> by name.** *(All emphasis in original document)*

**Reporting of HIV and CD4 test results by laboratory directors
is done using the State of Maryland HIV/CD4 Laboratory Report
Form (DHMH4492).**
The passage of the Maryland HIV/AIDS Reporting Act will facilitate
the transition from code to namebased HIV reporting in compliance with
a new federal mandate based on recommendations from the Centers for
Disease Control.

*   *   *

NEW YORK
(William Brangham, in PBS-posted transcript from program "The End
of AIDS?"):
"…Using Medicaid information, the state works in tandem with specialized insurance companies like Amida Care to identify patients who've
stopped having tests or stopped refilling prescriptions for their HIV meds.
Outreach workers then try to get them back into treatment…"

*   *   *

Note: All items are presented to show collection of personal information
occurs. All laws and regulations also contain requirements for maintenance of confidentiality; however, if breaches occur, unauthorized persons (e.g. hackers) may obtain the information or authorized persons may
use it for purposes not contemplated.

www.ingramcontent.com/pod-product-compliance
Lightning Source LLC
Chambersburg PA
CBHW021320250626
47155CB00002B/566